The Father

The first Sean Rooney thriller

TOM O. KEENAN

MᶜNIDDER & GRACE CRIME

Published by McNidder & Grace
Aswarby House
Aswarby
Sleaford
NG34 8SE

www.mcnidderandgrace.co.uk

Original paperback first published in 2015, reprinted 2017
©Tom O. Keenan

A catalogue record for this work is available from the British Library.

ISBN: 9780857161161

Designed by Obsidian Design

Printed and bound in the United Kingdom by
Short Run Press Ltd, Exeter, UK

ABOUT THE AUTHOR

Born and raised in Hamilton, this is Tom's critically acclaimed debut novel which was shortlisted for the CWA Debut Dagger in 2014. His experience as an independent social worker in the mental health field, writing expert reports for solicitors and Glasgow Sheriff Court informs and underpins his writing. Tom is now working on the second Sean Rooney crime novel.

ACKNOWLEDGEMENTS

To my mother, Maggie, Claire and Gemma.

For their support, guidance and belief in me as an author I would like to thank Andy Peden Smith, the publisher at McNidder & Grace, John Beaton and Linda MacFadyen as well as Peter Young, Bryan Kirkpatrick and The Crime Writers' Association.

CHAPTER ONE

"*You're a fuck up, Rooney,*" I say to him, in his head.

"Tell me about it," he says to me, in the dark.

I'm about to torment him some more, but then Mrs Gribben interrupts, her Irish brogue booming from the foot of the stairs.

"Get yourself up… di'ye hear?"

He's not going to answer her. *He* knows where's best.

"Jaysus, I don't know why I bother," she says to someone else. "He's been up there since Hogmanay, four days talking to himself – no bloody life."

Although a shiver courses up Rooney's arm, the one hanging out of the bed, his fingers feeling like ice, in his bed wrapped in a cocoon of blankets and coats tight like his mother's shawl, he's talking to *me*.

"Just leave me be," he groans, not that she can hear him from beneath his clothing-bank.

"Typical Glasgow January night, Rooney," he says, drawing his head above the coats to look through the ice covered window. "Dreich as sleet, cold as death, and unforgiving as spite. I'm staying put."

"They've delivered your booze," the Gribben says loud, then low. "That'll get him up."

"*They've delivered your booze.*"

"My order's arrived?" he asks, lowering the coats from his head to reveal his face.

"*Appears so.*"

Extricating from his humpy, he shimmies his legs out of bed, sits up and shivers, and clicks on the bedside lamp, turning a previously harmless dark space into a danger zone. Reality kicks in as he pulls his shambling frame up onto his legs, lifting a coat or two from the bed to rewrap himself. The lino's cold on his bare feet. He sits down to don a worn pair of sheepskin slippers. He straightens his half shape and orients by the lamp, from the light giving shadows, to the chair next to it, where he sits to get his bearings.

The thunder rumbles again: "Do you bloody hear me, Rooney? Are you coming down?"

"She'll send him away. She's done it before."

"Indeed, dear woman. Just detain the man long enough for me to get there."

Fumbling with his trousers, he finds a crumpled twenty; then, stacking another coat over his shoulders, he shuffles through the sitting room, into the hall, to the door of the flat, exposing only enough skin to turn the key and open it. He slides back the rolled-up draught-blocking rug with his foot, approaches the top of the stairs, only to realise he's been fooled. The Gribben is down there, but so is Jackie, his erstwhile colleague in crime, and one time spouse.

"Ah hah, the thought police have arrived." For Rooney, Detective Chief Inspector Jacqueline Kaminski, Glasgow Pitt Street, appearing there means "Big fuckin trouble."

"Well, Happy New Year to you… hermit," she says, in that smart-cop-way. 'Brass neck,' comes to mind. "No' answering your phone these days, nor your door intercom?"

"Might've done so, had it been a nice kind woman, not an annoying bad-hat like you. Why are you invading my privacy?"

"Privacy? Hibernation, you mean."

"What I do in the… comfort of my own home is my affair." He rests his elbows on the bannister. "Comfort being a very generous term," he lobs at the Gribben. "Why are you here, Jackie?"

"Just a multi-fuckin'-murder," she says staccato style; using profanities matter-of-fact in the way he well remembers.

"Oh. Fine. Cheerio," he says. He turns away, sweeping his coat around him like a Shakespearian actor's cloak.

"No' wanting to hear the gory details?" Jackie nods to the Gribben, knowing she understands her tactic.

"No' the least bit interested." He heads back to the flat. It doesn't stop her though.

"There's a psycho out there."

"So what, there's one here too," he says, gesturing towards the Gribben.

"You bring the best out in me," the Gribben replies, with one of those faces.

"He's one of yours," Jackie says.

"Feck-all to do wi' me."

"This guy does it in groups."

"Groups?"

"So do swingers…"

"Up on the Cobbler, four stiffs."

"Multiple?"

"An elderly councillor and a good whack of her family."

"Interested?"

"When?"

"Couple of hours ago," Jackie says.

"It's no' my stuff no more."

"I want you there, wi' me."

"She wants you there, wi' her."

"Jackie, this shrink retired on health grounds, mind?"

"Aye, I mind."

"Not that our breakup had anything to do with that, oh no."

"Rooney, we just need to get over there. Right?"

There's no contest between Arrochar and his bed. "I'm ill," he says.

"Aye, a walking liver disease. Your car's waiting, *Sir*," she persists, this woman with no sympathy for his sorry state.

"Better do what she says. She'll stop your order."

"What's that to you," he says to me. Defeated, he goes back inside, but not before he gives a defiant thrust. "She… ite, be good to get the fuck out of this igloo of an apartment…" He shivers, the coats falling to the floor as he puts on his shirt. "… into a warm bar." He grunts, struggling with his Docs. "Where I can find some… feckin'… privacy." The last word ricochets down the stairs.

He sits, takes a breath, and scans the room.

"An aesthetic nightmare, Rooney."

He nods.

He has been here since his last high, after hitting rock bottom. All he has of any importance are some self-produced paintings adorning the walls: a tiger, a great white, a mosquito – killers all, remnants of an old hobby and a retreat from a stressful profession. Some scattered books, textbooks mainly, lie across the floor; remnants of a life of Freudian analysis. An old winged-back Chesterfield chair, which, like himself, has seen better days. A drained glass lies on the table, flanked by a platoon of empty bottles. They'll remain standing to attention until his weekly environmental health sojourn, forestalling the invasion of flies, rats… social workers.

A dejected reflection of a man.

"You, Sean Rooney."

"And you're nothing but a figment of my tortured imagination. Me, I'm Rooney, get it?"

"You, mine host, are a forty-nine-year-old, divorced, ex-professional man, living in a shitty Partick pied-à-terre, with only a voice for company."

"I'm a Doctor."

"Ah, but no' the medical kind. No' how the body – "

"I'm a doctor, of the mind, and how it works."

"And how it doesn't?"

"I'm a PhD."

"An erstwhile… failed… psychologist."

"Fuck off, bastard." His name for me.

Rooney, forensic psychologist and profiler, as was, had the ability to track those who left something of themselves behind: patterns, characteristics, and sometimes clues. Men with distinctive ways and traits; types so dissimilar to their normal fellows, that the broad indiscernible road, in ever diminishing breadths, became a well-worn path.

"You telling them about me?"

"I am. They need to know."

It wasn't enough for him to find the man and establish who he was, however. He needed to know *why*: why *he* did what he did. So much so it made him sick, sick of it and *him* too. His men fell into similar patterns: been caused pain, will cause pain; been controlled, exploited and manipulated, will control, exploit and manipulate; no one cares for me, I don't care for others; people hate me, I'll hate them back; life hasn't given me anything, I'll take what's mine by right.

His job became a drudge. Then simultaneously, his illness and I arrived, invading him, tormenting him –

"Driving me mad."

"Making you… bad."

He had always hoped there would be one in particular, one who would interest him more than the others, but one who could get to him, get into him, damage him. He feared this, but so great his interest – his perverse interest – he… wanted him.

"What you saying?"

"You want him."

"I want – "

"Him."

For Rooney, mental illness arrived in his early-forties, just when everything was going well.

"I was on the crest of a wave, wi' the Strathclyde Polis."

"You hit the skids."

"I became… ill." Shoes tied and jacket buttoned, he moseys down towards these sentinels of his sure destruction. "I am no' up to this," he says, pulling his scarf from the coat rack, wrapping it python-like around his neck. "I just hope you're not taking the piss."

"The car's out there, hon," Jackie says, fearing a last stand at the door. "Get the fuck into it."

"Get into it, hon. Just do it."

"Abso-fucking-lutely," he says, realising the futility of argument.

"I see you're in your working gear; going begging?" Jackie asks.

"It used to be a white suit."

"Before it was a table cloth in a curry house, after a crowd of students ate from it."

"See your jokes haven't improved."

The Gribben smirks.

"Sartorial elegance no' my strong point, Mrs G?" he says, noticing Jackie's wellies, replacing her customary Prada heels.

The Gribben holds open his black Crombie, awaiting his arms, then adds his Derby tweed bunnet, an Oxfam purchase. "I've been worried about you," she says, through cig gripping lips, then folding her arms in a wee-washer-wuman-wie.

"I'm alive, alive oh," he says. "From Dublin's fair city, where the girls are so pretty – shame about you!"

He gets in the back of the car and pulls the door behind him. A uniform's behind the wheel. A group of weans gather around the car.

"Fame at last Rooney?" Jackie says, turning round.

"Right, dear," he says. "In this city, polis cars turn incidents into circuses."

"You're the incident Rooney, a circus clown."

"Fuck off and leave me alone."

"Just like old times... bastard," Jackie replies.

"Correct."

CHAPTER TWO

Klaxon blaring, the Police car batters through early evening traffic, heading out onto the A82, Arrochar bound. He's been on these journeys before. Courtesy of the ever-resourceful Glasgow cabs, he always delayed his arrival at an incident to just behind the paramedics. "I'm no good at stemming blood," he'd say.

"Takes me back."

"Aye."

"Talking to yourself again hon?" Jackie asks, from the front.

"As you know, happens."

Heading to an 'incident', Rooney would be on his mobile to Ben, his social worker chum and the leader of the major incident team. Ben had a sure and trusted diary, from which he'd track them through wives, liaisons, hotel receptions, pubs for professionals... professional boozers.

Rooney closes his eyes, pushes his head back, and covers his face with his bunnet.

"Aye, you get some sleep," Jackie says. "You'll need it where we are going."

"Right you are," he says. "You did drag me from my kip."

He slides down on the back seat, his arms folded.

We'll have an 'internal chat'. The two voices in his head: his and mine, our inner dialogue. As far as Jackie's concerned, he's having a nap on route. Not to be accused of talking to himself, *this time*.

"We were... professional listeners," he says to me.

So called no gooders, pain parasites; drinking large amounts of beer, and even larger amounts of wine, whisky, vodka.

"Our debriefing: to oust our feelings, put them to bed."

"Like flies in shit?"

"Pain relief, bastard."

Their reward... for the words of comfort.

"Years of learning what not to say."

"How's your tennis game? How's your broken neck?"

"Years of learning – "
"How not to stay... sober."
"I had... issues."
Ting! Revelation time!
"Your illness."
"My bipolar."
"Self-destruction."
"Messed up my... self. My – "
"Marriage?"
"Sanity."
"Mad man pursues mad, bad men."
"I was ill, they were – "
"Iller, badder?"
"Mentally disordered offenders."
"Psychos."
"MDOs."

Jackie's mobile interrupts our cosy chat. "Hello Archie. Yes, we're on our way."

"Where were we before we were so rudely interrupted?" Rooney says into the space between his head and the roof of the car.

"We were discussing your psychos."

"MDOs."

"Brian Harte, mind him?"

"Indeed."

"The nutjob."

"How is she?" Jackie asks into her phone.

"He was on his medical training. Had to abandon it with the onset of schizophrenia."

"That's what I said, nutjob."

"OK, be there soon...," Jackie continues.

"He had *beliefs.* A 'national responsibility for overseeing and punishing poor clinical practice'."

"Driver, get a move on," she orders the uniform.

"You assessed him... pre-conviction, in the Springburn Medium Secure Unit. He threatened a doctor with a knife."

"His mental disorder was evident, his predisposition for homicide less so."

"Yes... yes... yes," says Jackie, well out of our conversation and into hers.

"'Hates doctors... pathological need to attack health care staff... will kill eventually,' you said."

"I did."

"Your opinion: a nutjob?"

"OK bastard, whatever you say," he says, to the roof of the car.

"Rooney!"

He turns his head and gazes through the car window into a bleak, miserable night. He wipes the condensation with the cuff of his coat. The dark of the A82 bypass replaces the street lights of Dumbarton. The headlights of oncoming cars illuminate the inside of the car in strobe-like rapidity.

"*I* recommended a hospital order with restrictions," he says.

"*The sheriff released him on probation.*"

"With a condition to attend a forensic psychiatrist... for treatment."

"*Treatment he'd never accept.*"

Later, Harte, during his 'mission' took a dislike of and an iron crowbar to Doctor John Gilbert, an old friend and colleague of Rooney's, during a busy surgery. Fastidious in dress, with oiled, sweptback hair, he walked without hesitation or respect through a packed waiting room. "Time to protect the weak and vulnerable," he said, as he entered his friend's treatment room, where he casually and brutally bludgeoned him to death. Before he left, this man whom no one saw gouged out the GP's eyes with his fingers.

"You don't get evidence from onlookers about a man who kills. His characteristics were clear enough to me though. I tracked him down to that grotty homeless hostel in Brig'ton."

"*That you knew... well.*"

"I knew he'd seek sanctuary in a place where no one asks obvious questions – "

"*'Who are you?' 'Why are you here?' 'Where did you come from?' 'When were you last here Rooney?'*"

"Among those raving and talking in their sleep, his delusions set him apart."

"*In a salubrious hostel of the East End, where many a fine man graced their barren spaces, lay on their finer horsehair mattresses, with no more than inches between each mattress or body – *"

"My words."

"*– full of nutjobs.*"

"A man there would be conspicuous by his actions and attire."

"*'A real dandy,' the manager said of Harte's slicked back hair and smart clothes. 'I'm a medical man,' he said to him.*"

"With the assistance of a few pounds, I asked him, if he could check, perhaps when he was asleep, if he was carrying anything... particular."

"*Ethical?*"

"He found John's eyes in Harte's coat pocket."

"*And off to Hillwood he went, to the place where deranged folk like you and Harte happily weave baskets.*"

"I worked there."

"*You were sectioned.*"

"Bastard."

"Rooney!" Jackie scowls at him through her vanity mirror; meaning 'shut-the-fuck-up'.

"*You incarcerated him Rooney. He was a… sick man.*"

"I was pleased with *his* incarceration."

"*To treat or to punish; you wanted to hurt this man.*"

"He'd killed my friend."

"*He needed help. You were about helping.*"

"So I thought… then."

Rooney returns to his window gazing. Twenty-odd minutes later, the car pulls into the car park in Arrochar, at the head of Loch Long. He drags himself out of the car.

"Get these on," Jackie orders, handing him a fluorescent jacket, a hardhat, and a pair of wellies.

"Like a mammy wi' a wean in the rain."

"No lip Rooney. I don't need it."

He decides not to. It'll only confirm her long-term dominance of him. She introduces Detective Inspector Archie Paterson. He ate all the pies, Rooney thinks. He's to be his aide, again 'no lip'.

They transfer to a Police Landover and rumble up the forest tracks until they're around a thousand feet or so above the side of the hill. Then the walking begins. Rooney doesn't need this, albeit priding himself in being a 'bit of a walker in his time', having climbed these hills in his earlier life.

"*The old knees no' so good these days?*"

"You're telling me," he says, puffing white frosty breath into the dark.

Climbing paths looking down on Loch Long, Jackie leads like a Girl Guide leader. 'Keep up, boys!' she cries, forging ahead, fit and thin, us falling behind, fat and feeble. This is a bitterly cold night in the glens, and so says his ever-freezing feet and other protuberances. After thirty minutes or so of slog, she points "up there, on the clearing, just by the flood lights."

"Who's there?" Rooney asks, hearing the hubbub. He's in no mood to socialise.

"Some locals," she says. "The village GP, the local polis, firemen, the forestry worker who made the first call, some walkers, and some others, who the fuck knows."

"Fine thanks," he says, wishing he hadn't asked.

They crunch through icy boggy ground, moving up and over some hillocks. From Archie's puffing, Rooney wonders if his rotund body will give up on him and he'll expire right there and then. Then, as if to confirm he's well out of his depth there, Rooney slips and slides down the side of a hillock. Archie grabs for him, but his fingers rip from his coat as he falls. He knows the risks of this place from years of climbing around there, on the Cobbler, or Ben Arthur, its proper name, where he explored the caves on its slope. The 'New Year caves', where crazy Glaswegians, the Creag Dhu guys, spent New Year holidays deep in their recesses, around wood fires. There they smoked, drank, and told stories of famed climbs in these hills. As he slides, he remembers that sheep, dogs, even walkers, had fallen into fissures scarring these slopes. His slide comes to a crunching halt, ending with him in a sitting position.

"What the fuck am I doing here?"

"Sitting on your arse."

Jackie and Archie reach him.

"You alright?" she asks.

"Oh, just hunky-fuckin'-dory," he says, sitting in the icy mud.

"Get yourself up man."

"Go… away."

"You talking to yourself?" Archie asks.

"He has voices," Jackie says.

"Voices? I have a voice."

"I knew this was a stupid idea," says Archie, helping him to his feet.

Archie's right.

"He's fine, he's used to being on his arse," Jackie says, with all the concern of a Glasgow bagman.

"Thanks." Rooney turns to a sound of groaning. "What's that?"

"That is why you're here," Jackie says.

"We hear you're good wi' the auld wimen," Archie says.

Jackie leads him to her. "She's a city councillor, a kind of mother figure in the council."

"A coonty councillor and clapped out counsellor, perfect match," Archie says.

"Is that the best you can do?"

"I like it."

Rooney shakes his head, as if he's trying to shake me out of it.

"What do you expect me to say to her?"

"Just do what you do," Jackie says. "Talk to her."

"Take me home."

"To your humpy."

"Listen," she says. "You're here, and she's dying, and you need to talk to her."

"You brought me here to talk to a… dying old woman. Why isn't she in hospital?"

"Rooney," Jackie says, into his face. "The medics say if they move her she'll die on the spot. They can't get a helicopter in here. You're an incident counsellor. This is what you do – "

"Did."

"Did, do."

"I have to do nothing." He could walk away, but realises he's going nowhere without transport. "Get me down," he says.

"I will. When you do this…," she says. "We need what she can tell you." She knows how to exploit this once-was professional: emotional blackmail and professional demand in equal measure.

"OK, but don't expect me to do… anything else. No more, got it."

"OK, I got it."

He moves forward. He's to 'talk to her', so say the blue serge brigade with a problem talking to victims.

"Hello my dear, how you doing?" he says, leaning over the injured woman.

"Ridiculous question Rooney, she's far from doing anything."

She turns slowly to look him in the face. "I have been better, son," she says, with Eastern European vowels coming through the Scots.

"Rooney, she's wrapped around a rock, has multiple injuries, her life's ebbing fast."

"Do not worry, sir," she says to him. "I don't feel very much, and I don't need a doctor to tell me I am done."

"Indeed."

He edges closer to her and, as softly as his gruff voice will produce, he asks her name.

"I'm Irena, Irena Zysk," she replies, grasping his arm. She tries to pull him to her, like an old lady trying to put ten pence in a wean's pocket. "My family, they are safe, yes?" He grips her hand gently to say they're not. "Listen to me, I need to tell you," she says.

"I'm listening Irena, take your time."

"More crass statements Rooney, she has little time."

"There were these men," she says, "but one of them, this man."

"I'm no' the polis Irena. You don't need to tell me anything. I am just here – "

"Yes, good, but please listen to me." She's anxious to get it out. "They came to our house, when we were having dinner. They had guns and forced us into two cars. They brought us here. 'Get out of the car and to kneel down,' they said. Then this man came around to the front of us and stood over us. He was just looking down on us." She stops, her face grimaces with the pain. "Then he said something, in Latin. I knew it was Latin, I've heard it many times at our mass."

"The old mass and the Latin makes your skin creep."

After his illness, Latin words bring on shades of gold in his head, something to do with the colour of the vestments.

She continues. "'*In nomine Patris*,' he said. I know what that means." She made a mini sign of the cross. "In the name of the father. Then he turned to me and looked into my eyes, with the eyes… dead eyes. And a smile, not a smile, a grin – "

From her eyes, Rooney sees a flash of pain shoot through her.

"A funny voice."

"Not that funny Irena."

"A funny face and a funny voice without being funny; do you know what I mean?"

"I think I do," Rooney says, though not really sure if he did. She presses closer to him; her voice dimming as she whispers in his ear. "He nodded to one of the men, like an SS officer in Auschwitz giving the death command. Then one of them hit me hit hard on the head, then kicked me over the side of the hill. Down here, until the police arrived. It was dark, cold, and so, so long. I was scared son, really scared."

"I'm sure you were my darling."

Her soft tones remind him of his mother, dead three years. He sits there holding her hand, her fingers growing cold in his, the chill ascending her arm. The paramedics move in, to do what they can, but they've no chance. The tears well up in his eyes, the pain wells up in his heart.

"You are a psychologist, an expert on feelings, control them."

He can't stop them, the tears flow down his face, dripping off his chin.

"Who are they *for Rooney?"*

He feels the pain of the old woman, in his head and his heart. The darkness descends in his mind and his soul, as he sits there cursing whatever brought them together.

Joining him, Jackie says, "Our elderly councillor makes the full house."

"Four of a kind," Rooney gently sorts the old lady's hair.

"What?"

"Four of a kind, the family, and gran the ace."

"Oh," she says, standing corrected. "And the rest are up there, decapitated, laid out side by side."

"What do you care?"

"What do you mean?"

"You can't deal with this."

"We have a job to do Rooney."

"Aye, a *job* to do."

"You alright hon?"

"Just dinky-fuckin-doo."

Her 'hon' is far from 'alright'.

Archie helps him up to the path. He catches his breath. His mobile goes off. 'Ben' is on the screen. He holds the mobile tight against his right ear, to block out the whistling wind with his hands.

"Hi Roon, good to have you back."

"Ben, I'm no' back. It's no' official."

"Well, we'll see." Ben's unconvinced. "We're in a marquee in the car park, with some of the relatives and friends."

"How's it going?"

"I've just talked to a daughter. The family were snatched when was out of town. She's pretty... well you know – "

"I know."

"Not so lucky white heather."

"The family?"

"Murdered."

"Sure Roon. But any more, you know... the circumstances?"

"Not my business, you know that."

"Roon, you OK?"

"Just dandy."

"Sure?"

"Ben, with the greatest of respect, you're no' my social worker."

"Aye, sure Roon. Phone me later." He switches off.

"No' your social worker... Who looks after you Rooney?"

"I look after myself, you internal prick."

They return to the safety of the car park. Jackie's team is yelling above the din, trying to maintain the cordons. The paparazzi are getting through. Photographers or parasites, Rooney wonders. His mind flashes to stills of war correspondents taking pictures of victims being shot.

"What should they do?" he asks himself. "Take the pictures, tell the world, or put their lives in danger?"

"What would you have done?"

He doesn't answer, but he knows what he would do. A picture is as good as any evidence from witnesses, and Rooney likes his pictures.

"Where will they take them?" he asks Archie.

"To a makeshift mortuary. An empty barn, for forensics, for the night. The army set it up. They'll help search for evidence."

Rooney sees green Land Rovers spewing out camouflaged soldiers to head up the hill in horizontal waves. Just like the farmers when they burn off the bracken, the fire moving up the hill, fanning out.

"Well used to exercises in these hills." He recalls times coming down the hill, when he'd encountered platoons of paras in camouflage heading up.

Jackie heads off.

"Away to do police work."

"And don't worry about me," Rooney mutters. He lights up and coughs, drawing in cold air mixed with smoke, as he looks down Loch Long.

"Why should she?"

"No reason."

Archie escorts him to Jackie's trailer. She's there outside, delivering a statement to a BBC Scotland camera team. She's expressing "deep shock at a heinous crime," and offering "sincere condolences to the family and friends of councillor Zysk." She's in full flow in her best presentational voice. "The investigation is at a very early stage in establishing the circumstances and finding those responsible for the deaths of councillor Zysk and the members of her family." She's clearing her throat. "Our inspectors are carrying out enquiries and gathering details. Anyone with any information is asked to call Pitt Street on 0141 532 2000. Alternatively, Crimestoppers may be contacted on 0800 555 111, where anonymity will be protected." She finishes her statement and makes her way to Rooney.

"You've said that before."

"I try."

"What's the council saying?"

"Muir's released a statement from the City Chambers. He expressed 'deep shock'. Irena was a respected councillor, an ambassador for the multi-ethnic subgroup on the council."

"The Polish community'll be devastated." Rooney sees from her face she's too tired to enter into a discussion over local multicultural politics. "You look well and truly knackered."

"And you look like shit."

"She's right."

"Indeed." He feels his coat and muddy trousers. "I need a drink, you on escort duty dear?"

"Well, George Clooney asked me earlier." She looks around. "But, as you know, I've a real soft spot for the afflicted." She changes out of her wellies into her Pradas.

"Don't flatter yourself. Though you're right, he is afflicted."

"Well, you're no' going to catch the killers here."

"No' even wi' more filth than on Sauchiehall Street on a Saturday night?"

Rooney grins like someone with a voice in his head.

"Archie, take over," she instructs. His look says, 'Aye, on you go, leave it all wi' me.' "OK, let's get the fuck outta here," she says.

They weave through the cordons, the line of media and the onlookers – the 'disaster tourists' as she puts it – until they find themselves in the car park. Some people look stunned, locked in, refusing to move – rabbits in headlights – fearing they'll miss something. She seizes a local patrol car from an arriving officer, who's happy to be involved, if only to get them to the Village Inn, the local boozer, only minutes away along the head of the loch. At well past three in the morning the bar's still open.

She reaches the bar first. "Whisky, doubles, two of?" she says, no messing. "Correct?" she asks Rooney.

"You know me so well."

"Aye, no' the party pooper."

"But no ice, waters it down." He's in a hurry, downs it in seconds, and orders the same. They drink and they drink more. It's obvious to all there they're AWOL from the 'murders on the Cobbler'; something to do with his filthy clothes and his desperate need to get rat arsed.

Phil, the manager plays his part in the event. No local cops'll invade his domain and dictate local licensing times, liberal anyway. A guitarist and a fiddler, accompanied by some badly out-of-tune voices, are in the corner by the fire. "Free booze, they're no' complaining," Phil says.

"So, Jackie," Rooney says. "Why did you drag me here and out of my nest? If you wanted a wee highland bevy, you just needed to ask."

"Aye, happy as a dug rolling in shit," she says. "I knew you'd be good wi' the old lady, that's why." She slurps two mouthfuls at once. "You're a useful man, when you're not depressed, high or pished that is."

"Depressed and high permitting; but sober, when did that ever matter to you?"

"I need you sober *this* time." She taps varnished nails against the side of the glass.

"Look," he says. "I used to do profiles and therapy, but this is something different. I'm no' doing it." His voice's loud enough for the locals to turn away from their beers.

"I haven't asked you to do anything. Being here's good enough for now." She looks at him full in the face for two seconds. "Fancy some TLC?"

She heads off to the toilet, but returns waving a hotel key with a solid wooden fob at him. Sliding the empty glasses towards Phil across the bar she thanks him for the room, then takes Rooney by the hand.

"I had a feeling it would be needed the night," Phil says, leaning over the bar so's not to be heard. "It's no' for the tourist shite; it's for the folk who're involved in a… proper way?" He's happy to provide his small support and a bottle of Grouse from the gantry.

She leads Rooney out of the bar. Prematurely, he thinks, given it's still open. They head up the stairs, these two drunks, to find their room and a single bed. It'll do.

They sit on the edge of the bed and he reaches for the bottle. She reaches for him and pulls him to her. There was a time when it was for love. This time it's security, comfort, sex; for then, he cared not which. They hold each other, not needing more for then, but after a while they did. Then it's demanding, desperate. Clothes are wrestled upward and kicked downward. Flesh melds with flesh and drink mixes with adrenaline and basic human need. There's no script, neither lead nor follow, they just get on with it. His medication prevents him from getting a hard on, but they improvise. Then the agro starts, a scratch at first, then a flurry of slaps. He grabs her, and holds her tight, more for self-protection.

"You were a bastard, do you know that, a bastard," she says.

"I had an illness."

"You were a drunk."

"So why are you here; fuck, come to think about it why am I here?"

She sits up, the sheet slides from her revealing her breasts. She gathers it up and wraps it tight around her. Her shoulders look bony; he hasn't noticed recently.

"I couldn't let you die... in your... hole, Rooney."

"My... hole is quite appealing after tonight's escapades."

"I felt responsible, after the breakup. Not that I'm no' still bloody angry at your... behaviour."

He isn't sure what to do. He decides not to do anything, except have a nightcap. She turns away and, in time, a gentle snore says sleep has arrived as a salve for them both. A few hours later he's first to rise. It's still early morning. He reaches for the bottle and finishes what's left sitting by the window facing out across the Loch, the moon shimmering on the water. This is a quiet moment to himself, by then approaching dawn, and it's calm: deathly calm.

"Happy with yourself?"

"Here we go again. Monkey on my back."

"Done your bit, now the reward."

"I need it."

"You got out of the house, got on a hill, fell on your arse, talked to an old woman, tried to fuck your ex, unsuccessfully. You need it."

"What do you want from me?"

"To realise you're a pile of shite."

"I know that."

"Good."

"Will you fuck off then and leave me be?"

"Wi' your true friend the drink?"

"Guess so," he says, looking lovingly at the bottle of Grouse. He pours a large one, and another. "Fuck you, I'll do my thing," he says to me. "You're nothing but a hallucination; a figment of my poor, sorry mind."

He's right.

"The auld woman got to you. She reminded you of your mother."

"You who know everything."

"I know everything about you. I am you Rooney."

"I know you know too fuckin' much."

"I know you need to do this. Your mother would expect you to."

He's quiet for a while, then... "Jackie, we need to talk."

She wakes at the sound of his voice. "Please Rooney, no reconciliation," she says, groggily. "I need my wits about me before I commit myself *again* to a booze bag."

"Don't flatter yourself." He pours the last of the bottle and sees the scorn on her face. "It sorts out my thoughts."

"Aye sure, been there."

"Jackie, I can't do this again."

"What can't you do again? Us? Me neither."

"I meant this." She knows what he means.

"And what have I asked you to do Rooney?"

"Talk to the old woman."

"Right, and what did she say?"

The school-teacherliness pisses him off. It always had. So much so he could have blanked her, but he has to recount Irena's story about the man who said the '*In nomine Patris*' thing; to get it out.

" – of your mind."

He recounted it, as best he could.

"We know all that Rooney," she says, taking it in, "but what I'd like to know is what I don't know."

This is a skill for which he was well known. Her challenge gives him a sense of value. It courses across his synapses, stirring him. Something he hasn't had for a while, it's like an addict's hit triggering his spiel.

"Go on, you know you want to."

"Well then," he says, professorially.

"Here we go," she says.

"Right, this usually hinges on...," with the assistance of his fingers, "one, the modus operandi; two, the signature; and three, the victims. That is, A, why did he do it? B, what was his mark? And C, why did he choose these people?"

"Great Rooney, sounds like the old crap you used to talk."

"Fuck," he says.

Her mobile lights up. "Now, there's a strange thing," she says, answering it. "OK, we'll be there, soon."

He looks out of the window again. The sun is coming up. He wonders if he needs this.

"We need to go to Lewis's, to the gents toilets," she says.

"Buchanan Galleries in the January sales, for-fuckin'-get it."

"Shut-the-fuck-up, we're going."

"Shut-the-fuck-up, you're going."

Well out-numbered, he's going.

An hour later, they're in Lewis's department store in Buchanan Galleries. Two security men escort them into a gents toilet. For Rooney, this is a compromising situation.

Jamie, the toilet attendant is in there, recounting his story. "Well, it wis like this," he says, pulling up the sleeves in his grey work coat. "Ah dragged ma mop and bucket into the gents and tried tae get intae this cubicle," pointing through a now open door. "Ah couldnae see any feet under the door, but it wis loaked. Ah wis like that, 'Whit's wrang wi' the door,' ah said. Ah wis like that, 'Is thur anybidy in there?' ah said. I wis thinking some junkie or boozer hid fell asleep in there. Ah emptied ma pail intae the sink, turned it o'er, and pushed it wi' ma fit tae the edge ae the door."

He was milking this, his fifteen minutes of fame.

"Ah grasped the tap ae the door and stepped up tae edge ma eyes o'er and inside intae the cubicle. Ah wis like that, 'Jesus Christ, whit the fuck's that?' ah said. Right there, in big black letters on the back ae the cubicle, there it wis, 'Artir' somethin'."

"Let's see," Jackie says, moving into the cubicle. "It says, '*Artor... ius, ad... inter... nec... ion... em*'."

Latin! Gold flashes through Rooney's head.

"Jist look at this place?" Jamie says. "Hiv ye finished wi' me?" he says. "Fucking shit hoose," he says, his voice diminishing as he goes out of the door, visibly annoyed at the mess from the mucky feet of size nines.

"Aye, on you go," Jackie says. "But don't go too far, we might want to talk to you again."

"Aye, fine darlin', anytime," he says, then whispers to Rooney, "She's no' bad – you shaggin' her," and then back to Jackie. "Mind the bag as well, doll," he says, disappearing out of the door.

"It'll have to be checked," she says, indicating the sensitivity around unexplained baggage, evident after 9/11 and 7/7.

"Latin, the Latin," Rooney says to her.

"It's just graffiti."

"Graffiti... Latin," he says. "A bit of a coincidence, don't you think? Well, you clearly think so. We're here, aren't we?"

"Look," she says, "this is the kind of nutter that turns up at times like this; you've seen it before. They come right out of the woodwork. Must be the press attention or a perverse need to be part of something; makes their insignificant little lives interesting."

"The Latin."

"Aye?"

"Number two. The signature."

"Signature?"

"His mark, remember. Next comes three: why those folk?"

"See, you're getting into this Rooney," she says, turning to the bag. 'As per protocol' she would leave it for the bomb squad to check out. Then, in one fell swoop, she picks up the bag. "Stuff procedures, I can't stand the suspense," she says, grabbing and opening it.

Rooney steps back, coward that he is.

"Argh," she utters, dropping the bag. "A head, shit; a head, fuck me."

There's no need for description. The councillor's family were decapitated on the Cobbler.

"Hold on, what's that," she says.

"What?"

"A piece of paper, it fell out of the bag."

"Pleased about that." Rooney is relieved.

"Folded twice, let's see." She coaxes the paper open with a pen.

"Delivery note?"

"There're some words, 'Sal – va cons – ientia,' the same as on the wall."

"Latin," he says. 'Salva consientia' lights up his mind, just as Irena's words 'I knew it was Latin' echo in his head.

The words take him back to the days when he was an altar boy, when a particular priest used them to dominate him.

"A language of abuse."

"And what do you know?"

"After your illness, a glittering gold colour flashes through your mind when you hear Latin words, and you're transported back to those days."

"You know fuckall."

"This needs to be based on facts," Jackie says, interrupting our dialogue. She's clearly intent on stopping this getting out, not to allow it to cloud the investigation.

"Facts," Rooney says. "Five dead, four without heads, one with. One head found, three to come. What other facts do you need?"

"Fact, we have one big problem pal."

"We? You, you mean."

Smirking at him, she snaps commands at all there, in or out of her jurisdiction. "Nobody utters a word of this, right? Secure the area for forensics," she says, her words spreading throughout the room like cooled air from a rotating fan. She stops at Rooney. "I need to get to Control, but... I want you on board, officially. You up for it?"

"Get to... Jackie, I'm retired, mentally ill, useless; can't do his job, remember?"

"I want you on this, right? It'll keep you focused; something to – "

"Keep me off the booze?"

"Chance'll be a fine thing."

She returns a brief glance and she's gone.

"Fucks off, as she does, official capacity, job always comes first, always did, what about the Latin, me, but I don't do, I can't do…"

Rooney runs the tips of his fingers lightly down the cubicle wall, trying to feel the letters, trying to imagine how it felt for the person who put them there.

"It's graffiti Rooney,"

"That, bastard, is Latin graffiti."

"Latin, you know what Latin does to you."

"Jackie wants me to do this."

"What, be a crap psychosleuth?"

"Beats the life of a mole."

"Safer in your hole, Rooney."

"I could do it for her."

"Jackie, Irena… your mother?"

CHAPTER THREE

Rooney arrives back in his flat to "hit the bottle, wi' purpose." His illness, though "much improved," *he* says, has left residual hallucinations, intractable symptoms, i.e. my good self and the colours in his head. His medication helps, but his drinking prevents it working properly. "I'm self-medicating," he says to me. Ironic given he could get rid of me if he followed the rules set by his consultant psychiatrist – like taking his meds. He intends locking himself away for a 'medicinal binge', prescribed by Oddbins on the way home. Though his adventures on a freezing, wet hill leave him with a mother of all colds. Still a hot toddy of whisky, hot water and sugar will prove to be a combined 'medicine'. He wraps himself up in his old tatty robe, which like himself has seen better days. He perches over his halogen heater and sips the liquor slowly from a cup, stirring it occasionally with a spoon. He sniffs, snorts and coughs in succession.

Jackie phones. "I bought a Latin phrasebook," she says. "Let's see, *'internecionem…'* Here we are; it means 'slaughter'; and *'salva conscientia'*, that means 'wi' a clear conscience'."

"Jackie!"

"What?"

"You're no' hearing me." He coughs. "This isn't for me."

"It's no' for him, he can't do it."

"Just humour me. You're between projects. You got a cold?"

"Too right, something to do with being dragged up the Cobbler on a baltic night. Arthur?"

"What."

"You missed a bit, *Artorius*," he says, sneezing. "Arthur, Ben Arthur, the Cobbler? Latin for Arthur, *Artorius*, Wikipedia."

"Wiki-fucki-pedia!"

"You sound bad, you want me to come over – to rub Vick into your chest?"

"Nice idea, but you'll catch it."

"To slaughter wi' a clear conscience. Is this a message or a statement of intent?"

21

"Both," he says. With a slurp of his toddy, followed by a sneeze.

"Both, fantastic. Right, we're taking you on: on a temporary capacity."

"Jackie, this is serious. I don't, can't do, serious."

He doesn't do serious.

"Rooney, *listen* to me," she says. "There's the official investigation, that's my bag. Then, there's the other, the unofficial, and that's yours, less serious. Fancy it?"

"Fancy it?"

She waits a bit. "Rooney, you can give us something. You know the minds of these people."

"These people!"

"Hawd yer wheesht," he says to me.

"What?" she says.

"Nothing. These people; you're jumping to conclusions, are you no'?"

"We've over a hundred detectives involved, but we've no leads. And you know more about mega killers than anyone in the country."

"She's going for your ego Rooney."

"I know." He coories closer to the heater.

"Good. You're the man to explore the man with the Latin." There's a pause to replenish the Cabernet. "We'll do the investigation on the crew that did the dirty deed. There's a big push to bring these guys in. But the Latin man's for you." Another pause for a slurp. "It's your chance Rooney, to get back, back. Come on. You're on the case. Right?"

"A refreshing alternative to being a sad mad drunk."

In his present condition?

"To go back to the who and the why would do my head in." The days when he tortured himself with these demands remain so real for him. "It'd take me back to where I was. I can't risk that. You know that. It'd kill me."

"Will you think about it?"

"I'll think about it." With that, she's gone.

He pulls the halogen heater, the table, the old winged armchair, and equally old standard lamp, close. On the table, his necessities: whisky bottle, whisky toddy, cigs, ashtray, kitchen roll, and a glass. He lights up and stares blankly into the dark. It's difficult to read this man in this state. To know his fears, addictions, what floats his boat.

"I know you."

"You know nothing about me bastard, now leave me be."

"With your drink, your demons, your needs."

"We all have… needs."

"Drink is your need, but man is your thing. You're fascinated by man killing man."

"Beats listening to dispossessed voices."

I let him drink. By the fourth glass, he's mine. The alcohol is suppressing the cold; the sneezing and coughing are replaced by his raving. He's talking to himself, to me, and to his pictures.

"Predators," he slurs, pointing to his pictures, "continually seek out new ways of killing, taking prey, to become increasingly inventive. Their success is based on learning what works."

This 'how people kill' kindles his interest in a way which finding out 'why people kill' doesn't. He's stirred by the signatures of prolific killers of the natural world. I know what's coming.

"Orca use waves to wash seals off ice flows into the sea to be taken. Lions stalk and suffocate its prey. Crocodiles kill with patience and camouflage. Dolphins corral fish into the head of lochs, with no way out, sometimes drive fish onto muddy banks for capture. Golden eagles come in from the sun to snatch fish from the loch."

"Only man makes his own species kill."

"Man's ingenuity on how to kill knows no comparison in the natural world."

"The Nazis perfected it."

I can hear him thinking.

"'He nodded to one of the men,' Irena said. 'Like a SS officer in Auschwitz giving the death command'."

"The Nazis used proxies. They got fellow prisoners to shoot the Jewish prisoners instead of doing it themselves. They were told if they didn't do it they'd be shot as well."

"A proxy killer, psycho – sleuth; go for it."

"I'll do fuckall." He drains the last of the bottle in the glass, squashes his cig into a pile of butts in the ashtray.

Even although his body's drugged by booze, I won't let him rest. I nag him about Irena and the man with the Latin. This, though, would not be a normal investigation. According to Jackie, this requires an expert on the mind of a man who would leave that message that fateful night. The expert sips the last of the whisky from his glass. It has the desired effect as he slumps deep into his old winged armchair and falls asleep. He can't escape me there. Lately, his dreams, after some self-counselling, are relatively peaceful affairs, but the Latin words bring the painful ones back.

"Do you hear me?"

He stirs, slurring, covering his ears. "Can you no' even leave me alone in my sleep? Why do you torment me?"

"It's what a conscience does."

He moans in his sleep.

"You're back in St Mary's as an altar boy. You're lying naked on the altar. Father Healey approaches you and pours sacramental wine over you. He tells

you 'In nomine Patris' and he puts his penis in your mouth. It feels spiritual, powerful, enjoyable. Then he gives you a bag of sweets and sends you home. When you get home, your father asks you where you got the sweets. You tell him from Father Healey, for eating his willie. He hits you hard on the face and sends you to bed, saying never to blaspheme a priest again."

I watch him on the armchair. A dark patch grows on his trousers at his groin. He's pissing himself. He twitches, flails his arms, lets out the occasional scream, sobs and moans.

He wakes up mid-morning, by the oscillating sound from his answering machine calling out 'two', drowning out the diminishing voice of his father that keeps repeating, "never blaspheme a priest again".

The first message is from the hospital, an ex-colleague offering support. The second is from Jackie. "Rooney, it's me. Phone me."

He shuffles into his kitchen where he turns on the radio, spins the dial and surfs the stations. They are full of 'stark headlines'. From Radio 4, there's an 'unprecedented act of evil,' from Radio 3, 'a vicious murder of our senior councillor and her family stuns the world'. Radio Clyde says, 'Strathclyde Police vows to bring these maniacs to justice.' Real Radio says, 'Get the bastards.' He keeps up his listener-ship of Real and Clyde to provide balance in his life and to remain in touch with the gutter press view of his client-group's activities.

"Psycho-killer on the loose Rooney?"

"Shush."

Radio Scotland's Newsdrive describes the bodies being transported down the hill. It moves seamlessly to reports from its hacks at Buchanan Galleries, and there it is: *'Artorius, ad internecionem.'* It describes the booth in the gent's toilet. Jamie's getting a wee backhand, he thinks.

"Jackie'll just love this." He fills the kettle, reaches for the mobile and gets her immediately. "Did you hear it?"

"Believe me, arses will be kicked. How are you?"

"They need someone to blame. Oh no' bad given I had a skin-full last night."

"There's no one to blame."

"Someone to blame?"

"There's no one to punish."

"You catch them, then you punish them. I meant your cold."

"You don't. The bad you do. The mad you don't. My cold's a bit better, thanks."

Balancing the mobile between his neck and shoulder, he puts a teabag, milk, and hot water into a mug and stirs. Not like his mother did it. She used tealeaves, hot water in the teapot first, swirl it around, empty it, tea in, mask it, pour it. Milk and sugar always came last.

Jackie's voice brings him out of his dwam. "The mad you fucking-well do, Rooney. You stick them in Hillwood and you throw away the fucking key. Got it?"

"You have to understand them, their power, and thanks for the offer of – "

"Do you want to understand them, those who're behind this?"

"Have I an alternative?"

"You can crawl into your hole and die?"

"We need... I need something; anything – "

"Jackie, I'll do it, but I don't do hunches."

"No. Well. There's more."

"Go on." He flicks the teabag into the bin with a spoon.

"Hold on, two minutes," she says. A coffee is needed there, he presumes. She gets back.

"Coffee?"

"Got it," she says. "There was another note, on one of the bodies. Again, Latin, *'vincere aut mori,'* it says. It means 'to conquer or die.' I checked it out. Is this another message?"

"It's a Latin signature... from an Arthur who slaughters with a clear conscience."

"Great Rooney, we look for a man called Arthur who slaughters wi' a clear conscience." She slurps. "Is this what you got?"

"It's no' bad for a start."

"Fine, we bring every bloody man called Arthur in for questioning. If he speaks Latin, we have him. I'll get Archie right on it. I'll tell you what we have Rooney. They kill, they decapitate, and they leave messages. That's what they fucking do. Now, what we want is an idea of who or what could do that."

Rooney retreats the mobile to a safe arm's length. "Well, there's more to this, more to this man." He raises his voice to reach the mobile.

"Aye?" Even at a metre away, he can hear her.

"Well," he says. "If he's behind the murders, he's not directly responsible. He's hands-fuckin'-off rather than hands-fuckin'-on." He wonders if his growl will bring the Gribben to outside the door. He knows she likes to listen in.

"If he's behind it, it makes him as culpable as those who pulled the triggers." Her voice is softer now. He brings the mobile in close.

"It makes him different." His pitch is also less apparent; nothing for the Gribben to grasp.

"Different?"

"Well you know, he gets others to do the dirty deed."

"Less of the fantasies, Rooney. *We'll* find the bastards who did the dirty deed. You narrow *him* down. Just narrow 'im down."

"I'll give it some… thought, Jackie."

"You do that, hon, but no' by staring into the bottom of a glass. You bloody well stay off the sauce long enough to let your brain work."

"Right yar, ma'am." He gives a mini Nazi salute, not that she can see him.

"We will talk, later, Horseshoe Bar."

"Sieg Heil."

He gets the "always the crazy bastard" a second before she ends the call. Though she knows when his brain works, it's inquisitive. His mother said he would have un-knitted a jumper to see how it was purled, but it took him places his clients had already reached: 'up the fuckin' wall'. Jackie knows he's well equipped to profile this man, to give her something tangible, but this guy doesn't appear to fit the normal stereotype. Whatever, he appears to be instrumental in the deaths of the Zysks.

This one has killed through others, he thinks. The family and the messages are statements. But what is he trying to say, this man who slaughters with 'a clear conscience'? He needs to think. To do this properly he needs to free his mind from the sting of it all and to get some objectivity in there. He sits and doodles, and after an hour or two, and equal number of coffees, he needs assistance. And, as he does, he reaches for his ever supportive crutch, a bottle of Macallan 12-year-old, a Christmas present from the Gribben, saved for just this kind of need.

"Not a bad auld stick," he says, pouring a large one; then "Sorry Jackie, I need the inspiration," not that she's there to hear it.

He plays around with a hypothesis as he enjoys the feeling of the invading alcohol. "For a start, Irena didn't say anything distinctive; like he was old or young, fat or thin, black or white, bald, hairy," he says.

"A funny face, funny voice – "

"Pretty normal. White, 30 to 45, average height, weight, well groomed, an accent maybe, might have lived elsewhere."

"Narrows it down. A million men?"

"He may have a modus operandi. He's used others to kill – on his behalf? He leaves a signature. His victims have some common features. He may be an organised man, average to high intelligence, a stable lifestyle – "

"Half a million."

"Married, employed."

"Quarter of a million."

He prattles on for an hour or more, describing classic profiles. Then, after another large one, the drink hits home. An hour or so later, the 'I' arrives, and the 'poor me' stuff. The 'where the fuck am I in this?' diatribe comes out. "Why the fuck did I get into this? She seduced me into it. She fucking seduced me."

"Didn't take much, she knows you need this."

"She wants to get me out of my hole."

"She wants to use you. She always did."

"I can't do this. She knows I can't do it."

"You can't not do it."

The self-analysis comes next, then the self-loathing.

"I used to be a good psychologist."

"Most of your clientele were recidivists who went on to abuse again."

He had problems with this, in particular when the harm reoccurred on child victims. The drink, although dulling some of the pain, didn't help much here.

"I tracked people, gave profiles of who could do things. I understood these people, how their minds worked, what they could do."

"It was too much: the stress, the pain, the expectations. Whoosh, you got high, then higher. Then so far into the stratosphere you couldn't see the ground. You were unique. Your grandiosity knew no bounds."

"I was the best."

"You thought you were the best."

"I could see into people's heads. I knew their thoughts. I could feel their fear."

"You hit the skids, slid downward into a black pool of alcohol and you wallowed in it."

"I was ill."

"Alcohol induced."

"Up there, I knew nothing, cared about nothing. Down there, I was dying, screaming inside my head."

"Good rollercoaster ride, the ups, the downs."

"No sympathy there."

"Doctor Grant, your friend and colleague sections you. The polis arrive and crash your door in. You hit one of them wi' a vase. They cuff and bundle you into an ambulance."

"Paraldehyde injected into my arse."

"Three days later you come around, drugged to your eyeballs."

"I was three months in there."

"Where the unreality was real, the reality stark."

"I got my insight back. I knew what to say to get out."

"'I'm fine. Sure I'll take my medication. Sure I'll take the support. Sure I'll stay off the drink.' You got home, and started again."

"*He* looked after me."

"Most definitely saved your miserable life."

One night, as he staggered up Observatory Road, a distinguished elderly gentleman took him by the arm and walked him to his house. *He* is Nelson

Gray, an eminent artist and writer.

"He fed me, talked to me – supported me."

"That was eighteen months ago. Then three relapses; three admissions to hospital."

"I've been relatively well now... for over six months."

"You drink."

"Controls the symptoms; the hallucinations."

"Me?"

"It helps."

CHAPTER FOUR

Jackie and Rooney meet in the Horseshoe Bar, an old traditional pub just round the corner from the Central Station. Jackie, for that Friday après-work drink; Rooney, for more of the same, Friday or any other day; both of them to talk through the murders on the hill.

Rooney presents the profile he's been working on. She's not impressed. He catches sight of himself in one of the many Victorian mirrors decorated with horseshoes. He looks rough, his hair is longer than he ever remembers, brown but greying. He looks in his fifties rather than his late forties. He notices his teeth as he smiles at an old lady warming herself at the fire. His teeth are brown, stained with the cigs and the coffee. Jackie looks all the better for him not being in her life anymore. Looking younger than her forty-five years, she'd get away with late thirties. Dark green eyes deep set in a canvas of perfect skin. Styled blond hair to the shoulders. Designer jacket cut in at the waist. Nails perfectly manicured. The only consistent thing is the Prada perfume; she always wears Prada. He remembers in times past they would meet here after work. They had been thrown together in the first proper forensic squad, a multidisciplinary team: he the forensic psychologist; she, the new DI trained in all the latest techniques.

They sit for a while, not saying anything. I nag him to say rude things to her. "Fuck off, bastard," he says in a discordant way. Jackie's used to this, but asks if, in him, hallucinations and Tourette's go hand-in-hand, or is he just a "rude shite."

The place is buzzing with the killings. The chattering around the bar drowns out the usual rubbish talked there: football, politics, religion. "Murders... the gangs... drugs... wrang place wrang time," etcetera, provide a good alternative. They discuss what's known, which isn't very much. So far, the investigation is inconclusive, she says, but she feels it has the hallmarks of a mob killing. This is an innocent family, she maintains, with no connection to drugs, money laundering, prostitution, sex trafficking, or anything else.

"Three generations Polish, the Zysks," she says. "Irena, the son, his wife, their two teenagers."

"Sad," Rooney says. "She was respected in this city. Why her?" He waits for the "that's for you to find out," but it doesn't come. She gets the drinks up instead, Stella for him, Chenin Blanc for her. "No whisky for you, Rooney, you know what it does to you."

"It's my medicine." He looks the pint up and down. "Though it did affect my... performance, last time."

"Look Rooney." She gives him a look he's grown to realise will indicate something important is about to be said. "What happened at the Village Inn was... exceptional."

"It wasn't that good, Jackie, you know that."

"I didn't mean *that*." Her sigh says a lot on that point. "It doesn't mean anything... about us. You got that Rooney."

"You got that Rooney?"

He got that.

"Irina." She lifts her glass to check the clarity and whether the glass is chilled. "She and her long-dead husband arrived after the war, fleeing Stalin's communism." She takes a determined sip through rich red lipstick. "The teenagers were students at Glasgow Uni. She was a community activist in Partick."

"Nothing new there."

"Typical folk in a multicultural Glasgow." Rooney waves a kingly hand at the myriad of types around the bar.

"Nothing new here: neds, spivs, poofs, thugs... filth."

"Escaping fascism *and* poverty, to die here – "

"Wrong place, wrong time?"

"Right place, right time... for the killers." The Stella hits the mark.

"The local community's shocked. There's a multiple funeral in St Simons in Partick. Irena worshiped there for a good part of her life."

"A time to get together; you'll be there."

"We're there every Sunday."

"I know; it's a community."

"Dad likes to think so."

"Polish camaraderie."

"Reaching the alcohol-induced pain-in-the-arse stage?"

"We show solidarity in these times."

"Your dear father?"

"Just don't go there Rooney. I know what you think of him. You've made that clear over the years."

"I... respect him Jackie, you know that. I just can't fuckin' stand him."

She does that pause thing, where her eyes and mouth squeeze together simultaneously. Either for effect, time for a thought, or just to annoy him.

"You can't stand the fact he got me the fuck out of our marriage; that's what you can't stand."

Rooney knows he shouldn't push this line, not this time. In the past maybe, but now he knows where it'll lead.

"He's a well-respected man." She's pointing the glass at him. "Can't say the same for you."

"Aye, a big man, the Chief," he says. "Christ, where did that go," he adds, referring to the empty glass as a diversion.

"Evaporated!"

"Chief Constable, Rooney. And no doubt you'll be wanting another?" She knows he's not a man to refuse a drink.

"Why change patterns of a lifetime. Although he has a bit of a reputation."

"He fought the crime barons, the corruption, the cesspits they crawled from, in his way."

"His success was assured."

The eyes and mouth tighten again with the pause. "As you know, success comes at a price."

With a sympathetic smile, Rooney looks at her, knowing there is more to this.

"So says she... who intends similar success."

Another pause ensures this sinks in. "And what about the notorious glass ceiling?"

"Glass cutter, ice pick, or diamond drill... Or just your irresistible charm?"

"Charm never got nobody nowhere."

"Anybody anywhere?"

"Works though... for some women."

"Rooney, just what do you think I am?" For him this is said in an all too familiar way. "A career girl with an eye on the top job – "

"And a hand on any cock that'll get you there?"

"Incongruity!"

The whack on the chest is inevitable. "Here we are again; you and your filthy mouth. There's more to me, and you fucking know it."

He knows it. Just his way of making a stupid point. There was a time in their marriage when he wasn't sure if he could trust her. She was so damned determined to be the best officer possible, male or female. In a male dominated force, he had heard stories. He wondered whether she would be prepared to do anything it might take. She turns to the side, back straight, arms folded. This is a serious huff, aided and abetted by two older ladies 'tut-tutting' at the other end of the table. "That's it hen, don't let him away wi' it," she can just about hear them say. They enjoy their afternoon in the Horseshoe. Their free bus-pass takes them into town, some shopping along Buchanan Street, pie and beans in the Horseshoe; and if they are in luck, a barney to key into for a bit of light entertainment. "My money's on her," can almost be heard from across the table.

"Mine too!"

"I know." He defers to a fresh pint. "You have his support though."

"I got a chance through him. But everything else was down to me."

"The first in your family to get a masters in criminology."

"So right, pal." She points her glass at him to make the point. "Gaun yoursel' hen," is whispered across the way.

"Not to forget your reputation for pursuing the bad guys, just like father. Not easy for a – "

"Pole, Catholic... woman? What Rooney? Take your fuckin' pick."

"Jesus," is heard from across the table, prompting Jackie and Rooney to turn their way. "Whit was that you said, Mary, you know about the weather," provides a smokescreen.

Rooney and Jackie turn back to face themselves again. "Well, something drives you, makes you do... things." He's determined to push it.

"Keep it going, Rooney. Money, success... an alcoholic loser of a husband?"

"To please daddy. 'Sort out your life,' he said."

"It, you, us, needed sorted, Rooney."

"Fucked up our marriage – "

"You fucked up our marriage Rooney, you. He only helped me get out of it."

The silence at the other side of the table only confirms there's serious listening going on between Mary and her pal.

"You didn't need to be so enthusiastic about it. You had to show him *you* could sort it, us, me, out."

Mary looks at her pal. Is this some support for Rooney?

"I didn't need to show nothing to nobody, but myself."

"Anything to anyone?"

"Pedant."

"That the only way to get on is to be a man... be like a man?"

"Great Rooney, go for it. Punish her for the divorce."

"I'm the match of any police officer and –"

"And... you are a woman – "

By now, serous scowls are being transmitted in tandem across the table. "Birreli, mind him?"

"South side gangster, dirty money, teenage drug abuse, underage prostitution."

"This woman, Rooney, this woman."

"One smart-arse-lady-cop."

"Digging a hole for yourself?"

The glass points dangerously close to Rooney's face. "You, are getting... fucking close."

He sure is. No Relate counsellor here. "Don't dae it hen," whispers from the other end of the table. "He's no' worth it."

Rooney's hole digging continues. "A reasonable result, I suppose."

He's lit the touch-paper. "Listen, you pisshead." She gets right into his face. "I spent months getting into the Birreli family, breaking into their account systems, tracing the source of money laundering directly to Birreli himself. An operation carefully orchestrated, the case so sound, opposition in court hopeless, although their rich lawyers tried, and – "

"Battered, deep fried and dipped in curry sauce."

"An average sentence of ten years apiece, thank you, end of."

"Intensive and detailed policing, your hallmark."

"Too right."

"Your appointment as DCI?"

"Arsehole."

That's it; Mary and her pal are off to another table. "Used to be such a *friendly* bar," Mary says, as she passes them.

Rooney knows it's time to shut up. On similar occasions, the table would be upended, and a smack on the mouth would precede Jackie's serious stomp out of the door. But this time he knows the verbal retaliation will come sure and soon: the boozing, the women, his failings; his pathetic attempt at being a husband, etcetera. Then, as she collects two more to settle into a proper post-marital, they hear 'crack', 'crack' sounds.

"Fireworks tonight, in January?" Rooney takes his first swallow from a newly replenished pint.

"Those were shots," Jackie says bluntly, now on obvious alert.

"It's the convention, the convention firework display at the City Chambers," he says, from his take on the sound. "The convention on Glasgow kultyir?"

"Sure. All we need is a bit of fuckin' culture." Jackie gets up.

"It's Muir's annual bash, a celebration of all things great in this eminent city," he says. "Arts, sport, leisure, business; legitimate, illegitimate."

"Steady, Mr."

The commotion around them increases, leading them over, beers in hands, to the plasma-screens on the wall. There a news report sounds out above the din of the folk there. At the same time, her mobile's in danger of buzzing out of her pocket. The police klaxons only confirm her fears.

The TV blares out a Sky-TV 'breaking news' report. "There are reports of a major incident in the city centre. In Buchanan Street Underground. Reports are that some people have been shot."

Immediately, they understand the enormity of this; where, close by, politicians and civic leaders are arriving at the City Chambers.

"Fuck's sake, right. I'm on my way," she says into her mobile. She grabs her coat and heads for the door, only pausing to advise Rooney to 'stay-fucking-put'. He's going nowhere where bullets are flying.

He grabs her arm. "You watch yourself," he says. She returns a surreptitious glance, then pulls away to push through a crowd at the door.

"Still got the touch Rooney!"

He turns back towards the screen where the broadcast continues. "The incident happened as the convention finished its final day of debates, with delegates looking forward to the council dinner and the public to the fireworks display. Elected members are stunned by this tragedy." There's pandemonium in the bar, just a few streets from the underground. Mobiles light up everywhere. "I'm fine babe, don't worry." People are rushing their pints and getting out. Others stay glued to the screens, and to their pints.

Rooney feels compelled to go outside. A cacophony of sound fills the air. For him, sirens from police cars, ambulances and fire tenders are painfully evocative.

"Terrorist attack?" a young guy says, joining him on the pavement outside the bar.

"Who knows," Rooney replies, squishing a spent cigarette with a foot.

"It's been coming," young guy says, lighting up. "Afghanistan and all that."

Rooney accepts one and feels an outer-pub philosophical debate coming, well known to the smoking fraternity following the smoking ban.

"Suppose," he says, not to disagree nor offend. "After the Glasgow Airport attacks, Glasgow's on the hit list."

"Come ahead, we're fae Glesa," the guy mimics.

"Enough to strike fear into the heart of any terrorist."

"Lot of folk in the underground the night."

"Just headin' for a good night out."

"There you are, out for fun and frolics, and bang, just like that, you're deid, all fuckin' over."

"You never know the minute," says Rooney, ever the pub philosopher.

"Aye," young guy says, drawing smoke through gritted teeth, "fat cat city politicians missing their dinner while normal people are getting slaughtered."

"I know, doesn't make sense." Rooney tries to placate him.

"Does for me," young guy says, flicking his lit cig onto the pavement. "Fear is the expected response. It's called terror pal."

"Sounds like you know all about it?"

"Looking for a fat nose?"

"Don't use that shite on me pal. I was in the forces." Young guy decides Rooney isn't worth an assault or even standing out in the cold for and disappears inside. Rooney doesn't blame him. He knows he's right on both counts, the true dynamic of terror, cause and effect. Fear created by desperate men gets desired effect.

The dynamic thrills Rooney. Like a homing pigeon, he's drawn to the site of the action. Off he goes towards Buchanan Street, still inebriated, staggering. There's chaos there and he'll not get anywhere near. That's until he clocks the ever-ubiquitous DI Paterson standing at a cordon fence, just at the corner of West George Street.

"All in control Archie?" Rooney gets close, and tries to sound sober.

"Aye, it's all quiet Rooney, but there's a few deid folk in there." Archie gestures towards the station entrance.

"Indeed."

"Come wi' me." Archie takes him by the arm and leads him through the cordons and to the entrance to the station. Jackie's there waiting by a unmarked police car. They get in, Rooney to the back and Archie and Jackie to the front. Archie struggles to get his sixteen stones behind the wheel, his stomach peeping through strained shirt buttons. Jackie doesn't acknowledge Rooney at first. She's fizzing because he didn't 'stay-fucking-put'.

"OK, what you got?" she asks Archie.

Polis-like, Archie reports as if he had been rehearsing it in his mind. "Right, from a scan of CCTV recordings just before the shootings, we have a man we identified as the gunman walking into the subway at Hillhead, and alighting on Buchanan Street."

"Good image?"

"No, a baseball cap, under a hood, well down over his face."

"Great," she says, "a hoodie."

"A hoodie!" Archie says slowly, as if he's trying to intellectualise the possibility. "OK, the shooting. We have a busy platform full of evening commuters. We have him with a travel bag on his back. It didn't look heavy, but it contained handguns."

Jackie prompts him with a scowl. "Get on with it, detective."

Archie coughs to clear his throat. "Right ma'am. He made his way along the link corridor and down the stairs to the platform. Then we have him squatting in a corner, where he fiddles with an envelope, and then pulls this out." He delves into a standard CID evidence bag and hands Jackie what looks like a wet book of matches. Rooney asks to see it. She passes it over. Rooney rubs dark moisture between his fingers. In the dark of the car he wonders if it's blood. "It's from the La Patisserie Françoise," Archie says. "It's on the Byres Road."

"I know it," Rooney says.

"Of course you would," Archie says, confirming his smart arse persona. "You'll find some writing inside, in Latin. It says 'culpa' somethin'."

"Another Latin thing," she says.

Archie nods. "The man was anxious," he says. "On reaching the platform, he waits at the back of the crowd until the train moves into view.

Then he pushes through and onto the carriage. Inside, he never lifts his head, until the train reaches Buchanan Street. Then he gets off."

"*Buchanan Street station. You know it well Rooney. Mind the times you fell blind drunk from the Clockwork Orange onto the platform to hit the city centre pubs with intent?*"

"Fuck-off."

"Rooney, shut it. Archie, witness statements."

Archie struggles with his notes. "The guys have been interviewing, those able of course."

"Fine, get on with it." Jackie's impatience shows.

"Right," he says. "He moved onto the platform, looking decidedly suspicious. Security was stepped up for the Convention, what with the crowds gathering on the square for the fireworks."

"Detective."

"OK," he says. "He was attracting the attention of commuters. People were sensitive – "

"Enhanced police presence," she adds.

"Cup final policing," Rooney also adds, to their confusion.

Archie hesitates. "Right. Anyway, two armed officers are there, on the platform, security for people heading in. They become interested in this man, believing him to be a recognisable suspect in previous attacks, and move towards him. The man glances over his shoulder and sees them. He quickens his pace. They decide he needs to be stopped."

"The chef late for the council dinner?"

"Rooney, just shut-the-fuck up."

Archie snatches a glance of Rooney's face on the car mirror. *He's* keeping out of it. "Then he reaches inside the bag," he says. "Pulls out two hand guns, spins around, open fires without aim. Hits a woman on the side of the head. Empties both guns into the people there."

Jackie sighs. "How many?"

"Six dead, three seriously injured."

"Go on."

"Our men shoot to the head. People were moaning, calling out names. Some were motionless."

Jackie instructs. "Less drama detective."

"Right ma'am. Seems like the whole of Glasgow stopped. There's panic around the square. The car carrying Muir swerved, off-balancing the motorcycle outriders. One skidded, the rider and bike ending up on the pavement. The car raced away in the opposite direction – Muir's safe."

Rooney feels compelled. "That's good. Our celebrated Lord Provost has survived."

Jackie blanks Rooney. "Thanks detective," she says, "for being so... succinct."

"More on the man ma'am."

"Go on then."

"We ID'd him. He's a hit man, a freelance killer, works for the crime families that could afford him. He's hardly a hoodie." There's either witticism or sarcasm in Archie's voice. Rooney isn't sure.

"No, you're right." Jackie wishes she hadn't mentioned the hoodie thing.

Rooney needs to know. "Was he making for the square?"

"He was heading in that direction," Archie says, through the mirror.

Jackie coughs on purpose. "Well, he never feckin-well got there, did he?"

"Tell that to the poor buggers in the subway." Rooney brings the side window down. He takes in the buzz outside the car and listens to the babble of voices around. He focuses on the people hanging over the cordon barriers at the end of the road. He looks into their eyes and sees both fear and excitement. An intoxicating mix, as were the whiffs of smoke and the smell of sulphur wafting from the subway entrance.

Jackie shivers, reaching over to operate the electric window control, bringing up Rooney's window. "The Lord Provost and the First Minister have made media statements, expressing 'extreme distress' over the 'incident at Buchanan Street'. You listening Rooney?"

Rooney rubs the window to see out. "Indeed, Muir and Campbell getting together across the political divide to condemn the killing of ordinary Glaswegians. Now that is a public interest story."

"Ever the diplomat."

Jackie scowls at him through her mirror. "Per ... lease."

Archie reiterates the First Minister words verbatim. "We are shocked and saddened by the horrific and tragic circumstances in a Glasgow underground station," he said. "Our police forces are responding. My administration will do everything it can to support the people of Glasgow in this extraordinarily difficult time. We are committed to bringing whoever was responsible to justice, to ensure the safety of our people, and to care for those who have been injured. We offer our sincere condolences to those who have lost loved ones."

"Thanks, Detective."

"There's more on the hit man."

"Go on."

Archie girds himself. "Ian Baxter, a contract killer. Sold himself to the highest payer to whack those either not paying up or certain family members who are surplus to requirements."

Jackie says they know him. He's on a list of men with form on assault with a dangerous weapon.

"Hardly his kind of work though," Rooney says. "Too risky, too big."

"Squares with the increase in organised gang violence."

Rooney knows what he means. Glasgow's crime families had become violent factions; confident, ruthless; evidenced by an increasing number of murders, assaults; especially against rival migrant gangs. These were brutal organisations, not afraid of anyone; let alone the authorities. But this is unprecedented. "The mob targeting politicians, Jackie?"

"They don't care who they target."

Archie needs in on this. He started it. "Since Muir's reign, seems they target who they like."

"Less of the personal comments, DI."

"Aye, less of the personal stuff," Rooney adds.

"You better watch out, dear, with your form in the... underworld."

"You should do something else."

"Maybe I'll do something else."

Using a paper hanky, Jackie wipes the mascara from under an eyelid. The eyeliner'll be replenished next. "Well maybe we could use someone else," she says up at the vanity mirror. "Someone not so fucked up and intent on brain death courtesy of alcohol abuse. But you're good at what you do, Rooney, and you're here, so that's it." She has a pause for the other eye. "OK? Shall we just get the fuck on with it. It's what we are and it's what we do."

"It's what you are. It's what you do."

"In nomine Patris," Rooney says, masochistically flooding his head with gold.

"You weird fuck, Rooney."

That's it. Rooney's 'out of there'. He escapes the car. "Keep me posted," he says. "Police work going on here. I'm off to my office. Catch you later, no doubt. Cheeri'."

For him, for then, there's nothing more to do. The injured were taken to Glasgow Royal Infirmary, the bodies to the city mortuary.

"Right, you stay in touch," she says, then, "Rooney?"

"Yes, dear?"

"Stay sober, shit is happening."

"Indeed." He pushes out through the cordons. He's heading into the Merchant City. He knows he should pull out then, but something holds him like Gorilla Glue to the developing scenario.

"Enjoying this Rooney?"

"Go away, bastard," he says. "I'm going to get so paralytic; even you won't get to me."

"I'm in here. You're fucked in the heid pal."

CHAPTER FIVE

Rooney's not ready to go home. Even though it's pissing down, he's going to 'meander purposefully' from bar to bar through the Merchant City. The city's quiet, like a morgue. But there's laughter from inside the pubs, like a communal Irish wake.

In one bar, he hears, "They'd nothin' better to do in Arrochar ... keep the heid ... the subway needed decorating anyway!" Ah, how the Glasgow patter cauterizes the wound.

Glasgow's psyche thrives in its bars, where death and adversity are met by dark humour. He knows the caustic humour of the Glaswegians; their witticisms throwing a cloak over the grim reaper, as they have always done. The ripple effect of the murders will pervade the city; tragedy will enter lives. From the immediate families, to their extended families, their offspring, into the overall community, and on and on; multiple damaged lives creating more damaged lives.

"The net effect of terror," he murmurs to himself.

He makes his way through these dark and now deadly streets, now on a par with 9/11, with 7/7, with bombings on the streets of Northern Ireland and England during the Troubles – but the rain seems to calm things, normalise things. He's soaking and the rain's hammering off his bunnet and coat. The place is teaming with uniforms, and he should go home like the vast majority of folk, but what else can he do? He's drawn to this and he needs to immerse himself in it, to feel the fear, the pain, to be in the dark.

He wonders where this Latin man is tonight. Is he in Glasgow, on these streets? If so, what is he thinking, feeling? Would he feel pleased without being overly satisfied at his work? Would he want more? Would he want to be pursued, thinking connections will be made with him; where, through Irena, they have an image of him, a characterisation; and through his initial profile they have something to go on.

"Right, my good man, work done, time for a dram." He rubs his hands, as if to find an excuse to pamper himself for his resourcefulness. A tactic he often employed after a stressful day, an excuse for a necessary binge. He takes in Babbity Bowsters and O'Neill's at a trot, a drink in each, and then it's time for the Scotia Bar. He needs to be in the right mood for the Scotia Bar. He needs to put his traditional music, writer, socialist face on. A couple of drinks more'll do the trick. That done, he heads across the car park on King Street, the Scotia's lights in sight, like the lights of a welcome port appearing through a stormy sea. Before he reaches his destination, his mobile buzzes in his pocket. He takes it out to see 'Jackie' in the display.

"Yes, darling?" He finds a doorway, fearing this would take time. "Your timing's impeccable as always."

"My darling yourself. What you doing, getting pissed?"

He keeps the Scotia in his sights. "Indeed, just pursuing that objective."

"There's been an assault."

"Glasgow's one big assault."

"This one's... significant."

"What... assault?"

There's a perceivable increase in her tone. "An assault of a prostitute." He's not sure where this fits. "We have intelligence on a man who seems to fit the description in your... profile."

"Ah, the power of... intelligence, police or otherwise."

He expects the pause. "In *this* assault we also have the Latin."

"Latin?"

"Aye, Latin. Where are you?"

Within five minutes of telling her, he's in the back of the car with her and Archie . The car whizzes past the door of the Scotia. Like taking an ice cream out of the hand of a wean.

"In there." She hands him a brown envelope over her shoulder. "You can open it. It's been cleared."

Rooney opens the envelope to find a greeting card.

"There's nothing on it," Archie says. "No prints, no marks, nothing, just the message."

"It's in the same style as your Latin statement and on the book of matches."

Rooney grips it, trying to make out the print. "*In nomine patris alea iacta est.*"

Jackie translates from her book. "In the name of the father, the die's been cast."

"Indeed, the Father, again," Rooney says.

"Could be the same man," Archie suggests.

"Get real," Jackie says. "More like a crazy out for a ride on free publicity, that's the rational view."

Given his pub crawl was prematurely curtailed due to this, Rooney has to ask. "The assault?"

The rain rattles like a snare drum on the car roof, drowning conversation.

"What?" Jackie says, trying to project her voice above the bombardment.

"The assault, the prostitute."

"We've interviewed her," Archie says. "Much of this is her description." A police 'ah hum' precedes his pulling out his notebook.

"Come on then," she prompts.

"Right, well, she's from the South Side." Archie decides on a perfunctory tone. "Her name's Louise. She's a drug addict. She refuses to give her full name."

"Aye we know, her mother'll find out soon enough what she does," Jackie says. "Now get on with it."

"She met a man on Glasgow Green. He approached her without saying anything. 'You a visitor here?' she asked him. She looked at him and felt uneasy about the look on his face, his grin, but she needed his money."

Rooney shouts from the back. "The man who attacked Irena had a strange face, a funny face."

"I remember," Jackie says.

Archie continues. "They reached her flat and she invited him in. Once inside, he just stood there... staring at her."

Rooney wonders if this was the first time this man had attended a prostitute. Some of his clients used prostitutes. Not for the physical stuff, impossible for many, but for the mental stimulus; sometimes for the comfort; and sometimes from a need to engage sexually with a woman, without penetration, though often to be in control.

"Hardly opening his mouth, he told her to take off her clothes," Archie adds. "She looked at him for a moment. Another freako, look but no touch, suits me, she thought. The man waited until she removed all of her clothes. Then she reached for him to run her fingers through his hair. But this triggered violence. He pushed her. She hit her head on a glass table as she went down, causing a head injury and lacerations. She thought she was a dead woman as she saw him standing over her. Then, and almost in a dreamlike state, as she passed out, she heard him say '*mea culpa*', or something like that."

Gold floods Rooney's head.

"Latin," Rooney says.

Archie looks at Jackie. She indicates she knows what that's about. "Aye," Archie says. "And later she wakes up to find herself swathed in white and, for a moment, she thought she was in heaven."

"Unlikely, given her mortal calling," Rooney says.

Jackie's not amused. "So very fuckin' funny."

"Even heaven needs racy ladies." The drink is starting to talk for Rooney as Jackie's eyes drill into his via the car vanity mirror.

"HQ saw the connection between the assault, the Latin statement, and the murders," Archie says. "They put it down to a crank with a liking for violence on prostitutes, but they reported it to me just in case."

Jackie agrees. "The crank theory sounds about right to me."

"I went to see her," Archie says. "I held out the card to her; told her it was found lying on her when the cleaner discovered her. I read out the contents. 'Louise, do you know who did this to you or who wrote this card?' I asked her. She said she remembered hearing the words on the card, but could only give a description of the man who attacked her, based mainly on his strange smile."

"Can I see her?"

"Rooney... try to stay focused," Jackie says. "You've had a drink."

"I want to see her." Rooney employs his pissed-off-being-told-what-to-do voice.

"I expected it," Archie says. "She doesn't want to see anyone, but we've encouraged her to co-operate. She'll see you."

"Co-operate? A promise not to harass her; make it impossible for her to sell her wares; threats, per... suasion."

"Right, Rooney, when you are sober," Jackie says through the mirror. "Tomorrow, you two see her. Tonight, Archie, get him home. He's pished. Me, I have a serious briefing to give back in the office." Archie catches the 'back in the office' bit and heads off in that direction. On arrival at Pitt Street, she leaves the car without saying anything more, a determined look on her face.

The following morning, Archie arrives at Rooney's flat. Rooney's in no state to defend a long lie in bed. He settles in Archie's car, where Archie hands him a flask of coffee and a polystyrene cup; they have half of it on the way.

Soon they're in the South Side and at Louise's flat in Govanhill. She's on the third floor. Having got through the controlled access, they climb the worn stairs to her flat. The air's dank and musty but it holds perfume. Rooney visualises her and her guest on the same route. She would've been intent in getting as much money as possible from her client, to provide a pleasure that would prompt his return as a regular punter – valuable ongoing business. What was going through the mind of this man, Rooney wonders. He didn't think normal everyday sex was his bag, but what was? Rooney knows for most men who assault prostitutes, the attack generally came from a repressed conflict deep in their psyche. For these guys, power over women, expressed through an explicit act of violence, was the application of fear.

Archie is puffed by the landing of the second floor. "Out of condition, pal," Rooney says, reaching there first.

"You are not wrong there," Archie says, his face beaming red, hanging onto the bannister.

Louise is waiting as they reach the top of the stairs on the third floor, just arrived home after having her dressings changed. She discharged herself prematurely from the hospital the night before. Louise has work to do, but she wouldn't be attracting much custom in her present state. She's younger than he expected, early twenties, pretty, but older than her years, worn out.

She welcomes them into a cluttered sitting room and directs them to a sofa. They move a few fluffy toys to sit. She asks if they would like coffee in a west end accent, not the normal druggie, back of the throat, nasal accent. This woman's from a middle class background. They register their declines politely. She describes her attacker in detail; an excellent interviewee.

"I'll never forget his face – a cold blank face." She lights her third cigarette in succession, using fingers peeping through fingerless gloves.

She's intent in describing the encounter in detail. "It was as if he wanted to smile, but he couldn't. His mouth was twisted with a sneer that looked painted on. The last thing I remember was him standing over me, looking down at me with that crazy grin." She didn't need any prompting to continue. "I was only a way, a means, of giving that card – "

"To whom?" Rooney asks. Archie casts a glance. He's to do the talking.

"I don't know, to the world. I don't know, but why me?" Her voice reduces a couple of tones. She drops her head into her gloved hands.

"It's nothin' to do wi' you darlin', he just used you," Archie says, marshalling all his sensitivity.

Rooney scowls at him and moves closer to her, covering his mouth for fear of booze breath. "It's OK, it's OK," he says. "We don't need any more for now." He reaches for her hand, but she pulls it away. She gets up.

It's time to leave, but as they move through the door they hear her say: "'Et Filia,' he said to me." Then, without further ado, she moves into the bedroom and closes the door.

They touch base in the car.

"Et Filia," Archie says, pulling out the coffee flask. It's still warm. He passes Rooney a cup, half filled. "The son; first we had the father, now we have the son."

"Et Filii, is the son, Archie." Rooney takes a slurp. "Et Filia is the daughter," he informs from his rudimentary Latin.

"The father," Archie says. "And the daughter?"

"Indeed."

"No son?"

"No son. I'm concerned for her."

"I'll arrange cover for her," Archie says. "At least for a couple of nights. She's employed by a family who'll be worried about her... exposure."

"They won't want a prostitute with a profile with the police."

"Glasgow crime families are moving into high-class prostitution. Louise

Tom O. Keenan

is on their books. She'll be no use to them no more."

"Indeed."

"You'll remember the book of matches. The gunman in the underground. Our forensics checked it. It's the same lettering. The same hand too. And the '*Alea iacta est*'."

"The die is cast," Rooney says. "Means a war is always a gamble. Was Buchanan Street a gamble, a failed battle?"

"A battle, more like a war."

"A fitting statement to mark my departure," says Rooney. "Anything more before I go back to my leisure pursuits?" He had the Scotia in mind.

"The matches," Archie says. "We checked the café and we're following up some of their customers, there before the shooting."

"Excellent, to my club my good man," Rooney says to Archie, knowing he had read his code, dispatching him at the door of the Scotia.

"Stay alert," Rooney says, as he slides out of the seat and out of the door.

"Aye, sure, don't you worry about that," Archie says, from his open window.

"It's Saturday afternoon Archie," Rooney says. "The traditional Glasgow pub afternoon. In there, I'll think a few thoughts, bore a few folkies, listen to a few songs." Archie pulls away laughing.

In the Scotia, everything is a few, including the drinks; some of which he'll gratefully consume. He gets his first beer up. He'll enjoy this. That's until Jackie phones.

"Hello," she says. "Should we meet, later?"

"Love to darling, but I need to drink, I mean think. You know I need some space to... analyse." He lifts the pint of Belhaven Best to see it through the light. It's a dark beer, but normally clear; he wonders whether it's a bit murky.

"Aye, very good, Mr... Analysis," she says. "But just you remember you've to explore him, without highlighting to anyone he may be involved, because he may not be."

"There's nothing bad there." The beer hits the back of his throat. "Chief worried I may blab to the papers?"

"Just you watch," she says, as the second long swallow hits his gut, confirming the fine quality of the beer.

"Indeed, I will." He looks lovingly at his fine draught.

"I had to talk to Muir."

"You had to talk to Muir." The sound of 'Muir' gives him dyspepsia.

"He was... concerned," she says, "and not a wee bit shaken, as you would expect."

"He could have copped it."

"You wish he had?"

44

"Shut up."

"Copped it?" she says.

"If he was the gunman's target, had he reached the Chambers?"

"He wanted briefed, and I was not to talk to anyone, 'not anyone' without speaking to him first. The council is shiting themselves the guy was heading for them."

"No doubt in my mind." Rooney heads to the Scotia's toilet, where he balances the phone between his neck and jaw, struggling to release his tadger.

"There's consternation in there," she says. How did she know?

"I'm not surprised," Rooney says, with a shake.

"A political motive, maybe. The hit man. The families. Understandably, he wants to know if it was. He also wanted to know all about Louise. And guess what?"

"What?"

"He talked to dad. He's placed me in charge. So everything else, by way of police work, and my everyday-wine-token murders, is to be hived off to other units."

"Gee, thank you very much dad." Rooney settles back in his seat, her not any the wiser of his journey to the toilet. "We'll do your everyday killings – "

"And I'll do the multi-murders, great."

"And I'm left with the psychopaths."

"As you – in your own inimitable way – do Rooney."

"Indeed, dear."

After a minute, she says, "Hon, the prostitute, Louise."

"The only real live link with the man."

"Well not anymore, she's dead."

"Fuck, Archie says he was going to protect her, at least for a couple of nights."

"She was shot."

"He came back."

"Don't think so," she says. "Shortly after you guys left, two men in black coats arrived; two shots – point blank – as she opened her door. Then they walked off, out into a waiting car, and drove away."

"Sounds like she was a threat one way or other."

"The heads," she says.

"Talking heads. The heads on the M8. The heads of Ayr?"

"The decapitated heads, the Zysks, on the Cobbler, you dope – head."

"Indeed."

"Found, in a holdall, left next to Louise's body."

"You know how to cheer me up Jackie," he says, trying to keep his voice down. This's not a place to discuss decapitated heads or a dead prostitute. It could find its way into the lyrics of a folk song. "It's to create fear."

"Fear, people are shiteing themselves Rooney. What next?"

"More of the same Jackie," he says. "Fear and terror, and you know it. Feel it Jackie, feel the fear. It's lovely, go with it. Do it anyway, as they say."

"Rooney," she snarls. "You're a fucking pervert."

He gives her one of those crazy Mel Gibson looks that she can't see, but to him it feels good. The afternoon band strikes up. He finds it hard to hear her and moves outside. It's just as well; this is not a conversation to be had inside the Scotia, where the words 'fear' and 'terror' are normally associated with the call for last orders from Mary, the invincible bar manager. He lights up.

"The Chief wants action."

"Well, you had better give him... action." Rooney feels the chilled air and is more interested in whether his beer inside would be either drunk by another boozebag, as it would be, or Mary decided he was off and had collected the glass.

"Tough action, in this case, is justified," she says. "We're bringing in the gang bosses, all the known heavies."

Rooney remembers The Chief's Law, so called, when Hubert sent in squads, concentrating on one area at a time. In the schemes, gangs were rounded up, shoved into Black Marias.

"Into the courts Rooney, where justice is administered," Jackie says.

"Then right back out." They both knew, back then, that the sheriffs were in the pay of the politicians. They, in turn, were in the pay of the gangs. "Ergo corruption rules Jackie."

"Just don't, I don't fucking need it." Her voice drops off at the end of the sentence. Tiredness, boredom, and I've-heard-it-all-before sighs come from the phone.

"No, neither do I, nor do the great Glasgow public. There'll be big trouble in this little city."

"There *is* big trouble, big fucking trouble, do you get that?"

"Well, it's what the polis do; they do 'trouble'." He hopes his pissed-off-voice is heard by Jackie; though it only prompts a couple of boozers passing to tell him, them, to "sort it out children".

"That, you arsehole, we fuckin' will do," she bellows at him.

"That Jackie, is what you fuckin' well are, trouble." The 'trouble' is followed by a 'phiss' sound as he draws the last from the cig, flicking it into the air, his smoky breath creating a cloud in the cold air.

"You just do what *you* have to do."

"How did you get so much from Muir?" Rooney tries to sound interested.

"We had a drink together."

"Oh you did, a drink, and I thought you were mine."

Jackie's lack of response speaks volumes.

"It was necessary."

"Sure my darling," he says, lighting up. "Necessary for whom?"

"Mainly him; he's hurting. You outside?" She hears the 'tchip' of his lighter firing up.

"Hurting, hurting from what? Aye, can't smoke inside, you know that, it's against the law."

"I can't say right now."

"Oh you can't say. Right, I'll see you." This is serous huff; time to return to his beer.

"Rooney?"

"Hmm."

"Rooney, it's not a problem, OK?" He feels she's trying to offer him some kind of a reassurance, but not exactly understanding why. "And watch yourself. It's bloody dangerous out there," she says, reinforcing the doubt.

"You too my darling," he says, signing off, but thinking, 'Good god, Louise, Muir's daughter, truth *is* stranger than fiction.' How more correct could Mark Twain have been?

He goes back to his pint and sure enough it's gone. He gets in four more pints of Best in slow succession to catch up and to enjoy the craic and the music. Only then is he ready to leave the Scotia.

Like an auld bat, he bumps his way off the walls going up Glassford Street.

"*Mea culpa*, he says," Rooney voices. "Is he guilty?" he asks a young couple under an umbrella, who accelerate to get by this drunk man.

"*Mea culpa?*" he says to a group of woman out for a laugh. "Me a mamma," one says, drawing hysterical guffaws from the rest.

"Guilty, guilty, guilty." Rooney beats his chest in a religious way, as he turns onto Ingram Street, drawing looks from passers-by.

He ducks into a doorway to light up. "This man has to be pursued, but not openly," he slurs. "A police hunt'll only reinforce his importance, give him more reasons to either link himself with the killings or, if he's directly involved, encourage him to do more."

"*Sure, and if he knows you're after him that'll dissuade him. Chase me!*"

"Bastard, I need to try to understand this man, what motivates him," he says to me. "That'll be of some use... to her."

"*Someone like you?*"

"Someone of my sort. Not like her, a cop, who'd pursue him un... compro... misingly."

"*The tongue slightly over-loosened?*"

"My way is the right way."

"*The use of stealth, to track your quarry. Rooney, the hunter.*"

"It's the only way."

"*Being pissed, your prey'll spot or smell you a mile off.*"

"Go away, voice."

He moves onto George Square. The place where the politics were radical, where radical expression was found in the riots of 1919. But what's happening now is also radical. "Best thing that's happened here for ages," he mumbles to himself.

This time the politics were to do with the Glasgow Convention, with much of the debate in the City Halls. The city was full of local politicians from across the city to discuss the theme this year: All Communities Together. Muir declares the outcomes of the talks will be delivered, in respect for those who lost their lives. "Togetherness must be seen to triumph over discriminative acts," he says, publicly. Not bad!

He sits on a bench on the Square for a while to absorb the vibes of the people walking by. They crisscross the red tarmac, as they do, to and from work during the week, shopping and relaxing on the weekend, going to a fireworks display! Whatever, even though it's Saturday, their steps are more urgent today. Is his man behind all of this, he wonders. If so, would he be pleased he caused fear there, the killings and the wrecking of lives. Is this his objective? For most, including Jackie, this is mob violence. For Rooney, the Latin man has more than a supporting role.

"*He fascinates you. You fantasise that he is behind all of this. You enjoy the thought of it.*"

"Indeed."

"*You're curious about the Jackie–Muir thing, and about your own irrational reaction.*"

"Curiosity killed the cat, bastard."

"*Makes you think about her, them. Her wanting you to do this job and all. You and her. What's this about: unfinished business? Inevitably, you'll get pished. Jackie and Muir, your excuse, this time.*"

He heads into Merchant City, he'll have his dinner in Babbity Bowster: cullen skink and stovies and three pints of Deucher's IPA. Three hours later he hails a taxi at Candleriggs, fifteen minutes later he's back in his flat. The armchair does the trick: he's asleep in minutes, but only after consuming four glasses of whisky, putting paid to a half bottle. Normally, his dreams are dominated by nightmares, but this time there's a white stag, grazing in the morning sun. And there he is, Sean Rooney, erstwhile hunter, and Nelson Gray, his hero, and for then his personal ghillie, peering through the heather brush. "Just another few seconds my man," Rooney says. "The monarch of the glen, I've wanted him on my wall for some time."

"Arthurian legend says its presence represents man's spiritual quest, and the time is nigh for the knights to pursue a quest," Nelson says, digging into his specialist knowledge of Celtic history.

"Indeed, thanks for the information," Rooney says. "He's a cracker though. Look at him moving forward, imperious, royal. That's it, he's ready to go. Come on my beauty, come on."

"Get him now; go on, it's a good shot," Nelson prompts.

"Too soon, just about there, come on my sweetie."

The stag sniffs the air, looks them full in the face for all of five seconds, turns, and makes his run.

"Now, go on, do it, end him, squeeze it," Nelson urges.

In his dream, the shutter fires on his long lens SLR, like the far away crack of a high-velocity rifle.

"Why couldn't you have shot him properly?" Nelson says. "He would've made a very satisfying dinner."

"Am I a good man Nelson?" he asks him in the dream.

"Are you a good man, Rooney?" I say to him, in the same dream.

"I believe so," Nelson says.

"Have I always done the right thing?"

"Do *you* think so?"

"My father always said I was to be good."

"You've always done good Rooney."

"Thanks Nelson."

"You've done bad things."

"Leave me alone. Why do you torment me so?"

"In nomine... conscientia."

CHAPTER SIX

Rooney stirs, the dream resonates in his mind. 'You've always done good Rooney ...' He's not feeling that good though. After an afternoon in the Scotia, an evening in Babbity Bowster , and after finishing a good part of a half bottle on return home, what would you expect? He's half way through a carton of orange juice when Archie arrives at his door. He invites him in, hoping he isn't too fussy. Archie picks up the carton and follows him through to the sitting room. Rooney pushes some of the clutter off the sofa to have him sit there, where he knows is relatively clean. Archie sets about finishing the orange juice, without a glass.

"I guess Jackie sent you to get me out of bed and to get on with the job." Rooney takes the carton from him. "Not to mention to get off the booze,"

"Yup," Archie says, "I've no' to forget to mention to get off the booze." Archie loosens his tie and pushes deep into the sofa.

"Make yourself comfortable Archie!"

"Thanks."

"She wants you... informed."

"Go on then, I'm up and awake," Rooney says, guzzling another mouthful of juice.

"OK," Archie says, pulling out the inevitable notepad. "Following our enquiries at the café and using the description provided by Louise, it seems a man matching this description was seen drinking coffee there at around 11.30 a.m. on the day of the shootings; appears he glanced at his watch, repeatedly."

"Someone's late."

"Late?"

"Late, for an important guest, late for this meeting?"

"Meeting?"

"Indeed Archie, a meeting," Rooney has no need to take his hangover out on him.

"You've a weird imagination."

"Come on Archie, even for you it's easy to imagine two men there for a meeting. One, the Latin man, and the other, the hoodie from the subway."

"Why do you think that?"

"For the whys I need to play a mental game; that's a step up from imagination Archie. This generally leads to a SWAG, my shrink's wild arse guess. A SWAG, get it? Then, if I'm lucky, I'll move to a hypothesis."

Archie looks askance. "Do you have a SWAG here?" he says. "This... hypothesis?"

"Indeed, let's see where this takes us, right," Rooney says, embarking on an imaginary tour. "Latin man and hoodie, right?"

"Right, go for it!"

"OK, hoodie man appears," Rooney says. "He's a hit man. He doesn't say much. Action not words for him. He stands over Latin man. 'Yes,' Latin man says dryly, pulling out a chair. He gestures the hoodie guy to sit. He's the commissioner. He has the say."

"The paymaster?" Archie says.

"Puppetmaster."

"Puppetmaster?"

"He pulls the strings."

"Pulls the strings?"

"Indeed, pulls the strings," Rooney says. "They swap some coded communications. 'What's your business, my friend?' Latin man asks. 'Same as yours, big man,' hoodie man replies. Sorry Archie, hoodie men say 'big man.' I like it, I'm only five foot six. Anyway, Hoodie man's white tea with three sugars arrives."

"Well, we know... three sugars?"

"He's no' from the West End, Archie."

"Hoodie man or Latin Man?"

"Hoodie man."

"Right," Archie says, getting in to it. "Hoodie grunts at the waiter, and then leans across the table towards Latin man. He looks serious. The waiter says Latin man looked 'rough' and pushes an envelope across to... hoodie man, who sticks it in his jacket pocket, and then leaves."

"There was nothing else to say, the stage was set, the deal made long before. The hoodie man – "

"Selected for the hit, by the families?"

"Now we are developing our SWAG."

"Ah, but what about the hypothesis?"

"Don't get too smart Archie, it is no' like you."

"Naw, well, some more information," Archie says. "He had the right credentials. A twenty grand draft paid directly from an unknown Swiss account into his bank account, and a habit that needed funding."

"Ah hah, a hit man with a weakness, not good... Now, to the two Rs."

Rooney senses Archie's exasperation. "Archie, he wants recognition or revenge, maybe both."

"High profile, that recognition Rooney."

"Indeed, and high profile that revenge Archie."

"Got it Rooney."

"Good man," Rooney says. "There's more. Right, he's exhilarated. He's rattling the cup in its saucer. He's going over the plan. A perfectionist. An obsessive. He likes to get things right. He's in his zone."

"He's looking around, trying to catch people looking at him," says Archie. "'Look at the super confident bastard over there,' he's thinking. 'Wish I was as cool as him, I'll bet he's famous. Think he's on TV, or films?'"

"Feisty imagination Archie; should have been bipolar."

"Enough Archie, the master-class is over," Rooney says, getting up. Archie has a problem pulling himself out of the sofa; Rooney has to assist. "Jesus Archie you need to get some of the beef off."

"Rooney?" Archie says, going through the door.

"What."

"Jackie needs you to do this."

"I know Archie, bye pal," Rooney says, locking the door behind him. He's not getting back in, not without a warrant that is.

Rooney goes back to the orange juice, but he has something stronger in mind.

"This Latin man's connected to the hits," Rooney says to the juice. "He has to be."

Rooney knows though not to give this man some credence would reduce him to the realms of an eccentric, and he couldn't pursue a crank, a nonentity. *He'd* be a nonentity and he couldn't stomach that. This man's involved and he's convinced of it.

"Your hypothesis is a joke."

"What do you know about hypotheses?"

"I know everything that's in or comes from your head."

"Indeed, but you can't think *for* me."

"Your hypothesis is weak; not even a tentative theory; not even a hunch of why your Latin man's involved; it's his modus operandi that captivates you."

"God, but you are starting to sound like me."

"I am you and everything you dislike about yourself."

"Go away. Go where you go. Where I can't hear you."

"Jackie needs you to do this, but more than that, you need to do this."

We both know I'm right.

Later, Jackie invites Rooney for dinner at her place in Cleveden Drive, just off the posh side of Great Western Road in Kelvindale, a spacious Victorian flat. She won't eat at his place for obvious reasons. She 'wants to talk'. She's dressed for the occasion: a red track suit and a pair of Nike trainers, having just had her run. She serves macaroni cheese. What about your usual gear, Jackie? The wee black number, is that for Muir? Macaroni cheese and Shiraz, that's not for Muir. Filet mignon and Cabernet, for him, no doubt.

She talks her head off about Muir and her newfound status. She's now a 'high-powered official in the case'. Good for her, do her good to get a bit of ego stoking. Earlier that day, she had been called into Muir's office, she says, to 'brief the council on the investigations'.

"Fuck, there were about ten of them in there," she says. "As soon as I walked in, they fired right off. What a bun fight. 'Who's behind the incidents? Who's claiming the lives? What are you bloody well doing about it? We want action, action!' The get-the-bastards-tin pots, he calls them."

"Kind of reflects present day Glasgow politics," he says.

She resumes at the pace of a metronome out of control. "Muir says my 'undercover people' are to 'track and destroy these people'. 'No quarter, got it?' he said. His words stung my head as he banged the edge of the desk with clenched fists. So much so, a desk lamp and a tray of coffee mugs clattered onto the floor. It was dead dramatic. No one needed reminding of his temper, or to argue with him. They were to go quickly about their business. Then he turned to me. I was shitting myself and I didn't do very well. I've never done that kind of thing before. My voice was shaking and stammering. In my poleet wee voice, I said, 'I have to say Lord Provost, the investigation remains inconclusive. The only lead we have is this man who left the Latin messages and a tenuous link with the crime families.' 'Of whom I presume you are in pursuit,' Muir said. 'We have someone on it,' I said. 'You don't mean the shrink, do you?' he said."

"Me!" Rooney is flabbergasted. Muir has an ear to the ground.

"Then he gets up," Jackie says. "And, coming up close, so no one else could hear, he says, 'That'll do for the histrionics Jackie. It's for them, for effect, not for you. But you will get this sorted, right, for ...' And that was that."

"Well, you will rub shoulders with the high and mighty sweetie," Rooney says. "For to get this sorted. For what? For who Jackie?" he asks, taking a large spoonful of macaroni.

"For nothing Rooney. I'm fucked." The Shiraz kicks in, as her head drops to the side. She falls asleep on the sofa. Rooney carries her through to the bedroom.

"Story of my life," he says, coorying in beside her. Then, in what feels like a flick of a switch, it's early morning.

She wakes him up with a mug of tea. "Sir, your tea. It's seven thirty," she says, in a fake posh drawl, interrupting a deep sleep. "You have an... appointment at nine," she says.

"What?" Rooney growls, preferring to snarl rather than speak before ten each day. "It's seven-frigging-thirty. Sorry, it's not only seven thirty, but it's Monday, and it's seven-frigging-thirty, get it?"

"Rooney, you have a serious attitude problem, however..."

Now he's awake. "However, dear, you will piss off, kindly."

"Listen stupid, lives depend on your meeting. Muir wants to see you, so that's that," she says, getting back in, and sitting up.

"Lives and Muir don't concern me," he says, petulantly pulling the duvet over his head. "Oh, that's why you get me over her, ply me with dinner and wine, take me to your bed."

"Macaroni and cheese and a bottle of Shiraz, Rooney; and you took me to *my* bed, not that anything happened."

"Well, that wasn't my fault. I'm no' going."

"OK, I'll have you taken there in cuffs."

"You got me there Miss Moneypenny," he says, in his shit Sean Connolly accent. He tries to snuggle into the warmth of her body. She pulls away, reaching for her mobile to check her texts.

He'll have her for an hour or so, or so he hopes; then they'll have a good breakfast and go to the Chambers.

"He thinks."

Their taxi arrives at the Council Chambers, late. In truth, they fell back asleep, overslept, and panicked. After no breakfast and gulping down a coffee from a paper cup, collected from a McDonald's drive-through, they walk fast into the reception area. Rooney's in a right mood and smells of booze, and Jackie leaves him at the reception desk. He guesses he'll be seeing Muir on his own. He's ushered up the marble stairway through some long grand corridors and longer grand rooms until he hears that voice.

"Mr Rooney," bellows out. Muir's tenor reverberates through the halls. Rooney turns to see Muir approaching through an open door, an outstretched hand seeking a handshake. "I'm James Muir, come in Mr Rooney," he says. "I've heard all about you."

"Sean Rooney, call me Rooney," he says, feeling the insincerity of the man's grip. More typical of a health insurance salesman.

"Do you smoke?" Muir holds a cigarette case open.

"No thanks, unhealthy habit." Rooney does, but he doesn't take cigarettes from smart arse provosts he doesn't know.

"Yes, disgusting." Muir takes one and clatters the case shut, then laughs. "The ban on smoking in public buildings doesn't apply to me."

Democracy in action! He now feels embroiled in high profile stuff, epitomised by a Lord Provost with a Kelvinside tone, a silver cigarette case, and a disregard for his own rules.

They reach Muir's office where Rooney settles in a large leather bound chair adjacent to a large desk. Muir offers him coffee from a percolating machine in the corner of the room. The smell of the brewing beans reaches Rooney before the coffee does. If he wasn't so stuck on booze, he would've been a caffeine addict.

"I believe we have an interest in common, Sean," Muir says, taking a draw and pushing back on one of those large leather chairs that bend backwards.

"Rooney, I prefer Rooney, thanks." Rooney's determined to ensure this man doesn't see his nice side.

"Rooney, then."

Muir refuses to pronounce Rooney's surname properly, with no emphasis on the 'oo', nor the 'ey', making it sound like 'Ronny'.

"Our common interest... sir?"

"Just call me James, everyone else does."

"OK, Mr Muir, why am I here?"

Muir hesitates. "Well..., last night, well into evening," he says. Who's he trying to impress? "I was reviewing some reports and statements, from your colleague DCI Kaminski, on the case – your case."

"My case?"

"Well, *the* case," Muir says. "I have information which points towards hit men as responsible for the... incidents."

"Well, it's all sewn up then," Rooney says. "Can I go now?"

"No and no. Something doesn't quite make sense to me. The Cobbler and the Buchanan Street killings, and... Louise, were mob hits; crime family killings, no doubt, but... you say," he pulls out a report, "they were not... 'typical'." Then, with the tenacity of a starving dog raiding a Gregg's rubbish bin, "I have to satisfy myself about these extraordinary circumstances, as is my right."

"His right."

This man gives Rooney the creeps. He doesn't know why, but he does. He feels like he's being groomed by a sleazy paedophile. "No, I'm too old for that," he says to himself. Well, maybe the way an independent financial adviser seducing a life assurance policy candidate. That'll do.

"Why Me?"

"You Rooney, you can help me make sense of this."

"I don't know if I can make sense of much these days," Rooney says, "let alone all that's going on."

"Back to the reports," Muir says, dismissing Rooney's confusion. "I'd just checked the investigation portfolio and found this... file. He holds it up drawing Rooney's attention to the large bold print on the front cover: THIS FILE IS NOT PART OF THE OFFICIAL INVESTIGATION. Rooney wonders why it's there at all and why Muir has a right to it. "The more I read, the greater my interest. Latin phrases, Latin man, a statement from... Irena. And Louise..., a murdered... prostitute. And a psychologist, you, and your... unofficial brief. As you would expect, I needed to know more." He's now leaning over the desk like a cougar on a rock ready to spring.

"As you would." Rooney tries to think of how to get out of there if he launched at him, especially if he had a life assurance policy in his hand.

"As is my way." Muir walks around his desk. "Best to talk to those who know, I thought, and here you are."

"And here I am."

"This man, Mr Rooney. This man with a predilection to Latin statements, who seems to be around in the incidents."

"Yes?"

"In our incidents?"

'*Our* incidents now!' Rooney rises and moves to the window that looks over the Square, busy again, those crisscrossers, heading to work this time. In a past life, he would sit there on a bench with his drinking pals wondering what was going on in here. Shite, I'll bet, Rooney thought then; same now.

"We should share what we know," Muir says, joining him at the window with his cig.

"What I know isn't very much," Rooney replies. "But it may be ever so slightly more than you."

"Exactly why you are here."

"I need a drink," Rooney whispers to himself, hoping to get the hell out of there.

"You need a drink." Muir hears his whisper. "Well, you better go find 'a drink'," he says, stubbing out his cigarette brusquely on an ashtray as he turns away. "You will excuse me, Mr Rooney, I have things to do." And with that he's out. Muir realises he would get no more out of him in such a state of desperation. Muir advises the reception desk to tell Jackie to get Rooney 'the hell out of here'.

Outside, Jackie says they need to talk. Rooney suggests that he may converse better with a drink in front of him. She takes him, via a black cab, to the Scotia – by then just opening at 11.00 a.m. He downs a Guinness, she has Pinot Grigio.

"You no' got work to do Jackie, like apprehending some killers?"

"One drink and I'll be back in my office; first we need to talk."

Rooney is in his office.

"The consensus so far is that the firms are behind all of this, who knows why, we'll find out; but I know you have other ideas Rooney. Let's hear them, like not 'typical' for example?"

"Nothing fits Jackie. Why would the mob slaughter an innocent family on the hill, slaughter people in the subway, kill a prostitute, all for the sake of it? There's more to this and you know it. The Latin, *for example*, and the Latin man, and my fucking instincts Jackie."

He has two more and so does she. Her checking into her office advising Joycy where she is, confirms she is going to go with it. Drink overcoming duty, relaxation overcoming a great deal of stress; she'll catch up later, as she always does.

The drink kicks in for both of them. They return to her hobby horse: her ambitions to smash through that glass ceiling of Strathclyde Police, but how she feels she could never match her father, though she intends to die trying.

"Who wants to match their father?"

Rooney breaks into a hum as he hears Raglan Road, one of his favourite drinking songs, wafting through from an impromptu session warming up in the back of the lounge.

They leave there at six, she dropping him off by taxi, but not before she kisses him with a passion he hadn't known from her for a long time. And, within his nether regions, not a little stirring occurs. He invites her in, but she declines. She says she has a busy day ahead, and anyway "best not to get mixed up. Business is business, and pleasure is not getting reinvolved with a… liability." He goes inside and pulls out a half bottle secreted in his coat pocket by Mary as he left the Scotia Bar. He lifts it to his lips, and toasts –

"His true love!"

CHAPTER SEVEN

The mobile sounds as if it's about to take off. It's been buzzing for three days, since he locked himself away in his den to drink and sleep, sleep and drink, leaving numerous messages on its answer facility. He deletes them all. He can't stand the thought of going through them and hearing them one by one. And the intercom had gone off and the door rattled a number of times, as if someone was trying to break in. The Gribben, no doubt. This time it's refusing to give up. He gets up, kicks his way through a number of bottles, and reaches it. He ran out of booze the previous evening, which is just as well, and he'd slept for around twelve hours. He opens the door, not quite sure what to expect, but he isn't surprised to see Jackie there.

"Well, Lazyrus, I see you're up." She pushes passed him into the hall, her words like a foghorn in his head. "It's twelve o'fuckin'clock."

"Lazarus!" He pulls his dressing gown around him as he drags his body into the hall.

"Aye, well. Mrs Gribben let me in," she says, following him through.

"Hail Glorious Saint Gribben."

"You're no' answering my calls?"

"Indeed," he says. "Seen Muir recently?"

"My business, and that's why I am here," she says, in a pissed off voice. "This is not a personal visit."

"I'll come quietly," he says, in a no-state-to-argue way. "What's happening in the outside world?" He drops into his chair.

"Only a mass escape at the Springburn Unit," she says, as she pulls out a black bag from the kitchen. Then, one after another, she drops a number of bottles into it.

"You have been busy," he says, though shiting himself at the enormity of what she has just said.

"You are so abso-fucking-lutely right you piss artist."

"You here to chastise me? This is police harassment you know. When?"

"Tidy yourself up man." She stands over him like a sergeant major at roll call. "Last night, late."

58

"Oh fuck, please go away…" He's clearly not coping with this.

"We've a meeting wi' Doctor Grant, in Pitt Street."

"No' another fucking meeting," he says. "What's it got to do with me? Anyway, she'll feckin section me." He recalls a particular psychotic episode.

"It's just a wee holiday, Mr Rooney."

"Well, for one," she says, "you've worked wi' a good number of the heid-bangers in there. Some of whom are now out on the streets terrorising the gentle folk of Glasgow. Two, there's Latin involved. Three, it's the chance you take. So, get yourself ready, she's waiting."

He's in no fit state to argue, nor's he ready to face Doctor Martha Grant, consultant colleague, now medical director. Though, after a large cup of coffee, lots of orange juice, and a couple of Paracetamol, he makes the effort. But, after a binge such as was, he doesn't feel like it.

Archie is driving, and soon they're in Jackie's office, where Martha's waiting. Rooney's happy to see her, one of the better doctors he's ever worked with. And one who, apart from her sectioning him – wholly necessary – gave him good advice on his illness. She welcomes him with a big hug – difficult given her great girth. She smells good, expensive perfume. Good perfume usually turns Rooney on, but not this time. Jackie supplies a needed tray of tea and scones. He's happy to coorie into his Crombie, to sit back and listen.

"Well," Martha says. "It started late last night with the security controller reporting something strange. He scanned the monitors covering the ground and fences. All the screens in the security suite had gone blank. All except one, it said, *'In Nomine Patris'* emblazoned on a white background in large black letters."

"In the name of the father." Rooney stuffs his face with scone.

"Yes, I know," Martha says.

"Sorry."

"Desperately, he fired instructions onto the keyboard, and nothing happened. Then the dark descended throughout the site, and no alarm sounded."

"The security system was one of the best in the world," he says, under his breath.

"You were on the planning committee for the unit." Jackie heard him. "So much for the assurance."

"The local residents didn't want it," he says. "They feared an escape of a dangerous patient…"

"May *I* continue?"

"Sorry," Rooney and Jackie say in unison.

"Thank you. Well, in the wards nothing seemed unusual," Martha says. "Well not at first, said the night staff, until from 2B they heard a scream. Joe Dunlop, a charge nurse, was the first to die." Rooney remembers him. He was an unpopular man with the patients, viewing his job as custodial, not caring. "Georgie Giovanni, a psychopathic killer of women, took the chance. Joe was first on his list given this opportunity, throttled by Georgie's mastery with a violin string, and his eyes gouged out by a dessertspoon. Knives and forks were taken by others, and used on the security men trying to stem the stream of extremely agitated men."

"And like a swarm of rats racing from a house fire, they were on the run," Archie adds. "With no alarm, the doors opened like the gates of hell. Yes, some of the most dangerous men in the country were on their way out – "

"Yes, detective," Jackie says.

Martha resumes. "Twenty eight of them headed out on to the streets. There was no alert to the police."

"The major incident plan failed," Rooney whispers.

"The fail-safe communications system had been disabled," Martha says. "And there it was, emblazoned on every operable computer screen. *'Non revertar insultus,'*

"I shall not return unavenged," Jackie says.

"Death heads out onto the streets," Archie says.

There's the inevitable stunned silence.

Archie adds more gory detail. "One of them walked into the Maryhill Tavern, just before shutting time; he seemed OK, nothing unusual," he says. "However, he wore a long black coat, taken at knife-point from a drunk who had gone into a lane for a leak. Now dead, throat cut from end to end. One distinctive thing was the pump-action shotgun, drawn from beneath the coat."

"He had left this same bar some five years before," Jackie says. "That night he thought people were talking about him, planning to kill him. He had smashed a few tables, hit a few people, and survived only because we were on the scene to deter the locals from killing him."

Rooney remembers the case. "'Schizo-killer' the tabloids called him. John McCourt," he confirms.

"Correct," Jackie says. "Seems this time he would get them before they got him."

A man walking into a Maryhill bar with a pump-action means only one thing: knees or headshots. The barman would have shat himself, a profusion of sweat, panic; everyone frozen to the spot.

"His brains were splattered across the stained glass mirror at the back of the bar," Archie says. "He blasted everyone and returned to them repeatedly, their heads, faces, eyes."

Their eyes would not find him again nor command him.

"Enough Paterson," Jackie says, cheesed off with his rhetoric.

"OK, well," Archie says. "Then he sat down, apparently feeling safe, resolved. He was taken in happily humming to himself without a fight."

"Most of the patients have been picked up," Jackie says. "They were identifiable, drinking cheap wine in the parks. Some talking to themselves as they wandered around in the malls. Most gave themselves up; though some were significant by what they were up to."

"Some sex abusers brought grief to the women in the area," Archie informs. "Assaults, sexual."

Another inevitable silence.

They promise to 'do everything necessary to apprehend all of the men,' then say their 'byes' to Martha Grant and leave her to cope with only the worst escape of dangerous patients in the country, with explanations to give to many relatives and victims, and the inevitable inquiry. In his previous role, Rooney would have been there with her in this task.

There's a sense of relief most had been picked up, but also a sense of trepidation as they travel into town, though not for Rooney. He feels safer with the guys who had headed that way than most of the headbangers he would normally meet in the city. He knows, however, that a breakout at Springburn will evoke more than a sense of unease on the streets. It'll compound an already developed climate of fear and insecurity.

"There's one in particular," Jackie says.

"Marty Simpson?" Rooney asks.

"Correct."

"Bruce?"

"For me to protect," Jackie says.

Simpson was committed to the State Hospital at Carstairs, without limit of time. Then he was transferred to Springburn, because it was viewed he didn't need maximum security. An anti-social personality disorder, with a dangerous religious obsession and a prolific stalker of John Bruce, Simpson was a once very famous, but now very reclusive, rock star. He had a fixation of killing Bruce, dominated by his constant references to the bible. A rock-music icon from a housing scheme in Glasgow, Bruce made it big. For twenty-odd years, he led the charts and the younger generation on the university protest scene. Two years previously, Bruce noticed a man watching intently from the crowd. He had had many crazies before at his gigs, but this one was different – he stood out. The next time he saw him, he recognised him immediately, but now he sensed an immediate, palpable danger. Simpson approached him on the way out of the BBC studios in Queen Margaret Drive, where Bruce had just appeared on a late-night talk show. Simpson held a book open. Bruce thought it was an autograph book, but then realised it was a bible. He heard two or three words he thought to be Italian, then felt a deep dull pain from a bowie knife as it plunged through his stomach wall and into his left lung. For three weeks, he hung on to life. For over a year, he was a physical wreck. His star-like charisma and confidence were gone, a shadow of the giant he undoubtedly was. Gradually, he fought his way back to some physical health, but his emotional health was never to return. Eventually, he moved away from the rebel persona and became the type of conservative character he had previously despised, all so readily damned in his songs.

"Never had any taste," Rooney says.

"He's now a reclusive figure in a beach house-cum-fortress, on Loch Lomondside," Jackie says. "Even though he thought Simpson would be locked away for life."

Bruce fancied himself as the voice of the generations he had entertained, asking them to turn their backs on drugs, promiscuity and anti-state attitudes. His new friends were in echelons of the establishment, no higher than Muir himself, who had befriended Bruce as a symbol of his policy of 'togetherness' across the generations.

"Muir's buddy," Rooney says.

"Muir was informed as soon as we knew of the escapes, in particular of Simpson," Jackie says. "Then, of course, he passed the job of protecting Bruce to me."

"Of course, this whole thing is to do with Muir."

"I'm the detective here Rooney, so you keep your unconfirmed conjecture to yourself."

Muir was determined Simpson would never be discharged, despite the fact that over the past seven or eight years the Springburn psychiatrists had consistently put him forward for review of his detention. A review Rooney supported on the basis he was not amenable to treatment and, consequently, should not be in a psychiatric hospital. This was contradictory given that Muir's council had supported the drafting of mental health law to ensure psychopaths were kept out of mental health hospitals and were locked away in high-security prisons instead. For Muir, Simpson was different. So much so, as a restricted patient, Muir and Campbell had agreed long since he would stay 'restricted' and never freed.

"I remember how public opinion influenced the court decision to divert him towards a fixed custodial sentence – away from the state hospital."

"A suitable case for treatment I don't think," Archie adds.

"No, I don't think," Jackie says. "Muir called Bruce, offered him personal assurance, at the same dispatching orders to us all 'in criminal-justice' to make 'damn sure' we made no mistake in getting Simpson."

"I'll keep an eye out for him," Rooney says, getting out of the car.

"Aye, you do that," Jackie says. "Want some company, later?"

"No, you're alright; I guess you'll be busy tonight."

"Playing hard to get?"

Rooney gets to the Stirling Castle bar in Yorkhill. It's busy with Yorkhill

Hospital staff in for Friday lunch. He orders a pint of Stella, leans over the bar, watches and listens. After ten minutes or so, deciphering a number of voices from around the bar, he sees and hears Simpson order 'a pint of Guinness'. Simpson looks his way and next thing he's there in front of him. "Rooney, guess only you would've known I would've been here," he says. "You gonnae shop me?"

"And why would I do that Marty? You weren't Springburn material, not 'treatable'."

"That's right Rooney," Simpson says. "Psychopaths don't get treated, they just get incarcerated."

"What are your plans Marty; Bruce, maybe?"

"Got it in one Rooney, you always were quick."

"You know me Marty," he says, in a way not to provoke.

Rooney wants to know who's behind Simpson's break out. Although others got out, creating fear throughout Glasgow, he believes Simpson was the focus of it all, whatever Jackie says. Now this man is inches from Rooney's face and his breath stinks of booze and curry. He guesses that is what you would consume, having been locked up for ages. A shaved head, a growth on his face, and added weight, gives him some anonymity. He says he was 'encouraged' to continue 'god's work' through letters he received from an anonymous correspondent; a letter writer who seemed to prompt him implicitly, through coded messages, that Bruce should die. He says he was coached from afar to plan the demise of his anti-Christ and to adopt the ancient language of the true god, Latin. Simpson says to Rooney that he is safe, that he always liked him, and has no wish to harm him. Rooney didn't think he would, but it's good for him to hear the words; then he's gone and Rooney'll not follow him.

Rooney could have called Jackie there and then; after all, she was charged with protecting Bruce, but he decides to drink on. This's an intoxicating atmosphere and he wants to immerse himself in it. This's Simpson's bar and only Rooney knows that, as he had told him in one of their interviews. He didn't record it, though. It didn't seem relevant then, but it is now. He wonders whether he's still there, watching from a corner of the bar, waiting to see what Rooney would do: phone or drink. Rooney drinks; and, after a few, he staggers out of there around teatime, to wander down Old Dumbarton Road. With Simpson out there, there's a good chance he would get his throat cut that night; but he didn't care, he just didn't care.

He hails down a taxi at the Galleries. It takes him to the Aragon Bar on the Byres Road, where he nearly falls through its double doors. A couple of guys just inside the door pick him up and sit him at a table near the door and, without drawing attention to him, get him a pint.

He sits and scans the bar. The familiar faces. Old Howard, who says he won an Olympic gold medal at Archery in 1972, a group of bombastic teachers, who were there from 4.30 p.m. every Friday, and a hen party with an obligatory blow-up male sex doll, with all the bits.

The buzz is "Nutters on the streets of Glasgow... what else is new!"

Rooney's mind is on Simpson, not on his intentions, which didn't matter to him, but his 'correspondent' who used the Latin, the Latin man.

He manages to get home, god knows how. He leaves the radio on through the night and vaguely remembers hearing something about Bruce's death. He gets up for a nocturnal piss, and wonders whether he'd been dreaming; but then, around two, Jackie calls.

"Rooney, Bruce is dead. Muir wants to see us," she says.

"Why me, *you* fucked up."

"You're the fucking expert. I'll pick you up, eight-forty-five, we see him at nine."

"Saturday morning? Hold me back," Rooney says.

"Hold you back? Hold you up!"

They meet in Muir's office. It's freezing. Rooney snuggles into his Crombie.

Muir starts. "John Bruce was killed last night."

"He was murdered," Jackie adds.

"Yes, murdered, while in the protection of Strathclyde Police."

"There were... circumstances."

"We will hear of the complete circumstances... in your report," he says. "For now, I need briefing."

Rooney digs deeper into his coat until only his eyes and head are in view.

"Yes, fine." Jackie's shoulders slump as she sighs. She steels herself for the task and relies on her notebook for support. "Well, he was last seen on his balcony overlooking the sea." Muir is gazing with disinterest at the ornate ceiling. "He was holding a glass of Black Label whisky, as he did it seems most evenings, weather permitting it seems. Two armed guards saw him there as they paced the perimeter. A security camera recorded him moving inside to the warmth of his large sitting room, where it looked as if he saw something and spun around to call out to the guards. A large Bowie knife cut deep and almost severed his head from his body. A similar knife and cut as years before, but this time there was no saving him. Bruce's house-keeper, bringing him his nightcap, found him."

"Simpson?" Muir asks.

"Yes," Jackie replies, "Simpson. He was found about the same time in the Balloch Hotel. Customers saw blood seeping out from under a cubicle door in the gents. The door was heavy as the manager pushed it open to find Simpson hanging by his jawbone on the coat hook on the inside of the door, a note held deep into his back by the same knife that he used on Bruce. We found Bruce's blood on his knife. On the note was '*manu propria*': 'with one's own hand'." Gold arrives in Rooney's head. "Our inquiries confirm Simpson killed Bruce; how *he* died was inconclusive, but his hanging by the jawbone was a mob style of killing."

"Still to be established," Muir says. "You can prove this?"

"We've also established the release of the Springburn patients was made possible by a computer virus," Jackie adds. "It wiped out the site's security software, allowing a team to enter the campus and the wards. They overpowered the security men, released the patients."

"You have established nothing – "

"You'll be upset... about Bruce," Rooney interrupts, popping his head out of his coat, trying to take the pressure off Jackie, but only giving Muir another target to vent his spleen.

"No, Rooney, I am bloody well livid about Bruce, beside myself, bloody raging. A clear lack of responsibility, bloody poor practice."

God, how this man resembles Basil Fawlty.

"Sure," Jackie says, "we messed up. We should have saved Bruce. We knew he was at risk."

"You were charged with his protection. You!"

Rooney decides to stay quiet. Muir is huffing like a bull on the make and Jackie's ambitions are evaporating before her eyes.

"That is all there is to say." Muir ends the discussion, while directing a long look towards Jackie. "It's Saturday morning and I have a life," he says, showing them out.

CHAPTER EIGHT

They walk to Sloans Bar, just off Argyle Street.

"White wine?" Rooney asks, reaching the bar first.

"Aye, Sauvignon Blanc. Make it a large."

He gets the drink in. The place is mobbed with Saturday imbibers taking respite from the madness of Argyle Street's shopping zone. No cozy booths available, they move to the corner of the bar. They pull out a couple of bar stools to settle for a debrief. Jackie's gutted. She admits she messed up over Bruce's murder. There had been 'extenuating circumstances', she says, which, at the time of the murder, she could not divulge. Then she goes on to assault Rooney's ear about Muir. She's sure Bruce's murder had marked her card with Muir, and his influence within the Strathclyde Police Authority would soon confirm this. The Chief didn't like Muir much. He saw him for what he was: a corrupt, power-grabbing, politician. Hubert had been determined to 'clean up the city', and that, including the crime syndicates, meant the council as well. He just needed the evidence. So, the possibility of support from Jackie's dad on this one was unlikely. They discuss how 'dad' would view this. He didn't take fools gladly, whether it was his daughter or not. In her career, he had never given her a cushy journey. She had been sent to Partick Police Station in her first placement, a tough area, no easy number for her. Despite that, she had fought her way up. Jackie had a lot to prove then, but even more now since she'd been accepted into HQ at Pitt Street.

"Guess the glass ceiling just got thicker," Rooney says.

"Thanks, I knew you'd understand."

"Indeed. You know me, supportive."

"Aye, always been your hallmark; anyway I don't bloody well need your support. Not then, not now." He's pressed a button. "I support myself; you know that, do you fucking hear me? I do it myself. I've always had to stand on my own two feet. Dad didn't make it easy for me. No way, no hand-ups for me pal. All my friends had everything they ever wanted. I had nothing. 'Character building,' he said. He had nothing in his life, and he made it. He would make damn sure if I made it, I would make it in the same way.

He failed to realise it was doubly hard for me as a woman."

"The same cultural challenges, you know being Polish in Strathclyde police and all. Didn't have the square and compass, did he?"

"No, damn-fuckin'-tootin' he did not." She gets to her feet to gain a better perspective on him. "He fuckin' well used his brain rather than... contacts."

"His fists too," Rooney adds. "They say he put a few Brig'ton hardmen on their backs."

"He fucking gained their respect," Jackie says, getting on her feet.

Hubert had reached into the no go areas of Glasgow and the traditional territories of the established gangs. He took on the gangsters and made enemies in the City Chambers by promoting a tough approach. He was forced to resign after a local hood, who battered and raped an old woman in Govan, was taken into an alley by three local policemen and ended up hospitalised, to leave disabled some months later. Hubert was interviewed on TV and was unapologetic, saying the man deserved it; and, if he had been in the alley, the man would have gone to the city mortuary rather than to hospital. A new regime arrived at Pitt Street promoting a softer community-based approach. That worked until successive politicians became steeped in cronyism and corruption. Following 9/11, as the crime syndicates began to exploit the national focus on terrorism with a reign of fear on the streets of Glasgow. This prompted a return of a tougher more protective police force able to meet the challenges of the new millennium: drug-related crime, organised crime, and international crime barons. It was clear the man to lead the SPD was Hubert Kaminski, and when the Chief Constable position was 'made available', the job was his.

"He has a way of demanding respect. Come on, sit down." Rooney pats her chair. "Though the gangs' new respect for the Chief was well matched by the Provost's seedy links with them."

"The politicians fucking undermined him." She sits and faces the bar, and pushes her hair back from her face.

"Sure did. During his investigation, he established that Muir had used 'undue influence' to secure a six-figure contract for his friend and fellow councillor Bill White. Uncomfortable to say the least, but he viewed there was 'insufficient evidence' of criminality; 'no further action' was viewed as appropriate."

"Fuck off, he's no man's man."

"A strong man, your father."

"And you're a weak man, Rooney."

"I had you."

"You lost me." She gave him a stare that went into his past.

"I couldn't... trust you."

"What, with our marriage or your soul?"

"Both."

"Do you trust me now? No marriage to risk, your soul is now your own." He could feel her eyes penetrating him.

"I couldn't tell you… everything."

"Oh, and what about the dreams? I've been there Rooney. I held you as you woke up screaming about you and your mam. I know about your demons."

She goes on and on prompting him, goading him, inviting him to bare his soul, his inner feelings. Sober he would have been careful not to go there – danger, danger, danger. Drunk, he's like many in the pub after a few when it all pores out.

Then, until he feels he's about to explode, in that midway point between stupor and 'taxi', it comes out.

"OK, I will say this only once, as said." He also turns towards the bar, to avoid her eyes. "Then it will be said no more, never again, kaput, finished, over – got it?" She nods. "Shite, why am I doing this?"

He wrings his hands and hesitates before he starts. "Right, there were times when I lived in my head." He takes an unnecessary drink of his beer to emphasise this. "I imagined I was Rod Taylor in the movie version of HG Wells's *The Time Machine*. At the controls of the machine, I travelled back forty years to my childhood, and back among my family."

"You sure – ?"

"You started it, now listen."

"I'm listening."

"It's a cold winter evening, and my mother's at her sewing machine – a Singer, next to the open fire. It's quiet and warm, and there I am in the corner playing with my toy soldiers, an eleven-year-old boy. The radio is on. Doris Day is singing '*Que Sera Sera*' and my mother is humming away to it."

This scene that fills his heart and his head, a mixed emotion of joy, love… and fear.

"Every few minutes my mother looks anxiously at the old mahogany clock on the mantelpiece. 'Time you were in bed wee man,' my mother says as, again, she looks at the clock. 'It's nearly nine o'clock son.'

"'Aw, no' yet mammy.'

"'You need to be in bed before your daddy comes in.'

"Just then, there's the sound of the outside door closing. There's fear in both of our hearts and eyes. Both of us sit up startled, the living room door opens, and there he is, just as I remember him, standing there in all his glory, and in all his brutality. I want to intervene, to protect me, my childhood, my mother. But I understand to change this would be to change myself, and to do that – to change my history – is not only impossible but too much to risk."

"You need to get it out," Jackie says.

"Get it out Rooney, trust her."

"'What you doin' up at this time,' my father growls.

"'He's just goin' now; you're home early the night,' my mother says.

"'Well, they said I had too much,' he says.

"He slumps into the large armchair, drunk.

"'Should you no' be goin' to bed yourself,' my mother says in a trembling voice.

"At this, his demeanour changes, as he rises and towers over the both of us. We hold each other and wait for the inevitable. We both feel the bony back of his hand as it hit us both, almost simultaneously. She cries out loud. I just cry inside."

"Rooney, that is just sad."

"Aye, pathetic, I know," he says. "Well, you brought it out, but that's it, no more, no more," He's shaking. He shouldn't have said it, but it came out. "You've not to mention it to anyone Jackie, got it?"

"Rooney?"

"Aye," he says, waiting for it.

"Your mother committed suicide."

"You know about that?"

"You told me Rooney, after she died."

He pauses to signal to the barman. "Two more."

"Maybe I should have kept my mouth shut."

"It was after one on those nightmares."

"I have just about come to terms with it."

"Rooney, you never come to terms with something like that."

"Ah well, we all have something."

"You poor sod, you have been through it."

"Said the spider to the fly."

She puts her arm around him and pulling him in. This feels good, and in a strange way not unlike the way his mother used to hold him. He tries to remember his mother's perfume to make this feel as real as possible, but he can't, which worries him because he would normally be able to. For the meantime, Jackie's Prada fragrance does the job.

"I always wondered why a man who works with the mentally ill becomes... ill himself."

"Well, depression comes from loss."

"So psychopaths then, what about them, for example the Latin man?"

"We are a bit premature on that one Jackie, but that type of mental disorder isn't organic, biological or functional. It's to do with personality, a personality disorder. It's a different thing. It's a mental disorder under the Mental Health Act, but not a mental illness. It's different."

"Personality disorder – "

"Narcissistic personality disorder, where a person is excessively preoccupied with power, prestige and vanity, mentally unable to see the destructive damage they are causing to themselves and to others."

"Psychopaths, I call them."

"Why do I bother?"

"Rooney," she says. "I'm not a psychiatrist, psychologist or any other kind of ' – iatrist or ' – ologist, so don't expect me to understand this, but what causes it, you know… the mental illness? Do you catch it?"

"Yes love, you better watch, it's contagious."

She looks around the bar; 'contagious' is not a good word in this place.

"I know you hon, you're not crazy, not psychotic, not a nutjob. You're 'bipolar'; you told me."

"Bipolar disorder, bipolar affective disorder, affect, mood, up or down, or up and down, big ups, wee downs, wee ups, big downs, cycling pole to pole – "

"That's where the polar bit comes in."

"Correct, over days, weeks, or months."

"How's it caused?"

"Who knows? Genetic, triggered by trauma, development factors. It sneaked up on me."

"Something to do wi' the mother and father stuff you talked about?"

"Who knows?"

"What about the… relationships?"

"You know about the relationships."

He doesn't like talking about his 'relationships'; especially not with his ex-wife; his relationships were disastrous to say the least, a succession of failures, leading to a failed marriage. Then the illness kicked in, prompting massive disinhibition; 'experiments' followed.

"It may have caused the breakdown," he says, hoping he could move away from this.

"And what about deeper relationships, your mother, your father, for example," she says, with a degree of sensitivity he'd forgotten.

For Rooney, this is going too far into dangerous territory. "Who knows Jackie?"

He notices the barman raising an eyebrow in his direction. This must be a non-smoking, non-swearing, non-aggression, non-confessional pub. God, how things had changed in Glasgow.

"I remember when I first noticed it." This was new and somewhat more comfortable.

"Oh?"

"Aye, you became very defensive, paranoid. Everyone was against you, you said, talking about you."

There were those times when his paranoia focused on certain individuals. Like Ben, who he was convinced was conspiring against him, trying to destroy him for his own gain. Though, most of his paranoia was pointed essentially towards his health board employers.

"The powers-that-be never understood. They got me in the end, though."

"'Paranoia is just a heightened sense of awareness,' said John Lennon." This stopped him in his tracks. God, was that what was going on?

"Some people were talking about me."

"Aye, because of your stupid behaviour; you were out of it, in your own world. You were out-fuckin'-rageous."

"I wasn't able to sleep for weeks. Talking like a Gatling gun – "

"Your addictions – "

"Great for getting things done."

"The paintings."

"One a night."

"The photographs."

"Thousands."

"You were flying at the speed of light."

"Mad she means. Fucking-well out of it. The delusions, the paranoia, the beliefs. Bonnie Prince Charlie for a while. Mind the tartan, the kilt? Then the hallucinations, me, the voices, the colours."

"I still have the bastard."

"Your voice."

"Got it."

"Hello Bastard," she says to me.

"Hello cow."

"He called you a cow."

"A cow. You cheeky bastard."

"You got it."

"Then the downs."

He doesn't like talking about the downs. "Don't, I can't do the downs, can't even think of the downs."

"It messed up your job."

"The detentions did that, cyclical admissions to hospital. I had months in there."

"Bloody shame." She reaches out and takes his hand in both of hers. "Roon, you were doing well at what you did." If this is a compliment, he doesn't believe it. "You must have been messed up pretty badly, to give you this, that?"

"I'd prefer not to go further down this road, Jackie."

"Oh come on Rooney, you know your secrets are safe... with me."

It's in the way she hesitates that prompts Rooney to reveal no more.

"*Not safe?*"

"And what about you Jackie?" he says, turning the spotlight towards her, and away from him.

"Me?"

"Aye you, your... psychology."

"Don't go there Rooney, you know I don't like it. You know you can't... analyse me."

"Would I dare?"

"*No?*"

"You loved your mother – "

"Don't Rooney."

He knew he shouldn't, but he needed to balance the emotional books.

"There was only you and her. Hubert was away. You never said why."

"Fucking hell Rooney – "

"*Get in there!*"

"He comes back. She turns to him. He intrudes on that ideal mother-child love, the dyadic relationship; with which according to Freud we will always seek to be reunited."

Jackie looks on blankly.

"Your mother dies and your father gets a new wife."

"You're right, I loved my mum. It was a beautiful relationship. I missed her so much. I still do."

For a few seconds he looks into her green eyes and sees a child, then a steely gaze takes over.

"Well, you know something about me Rooney and I know something about you."

"*Depends what you with it... Hon!*"

CHAPTER NINE

Sloans always had a buzz, especially on a Saturday, but for Jackie and Rooney a familiar hubbub grows around the bar, the kind they had grown to know recently. Something catches Jackie's eye on the TV above the bar. "Turn it up, bar man, please," she says, "if you don't mind?" Her voice breaks through the chatter until the volume on the television's turned up, and familiar terms are now coming from it. 'Explosion... casualties...' Here we go again, get the flak jacket on! Now audible, the commentator's report draws attention to the television. Those continuing to chatter are shushed.

The commentator continues. "The bomb exploded at noon, as Lord Owen began his keynote speech."

"Topic, the rise of organised crime," Rooney whispers.

"The Grosvenor Concert Hall has been destroyed," the reporter says, "bringing the ceiling down on around forty guests. It's difficult to know the number of casualties, but remarkably initial reports suggest close to twenty, possibly more."

"The crazy bastards." From the speed of the beeps Jackie's thumb is dancing furiously around her mobile.

"My man," Rooney says, well under his breath not to disturb her.

"Owen's annual seminar. I wondered if it would be a target. I said it would. They never fucking listen."

Owen, Lord Spencer Owen, a Labour MP before he moved to the Lords. Everybody at the bar was stunned. All except Jackie, as she pulls Rooney roughly from his seat and out onto Argyle Street.

"Christ, you know how to haul an auld man about."

"Taxi," she calls, then whistles until a black screeches to a halt. She pushes him in, then following him in instructs the cabby. "The Grosvenor Hotel, fast."

"You'll be lucky hen," the cabby says in gruff Glasgow. "The place is surrounded by polis, press, TV, tourists. Even before you get anywhere near."

"Just get us close." She knows he'll try.

Rooney phones Ben and leaves a message. "En route."

73

The taxi edges through unfamiliar back streets.

"Towards the flashing lights, driver," Jackie says.

Great, Blackpool illuminations, Rooney murmurs to himself, but checks himself from suggesting so. Black Glasgow humour wouldn't go down well there, with her in crises mode. The scene in *Apocalypse Now* goes through his mind, where a US patrol boat edges towards the shore, somewhere in Cambodia. Like Dante's Inferno, smoke, an acrid burnt smell, flickering images, the air thick with fear.

They slow to a crawl on Great Western Road, a few blocks from the Grosvenor. It becomes clear they aren't going much farther. The police had cordoned off the scene all the way around the hotel and the top of Byres Road. She pays the man, unrepentant about not getting any closer.

"Close enough," she says. "It'll give us time to get our heads into gear."

Rooney had similar feelings approaching the Cobbler. The same surrealistic vision in his mind, the tension building the closer he got. He feels 'in his watter', as they say in Partick, his man has been active there. They move easily through the cordons with the help of her badge and reach the hotel. There they find an impenetrable barrier of fire tenders, ambulances, police cars; a complete disorder disallowing any vehicle's movement in or out. Ambulances act as stationary first aid stations, the crew stabilising people, performing lifesaving surgery – hopeless for some of the seriously injured. A temporary mortuary has been hastily set up in a wedding marquee in the street, screened off with large bottle-green tarpaulins.

Rooney and Jackie glance inside as they pass by, the flaps open to admit another stretcher victim covered in a white bloodstained sheet. Inside, multi-coloured shrouds lie side by side, broken occasionally by huddling bent figures inspecting clothes, faces, personal possessions, looking for identity. The noise is deafening. People, relatives mainly, are crying, calling out names, and sobbing painfully. Radios crackle with directions and orders; voices sounding confused with no clear intent or purpose. The aurora borealis appears in his mind once more.

"Fuck these people," Jackie gasps, lighting up, as television commentators speculate out of all control or license.

They move closer to the scene, not saying anything to each other. Until they reach a large man, acting on behalf of black coated figures behind him; a CID silhouette, even down to the mobile phones held tight against the side of their heads. She knows him. "It's John, an old colleague," she says.

"Oh John." Rooney half hopes that Archie would've been there; not this time.

"John, Hello."

"Jackie, hi there, come on through."

She doesn't have to pull rank or show her badge there. John returns to his telephone discussion. "No sir," he says into the mouthpiece. "It's the

Chief," he says, turning to her, putting his hand over the phone. Then, returning to Hubert, "We've interviewed everyone we can sir, and no one noticed anything unusual." They become interested in his conversation. "Owen had just started to speak and it went up. Then the ceiling came down," he says outwards to Jackie, then gestures towards Rooney.

"It's OK. He's with me... a colleague."

"Yes sir, one minute, sir," John says, then muffles the phone with his hand. "Do you want to talk to him?" he asks her.

"Suppose I better," she says, flicking her cig to the pavement, squashing it with her foot. "Hello dad."

'Dad' is asking the questions, from the 'yes, yes, yeses' from Jackie.

"They've admitted liability," John whispers to her.

"Who has?" she says, handing back the phone.

"The Taylors. Never heard of them, have you?"

She doesn't respond, although later she said she knew this crime family. Rooney decides to do some investigating on his own, as he does – not advisable given his predisposition to hallucinations, drink, and danger, but he's determined to not let these things disable him. He moves into the hotel. Yes, he knows it's stupid, given the place could've come down on him, but Jackie's soon at his side.

The humming generators lead them into the devastated reception area. They follow trails of wires into what was left of the concert hall, and tread warily across a crumbled mess that poured out of the double doors. This would've been the first floor, previously above a large ornate ceiling. Every now and then, there's a call for quiet as all listened for taps, scratches or moans, to guide them to victims hanging on to life. They move on, clambering over equipment, broken furniture, and rubble, lots of rubble. Rooney strokes a large marble pillar; this one appears untouched, dominating what remains of the hotel foyer. He presses his face against it. Wrapping his arms around it, he feels its chill against him. It impresses him. He'd have loved to see the top of the column. "If the capital is highly decorated," he says breathlessly as they crawl through, "it means it's Corinthian." He remembers visiting the temple of the Olympian Zeus in Athens, which has Corinthian columns. He remembers their smooth feel, at a time when you could get close to them. "Also, I hope very strong," he says, hoping they were marble as they are holding up a very precarious-looking ceiling. These mental diversions help reduce his predisposition to panic.

"Where the fuck are we going?" she asks.

"Evidence, as you say."

He wonders if there's a sign, but if so, where? The registration book seems plausible. They find the reception desk, to the side of the main stairs, where it would usually be. Then on the floor, behind the desk, he finds a large book, surprisingly intact albeit covered in dust. It can only be the registration book. The spine of it sticks out, covered in rubble alongside the contents of the desk. Jackie frees the book from the grip of its surrounding mess. She thumps it on the desk.

"I can hardly see a thing, but let's see," she says, reading some of the entries.

"Second of January. Marybell Carter-Jones, Louisville, Alabama ... just loved the Hogmanay party, especially the Highland bagpiper.

"Fifth of January. James Parker Bowles, Kensington, London, England. I was cold. The soup was cold. Just like Glasgow. I will not be back.

"Fair enough," she says, as she continues 'through the singed pages', flipping forward in time to the last entry.

"Fourteenth of January. Lord Spencer Owen. So good to be here. Thank you so much for the warm reception.

"Jesus, Owen. Poor man didn't expect this."

Then her voice, following her gaze like a magnet, skips back to the previous page. There she exclaims, "14 January: *empta dolore docet experientia.*"

"Wowheah, bingo," Rooney says, vibrant gold appearing in his head.

"You found something Jackie?" John bellows as he enters the reception area.

"Naw, nothing of importance." She says, ensuring he doesn't steal a lead on her.

He's now beside them. "You guys need to be out of here. The place isn't safe."

"This Taylor family. What're your thoughts?"

"Crazy bastards."

"You know them?"

"I've heard of them."

"Names?"

"We know who they are. We're going to engage them."

"*We* need to be involved."

"They're held up in a posh townhouse down on the Broomielaw, by the river. Special Forces go in tomorrow morning, at 6.00 a.m. We've been in touch with your people."

Almost instantly, she's on her mobile, to inform 'her people'.

Rooney hears John whispering, appearing to push his old friendship somewhat. "Jackie, listen, the Chief wants no prisoners. He wants a message to Glasgow's criminal underworld, that 'no organisation's bigger than him'."

"Maybe so, but no prisoners mean no information," she replies. "You want to be around when they move in?" she asks Rooney.

"Indeed, have I anything better to do? Are you sure it's just a 'them'?"

"What?"

"Maybe it's a him?"

"Look, we've got them. That's enough for now."

It's her job and she's going to do it. So he leaves her there and retreats from the dust, the noise, and the despair; out onto the street. He could offer some support to the stretched services swamped by families arriving at the scene, but Ben's team would be well on their way there, and this would distract him from the task of pursuing the entity who seems to live for the grief caused to others.

Rooney gets home and opens a bottle, finishes a glass and pours another. Over five hours he finishes the bottle, to slump back in the chair and fall asleep.

"As he does."

The knocking on the door startles him out of his slumber. It's 5.30 a.m. the following day, and he's still sitting there, glass gripped in his hand. He smells whisky and feels his damp trousers. "Shit, I must have spilt the stuff. Either that or I've pissed myself. Why the hell did I give up a normal boozer's life for this?" He gets up and moans as he tries to wipe his trousers with a damp towel. "Feckin hate this," he says to himself. He reaches the door to find the Gribben standing there.

"You've to come now," Mrs Gribben says. "And I'm in no mood to be arguing with you. Jackie said to say that."

The Gribben points to the car. Jackie and Archie are there waiting. He gets in and off it speeds, Archie at the wheel. "The SAS are there," Jackie says, not taking her eyes from the road. "They've taken up position just out of sight of the house where the family are."

"SAS!" Rooney says. "Not taking any chances eh? Heckler and Koch MP5 assault machine guns?" His detail isn't appreciated. "Ideal for confined spaces, like the Iranian Embassy siege in London?"

"You still drunk?" Jackie sniffs; obviously the smell from his trousers.

"He had no time to change, Jackie."

"What does the family have, blades and bottles?"

"Rooney, this isn't the days of the Billy Boys or the razor gangs. These families have sophisticated weaponry."

"Sawn off shot guns?" Rightly, she ignores him.

"They've listening devices through the walls. Taylor and around fifteen of his soldiers are inside. They're a violent group, but not a disciplined force capable of coping with the SAS."

"No quarter offered, nor given?"

"Correct. Diplomacy and dialogue, normal in these situations'll only delay the inevitable fire-fight and give these people protracted attention. You got it? This is not to be allowed. They've shoot to kill instructions."

"Sounds like the Chief's words. The media'll just love it. What's the legal basis for this?"

"It's father's law," she says. Rooney doesn't enquire further. He knows what she means.

Archie and Jackie close the car doors gently as they leave. Rooney is to remain in the police car and to 'mind his own business'. On the stroke of 6.00am, he hears windows going in on all levels of the townhouse; stun grenades, he presumes. Sporadic gunfire entertains him for around ten minutes. They return to the car.

"The group's liquidised." Jackie puffs smoke into the car.

"Executed, you mean."

"Overpowered. A successful operation," she says, pouring coffee from a flask.

"You'll now have great delight in informing me," Rooney says, asking for 'one of those'.

"Archie tell him," she says, setting up two more polystyrene cups.

"Well," Archie says. Rooney settles in for another soliloquy. "They were dazed from stun grenades and fired into the fog created by the smoke canisters. The SAS held their positions as Taylor's men continued to fire. He was screaming orders indiscriminately around him, and they fired on until there's a pause; as if every one of them stopped to breathe, rub their eyes, think, until the second grenade attack knocked them to the ground."

Archie pauses for breath as Jackie passes the coffee. "Milk?" "Aye." "Sugar?" "No." Rooney has the same.

"They were wearing infra-red goggles. Made it easy to get on top of them. The first few went down where they were; some were caught in rounds from both sides, not able to see the laser tagger red dots on their foreheads."

"Looking into the eyes of executioners," Rooney says. "As you would expect from the SAS."

"They have... protocols to ensure maximum effect and minimal loss," Jackie says, like reading from a training manual.

"Maximum effect, no prisoners; minimal effect, single pistol shots through the frontal lobes."

"If you want to see it in that way."

"Taylor stood there alone, surrounded," Archie says. Rooney sees him in his head surrounded by ghoulish helmeted figures. "He was determined to go down with his group. He raised his sub-machine gun, and then a semi-automatic pistol was pushed into his face."

"A taste of hot metal in his mouth, his last experience, like a firework going off in his head," Rooney suggests.

"Sure is graphic Rooney, but sorry to disappoint you, he didn't fire," Jackie says.

"No?"

"He's needed."

"The 240 volts on the testes comes next." Rooney knows he's pushing it.

"Listen, if you are getting something constructive out of this, fine. But if you are getting some sort of a weird kick – "

"It's the way my mind works, visualising things."

"I understand that, but you understand this, I am a police officer, and I need evidence. Truth and justice, *veritas et aequitas*."

"The Latin phrase book's going to your head Jackie," Rooney says, but he's impressed. She's determined to challenge not only 'orders', but her father's orders; not a good idea, but the right thing to do.

"The fire-fight was over. Seems the Chief's pleased at the exercise," Archie says.

"Punished the gangland fraternity."

"None of ours were lost, Rooney," Jackie says.

"The slaughter won't be popular though."

"No, not the best of publicity, but sends out a message."

"And counter-reaction," Rooney says. "Methinks, a more sophisticated plot's at hand."

"They did it. They admitted it," Jackie says.

"We'll see."

"Aye, we'll see."

"Aye, we'll see," Archie says.

"That's all detective," Jackie says to him. That's him told.

They move into the townhouse after the all clear, but only after a cargo of corpses is bundled into a large freezer van. They're warned of booby-traps and to avoid the blood-pools where the Taylor clan once lay. The air is heavy and vaporous as they move through the house where this brotherhood lived and planned destruction. Sleeping bags lie across the floor, covered with beer cans and littered with cigarette butts. These men had not been expecting visitors – well not initially.

Both of them know where they want to reach, which is Taylor's desk, in what might have been an office at the top of the stairs. There, they'll seek what they're looking for, but will it give them what they're interested in? For Rooney, anything which will help to confirm the Latin man was involved; for Jackie, evidence for the following inquiry. Taylor's desk diary, notes, files, records, anything, are scooped up and bagged. The air in there is unhealthy, and they get out post-haste, retreating to the relative comfort of Jackie's office. But he really wants to return to the room he had left prematurely that morning, to get a bath, change his clothes, get a bottle out. She settles to work on; while Rooney, respecting the resolve of the woman, makes for the door and home.

Taylor is transported, unceremoniously, to the high-security unit of the London Road Police Station, designed to hold terrorist suspects. It was intended mainly for a terror campaign following 7th July 2005 that never happened, although the Glasgow Airport attack in June 2007 confirmed fears. Not until January 2011, however, was it needed, proper.

Jackie and Rooney agree to meet there the following afternoon. She needs to clarify any connections with the shootings, and he 'needs to be there' for a prearranged interview with Taylor, who had undergone intensive questioning by the CID since he arrived. Rooney hopes to confirm or not any connection with his man.

Rooney has the bottle, though no bath nor change of clothes. He arrives late at London Road. The desk officer is about to show him out and to point him towards the Belgrove Hostel, a wet house where alcoholics can drink and keep their room, something not possible in most hostels. After asking for Jackie, she arrives in the reception, looks him up and down, sniffs, shakes her head, and hands him a weak coffee. Rooney takes it and follows her inside, where she reiterates the report obtained by CID agents; important information in anticipation of their interview.

"Taylor's a son of a restaurant owner from the South Side," she says, reading from the report. "Raised in Crawford Street, a predominately Asian population, he's a confirmed racist who fears the changing cultural scene. He dabbled with the BNP as a younger man and violently demonstrated the racist traits he learned there. He hates all non-whites, Eastern Europeans, in particular Asians, south and east, whom he views as a growing threat to his family interests."

Rooney nods. The strongest minority groups had moved intently into the cities where the opportunities were greatest. Chinese Triads had expanded in strength and built their own crime families, exploiting and using the Chinese incomers from the new territories, obtaining new soldiers, developing armies, making millions from extortion and internet gambling syndicates. Indo-Pakistani groups grew their businesses into massive multi-million pound concerns, built on illegal migrant workers prepared to work for pittances in back-street restaurants and 24-hour shops. Eastern Europeans developed massive drugs and sex trafficking empires, assisted by asylum seekers and Polish, Latvians and Lithuanians moving into the country.

The growth of migrant gangs threatened the traditional Glasgow crime families' power base and businesses. Initially, the families exploited the impoverished migrants, a cheap source of manpower and soldiers. As their numbers grew, assaults became rife, until they formed their own groups and fought back. Pitched battles were common, tit-for-tat killings the done thing.

"The Taylors defended their patch with brutality," Jackie says. "Their attacks on migrant groups were notorious by their savagery. They grew their family into a military operation, resourced through a kinship that had money, resources, and, ultimately, arms."

"Got too greedy." Rooney slurps his coffee. "Greedy people can be used."

"Apparently... We've offered Taylor witness protection."

Rooney realises this isn't a bad move. She wants to establish links with other families and at the same time justify the SWAT attack on the Taylors. He wants to find out who's behind this and if this was orchestrated. He can see next day's gutter press: 'Witness protection? Hang the bastard!'

They move into the interview room, a highly sophisticated space equipped with the latest recording and monitoring devices. Taylor is monitored through two-way mirrors by CID detectives outside, with two inside. He's seated and they take a position sitting directly across from him. He says he's relieved a 'doctor' is there. Stethoscope at the ready! Then he launches a rant at them, proclaiming his task has been successful, his mission justified, his cause announced to the world.

In answer to Jackie's question, Taylor said he'd be happy to describe his organisation. He had assumed the clan chief position within the family. They were responsible for a number of attacks, including on a multi-racial cultural centre in Govan, which he burned down to some publicity, but this was not enough for him; he wanted more. He said his group called themselves the Taylors of Govan, which they shortened to the Taylor's. Then, when they felt ready, he decided they should act 'decisively'.

"Why?" Jackie says, getting right in there.

"We missed the last time, but not this time. This time we were determined."

"Determined?"

"To succeed – "

"You cocked up at Buchanan Street," Rooney says.

"Easy Rooney," Jackie says. "Well?"

"Your colleague seems to think so," Taylor answers.

"Owen, why Owen?" she adds.

"Just a means to end, that's all."

"Anything to do with... Muir?" Rooney asks. He doesn't expect an answer, he just wants to see the reaction on his face, which remains impassive.

They had around ten minutes or so on how they as a family were determined to hit those who threatened their business, livelihoods, power bases. Taylor's a large gutted man who would – when not in jail that is – be wrapped up in a business suit and a cloak of normality. The family chiefs are businessmen, wheeling and dealing with the financial institutions, politicians, and assuming godfather presence within local communities, where they exploit the fears of indigenous communities against the threat of incomers. Rooney had met his type before, a Glasgow godfather, a rough personal authority belying an innate intelligence.

"Was there anyone else involved?" Jackie asks.

"Were you... assisted?" Rooney adds.

Taylor remains quiet, for then. For Rooney, indicating affirmation.

"And who might have assisted you?" Jackie says. "Answer, and we'll have you out in less than ten."

Ten years! This man should be going down for good.

"A man called Fraser," Taylor says, his tongue freed.

"A man, don't you mean a gang? The mob, for instance?"

"I said a man."

"What man?" Rooney asks.

"Angus Fraser was his name, or so he said," he answers, almost too easily. "We met him in the Argyll Hotel, off Park Road. He had the expertise we needed."

It's time to turn up the gas; he's sure his man's behind this. "You lot didn't have the wit to plan all that stuff," he puts to Taylor.

"Rooney," Jackie says to him, meaning, 'you know fuckall about investigative interviewing,' before turning to Taylor. "Fraser?"

"A strange-looking man."

"Damaged mouth, affecting his speech?" Rooney enquires.

"That's as much as get," Taylor says on the description, then continues as if he wasn't asked. "'We want to make a statement to those in office,' I said to him. 'Exactly my purpose too,' he said."

"Why did you need him? Or more like, why did he need you?"

'*We* were in control. We are the heavy team and we take action," he says. They threaten our business environment. We needed his... knowledge.'"

"Knowledge, what knowledge did he have?" Jackie asks.

"What you could do for him was more important," Rooney adds.

Taylor looks intently at Rooney. "Fraser said we were ineffective... the last time," he says. "We had failed. He assured us the next time we would not. It would be a bold blow. 'You will be ruthless, without compassion,' he said. 'A lack of resolve would be seen as weakness.'"

"What did he offer?"

"He said he could maximise the effect."

"What were his demands?"

"That we were ready to lay down our lives for our cause."

"You weren't the last time," Rooney says. "You got someone else to do your dirty work for you. The hit man in the subway?"

"*I* faced him up." Taylor slaps his hand on the table.

"Alright, calm down man." Jackie sees he's clearly animated by Rooney's words.

"'We are and more, Fraser,' I said. My actions seemed to please him. Then the detailed questions came. He said he wanted to confirm our plan was well thought through."

"He helped you?" Jackie asks.

"Yes."

"Why?"

"We needed his expertise."

"No, why did he want to help you?"

"He believed in what we were doing."

"You're lying my friend," Rooney puts to him, wondering who is using whom: Fraser using Taylor or Taylor using Fraser? "Far from your usual kneecapping, hitting rival gangs, you didn't have the expertise; you know... this was a big political hit?"

"We did it, didn't we?"

"What about... dispatching, decapitating an innocent Polish family?"

"Rooney!" Jackie says, meaning 'lay off, this is my territory.'

"That wasn't us," Taylor says.

"We'll come back to that," Jackie says.

"But you needed his help," Rooney suggests.

"He helped."

"And where is this man, Fraser?" Jackie asks.

"I've no idea."

"No, I'm sure you haven't," she says. Then, shifting tack, mentions, "We found this on your clothing: this card." There's silence as Taylor reads the card in her hand.

"What is it?" Rooney asks her.

"Another card." She spells out the phrases deliberately in chunks. *"In memorium spatium... est ad pascendum et spatium... est ad morendum... sed solum volat qui... voluit et perpetuo... sublimes tuus volatus fuit."*

"Bet you couldn't say that pissed."

"I'm reading it Rooney. Translated it means, 'To everything there is a season, and a time for every purpose under heaven, a time to be born and a time to die... etcetera, etcetera.'"

"I know it. 'Turn, turn, turn'."

"This is our time," Taylor says.

"But only he who wants to, will fly, and your flight will be forever sublime," Jackie reads eloquently.

"A message, an order, a trigger for action?" Rooney says.

"We have only begun to fly," Taylor says, in a sinister, prophetic way, conversant with Jackie's quote.

Taylor didn't have anything more to say. He had said enough to convict himself, and he didn't appear concerned about this. They left him there in the glory of his deed. This man is self-assured and this is only the start, even if he's sent elsewhere for a few years. When inside, his family would continue; his dead soldiers will be replaced. It's clear 'Mr Fraser' has a confirmed profile with this fraternity.

They leave there, Jackie dropping Rooney off in town. She has 'more work' to do. He wonders if he had stolen her thunder. He needs to get this information out of his head and onto paper; a session with his computer looms. Then he could think, maybe have a drink, to help him think. He's sure of two things: one, this whole fiasco is steeped in local politics and crime families; and two, he has a man, for the present, a man called 'Fraser'; and he has more Latin. Is Fraser the Latin man?

He finds a bar to work it out.

Fraser's the man with the Latin, he believes. For this, he is happy; now he has a physical presentation, and for the first time a link and a start of a proper profile. He has a description from Taylor, consistent with the one given by Irena and Louise; he has the Latin messages, and he has a possibility his man is involved with other crime families. He believes this is a breakthrough.

"Now I can start piecing it all together."

"You're being led down the garden path, dummy."

"How's that. The Taylors were aiding him, doing his dirty work?"

"Fraser assisted the Taylors. You've no proof of the contrary."

"What do you know?"

"More than you think."

He sits for a few minutes thinking. Then 'fuck it," he says, and heads home, by then the early hours, to open a bottle. He phones Jackie to talk to her answering machine and finishes the bottle listening to Vivaldi. Then it's early morning. He has that nice drunk and carefree feeling where it doesn't seem necessary to go to bed. He pulls out vinyl after vinyl, 60s and 70s stuff. It doesn't seem necessary to do anything strenuous that day either. He'll open another bottle, and so it'll go on, and wonderfully on.

Too cosy, though. It's time to sow the seed of uncertainty; to get him to retreat into his world of self-reflection, self-doubt.

"What do you know about tracking the best?"

"I did OK."

"Aye, great CV. The real job, forensic psychology; past tense since your psychotic episode. Right? Went right downhill with the booze."

"I was working my buns off, burning the candle at both ends; behavioural work, anger management, sexual, violent offenders – "

"The criminal bloodhound stuff got to you; the profiling, the tracking. The stresses get to you, and then you're all-powerful, invincible, destined for greatness. Then, you shoot way out of orbit. Crazy investments on overseas businesses. You lose your house…, Jackie!"

"They were stupid affairs."

"They were delusions Casanova. Manic sex maniac for a while, then the

Black Dog, you plummet into depression."

"I had to hide."

"You contemplated suicide."

"The alcohol helped."

"Sectioned and detained in the local loony bin?"

"My place of work, where I did my training. Not a comfortable experience."

"You didn't know fuckall at the time... to be 'uncomfortable'."

"Jackie was there."

"Who else would have put up with your... liaisons; dragged you back to earth, picked you up from the pits?"

"Jackie," he says, and tries her number again. "I'll do this, I have to."

"Who for, loser?"

He shrugs me off and settles down to do the profile. He boots up the laptop.

"OK," he says. I'll do her a report. What do I know?"

He knows the where and the what. He knows something of the how and who, but he doesn't know the why. He knows the report has to reflect progress, or lack of more like. He types and talks at the same time.

"OK, chronology," he says. "The Cobbler: the Zyks. Irena, the respected councillor, a 'kind of a funny face'; Latin: Arthur, slaughter with a clear conscience, '*In nomine Patris*'; the Mob? Fraser?; Buchanan Street: the shootings in the subway; Glasgow Convention; Latin messages: book of matches on killer; the politicians, mob cock-up?; Louise: prostitute, assault, 'something of a gruesome smile', Latin on a greeting card, the '*Et Filia*' statement; her murder; the heads; Springburn, John Bruce, Simpson, high security patients, Latin on security screen: Mob hit? Simpson is freed, Bruce is killed, Bruce is Muir's friend; the Grosvenor and Lord Owen, Muir's mentor; and the Taylor Clan assisted by 'Angus Fraser'."

"Very good Rooney, that's the easy bit."

"Shut it; right, the incidents. The Polish family, Glasgow Convention, Buchanan Street, Louise the prostitute, Springburn, Simpson and Bruce, Lord Owen, the Grosvenor and the Taylors. Family, the mob involvement. Latin, the Latin man is Fraser?"

"Easy."

He types and talks.

"The Latin man: identified by three people associated with the hits; age: 40s?; race: Caucasian, mixed North American accent, some Scot's; appearance: distinctive scar on the face, a grin?, affecting speech; distinctive aspects: grasp of Latin. his signature: leaves Latin messages, serious need to be involved in family underworld, high profile killings; psychology: wants to create mayhem, gain recognition, to lead pursuers along a path; why?:

damaged, pain, no other way to ameliorate this, wants to reflect this pain, see it in others?; objective?"

"All hunch and hypotheses, not even a SWAG Rooney."

"We'll see bastard. Let's see then. Summary draft profile – "

"Unconfirmed."

"An able, intelligent, albeit highly disturbed man, who may have something to prove, a mission, a quest, a big hang-up, an obsession. He has an ability to exploit and manipulate groups. Has an interest in Latin, lives in Scotland, most probably West Central, has either spent some time in North America, perhaps a US citizen; most likely to be married, in full time employment, and middle class; has a scar on his face affecting his speech."

"Fantasy."

He types and adds a heading: 'Latin Man SWAG'; then he transfers it into an Adobe PDF, which had a read out facility in a kind of Stephen Hawking voice. It recites the report back to him, which is scary, even more so as his mind is engulfed in gold. He concludes it: 'Look out for a local, possibly academic, man with an accent, knowledge of Latin, a scar; and an ability and a reason to kill.'

"Delusional."

"Go away. OK, what's this guy trying to say?" He googles *'Empta dolore docet experientia.'* "Here we are," he says, finding it. "Experience bought with pain teaches effectively." He speaks the words in chunks, adding other Latin statements. *"Ad internecine*, to slaughter … *Salva conscientia*, with a clear conscience … *Artorius*, Arthur, *et vincere aut mori*, and to conquer or die … *Culpae peona per esto*, let the punishment fit the crime."

Rooney's fighting three forces here: one, the Latin, which is blinding him with gold; two, I am undermining him; and three, he's struggling with his own self-doubt.

"In Nomine Patris, Et Filii or Et Filia. In the name of the father, and of the son… or of the daughter, but no 'of the holy spirit'."

He recalls the prayer from The Boondock Saints, where Connor, Murphy and Il Duce, the 'Saints', felt they were acting on behalf of god, the Father, in their murderess response to organised crime, acting as proxies for god.

"Was this man using organised criminals as proxies for his mission?" he asks himself, recalling Il Duce, played by Billy Connolly, and him saying, 'And shepherds we shall be, for Thee, my Lord, for Thee. Power hath descended forth from thy hand …'

"In the name of…"

CHAPTER TEN

"I have a hypothesis, on my man."
"Your man, you've no idea."

It's his professional hunch, however, a SWAG, and his best attempt for now. Deciding to thank himself for his work so far, he meets with Ben in Tennents Bar on the Byres Road, for a 'couple of pints'. They talk about their respective roles. Ben's, on counselling what was left of the Polish family, critical incident debriefing for staff bringing out the bodies, and those supporting the families turning up at Buchanan Street and the Grosvenor. Rooney's, on the pursuit of the 'Latin man'. They have a few drinks that'll lead to a few more, inevitably.

Leaving Ben in Tennents Bar, Rooney decides to take a booze cruise down one side of Byres Road and up the other side, intending to finish, if he's still on his feet by the time, back in Tennents. Something of around ten pubs on the road and another five in the lanes just off; but if he gets stuck in one, that'll do. Multiple drinks in multiple pubs or multiple drinks in one pub, it's OK. As it happens, he gets as far as Curlers, well over half-way up, and he's about ten drinks up and feeling no pain. It's around seven p.m. and he likes the feeling. He's drunk and most people coming into the pub are just starting and sober. He has a good head start on them, but he needs more, and he needs to immerse himself in the world of drinkers, to head into this city of and for drinkers. He turns left onto Byres Road and makes his way to Hillhead Underground. Although he knows the underground system well, he still feels his way along until he reaches the platform; but more, because he's morose drunk. He knows he shouldn't have, but when you're pissed! This's a pursuit of a serious binge, and in there he starts to mouth his thoughts in lumps of alcohol-induced bile. Alcohol makes him say things he wouldn't normally say, but that's no excuse. He swears, curses and causes trouble; out of character, out of his mind, out of control.

"This city is shite, it is, don't believe what the Lonely Planet says, it is just shite. Unique and interesting characters, that's what's said in the tourist blurbs. Just don't believe it. The people are shit; it's all shit. Me, your unfriendly, not very jovial, shrink is going to prove this to you. Then you can make your own feckin' mind up."

The platform starts to fill up; disaster tourists at the Grosvenor Hotel, some hoping to catch sight of Buchanan Street, now closed after the shootings, and normal drinkers heading into Glasgow for a meal, cinema, or a normal drink. He's becoming obvious.

"Fucking subway, fucking shot up the fucking place and everybody in it, people just like you bastards, *ad interneci...* you bastards. That's Latin for slaughter. You get that, slaughter, down here a couple of weeks ago you lot would have been slaughtered." He's clearly out of order. The police officers, now on constant duty there, shake their head rather than take any action. He's only one of a hundred drunks they'll come across this day.

Something tells him to 'quieten it'. He can hear the 'disgusting man' murmurs, and recognises a nurse from the hospital. She's aghast at him.

"Sick in the heid," he shouts, hoping she'll turn away.

The underground station smells reasonably clean, except for the water running between the tracks that smells as if it contains shit from the pails used by the mechanics. The twentieth century navvies, tunnel rats, who only come out of these tunnels in the dark; from the dark to the dark, just like the miners of old, down before sun up, up after sun down.

"Poor bastards."

"Right sir, enough," comes from an 'official-looking' man behind him.

"Fecking get my face punched, if I don't," he murmurs.

The train explodes into the station like a desperate man into a willing woman. Would he wave to the driver, a warm gesture? Why would he, nobody else would? How mind numbing it would be to sit in the driver's cab, continually underground, going from the dark of the tunnels into the light of stations, round and round the same route; all day, every shift, and all your fucking life. "Poor bastards," he says. "No one respects your presence, let alone your existence." He decides to leave it this time.

He stands with his back to the wall until the train comes in and the doors separate. Then he walks forward and fumbles his way to the entrance, where – crouching – he mumbles his fake old man crap: "older man, older man." As he does, he waves his hand before him. It always gets a supportive hand on his arm that one. Well, some people use their dogs to get women; for him, the old man stuff always works, but not this time. People are naturally avoiding him. He looks left then right as he enters the carriage. Sober, he would have found the older person/disabled seat at the door, well away from the drunks or the junkies, but he's drunk and he has to engage with his peer group. The carriage is, as he would have expected it to be in Glasgow, something akin to a council refuse dump. He kicks crushed lager cans, bottles, and polystyrene boxes as he makes his way through the carriage, kicking an empty bottle that rolls into the midst of the drunks where it came from. "Fuckin' empty," one of them says, checking it out. He sits down adjacent to them.

"Got a light pal?"

"You're no' supposed to smoke in the tube," Rooney growls.

"None o' your fuckin' business pal," his 'pal' says, as his lighter and cig fires up. "You wan ae they smoke polis?" he says, the words expelling with the smoke.

"No' me," Rooney replies. He has to get him on his side. "I like a fag myself, gie's one."

"Fuck off and get yer ain then."

So much for the camaraderie! He smells of piss and looks like the corpse he will soon become. He's one of Glasgow's sons, its statistics, its record; the sick man of Europe.

"No problem sir," Rooney says.

He takes another few draws and looks Rooney straight in his face. "You a fuckin' poof?" he says, wondering why he choose to sit closer than is necessary to avoid the smell.

"I may be many things my friend, but on this occasion I am not of the homosexual persuasion."

"Well, fuck off and die then."

"Right, you get a fuckin' grip," his pal says to him, "he's an auld man."

"Don't worry, he's windin' you up," he says to Rooney.

"No problem friend," Rooney replies as the corpse gets up. Then he feels the cold steel of a blade on his face.

"This, you toffy cunt, is going to stretch your smile," he snarls, pushing the blade flat against Rooney's cheek.

There he is, from trying to understand psychopaths and their view of the world, to trying to understand a city through the perspective of its underlife.

"Go on then, it might make me look a bit happier."

"Right brother, put it away – you crazy?" his pal says, interceding.

"Indeed, do it and you're locked up, and the next thing you're in front of someone like me doing your assessment and recommending treatment, anger management, and alcohol rehabilitation; your choice."

Rooney survives the blade and gets out at the fourth stop at St Enoch's. It used to be the fifth, but that was when it stopped at the Buchanan Street station, now a crime zone.

He makes his way along Argyle Street until he reaches the Mecca Bar in the Trongate. For him, it is the right place to go: a boozer's paradise. He bumps and staggers his way in. They identify him as a soft touch as soon as he walks through the door; might've been something to do with him being clean.

"You fae the social or somethin'?" one says.

"Mibey he's wan ae they social work students 'looking for experience'," another laughs.

After explaining he's trying to get well and truly rat arsed, they appear to accept him. He heads for the toilet to make room for some more liquid courage and in there sums it all up. There's a rubber hose spewing water into the sink, swishing away a goodly proportion of a punter's blood, he surmises. A fellow piss artist joins him there and says there was a stabbing earlier that night. It seems an asylum seeker had wandered in. The accent gave him away as he ordered a drink, and he was chibbed in the lavvy. The hose, which sloshed the blood from the floor, now spews into the sink, ready for the next time.

The Mecca Bar has in and out doors, just like the kitchen area of a restaurant where waiters would go in the in-door with empty plates and come out of the out-door with full plates. Here the punters go in the in-door empty and out of the out-door full as breweries. The door out is two doors, swing doors, not unlike those you see in saloons in cowboy movies. Why, he finds out a bit later when there's a fight on the tiny dance floor. The bouncers grab both of them, a man and woman, the woman getting the better of the guy. Both are lifted by the neck off their feet and transferred to a horizontal position, heads pointing towards the door like aeroplanes ready for take off, then simultaneously they're dispatched through the door, their heads acting as battering rams, to land in the pavement outside on torn faces, skinned hands and knees. Up they get, dust themselves off, and "ya bastard... ya nyaff ye," they yell, before launching themselves back into the fray. Again, the woman gets the upper hand. Her head crashes into the man's, while he's still sorting himself out. Sore one.

He finds a seat away from the affray, close to, by then, 'his best friend', to get into the alcohol, where he pulls out his Sony and starts to recite. His best thoughts arrive in his head when he's pissed. He toys with his hypotheses and speaks aloud as he does.

"He wants to cause pain, get recognition, taunt and tease; a highly disturbed man with a big hang-up, expert in Latin, with a strange grin; a bit of an accent and a speech defect. He needs a front, so most likely to be married, in full time employment, maybe academic, middle class." He plays around with the words and repeats some of them. "Very able, intelligent, Latin, strange grin, speech defect, accent, academic, middle class..." He stops. "Jea...sus, I know this man," he utters.

"You gonae shut it o'er there," comes from an exasperated bar man.

"Aye, sure." Rooney decides it's best to keep his thoughts to himself, as he snuggles into the wall. In his drunken stupor he's trying to see this man in his mind's eye, standing there looking down on Irena. "'*In nomine Patris*,' he said."

Irena is in his mind a lot that night, so is his dead mother. So am I, not like me to miss a chance of a bit of sport. He gets an image in his head of a man, but he wonders whether this was created from those images he had as a child of a drunken father as he fell in through the door, rising with those eyes full of drink and hate, to draw his bony knuckles across his mother's face.

"*Your father Rooney or your man. Are you morphing?*"

He doesn't answer, but it hits home.

He can't remember getting back home in his drunken state, but vaguely remembers two calls registering on his answering machine: one from Jackie and the other from the nursing home. He can just about deal with the nursing home: 'your father needs cash for his whisky', but Jackie, maybe less so.

Falling over the coffee table, he's violently sick. Getting on his feet, he staggers into the toilet and places the flats of his hands in the mirror. The man in the mirror, him, looks like a man he feared. That face, the face of his father; bloody eyes, hair a mess, blood vessels in his cheeks and nose, protruding like tributaries of a subterranean red river running just below the skin of his face. This is what he has become. This is the man he fears he would become, the failure, the drunk, the father.

It takes some time before he can bring himself to press the play button on his answering machine.

Jackie: "I tried to reach you, but after trying a few times, I knew you would be out of it, intoxicated somewhere, possibly at home; so much for your tentative profile. Are we still paying you? I've put out an all-points, to inform me if anything comes in relating to Latin man re description. Call me."

He deletes the nursing home one; he knows what that's about.

He's drunk and useless, and it's two days before he's in any fit state to contact anyone. By the morning of the third day, his binge is over. He phones Jackie.

While ringing her, he half hopes she wouldn't be there. He'll leave a message and perhaps have another drink, but she answers immediately. "I knew you were on the sauce you useless bum. Fucks sake man, you need to get a grip or you're going back to Hillwood; not to your old job, but as an inpatient, again; this time for good. I just hope your profile turns something up."

"Indeed fine dear, let's hope." He tries to disguise the fact he's still drunk.

"Anyway, as I am required to do, I met with Muir. He wanted to discuss the hits, and my involvement, and exchanged some words about Bruce and the Secure Unit breakout in angry terms. He says the Glasgow polis is shit scared of the families to do anything; oh, and, by the way, and I'm a gangster's moll. He's not very happy about me, Rooney, but then he talked about you and I, in personal terms. He wanted to know if you were up to it, then asked if I'm fucking you. I didn't answer."

"I don't need that kind of shit." He nearly asks if this is a lover's tiff between Muir and her.

"Are you still drunk?"

"Indeed, I fucking am. And, although I find this interesting from a social and anthropological sense, which pampers not a little this letch's ego, where the fuck is this going?" His mood is apparent, so's the fact he has just about drunk himself sober. She says Muir had talked to her father, who says *he* would take over.

"What could I say to this?" she says. "Have you anything on our man?" she snaps.

"I'm fecking-well-working on it." He returns the snap. "I've done a… report." He decides to resist telling her about 'his man'.

"Well, just keep a civil-feckin'-tongue on you," she says, this time softer. "I'll look forward to seeing your… report." Then the line goes dead; her way of making a point.

For Rooney, the morning after such a binge is not a good time of day. He should get out of this he feels, with this wannabe delusional cop and a sick sociopath. However, he would stay in, if only to whet his appetite for head-bangers, but more likely to give him a reason to drink. He changes his clothes and tries to cover the stink of booze from his breath with toothpaste, mouthwash, and chewing gum.

His tentative profile needs testing though, and he has this man in mind. But rather than involving Jackie, he telephones him at the university, to be told he hasn't been seen for a few days. At least he can 'remove him from his inquiries'. He can't believe he would be involved in this stuff, but anything is possible. He either wants to confirm his thoughts or dismiss them, confirm and pass to Jackie, or dispel and let the man get on with his life. Never in his life did he think this man would have been a threat to him, let alone others. He tries his number again: no answer, no answering facility.

He decides to go to his place, a posh Victorian flat in Polwarth Street, off Clarence Drive in Glasgow's salubrious Hyndland district, within ten minutes of his own. He enjoys walking through the West End, through the Victorian mansions, musing at the rich Glasgow traders who used to live there. Now they're multiple occupancy, residents unable to afford to own them.

As he turns the corner off Clarence Drive into Polwarth Street, some of the feelings he's been immersed in recently re-emerge. Police officers and ambulance men are there outside the house and an ambulance stands at the gate. Here we go, been here before! He approaches with a degree of caution, reaching the gate of the house where a police officer stops him. He pulls out the Criminal Investigation Department ID Jackie gave him when drawn into the investigation. 'May come in handy,' she said at the time. He's allowed in and enters the house through open front doors. Forensics is dusting the place. A young CID officer approaches him. "I'm Ferguson sir, officer in charge."

"What's the story detective?" Rooney asks. "I have an interest in the people here." He shows his ID.

"Well, she's in the ambulance, bruised and battered; and, from other bloods, we believe others had been injured. We can't trace the husband."

He makes to go in.

"Don't sir, lots of blood, the place is in a mess."

"What's there?" He moves inside.

"A desk, a couple of computers, lots of magazines, books."

"The books, what kind?"

"Oh, politics, etcetera."

"Oh, etcetera," Rooney says, interested. "What happened in here?"

"Not confirmed. She was found in a pool of blood after the local police got an anonymous call, from this number."

"From her husband?"

"Who knows?"

"Who is he?"

"Arthur Johnston, professor at the university, urban conflict. I know him through major incident planning meetings." After gang violence increased, Johnston was co-opted onto the group to inform the plans.

"Invading a man's home; appropriate?"

Probably not, but he can't give up this opportunity to have a rake around this guy's things, to get a sense of him. "All a misunderstanding, Mr Johnston, we are very sorry," he'll say if he has to, if it turns out to be nothing. From Ferguson's description, 'desk, computers, books', he sees this is more a working environment than a homely one. Is he the man, he wonders. He has an interest in conflict, as is his job. He's professor of the subject, why wouldn't he? But does he have the links, the influence, and the motive? Is he *the* man?

'His man' though would be careful. Rooney knows if he had a hand in the violence going on he'll know there'll be a point where contact will be made. He'll know that eventually he'd be tracked down. A clever man, albeit psychologically damaged, would plan for this possibility: slow his pursuers down, tantalise them, gain more time to do more.

Rooney has an eerie feeling in there that unsettles him. Is this where plans were made to create havoc? Did a campaign of terror originate here in this room, in this house? It doesn't seem possible or feasible. He moves to the desk and finds the laptop is still open.

He hits Enter to bring up the desktop. The Internet is open on Wikipedia, on 'James Muir'. He hopes this webpage is no more than a passing everyday interest.

The room is a room of an academic, not a mass murderer. He has been in houses of multiple murderers, some turn their places into shrines for their activities, but he shouldn't be fooled, as might be the intention. His man may want to present as a normal man, to have influence and opportunity to do what he does. Other more pressing questions come to his mind.

"The husband, any ideas, abducted, you say there was blood, from another?"

"Don't know sir, we're working on it."

Once home, he calls Jackie. She knows about the assault. She wastes no time in getting there.

"Well, is he *our* man?" Her smoke invading the flat as she arrives. "And this time you will fuckin' well answer. After all, this is why you're involved."

She's right, but he doesn't like her manner; now changed from her normal soft-cop-warm to tough-cop-cold mode. Police strategy rolled into one.

"I doubt it. He's an academic, and this is his work. I don't know, but I need to check him out. Right, Mrs Marcos?"

"Right, good, you know your place, and his background, and any links with the Latin, and I want your report, with detail."

"Sure, but what we have here is a respected academic, his wife attacked, taken to an inch of her life, him possibly kidnapped."

"This is still a police inquiry, that's my work. You explore him, that's yours. What about her?"

"She's in hospital."

"Yes, she's in hospital."

They had run out of things to say at that point. Something to do with the long hush and the way she tapped her cigarette in the ashtray, standing gazing out onto the street. He notices her green eyes sparkle from the light coming from the window, her blond hair, looking almost white. She catches his gaze.

"A respected academic?"

"Apparently; have you got anything on him?"

She blanks him. They go for lunch, where they warm to each other, and end the afternoon – the worn out old book and the glossy magazine, via a couple of West End bars – in her bed. He enjoys holding her. She smells good, the Prada. She feels great to him: she's bonier than he remembers her, but her bumps are all of the right proportions. She's drunk, randy, needy, or something else. He can't believe it's because she wants him.

CHAPTER ELEVEN

The next day they travel to the Western Infirmary to see Marlene Johnston. She's in no state to be interviewed and the medics are reluctant to allow them access. Jackie pulls out her CID badge. "Utmost importance," she says. They're escorted to Marlene's bed. Her head's wrapped in bandages. She looks like death warmed up, but she's awake and determined to give a clear and honest statement.

Earlier, on the day of her injury, she says, she was in a hurry pushing her way through the meanderers strolling along Byres Road. She says she was lucky, not a care in the world. She says she wanted something more than she could find on the street that night; for her, more than life itself. She seems confused, dreamlike, maybe the medication or her head wound; she's talking in fantasy-speech. They wonder how much of it's real.

"I was getting in deep, but I needed him," Marlene says.

Rooney wonders if they need to know this.

"It was raw, uncontrolled," she continues, "but he was getting close, too close, and he was prying about my husband. Why was he interested? I didn't care. I couldn't deny myself. After years of neglect from my husband, my own needs denied. I could have succumbed years ago when he was off on his projects, but I didn't. Now I could, I just could. I raced up the stairs heading for his flat. He was just leaving or else he was making as if he was, perhaps to appear indifferent towards me, to draw me further to him. I pushed him back through the door and we both collapsed onto the floor, kicking the door shut as we fell."

"Your husband?" Jackie prompts, hoping she would give her something real, substantial.

"I left *him*...," Marlene says, taking a gulp of air, "hidden away in his study in the flat, where he had been for over two days, surrounded by his books, radio, the internet. My only role was to provide food, constant coffee, and every highbrow paper I could find. I couldn't understand why the hell I was with him. He gave no physical release, no love, no care. The only comfort came from his money and anything his position provided. He was complicated and obsessive, and loved none but himself and his work, whatever that was, because he never discussed it. But I loved him, or so I thought. Or was it pity? But I knew he had pain locked away somewhere in his head, in his soul."

Sounds like my man, Rooney thinks.

"Jazz said he knew people who wanted him," Marlene adds.

"Jazz?" Jackie asks.

"My lover, he was involved – "

"Involved?"

"Yes, with a heavyweight crime family; drugs, prostitution, all that stuff. I knew this… but he wanted me."

"We need to know more about this Jazz." Jackie leans closer to her. "Are you alright? Do you want to go on?"

"No, I'm OK. He said it would help us, to start again. He was pushy, no longer just prying, he was insistent. He would not give up and I would have to decide: my husband, my love; or him, my lover. I knew, though, deep down I would lose both of them; it was just a matter of time."

Rooney feels sorry for this woman. Jackie notices it in his face.

"We went to my house. I was home earlier that night, earlier than usual. My husband knew of my affair, but it gave him space; it kept me out of his hair. I was not to disturb him at his work. I would be eager to tell him of my activities that night, meeting friends in town, going to the cinema. Whatever. It didn't matter. What mattered more to him was I left him alone to get on with his work. I opened the room door and he said, in a loud and aggressive voice, 'You're home early, don't disturb me, go back out, I need my space, go away.'"

"Maybe he didn't mean to hurt…" Jackie looks at Rooney as if to say 'shut it and let her talk'.

"I didn't reply to his words. Instead, just then, Jazz hit him as he spun around in his chair. He hit him a second time, this time square on the front of his head. A cosh, I think. 'Did you have to hit him so hard?' I asked him, my voice shaking as I fell to my knees next to my unconscious husband. 'I had to, babe,' Jazz said. 'I couldn't take the chance he would come back at me.' He had convinced me our life together would begin. 'I know people who want him bad and will pay good money. The kind of money that'll give us the start, a new life together,' he told me."

"Where was this… man from, Marlene?" Jackie asks, but Marlene is on a desperate rant.

"Jazz knew I wanted him, but he knew I would go so far and I would call it off… at a point, just where he was then. I would tell him to leave, having taken it as far as serious assault. I would bring my husband round and tend his wound, thinking this would knock some sense into him and we could start again, but Jazz thought his plan was better. 'Too late sweetie,' he said.

I barely heard the words as I got the cosh. He intended breaking my skull; just as well I've a thick head."

Rooney waits, wondering if she was drawing breath for more, but she becomes silent as, as if all her strength had ebbed from her. Just then, the young medic interrupts. "She's tired, you must leave. Now," she orders. At this, their interview is over.

Later Jackie is informed Marlene had died shortly after their visit. "'Brain lesion, bleeding inside, unable to save her,' they said."

Another casualty, Rooney thinks, knowing there'll be more.

Jackie heads to her office to work, to report. Rooney heads off, to drink. Next thing he remembers is waking up at home with a big head and a desperate thirst. He arrived late the night before and was pleased to be there, if only to finish the Macallan. By morning, he has run out of whisky and calls his understanding taxi firm to deliver a forty ounce bottle of whisky. That's done in by the Sunday night.

From his bedroom, he zigzags through the sitting room, chindit-like, along a well-worn route through a jungle of empties, bottles, beer cans, and books. The morning light peeps through the break in the curtains as he shuffles his way through to the kitchen, wrapped in his ragged robe and shabby slippers. From the fridge, he digs out a litre of orange juice, which he finishes as he empties his case and dictation tapes onto the kitchen table. What now, he wonders. Update his report with Johnston and his now dead wife, or …?

Jackie phones. "Are you all right?"

"Why are people always asking me if I am all right?"

"Just thought you –"

"Just thought nothing, you phoned me remember."

"All right, but don't you think after all it's done to you, you should do something about it?"

"About what?"

"Don't treat me like an idiot, your drink problem."

'Drink problem', this sounds strange and somewhat unconnected to him. He's a manic-depressive and a boozer sure, but drink problem? This's the official voice she puts on when she's in role; a right pain.

"Apart from casting aspersions about my predilections, what do you want?"

"I have some information, a… portfolio on your man. Can you come over here?"

"It's five-past-nine in the morning Jackie. We *alcoholics* don't get out of our bed until after way after twelve and only after a good dose of Iron Brew."

"Just get the fuck over here, right."

He shakes his head, but this's no more than a small act of defiance. He has no chance of resisting Jackie.

He gets there feeling like death after the heavy night with the whisky. Black cabs in Glasgow calculate their takings in minutes rather than miles, so his plea to the driver to hurry along had no effect as the cab becomes jammed in a busy commuter street. "Was this intentional?" he asks the driver, trying to be funny, but this led to a convoluted argument about the growing discontent among Glaswegians about foreign workers flowing in to fill the jobs nobody wanted. He's expecting it. "Look, I don't give a fuck about the neither work nor want, who expect everything on a plate," he says. "Can you not just bloody well get me there?" His gross manner is evident, perhaps also is its origin.

"Guess you're a fuckin' social worker pal," the driver parries with Glasgow sarcasm.

He didn't dare enter this duel of discussion, but he has a surreptitious smile to himself at the dry wit. He gets there late as Joycy arrives with a tray containing a cafétiere of coffee and cups.

"You want one, Mr Rooney?" Joycy says, escorting him in. She has a way of dropping unintentional innuendos.

"Indeed, I need one. I need one," Jackie and Joycy look at him suspiciously. By return, his sexual innuendo is messed up by the shakes; what he needs is a drink, and it shows.

"You're bloody late," Jackie spits.

"You'll get over it my darling; but you're trouble and I won't."

"People are being killed you know."

"So what the fuck, it's Glasgow."

Resting his hands on the back of her Chesterfield, he leans towards her, hoping his serious and challenging face shows behind the bloated face of a drinker; his irritable, twitching, bleary eyes.

"Listen, get this. I don't give a flying-fuckin'-fart for this impenetrable shite anymore." He slams his report on her desk, then sits down and gulps the coffee, muttering to himself. "Christ-sake, you jump into bed with a woman and she thinks she not only owns you but she has a right to your fuckin' pension."

She shushes him, scared they would be overheard. "I know; not one of my brightest ideas, and if you say anything that may affect my... my.... Anyway, I've got my own fuckin' pension, thank you very much." He doesn't think she hears that bit.

"'Career' is the word you found hard to say."

"Anyway, you... invited me here."

"Arthur Johnston."

"Indeed, interested?"

"He has form."

"Criminal?"

"Not, significantly so."

"You bring me all this way at the taxpayer's expense, for this?" He leans over her desk and the folders she's been poring over.

"Conflict academic, student activist, son of a diplomat; it's all there."

"Definitely implicates him in the death of dozens. Is that it?"

"Here."

Ignoring his retort, she pushes a folder into his chest. "*That* my friend is a detailed portfolio. When we do an investigation, we do it... properly." She moves off to top up her coffee.

Rooney slides onto one of those precarious seats on castors which has a habit of disappearing from beneath you. "Is there pathology?"

"Pathology?"

"Hang-ups, dear."

"Hang-ups? Well, he always had a thing about the council."

"Really," he says, seeking more information.

"Two years ago, an illegal asylum raid, up in Lincoln Avenue, in the high flats, an asylum seeker being deported. He got in the way. He was arrested and held in custody for a few days, after being roughed by the police officers. Appears the council wanted to establish if he was an illegal migrant.

"I don't remember seeing that on the news!"

"Would you prefer the old policy, when thousands of scroungers piled in? Making a fortune for your social worker friends, treble time after hours, running after them hand and foot?"

"I meant the police brutality. Used to be truncheons in the belly, gripping the balls, the back of the thigh. A few kicks with the boots off so's not to leave any marks." He calls on personal experience as a younger man; when, on a drunken night in Glasgow, he was bundled into a back of a police car, taken to the police station, and given a good kicking by the cops.

"Doing a very difficult job."

"Right wing politics, right wing police, right wing police state. Good grounding for you Jackie, I would say."

"*You* would fuckin' say. What *do* you know of me?" she says. He doesn't really know *her*. He knows her, but he doesn't really know *her*.

"I'm learning Jackie."

"So pleased."

"Anything before this?"

"Eh?"

"You know, signs of an angry man?"

"Oh, angry young man? Sure was. Many arrests, petty student saves the world stuff, taking on this, taking on that, anti-establishment. You know the behaviours we all had, but grew out of."

"You?" He can't resist it. "The behaviours we all had," he reiterates. "What were your behaviours?"

"See Rooney, what do you really know about me?"

"OK; you are a good cop, well qualified, high profile father, Polish background, ambitious, etcetera. Will that do?" he says, hoping it would, but knowing it wouldn't. "Oh, and you have a predilection to alcoholic, mad shrinks."

"In-fuckin'-deed. You think you know me, but you know nothing about me."

Rooney guesses she has been waiting for a chance, sober, to confirm a proper reflection of her since he launched his psychological assessment at her in the Horseshoe Bar, before they were so rudely interrupted by the guy shooting up the underground.

"So, was my... hypothesis correct?"

"What all that Freudian shite?"

"It was just my view."

"Your view Rooney; just your fucking view. A demented ex-psychologist, ex-husband, drunk's view."

"Well, was I close?"

"Close, Rooney, close? Let's give you some facts."

"I know the facts, I lived with you... remember?" He pours himself another cup of coffee, wishing it was something stronger. "Right, you were schooled at Holy Cross High in Hamilton, to the age of 18, before going to university. You were into sports in a big way, hockey, swimming, football."

"Good. My family?"

"Your mother died when you were six. You were an only child. Your dad married again when you were eight. Mary, your stepmother is upper crust. You have three younger stepbrothers and a stepsister. They all hated you."

"Thanks Rooney. Very good, you remembered."

"Daddy adored your new mummy because she was posh."

"They detested me. They went to Hamilton College, a private school. We had a nanny, a horse, and a car each. I didn't fit."

"You just wanted your old life, with your mother; your father out of the way."

"Psycho-shite coming my way, again!"

"Where was he Jackie? You never told me that."

"Never you mind where he was, but he wasn't with us, that's all. But he was quick to forget my mother, to take on the Barbie girl, embrace the high life, and have the perfect children."

"He supported you though"

"I did it all on my own. I was determined."

"You're still determined."

He's opened Pandora's Box, which contains Jackie. To open Pandora's Box is to release something that can't be undone. Rooney has to put the lid back on.

"What else do you have?" he says, trying to open the folder – and close the box.

"Fuck's sake Rooney, I bare my soul and – " She grabs the folder from him. "Some of this isn't for public viewing."

"Sorr...ee."

"*That* is as much as you get." She pitches him a file, which slides off his lap onto the floor. "Far be it from me to do your job for you; *that* is a special investigation file on the man." Rooney leans forward to retrieve the file from the floor, almost slipping off the seat and onto the floor himself. "It concerns his... subversive activities, and various communications, including the Lord Provost." She sits back, satisfied having shown the value of 'good policing'.

"Christ," Rooney says puffing, after bending to pick up the file, "he was being watched."

"As were other 'political agitators'. Dangerous times call for robust intelligence."

He wonders whether his support of the Palestinians, his membership of the CND, and his marching against the war in Iraq, are in one of those files.

"Dangerous times call for bloody state abuse..."

She dispatches a determined glance at him. "Just look after it, it's sensitive data." This is her zone and she's defending it.

Rooney's more determined now than ever to challenge 'best practice'. "Does it describe his state of mind at the time?"

She's resolute in matching him in this. "In there, a police psychologist's report; describes him as a – "

"I don't need... descriptions. I want to know what it says." He pushes the file back across the desk,

She looks him up and down. "It *says* the intervention did not result in any significant physical or psychological trauma. He's a remarkably robust individual."

"I guessed so, nothing of note."

"Oh," she says, "and Police shrinks know nothing about trauma."

"Sure do," he says. "They work with it all the time, but they're more likely to report on fitness for duty, given they only assess those in the force."

Her face shows her disapproval.

"This man was a bit of a... a troublemaker."

"The question is: is he still trouble?"

"Christ, you are just so sancti-fuckin'-monious."

"Now, that is a good assessment."

"What do you know of him?"

"He's into conflict."

"Eh?"

"He's an academic; urban conflict, from the University. I was bound to know him. I did my PhD there. I interviewed him on anger and aggression, peer group control, and behaviour management; all that kind of stuff."

"Very interesting. All you have to do is to match your profile with him. If it fits, bingo we have him. It's so easy."

"Indeed, dear," he says. "Easy. But if he is our man, he'll know we'll locate his path eventually. He'll have prepared for it; especially if he's giving out regular calling cards."

"If he has something to do with it, we need to stop him calling in the first place."

"There says a good cop."

"And there says the psychic bloodhound, I don't think."

"If he fits my psycho-friggin'-photo-fit, maybe we'll get some results."

"*My* investigations will produce results. Now start doing your job." She throws him back the file, this time like a paperboy spinning a newspaper towards a doormat.

It's clear his credibility is on the line with cop-superior. "Don't you worry about that my darling; however, although you may have discovered a shred of the Dead Sea scrolls, I have read the missing friggin' gospels," he says in his own defence, opening an ALDI bag and tucking the file in there alongside his report.

Her pause says she's searching for words.

He continues. "OK, but if the man – "

"The Latin man?"

"If the man – as yet to be determined I agree – is behind the killings, he'll have planned everything. Right up to his eventual arrest. He'll tease and tantalise until near the end and his possible incarceration. And then he'll go down, to prison that is, with a big ego publicity trip; to live the rest of his life basking in the glory of his deeds."

"I suppose our sympathetic no-death-penalty will confirm that."

Margaret Thatcher comes to his mind. "I personally have always voted for the death penalty."

"Bloody right," Jackie says.

"As far as *this* man is concerned, he can't lose," he says. "He's in his zone, wreaking havoc, in control of his domain. He'll go on, and on, like any pattern killer or serial killer, until stopped."

"Serial killer?"

"What?"

"You said serial killer."

"It just slipped out."

"This is serial killing with a big difference."

"Tell me about it."

"What we need from you is material evidence. If this man has something to do with or even orchestrated the recent hits, he is slightly above the everyday normal two or three murders a day serial killer. This is in the tens – "

"Indeed... dear."

"I'm no' your *dear*, Rooney, no more; and don't bloody patronise me." It's clear his 'jacket is on a shaky nail', as they say in Partick. "This is your task; you find him, and find out what he is about. This is still unofficial, an unofficial brief. You got it?"

"I got it a long time ago."

"Good, we need facts, facts. Fact he's involved or not. Fact he's connected wi' the hits, or not. OK?"

"Understood, but he may be way above what he would consider the tacky business of killing individuals."

She gives him a long, hard and cold stare.

"Hypothesising again Rooney, facts, remember. You give the file a good going over. It includes some interesting stuff from our people. We'll talk tomorrow." She takes him to the door at the same time instructing Joycy to get him a taxi. "He'll be outside."

"Fantastic, made a real impression there."

Rooney rolls the ALDI bag up, puts it into his inside pocket and heads out. "Who needs fancy attaché cases?" Time to retire to *my* office, he thinks, as he heads off to any decent boozer to consider the stuff. "Bye, Jackie."

"Hon?" she says, as he stomps down the stairs.

"Aye?"

"Sort it out."

"With the greatest respect... dear, fuck off – "

And with that, the door is slammed behind him and he's well and truly dispatched, but the words 'sort it out' ring out in his head.

He reaches a bar recommended by the cabby. He orders a pint, pulls out the file and starts reading it there. By the fourth pub, he's getting a grasp of this man, some of his history, his path to becoming a professor at the university, his interest in political conflict and urban affairs. Apart from this, he isn't sure what it says, what it really says, and that worries him. It reflects a composure and a lack of emotional response he's more than well acquainted with. But more, it reflects control. The incident in Glasgow, though, is significant for him, where he got a kicking from a police officer; when he was inculcated in what was thought to be subversive activity.

"There's pain there, I know it," he says to himself. The drink is kicking in. "It's pain alright, subversive, hidden, destructive. Physical, mental, emotional, and a need to reverse and propel it back to towards others. You hurt me, and I hurt you or yours. To cause as much discomfort to you as you can; a classic pretext for causing mayhem."

"*A classic pretext for some serious boozing, I think.*"

"*You* don't think, *I* think."

Rooney is in truth only getting a grasp of getting progressively pissed. This's a good history, though. He did his best histories when he was a student, when he was interested, keen. Later that evening, after falling out of the bar very drunk, he reaches his flat; and, having picked up a bottle on the way, he sets about finishing it. Then he falls asleep in his room to wake a couple of hours later in a sweat. He's shaking violently, and he's brushing off rats. They're coming out of the walls in their hundreds, crawling over him. Is he dreaming or hallucinating? He's not sure.

"*Like the rats? They're in your mind. They're on you, in you, coming from you, crawling into you.*"

"Argh," he moans, brushing them from him.

"*The snakes'll be next, then the spiders.*"

He gets up and is violently sick. The sick has a good proportion of blood, it's sticky, but it doesn't smell like normal sick. It passes after a few hours; and, after cleaning up, he accepts if he's going to see this through he needs help.

CHAPTER TWELVE

Rooney as weak as dish water, and his vomiting continues for a bit, but the DTs don't. That morning, he gets an emergency appointment with Dr Dawes, his GP at Northcote Surgery. He leaves there with a prescription for Diazepam, Omeprazole for his stomach, and his advice: "You need treatment Sean." After walking to Byres Road Boots and collecting the prescription, he gets home, just as Jackie calls.

"Johnston walked into Partick station. He said he'd been kidnapped, but freed himself. He wants protection. He said certain people were intent in killing him. He also wanted to, in quotes, help with the investigation into his wife's murder. Next thing Special Branch finds some of the Murphy family in a Govan apartment. Three dead and one lucky, and a Latin statement scrawled across the wall. You know the kind I am talking about: *'Partitur pax bello.'* Peace is borne of war, it means." Gold appears. "We have him in a safe house. We can't charge or remand him. We've no evidence, but the chief says we've to watch him. So we had better watch him."

"Thanks," he says.

"You sound ill."

"I'm fine."

"Do you think you should get help?" she says, in a way which sounded like she wouldn't be providing it.

"No, dear, I'm just dandy."

"Johnston. I want you to see him, to use this opportunity. First, though, I want you to go to a media conference with me. I'll pick you up."

"Then, no fucking more," he says. He'll do this, then go home and get better. He'll see Johnston and maybe go back to work, normal work; and get back some routine. That'll sort him, he thinks. Jackie arrives shortly after and has to help him into the car.

"You look like shit Rooney. Can you do this?"

"I do not look, I might see something I don't like," he says. "What the fuck do you care?"

"We've a job to do," she says.

"Why's this so important?"

"Muir's to talk to the public. We've to be there for back up, to provide detail on the investigation."

"Oh, just fantastic."

They reach the City Chambers and move into a packed foyer, where they push to the front. Muir's late, and goes straight into his statement as he saunters down the stairs. When Rooney hears this man's voice, he gets a Michael Portillo type of figure in his head. When he sees him, he's not far wrong.

"Good evening ladies and gentlemen," Muir pronounces, from the middle of the stairs. "OK, let's make a start. I am here to talk about the incidents," he says to all, in particular the gathered hacks.

"Terrorists," comes from a man at the back.

"No terrorist group has claimed responsibility. This is not terrorism."

"It's the gangs then."

"We have engaged certain… organisations, and we are exploring gangland activity. Please rest assured arrests are… imminent."

"Aye right, the crime families are well above the law," comes from a pushy man sitting in front of them.

"The police are investigating these organisations and pursuing inquiries – "

"We hear there's a man. What's his involvement?" says the man, persisting.

"Who's he?" Rooney asks Jackie, quietly, so's not to be heard.

"Matt Hurley. He's been with the Herald long enough to spot an opportunity to push a Lord Provost into a corner."

"No, I meant who is *he*?"

"*He* is Arthur Johnston."

"Johnston!"

"We can't be sure, Mr Hurley," Muir says.

"They are saying there is man central to all of this Lord Provost. Is this the man? Is it over? Can you confirm?"

Hurley looks around as if to confirm his place as an agent provocateur among his peers.

"What is this?" Rooney asks Jackie.

"Shoosh, listen."

Hurley presses his question home. "Lord Provost, will you assure the city it is over?"

"I sincerely hope so," Muir replies, looking away.

Rooney looks at Jackie.

"The man you have, is he a… the leader… of these gangs? Some people are calling him 'the Father'. You know, his calling card, 'in the name of'?"

Hurley prevails.

"The Father..."

"Interesting, Mr Hurley?" He spans the room. "Are there any more questions?"

Hurley sneers around at his colleagues. "Which means you won't give us detail."

"Anyone else?" Muir asks, ignoring Hurley and trying to engage others.

Hurley brings him back. "Lord Provost, people are saying these killings are linked?"

Muir spins around to consult his press secretary behind him, then turns back to face the journalists. "No... link exists," he says.

Hurley seems to sense he's on to something. "Multiple murders over a number of weeks; so what is it. A bit of a coincidence, don't you think?"

"No links, no coincidence, just a number of despicable atrocities," Muir says, slapping his hands on the podium. "Right, is that it?"

"Jointness?" Hurley says, continuing to harass Muir.

"No jointness, none," says Muir. "Glasgow remains a safe city, but we are not immune to the national problem of gang violence. Now, if you'll excuse me ladies and gentlemen we need to get back to our business of keeping us all safe." At that, he leaves the room, ending the press conference.

Again, Rooney turns to Jackie. "Johnston, the Father?"

She shrugs. "We need something just now."

"Muir needs someone you mean. This is a feckin' lie, and you know it, there are no links; nothing established that is; except to Muir, that is."

"What do you mean to Muir?"

"Links, associations; mostly with him."

"Let's hear it?"

"Councillor Zysk, on the council, Muir's council. The hit man in the subway trying to reach the Square, City Chambers, to get to the council. Owen, Muir's mentor. Bruce, Muir's friend. Muir."

"And Louise?"

"You got me there."

"Mob killings Rooney, there're the links, the associations."

"Yes?"

"Well, Johnston links them, not Muir. You said so yourself. There's a pattern, the Latin messages. We'd be irresponsible not to implicate Johnston in all of this. We need to find out why he is doing these messages, why he features in these murders."

"*If* he's responsible."

"The public need answers. We are getting nowhere, nowhere."

"It's a diversion Jackie, away from Muir, and you fuckin' well know it. What about the mob?"

"It's all we have, for now. Don't worry, we're exploring the mob. You just do what you're supposed to be doing, get into the man's head; evidence, right?"

"Into his head man, not out of yours."

Rooney arrives home. "I need to paint my picture," he says to himself, "to fill in the blank bits." He walks up and down his living room speaking aloud, with what he has by way of information, and what he understands. He gets a fresh 300 by 400 mm canvas out, bought online, takes his easel, oils and brushes out, and places the oils and brushes carefully in a pattern on the table. He was an avid amateur artist before and during his expressive episodes of his illness, less so these days. It provided continuity with his normal world; therapeutic for him and cathartic to try to translate what's happening in his mind; whether it's his pained thoughts or feelings or the colours that invade his head. And, converse to what he believes in his heart, his paints describe what's possible in his mind.

"Now," he says to himself, "what do I know about this man?"

From the file, and his personal, albeit limited, knowledge of him, he ascertains this man has 'led an ordinary life, but is far from an ordinary man'. He emphasises 'a bit of an eccentric', a 'solitary man', not an 'in your face type of character', a 'listener, not a talker'.

He talks to himself, marching up and down the room, voicing the details in chunks.

"Doesn't appear to have any friends ... Canadian-born professor of urban conflict at Glasgow University ... a subject close to his heart and his life ... UK citizen for two years and married to Marlene for three ... met her on the campus in his first year there ... appears to enjoy the cultural fusion in this metropolis ... arrived in 1996, after leaving his native Cape Breton, and having travelled around Europe ... achieved excellence in his field, commanding international respect as a leading expert in political and urban culture ... specialised in the migration of people and its effect on a local cultural scene, and in particular a growing antipathy between the incoming and local folk ... interviewed by BBC on the rising aggression against incomers ... viewed as the eccentric academic with the strange grin."

He sits down at his canvas and runs his hands over it, to get a sense of its proportions. He squeezes the oils in order onto his pallette on the table. He speaks the words 'mood, soul, heart,' and the colour black appears in his mind. He paints a black face; not a black man's face, a Caucasian face with the light removed; then the words 'angry, spiteful, contemptuous' prompts red. He paints staring, red empty eyes, with small pupils. The words 'no emotion' and 'cold' prompts white. A white mouth, a grin, a sneer, and he has more of a straight line. The words 'blood', 'retribution', a red scar from mouth to his cheek. He thinks about the Latin, and gold comes. He paints gold hands, splayed fingers, covering his face, protecting it, but ready to strike out. He hopes it'll turn out something like Edvard Munch's Scream, but it's almost the opposite: from a fearful depiction to a sinister aggressive representation, a bit like a dark Nosferatu Dracula.

"An evil face, the kind of face that interests you, excites you."

"A face of a man who doesn't care; no moral conscience; an arrogant contempt for the human race. This is nihilistic man. Compared to prehistoric man who has just got on his feet, this man has yet to develop a social, moral or human conscience."

"You can do with some of that."

"Jea... sus."

"Your life's about caring, healing. With all that comes with it. A damaged psyche?"

"My psyche is fine pal."

"You've painted a picture of a man you have in your mind."

"I have."

"But it's not Johnston. Johnston's a distinguished looking man, greying. An angular face. The scar's not as evident as has been described in the Latin man descriptions, with a Canadian accent. Though not as evident since his time in Europe. Why did you do this?"

"What do you mean bastard?"

"He's not the same man."

"It doesn't matter. He's *my* man."

CHAPTER THIRTEEN

Rooney travels to the safe house; nothing more than a nondescript flat on the fourteenth floor of a tower block in Shawbridge Arcade. Anonymity and privacy maintained through a protected entry manned by a concierge, a one-lift access and one stairway to all of the sixteen floors. It's 11.00 am, but Rooney believes this man will be at home whatever time of the day it is. Rooney gives his name through perforated holes and asks where 14/8 is.

"Easy. Fourteenth floor, eighth door on the left as you come out of the stairs. Forget the lift. Out of fucking order, again," the concierge informs. Having entered many similar blocks of flats in Glasgow, Rooney knows a lift that works is a luxury.

The smell of urine and shit fills his nostrils as he enters the stairwell. His feet crunch on broken bottles, glass syringes, and aluminium-foiled papers, as he climbs. He counts each floor by two sets of ten steps.

He reaches Floor 14, breathless. He didn't expect anyone there to greet him. He may have expected a SWAT team with automatic weapons guarding the floor; but no chance, nothing. He walks along, passing flats without doors. Loud Bollywood music comes from darkened inners and a smell of curry and oriental food nearly knocks him off his feet. This is an illegal migrant floor. Orientals in sweatshops providing cheap designer copy clothes, and Asians, in an industry of food production, coexisting for mutual benefit. He can hear eastern European accents. He presumes they're employed in a factory for illegal commodities, copy DVDs, computer games, to be sold around the pubs, the Barras, supervised by migrant lieutenants, policed by frontline soldiers. All part of the burgeoning migrant gang industry; no work visas there, no council management there: a migrant enclave. A police safe house here would have had migrant approval or at least acceptance, he wonders.

He counts the doors as he moves along the hall, until he reaches the eighth. As he approaches it, he accidentally kicks an incongruous plant pot with his foot. He knocks the door. There's no answer, initially, then "Who is it?" comes from within.

"Rooney," he replies, in a serious voice.

A heavy-metal door opens inside, followed by the outside door.

"Mr Rooney. Why are you here?" Johnston pushes passed him to look out into the hall. To Rooney, he looks younger than he remembers. He appears him thinner, gaunt, and with a distant look in his eye. Not that he could see his eyes. This man avoids eye contact.

"I was asked to see you." Rooney follows him into the hall.

"Oh yes, why?" Johnston says, with an arrogance Rooney didn't expect. "What have *you* to do with me?"

"I've to talk to you."

"Who asked you to talk to me?"

"The CID."

"Oh, the CID!" Johnston's clearly confused over why Rooney is there on behalf of the CID. "I suppose you'd better come in."

Rooney follows him along the corridor and into a sitting room. He notices a neat line of shoes along the wall of the hall, all black. The house smells of cleaning materials. Johnston tells him to "sit there, please," pointing to a particular chair. Johnston moves to the opposite end of the room. The room is dim, nearly dark, with dark brown curtains pulled tight shut and fastened together with bulldog clips. He hears a 'chirp' and turns to see a small cage on the dining table containing a couple of birds, Zebra Finches, he thinks. He had seen Finches as a boy in his local pet shop. He wanted one, but his mother said they made a lot of mess.

"The CID. I haven't been charged of any crime," Johnston says, cutting a piece of apple to squeeze it between the bars of the cage. He's sitting upright on the edge of a dining chair leaning over the cage.

"I believe you're here, for... protection." Rooney has to turn sideways on his chair to see Johnston properly.

"I came forward voluntarily. I know my righth."

Rooney hears a discernible lisp. Irina said the man on the hill had a 'funny voice'.

"Ah, but does he have funny face?"

"Indeed. And what about the Murphy family?"

"I've no idea," Johnston says, hesitating. "My wife was... involved."

Craning his neck, Rooney tries to face him. "They seemed to think you were important to them."

"Well, they would." Johnston moves to the other side of the cage, further to the side. "Kidnapping is a lucrative business."

Rooney settles with the possibility he will not be engaging face-to-face with this man.

"They seemed to have had a particular interest in you."

"Why are you here?" Johnston pushes his chair further into the dark of the corner.

"I have a role in the investigation."

"What's your role in investigating... my kidnapping? You're a thychologith."

"You're a thychologith."

"Indeed."

Rooney hadn't noticed Johnston's lisp so clearly in the past when he met him in planning meetings, not like this. "I am concerned about other things, bigger things, Mr Johnston." Rooney extends the latter words for emphasis. "The murders, for example."

Johnston gets on his feet. "Mr Rooney, do you know how damaging thith could be to my career?"

"Well, there have been other killings."

"You're making me very nervous."

"I assure you this is a discreet inquiry." This prompts a silence. "I am sorry about your wife. You must be feeling it right now."

"You know nothing about my... feelings, nothing," Johnston moves back to his corner.

"I am sorry Mr Johnston, but there's a murder investigation open on your wife. Why didn't you come forward... initially? You avoided giving a statement to the police."

"I don't like talking about... some things."

"The police think you were taken forcibly from the flat, after being assaulted in the process. They have the forensics to prove this. Were they your wife's killers? Were you abducted? How did you get away from them?"

"Just too many questions Mr Rooney," Johnston says, emphasising each word.

"Indeed, but there's a link between your wife, a Glasgow crime family, and –"

"What?"

"The recent atrocities: the Cobbler, Buchanan Street, Lord Owen, the families, et al, et al."

"I said, I don't like – "

"I need to ask you..., are you Angus Fraser?" Rooney projects this into the corner holding Johnston.

"Please, I don't need this." Johnston moves behind Rooney. Rooney keeps his gaze on the corner. He hears Johnston pacing the floor behind him, murmuring to himself.

"You sound... a bit... agitated."

"I thound... ah yes, tones, timbre, intonations; it's the way you people work. Forensic training; a voice tells more than the eyes when it comes to telling the truth; a verbal lie detector it is." Johnston circles him like a lion with its prey. "Like Sposeto, the blind advocate. He could tell when someone was lying simply through the shift in their voice. A reporter once asked Sposeto to assess his age through his voice. Without hesitation, he correctly answered thirty-two. He could detect profiles. Obese people, for example, have a certain profile, criminals have a certain profile." Rooney detects a pause in Johnston's voice when he is about to say something significant and a drop of tone when he does. "What kind of profile do I have Mr Rooney? Is thith what you do?" His lisp sounds more sinister in the lower tone.

"Could you sit down? I need to talk to you."

"Ah, the body language, the cueth, the thigns." After Johnston's rant, his breathing returns a calm voice, his words composed, albeit he's using words with an 's' which gives multiple 'th' sounds. He returns to behind Rooney. It disconcerts him, as intended.

"Why did you turn yourself in?" There's no answer, the silence is clearly tactical, but Rooney moves in before it matters. "You turn yourself into the Partick Police Station saying you want police protection from the gang which was hunting you, intent on killing you. The next thing they find what was left of it in a Govan flat. Three dead and one survived, a Latin statement scrawled across the wall. You know the kind I am referring to? What was that about?" Again, there's no answer, but Johnston's breathing is faster again, more animated. Rooney wonders if there's a grin creeping across his face: a smile, his scar? "You've been tracked by a dangerous family. What did they want with you?"

"I have a... a profile. Conflict politics, it's what I do. I'm an ekthpert. The families are part of the political makeup of this city. They're as powerful as the civic leaders, some of whom are in their paid employment. It's my work."

"Apparently, this is dangerous work."

"I don't fear for myself..."

"And what do you fear for, in your... work?"

"After Marlene, I needed a safe place. So I went to the police."

"Your wife's murder and the three dead men in Govan?"

"I will co-operate with a *police* investigation," Johnston says, ending the discussion. "Now if you'll excuse me."

Rooney turns to see Johnston is no longer in the room, neither is the bird cage, obviously taken as he left.

"He's no' going to trust his birds with you Rooney."

Rooney gets up and leaves. This man made his blood creep, something unusual for him, but he intends going back there, when he has more ammunition. He leaves there sorely needing a drink, but he has to see Jackie first. He heads to her flat, not being very sure why.

"Guess you've something to say," she says, leading him in.

"Yes, I have," he says, though not sounding very convincing. Since they split, Rooney has never spent more than one night in her new flat. They sit at

113

opposite ends of her settee.

"We interviewed the surviving member of the Murphys," she says. "Higgins. He said that in the middle of the night a door-breaker battering ram busted their door in. Drugs bust, they presumed. They were put on the floor, on their knees, arms tied behind their back, and blindfolded. Then, systematically, three of them were shot in turn on the back of the head. All except him, who survived we think on purpose. And, guess what, not surprisingly he's been somewhat forthcoming with information – "

"Silly man."

"We've offered him anonymity and protection from the men who'd surely kill him. He's no reason to lie. He said the man, Jazz, who killed Marlene and assaulted Johnston, was one of their group. He's dead. *They* took Johnston. I have the Higgins testimony here." She lifts a document file from the coffee table.

"A family hit?"

"It has the hallmarks." She talks to a report pulled from the case file.

"Which one?"

"None have claimed responsibility, but – "

"There's a letter, a message. Latin again."

"Go on then."

"*Bellum lethale, familia familias*. A deadly war, family of families."

"A family war."

"Bigger." She pauses in a strange, indifferent way. "Now, the testimony."

"Go on then. I suppose I should hear this."

She recounts the statement in detail. He's to listen intently. More because he intends confirming this with Johnston. He might have stayed there with Jackie, but realises there's no chance of that; she has work to do. She shows him out, and then a strange thing. As she helps him into his coat, popping his hat on his head, she puts her arms around his neck and kisses him square on the lips. Then she says, "I may still love you, you bastard, but I still don't fucking like you. And I no longer need you."

Rooney tries to say something, but it's as if his tongue is stuck to the bottom of his mouth. He leaves. Then, as something is about to come out, he turns to find the door closed behind him.

"Conflicted, Rooney?"

"The monkey on my back, the voice in my head, and the pain in my arse."

"I'm the best and worst of you."

"You think you know everything about me."

"I'm in you, I'm of you. I'm from you."

"Can I turn you off?"

"Take your meds; stop your drinking and get well."

"Bastard."

Back to the safe house he goes.

Once there, Rooney recounts the Higgins testimony to Johnston. "Go on," he adds, this time facing him across the dinner table. There's even less light, but Rooney can see his face that bit clearer, his scarred mouth more evident now.

"OK, you will hear my story," Johnston says. "Well, I was hit. We know this. I was unconscious. When I came to, I was not very sure of what was going on. I was in the dark. My arms were tied tight to what felt like an iron pillar. I was on the floor, and my legs were tied together at the feet and the knees. I had a muslin hood over my head. Even so, I could see some shapes silhouetted by a light in the corner of the room. I understood two things. One, I was alive and whoever my assailants were they wanted me so. And two, I was not in the hands of petty criminals. More probably, given my background, I was in the control of an organised gang. I didn't have long to wait to confirm this. A number of figures approached me from beyond the light. Nothing was said until I felt their prethence around me. I could smell their sweat. Then they spoke. 'Mr Johnston,' one said. Instantly I detected a familiar voice. Not to make rash judgments, I thought, but if my instinct was correct – "

"You said if you mentioned some connections, you would be released immediately."

"Well, you would say anything in that position, wouldn't you?"

"What do you know of this gang?"

"Well, Marlene had a lover. It kept her out of my hair. I realised how careless I had been not to find out more about this man; him being part of a family."

"It's not like you to be misinformed."

"You know nothing of me, nothing."

"Indeed," Rooney says, questioning his counsellor-client rapport.

"I wondered if they would hold me for cash, to further their criminal activities; for kudos, a symbol of power with other crime families."

"Higgins said they were one of the most dangerous gangs in the city. The Murphys, an East End family, Irish origins, roman catholic, links with the IRA."

"'Indeed, Mr Johnthon,' one said, this time with a push on my shoulder, and louder. 'I hear you,' I said. I had to stay in control and keep my nerve."

"He said they knew you were big, Mr Johnston, but didn't know how big. What did he mean?" There's no answer. "He also said you were worth big money to the right people, big money they needed. Why were you worth big money?"

"Well, at least we know what their motive was for taking me."

"What big money people are we talking about?" Again, Johnston doesn't answer. "Higgins said your expertise was in demand, by the families, in a time of incomer gangs. He said they were very much aware of your value to some serious organisations in the fraternity to which they ascribe. What, may I ask, did he mean?"

"I guess they wanted to cash me in."

"Why?"

"I don't know; maybe because I know things."

"You know what?"

"I had some knowledge... about them. So much so they could not release me."

"Higgins said something similar, but what he said next was interesting. You said to him, 'Unless I can barter a deal with you that would make it more than worth your while to keep me alive?' What was that?" Rooney says.

"Well," Johnston says. "I was in danger, but I was convinced of the greed for power of these men. This was a dangerous group. I knew it could track me. They had killed my wife... they could hurt me. Now, no more, that is... it."

"I think your feelings were hurt more by their audacity and their disrespect, rather than the death of your wife. She betrayed you and she got what she deserved. When they understood who they were dealing with, maybe then, there would be some respect." He lets this sink in. "It appears you said to Higgins, 'Tell me, what is the biggest desire for your family, the biggest challenge, your ultimate goal?'"

Johnston remains quiet.

"Then Higgins mentioned you said something very interesting. You said you would help them achieve this. And when you did, they would release you in absolute gratitude. To which Higgins replied, 'We may never release you, Mr Johnston.' I think he had just ordered your death. And that was the point you realised you couldn't persuade them; the time you decided to turn the tables."

There's a pause. The silence speaks for itself.

"You continued as if you hadn't heard Higgins, or at least never believed it could've happened. Instead, you said, 'My friends, when you become aware of my influence, you will also become aware, should you remove me, your insignificant team will be squashed like an ant underfoot by some heavyweights you can only dream about.' Was this your *bellum lethale, familia familias*', the family of families?"

Rooney stares him square in the face, but he doesn't want him to respond right away. "And what happened next was significant," he says. "Higgins said he was given information which both confirmed your credentials and ensured your release. What did he mean by this, Mr Johnston? He also mentioned particular words that were emphasised, something along the lines of 'kill him and you, your family, your dog, and your bar man, are all dead.'"

"You should use your head."

"Use your head."

"Indeed."

"Why do you drink?" Johnston says, his mouth tightening at the ends.

Where did that come from, Rooney wonders. A distraction he knows, but it stabs deep into his consciousness. What did he know of him? This man could get into your head. I could get on with him! Rooney knows he needs to get the hell out of there. Anyway, he has no more questions and Johnston has no more answers. He doesn't intend to respond to his attack. He knows it's deliberate. It's a thrust, but he isn't ready to parry; no defensive strategy, other than to get out of there.

He is satisfied though. Albeit hurt by Johnston's words, he put pressure on him, and maybe even got under his skin a bit. Now he'll let him stew. If he isn't his man, he'll apologise. 'I was only doing my job, Mr Johnston, no hard feelings.' If he is, he'll enjoy turning the screw. Next time he'll be ready for him. But, as is his want, he needs a drink.

He hails a taxi that drops him off on the Byres Road, and makes his way into Jinty McGinty's, an Irish Bar in Ashton Lane. The irony doesn't escape him as he orders a double whisky; slightly out of place in a bar where Guinness reigns. He drinks it slowly and absorbs the Irish canned music. He wonders where Higgins is that afternoon; might even be in there, or in the East End of the city, the traditional Irish area. He scans the bar, studying the famed Irish writers adoring the walls: Sean O'Casey, James Joyce, Oscar Wilde, et al. Under the picture of Oscar Wilde, there's a passage of *The Ballad of Reading Gaol.*

"Yet each man kills the thing he loves –
* you'll kill her*
"By each let this be heard –
* everyone will know*
"Some do it with a bitter look –
* you can only*
"Some with a flattering word –
* love*
"The coward does it with a kiss –
* or fuck*
"The brave man with a sword! –
* through another."*

"Thanks bastard."

He absorbs these words and appears disturbed with the possibility they're from him. The Latin man, the proxy killer, doesn't have the courage to kill himself. "Not with a sword," he says. "Not even with a kiss." As a Mafioso boss or capo would do to mark someone for death. But, in this man's case 'more with a bitter look'. Irena on the hill comes into his head. "'He looked into my eyes, with those eyes... dead eyes,' Irena said."

"You talking to yourself?" comes from a guy shouldering by to reach the bar.

He dwells on the migrant element to all of this, Irena, Polish; the Murphys, Irish; the Taylors, indigenous Scots; Muir's theme: better together, etcetera. He's immersing himself in all of this, as he does.

"Morphing? Migrants old, migrants new?"

"The Irish poured in after the great famine of 1846."

"Like the migrants of today?"

"Just like them."

"Like them: poor immigration control?"

"A political and social imperative to promote a multicultural society."

"Welcomed with open arms?"

"The Taylors, Asian haters? The Murphys?"

"The pernicious and dangerous face of migration in Glasgow."

"Piled in then, piled in now."

"The Irish came looking for a life without starvation and despair, escaping near certain death in Gorta Mor, the starvation; doing what the new wave of immigrants are doing now, trying to find a better life, free of starvation and poverty, but facing aggression and hate."

"Higgins and his cronies have done very well."

"Some have."

"Do you think he might be here?"

"Where his ancestors had come before him?"

"I meant in here Rooney. In an Irish pub, with Irish boozers, everyone an inveterate drunk, just like you."

Then, unexpectedly and involuntarily, the contents of his stomach spew out over the floor of the bar. He gets out of there fast, leaving the barman to clean it up. Maybe I said something important. Were his feelings conflicted over migration; migration that was in the Latin man activities; something about his own roots; inveterate drunks?

Rooney accepts he needs help. He'll see his doctor about his 'stomach problems'. Another emergency appointment beckons the following day. After describing some of his symptoms, Dr Dawes says he may be an alcoholic. Rooney is stunned in disbelief; but takes a card for the local alcohol project, saying he'll check it out.

He walks to the project, if only to dispel the diagnosis, hoping someone there will say the doctor is wrong and he'll go back to him with his drinking hobby intact. Maybe he'll give him something for his stomach. What happens there, though, just about floors him. Within minutes of meeting the counsellor, Geraldine, he's recounting his innermost feelings and he's sobbing profusely. She says he needs to grieve properly for something; there's something deeper within him that needs to come out; something that'll trigger his illness.

"Counselling you, Rooney?"

CHAPTER FOURTEEN

Rooney retreats to his flat, intent in committing every piece of information from his mind into his dictation machine. The emotional stuff that came out in the alcohol project would be parked meantime. He buys some still water on the way home. He'll let his stomach heal a bit. He knows if he doesn't 'screw the bobbin', he'll mess the whole thing up, and himself with it.

If Johnston *is* the man, Rooney wonders what would have set him off on such a series of savage events, and what chance would he have to either pin him down or stop him? More unanswered questions and no crutch this time to cope with them.

Over the following couple of days, if anything to trump Jackie's phrase book, but more importantly to grasp what this man was trying to reveal through the Latin statements, he enrolls on an online beginners Latin course. The gold, though, attacks his brain in conjunction with each word and phrase. He wonders whether the 'flooding' might reduce the intensity of the colours which lights up his mind when he voices or hears the words. No chance, in his present state he fears this'll trigger a psychotic episode. He abandons the course and arms himself with a Latin phrasebook by C. Messiner instead.

Through his online course, however, Rooney discovers Glasgow University to be a particular centre of excellence in ancient Latin. Latin poetry of the ancient Scots called '*Deliciae Poetarum Scotorum*', mentioned in Dr Samuel Johnson's *Journey to the Western Islands of Scotland* in 1773, is held there. He also establishes Dr Arthur Johnston, Johnston's namesake, a seventeen-century Principal of the University, achieved international recognition for his editing of the works. Johnson viewed Arthur Johnston to be one of the most prestigious of Scottish Latin poets.

Consequently, he needs to do some family finding: some genealogy. From the Scotland's Archive's website, he finds a bio on his Arthur Johnston, to establish he's indeed a descendant of the Arthur Johnston, the Scots Latin poet (1579–1661). He confirms his great grandson, his man's great great grandfather, settled in Sutherland in late eighteen-century Scotland; and, despite attempts by the academia which was protective of the offspring of its great master, they were cleared from their land in 1814, during the mass clearances of indigenous folk in Sutherland. He's to ascertain they were shipped off, on a one way trip, to Nova Scotia. There, the Johnston family settle on Cape Breton Island, until a descendant arrives back in Scotland in 1996, *the* (his) Arthur Johnston.

Rooney decides it's time to explore *his man*'s psychology. He recalls a mentor of his, Dr Michael Stone, who profiled some of the most evil killers of all time. In his research, Stone rated them from level 1: people who killed in self-defence, to level 22: the most evil of psychopathic killers, who killed without any remorse and tortured their victims for fun. His man, if he is responsible for the killings, would be around level 18. Rooney consulted Stone over a difficult case at the State Hospital over a sociopath with an aptitude for extended torture. His advice was essential given the debate that occurred in Court over whether this man was mad, psychotic, with no control over his actions; or bad, who enjoyed torturing his victims until they begged to be killed.

His man though doesn't kill by himself, however, but he'd have been just as sinister and just as evil. Like the Nazi overlords who gave the orders, who had the power to save or kill, who didn't dirty their hands with the blood of others, but stood back and enjoyed the feeling of it. No, he's level 22, he reassesses. He is just as evil, or just as sick, or just as ill.

What would create such a man: the usual pain and conflict? He has *act* and he has *antecedents*, but he has no *why*? He has questions and dilemmas; with no help from the whisky there; not that he could let it cloud his head.

The man's plans need to be next, Rooney decides. He asks Jackie to get her boffins into Johnston's computer. The hard drive is taken to search for any evidence. If he's the man, he wonders if he has a number of secure web storage sites to which he'd secretly uploaded information. He might also have had some CDs in safe deposit boxes, always updated, and always ready for this possibility, this eventuality.

Jackie gets back to him within an hour.

"We found a file folder, deep in his hard drive. A long list of files, including some incriminating information on the Cobbler killings, Springburn and Bruce, the Grosvenor and Owen, Buchanan St, and Muir. The Muirs to be correct. Rooney, we are arresting this man."

'This man' has information only his Latin man could have had, and later that day Rooney goes to Glasgow's Barlinnie prison: the Bar-L, as known locally. Johnston, as Jackie said, had been arrested and charged with suspicion of conspiring to assist murder and holding information which might have been used to assist murder. Then he was taken before the Sheriff and remanded in the Bar-L until trial.

Rooney arrives at Barlinnie by taxi and presents himself at reception. Jackie's cleared him to see Johnston. Everything he has, including his jacket, money, digital camera, mobile phone, propranolol, are squeezed into a tiny locker. Then, after being frisked from head to toe, his mouth examined for drugs, he's escorted through the grounds by an officer acting as his personal tour guide. "That's where Peter Manuel was buried," he says, as if he has to. "Last person to be hanged in Glasgow," he says, in a dry monotone voice, "killed at least eight people." Small stuff in comparison to what was going on now. "Over there on that area of grass, an unmarked grave," he adds. "And that's where the riots took place," he says, without lifting his head. "Three prison guards taken hostage and held up on the roof for five days; dropped slabs on the riot squad officers below." Rooney can't help looking up wishing he was wearing a hard hat.

Rooney is escorted to an interview room in the maximum security area that is segregated from other prisoners. The room feels barren and impersonal, having the regular two chairs and one table set central in the room. One prison officer's there, standing in the corner, arms neatly clasped in hands behind his back. Rooney enjoys the peace there, before the prisoner is escorted in that is. It impresses him on how relaxed it, prison, is, compared to his day job, as was. He recalls a busy schedule of reports, interviews, counselling sessions and court hearings, and the occasional major incident. How seductive it is here, away from the pressures of life. A place to find respite from your problems, to get some structure into your life.

Sounds good, not having to do anything there; a real antidote to the outside world of hassle and stress. It's easy to see how prisoners become institutionalised, similar to many long stay patients, losing skills, abilities, growing to fear the outside world. He wouldn't have minded some of this. His daydreaming ends abruptly, as *his man* is brought in.

Johnston's told to sit at the other end of the table, which he does, his hands spread out on the table, as if he's about to commence a piano concerto. This man at the center of a massive murder investigation; with a fiendish look caused by his scar; but this is being judgmental and Rooney shouldn't do judgmental. He tries to tie him to a figure or a character, but he can't; there's nothing in his repertoire of baddies that illustrates this man.

Johnston opens.

"You again?"

"Indeed, me, again. No birds?"

"You are an infernal nuisance and I'll see you in Court for this," Johnston says, indicating the client-professional relationship has no chance. "I've been wrongly charged and I will fight this."

"And why did you have the incriminating stuff on your computer?"

"Always lead with a question Mr Rooney? Did you get this on your investigative interviewing course? My job, Mr Rooney, is conflict. This is my interest. I was researching. I was playing your part, tracking these murders, my interest paralleling yours."

"You had information on your files, highly confidential, secret," Rooney says. "Where did you get this information, unless you had first-hand experience of it?"

"I... study things."

Rooney needs to move to something more solid, tangible. "And what about the Latin?"

"The Latin?"

"The Latin."

"Many people are interested in Latin."

"Apparently. Your namesake, Arthur Johnston?"

"Genealogical research Mr Rooney. I like that, impressive."

"Indeed, can we drop the 'Mr's'?"

"Yes Rooney, it's too personal, and in here there is no personal."

"So, what about Arthur Johnston and the Latin?"

"My family is privileged to have this man as an ancestor and we enjoy the expression Latin brings to our lives."

"The links between the man, the Latin statements, the killings?"

"What linkths?"

The tone drops, the lisp arrives. Time to raise the tempo. A small taste of Caplan crisis intervention. Create the crises – crisis provides the energy – use the energy.

"Look, I'm not here to mess with you," Rooney spits. "You're responsible for your wife's murder, you're a suspect in multiple murders, and you're an academic with a perverse interest in the killing of others. Three of a kind, I call that."

Johnston doesn't rise to this hostility, not initially. He returns to a quiet and composed bearing; but then he attacks, and when it comes, it comes.

"Why are you here? What is your game? What are you? What is your perverse interest in me? Is this your kind of work? Truth is you can't do it anymore, No sir. Can't cut the mustard no more. Can't even understand his own psychobabble. A sad mad man, and you drink – shrink."

"He's up for you, sad man."

Rooney's stunned. As in the last time, the man can assault a psyche. Johnston's now on his feet and circling him. The officer moves farther into the room. "Sit down you," he orders. Rooney feels vulnerable. He feels Johnston is a predator ready to strike and he wants to see this in action.

"Leave him," Rooney says.

"You are an excuse for an interrogator. Why did they send you?"

"I am not a fucking-well interrogator." Rooney bangs his hand on the table.

"Well, why are you here, you alcoholic excuse for a man?"

Rooney wonders how he knows anything about him. He'd met him on no more than a few times at meetings. Is he just chancing it? Rooney tries to gather his thoughts. He knows Johnston's intent in getting to him, and he is succeeding.

"Why you're here is more to the point."

Again, there's silence from Johnston, until then he turns and says, "*Vide et crede*, Rooney, see and believe. What do you *believe*?" Johnston touches something in Rooney. Gold comes flashing in. Something stirs deep within him. "*In nomine Patris*, Rooney, in the name of *your* father."

Rooney's mind implodes into a firestorm of yellows, magentas, and golds; like fireworks going off in his head. He rushes across the room; uncharacteristic of him, as he would never leave his seat at an interview table for obvious reasons, being a coward being one of them. Reaching Johnston, he grabs him by the neck. "Listen you... you torn face bastard," he says. "The Latin, you've used this before, haven't you? Remember Irena? She heard you say '*In nomine Patris*' on the hill, just before you dispatched her family and her over the side of the hill. *You* are the Father," he says, spitting the words into his face. This is raw aggression. Where did this come from?

The officer moves forward to intervene, fearing a situation that would require an 'incident report'. "*Mr* Rooney," he says in an authoritarian tone, as he releases his grasp of Johnston.

"It's OK," Rooney says. "It's OK."

Rooney's voice is quivering, shaking. Never in his career had he felt this, far less shown this kind of emotion. His professional defence system always kicked in. Even when confronting child killers, or someone like Brian Harte, who brutally killed his colleague John Gilbert, his safety shield, as he called it, had protected him and allowed him to be dispassionate and impartial. Johnston has stirred something significant inside him, in a way that scares him.

"You know how to get to people, you bastard, and you know that," he says in a trembling voice.

Johnston breaks into a grin. "Your display doesn't... trouble me Mr Rooney."

"No, don't suppose it does," Rooney says, backing off a bit. "And what does scare you?"

"Not being able to... control mythelf," Johnston says. Rooney looks into his eyes, and for a few seconds this man scares him. The lisp, however, returning at a point of calm, interests him.

"Control what? Killing people?"

Rooney waits for an answer he knows won't come. He'll try a different tack. "Are you angry about Marlene? They killed her to get to you, you know."

Johnston retains a calm composure, stoically folding his arms and sitting upright. Rooney'll get no more from him, but he questions his ability to interview an 'intelligent man'. He takes a mental note to ask himself about this later. He underestimated this man and realises how poorly prepared he'd been. He'll leave him there without saying anything more. More words are unnecessary, any more a waste of breath; but he got to him, that's for sure; but he can't resist the compulsion of having one more swipe at him.

Johnston's sitting squarely at the table across from him. Lacking his camera, which is at reception, Rooney feigns one in his hands and points it at him. He says 'click' clearly, as if to catch a full frame of his face. How 'his kind' didn't mind posing for mug shots and being caught by TV cameras as they left courtrooms, but not like this. Rooney intends creating an intrusion, capturing something of Johnston, a mental photograph. He intends disturbing Johnston because he had upset him; to make a personal point, because *in there* he could.

"I will respond to thith, Rooney... in my own time," Johnston says coolly, his eyes penetrating determinedly into Rooney's.

"Decapitate, blow me up, or shoot me," Rooney says. It's his turn to smile at him. Touché. How unprofessional can you get? His demise is now a strong possibility. Johnston's words come from a man with no emotion, and yet an emotional situation has been created, a sociopath context. But who created this? Rooney would like to think it's him, by employing Caplan, using the energy, confronting, creating a new homoeostasis, but he realises Johnston may have trumped him on this; he may have provoked the scenario. He settles on the fact whoever prompted it, it is valuable, to see Johnston in action. It may have become too cosy, too embroiled in an intellectual mind game which sociopaths love, especially when it focuses on them. Johnston returns to the silences. Rooney wonders if he'll dwell on this encounter until they meet again. If so, Rooney will use this to his advantage.

For Rooney, it's time to leave there, if only to compose himself. He leaves the room without saying any more. But, rather than any professional goal achieved, he retreats feeling somewhat ashamed of himself. Never before had he acted like this. He had allowed his professional armoury to slip, his personal foibles have revealed themselves. Was this *his* intent? He'd lost discipline and all sense of professional values. He'd stepped out of line. In his business, working with seriously mentally ill people, this shouldn't happen. He also wondered whether he is melding Johnston with the Latin man, as had been suggested. He let his heart rule his head. He condemned him, without confirmation or substance; but, it's clear he wants him to be *the* man.

Leaving the prison, Rooney enters a taxi and exits it at the Clutha Vaults in the Saltmarket, on the north bank of the River Clyde, known for its poetry, politics and folk singers – a heady mix. Adjacent to the Scotia Bar, it's another of his favourite watering holes. In there, he hits the whiskies, against all his fears and all the advice, the DTs, the crap stomach, the self-disgust, the inability to function. He'd get to them after a few beers, but this night he's in a hurry. The pain in his mind needs immediate amelioration. He knows this is complete madness; he should go home to think the thing through, but no.

It's Friday night and people are out for a drink and a blether. This is a healthy antidote to being in the Bar-L with Johnston. It's loud in there. A band is blasting out joyful, upbeat music, pushing the humdrum of the working week aside. It's mobbed, and just the kind of environment he needs, where he can lose himself and recover from his encounter with Johnston.

He finds a seat by the fireplace; easier to get to the toilet from there and out the back to the beer garden for a smoke. There he'll drink and contemplate his encounter with Johnston, how he'd allowed his professionalism to slip. He lost control. Did Johnston fashion, he wonders, to test him.

Around ten, he staggers out of there. Well 'recovered', drunk and wavering around on the street outside the pub, he feels the ground coming up to meet him. He grabs the traffic light pole on the corner of Clyde Street, and is about to mumble 'taxi' to passing traffic, when he hears a voice from behind. A voice he remembers from the past; a voice he had hoped he would never hear again.

"Hello, Doctor Rooney, do you remember me?"

The 'do you remember me' is only just preceded by a sharp pain in his lower back. The voice prevails. "Do not worry Doctor Rooney, the knife has only minimally entered your *latissimus dorsi* (and a stab of gold in his mind). Hence not a vital organ, therefore, you will bleed, but you will not die. Well not quite yet, and I've calculated you will lose approximately eighty grams of blood before it clots and stops. You are in the hands of a proper clinician and, if you follow my clinical guidance, the knife won't go much deeper; don't, and I'll be inclined to administer a deep and fatal incision to your liver."

Even in his drunken state, Rooney knows this is a dangerous situation, and he's in no fit state to resist. He obeys this assailant's orders to go towards the river Clyde, only metres away. He could have called out, but if he did this man would drive the knife home and calmly walk away. To any inebriate observing, he's only a fellow drunk being helped along on his way home. They walk deliberately along the riverside causeway, well known as a haven for drug taking, prostitution, alcoholics, and those just going there for a piss after some heavy boozing. They're well at home.

"You're Brian Harte, aren't you?"

"I am lead physician Doctor B Harte, and you are Doctor S Rooney, PhD. You will well remember your involvement in my locum secondment to the State Hospital."

"As you say. What do you want?"

"Me, I want to kill you."

"And why?"

"Because your clinical practice falls below what is deemed to be acceptable standard." God, if he only knew. "And if it had been left to you, I would have remained in an inappropriate placement, outwith that which is clinically necessary."

"We could discuss this. How did you get out?"

"I had assistance."

He reaches an immediate assumption Johnston is behind this, but he rules this out. How could he do this? This man was on a restriction order in the highest security environment in the land.

"Kill me and you'll find yourself back there for an indefinite placement, you know that."

"I have the means to control my clinical destiny," he says. Rooney feels a large bundle of notes being pushed into the back of his head.

"I guess you have an exit route."

"You are correct. I'll be well on my way to deliver my clinical duties unhampered by... wrongful interference, well before they find you."

This man has been enabled in this. Rooney knows this. He has to make a move. He swings around to strike him, but he only succeeds because of his drunken state in falling flat on his back.

"Silly doctor," he says, as he pulls him into a sitting position and, using plastic binders, ties his hands together through the railing by the side of the river. Then, almost as part of the same movement, he puts the knife inside his mouth, and with a deft cut pulls the end of the knife out through the side of his mouth, extending it by an additional half-inch. Rooney screams in agony, but he has little chance of help there in that isolated spot. "This is necessary to remind you of your clinical responsibility towards others who may have suffered such injuries."

'Torn face,' the last words he delivered to Johnston, echoes through his mind.

"I am going to leave you now Doctor Rooney, but just remember I may come back to administer a greater medical procedure. I hope my clinical intervention today acts to deter you from further poor, or even malpractice."

His mouth is aching, but still he manages to say, "You want to kill me."

"I do, but this is not within my clinical remit or instructions."

He walks away, and in the dark Rooney hears some murmuring, close by. "He's been chibbed. Let's shift before the polis arrive." They sound like a bunch of homeless men, who, on skippering there, are stirred from their cardboard mattresses. He knows they'll not help him; they wouldn't want to be witnesses in any serious assault, having to go to Court and all that. They drag their bedding off to head up the pathway to a more private site, and then he's alone. "Thanks a fuckin' bunch," he shouts.

He sits there spitting out blood, trying not to separate the end of the wound, in the hope a few stitches would sort it, and in the knowledge he'll have something permanent on his face as a memento of his meeting with Harte.

He'll now have a 'Glasgow smile', a scar some Glaswegians known for using a blade would be proud of providing. The blood runs down his neck and, from the wound in his back, down onto the cobbles where he sits. His hands are dipped in a pool of blood, but not enough to concern him that his wounds are life threatening. Only then did he realise he had shat and wet himself, the blood mixing with his urine and shit. He's never felt so miserable in his life. Nearly an hour later, after he had dozed off, a hand on his shoulder brings him to his senses. He's been discovered by two police officers patrolling the path on bikes. They walk him up the path and up onto the Broomielaw, passing the Clutha that was still in full swing. He wishes he hadn't left.

Rooney spends an uncomfortable three hours in Glasgow Royal Infirmary A and E, unsuccessfully trying to explain to the medics he isn't a drunk and his being tied to the railing and his face being cut wasn't part of some gangland fight or feud, or he wasn't just set about as happens to drunks in this city. His pockets had been emptied as he sat there on the path and his wallet taken, only reinforces the belief he's a drunk, or a rough sleeper. Only when a nurse agrees to contact Jackie, he feels he might be treated with a respect not accorded to those who were stitched up, cleaned up, and put out of the door to fend for themselves in the small hours of every weekend. By the time Jackie arrives, he has indeed been stitched, on his back and face, and washed, and he's waiting there in the corner of the waiting room. His soiled clothes smell so much of shit he commands a good proportion of the waiting room.

Jackie delivers him home and into a warm bath, putting his clothes in a black bin bag tied tight with duct tape, to be delivered to the council incinerator the next morning. He says nothing in response to her questions. He is sore, tired, and his brain feels numbed by the experience. Helping him into a comfortable bed, she says, "You're out of this Rooney. They'll kill you."

"They'll kill you" resonates in his head as he falls into a deep and protecting sleep. 'He'll' kill me more like; 'they?'

CHAPTER FIFTEEN

It's two weeks before Rooney recovers from that night. Two weeks in which he sits quietly in his tatty robe trying to come to terms with what had happened to him, his attack on Johnston, him being assaulted. Two weeks of detox in which not a drop of alcohol passed his lips. He had been back to Geraldine and cried his eyes out again, this time when she asked about his childhood. Two weeks in which he reflects on his abilities and his sanity, and wonders if he should get a review of his medication, to get rid of the stuff in his head, including me!

Jackie arrives back in his flat and produces a card she found in his jacket pocket on the night before committing his suit to the bin.

He makes tea, and brings through a porcelain tea pot, one of the only wedding presents he possess, two mugs and a carton of milk, on a tray.

"I think you should see this," she says, handing him the card. In return, she accepts a mug of tea. "I mind the tea pot," she says, "Glad *you* got it."

"Sure, better than nothing," he says. "The card?"

"I've held on to it until you were well enough to cope with it. It says '*empta dolore docet experientia*,' in familiar font."

Rooney runs it through his fingers, as bright gold glitters in his head. He can see the indentation caused by the pen as it leaned into the card, maybe even the font.

"It means 'experience bought with pain teaches effectively'. I looked it up in my Latin book."

"I know what it means," he says, dropping heavily onto his sofa. "It's been used before, in the Grosvenor, Owen."

"What does it mean; to do with you, I mean?"

"It means, 'butt-out, got your fingers burned, learn from this'," he says, looking very much the older man, a grey face, a two week beard, and his hair tousled and growing over his robe at his neck.

He gets up to replenish the mug, pouring more for Jackie. She notices his pallor, and his gait, slow and deliberate.

"I should learn."

"So you should," she says, adding milk from the carton. "Harte, some more info."

"I'm listening."

"The official or the unofficial line?"

"Both."

"Well, the official bit is Harte was recommended for conditional discharge, a couple of weeks before he sought you out. Backed by the council solicitors and two consultant psychiatrists who said he was no longer a risk to the public. Treatment would continue in the community, supervised by a social worker and a consultant psychiatrist."

"Twats," Rooney says, criticising and demeaning his colleagues at the same time.

"Unofficial?"

"Go for it"

"Political involvement."

"More?"

"Recommendation by the council?"

"A Lord Provost diktat?"

"Can't say; don't know. Only know it was something to do with, let's say 'political influence'."

Rooney would usually rise to the mention of 'political influence', especially when it confirms his view of a corrupt council, but not this time.

"What's wrong man?" Jackie asks, getting up and standing over him.

He doesn't answer, only raising his eyebrows in her direction and shrugging his shoulders in a gesture of indifference.

"Roon, something else."

"What?"

"Harte's body has been fished out of the Clyde, not so far from where he attacked you."

Rooney pauses to think. "Listen Jackie, I don't give a jiggle-jot for Harte," he says. "It's a kind of justice, but this has gone too far. I am a forensic psychologist, not a detective inspector. I am doing police work here, and it is high time I returned to my normal nine to five woodentops, or at best to retire." He drags himself off the sofa, almost revealing a lack of anything underneath, but Jackie's not interested in this man who would not be out of place in a nursing home. "I'm too long in the tooth for this," he adds.

"Dead right, crosswords are much more your thing."

"I've had enough."

"Rooney, you want out, but you bloody well need this."

She gets up to leave. He asks her to stay, but she perceives it as meaning 'let's go to bed'. "Darling, a good fuck would kill you," she says and leaves.

He shakes his head and returns to his bed where he remains for a further couple of days. In there, he indulges in some exploration, into his heart and soul. Johnston got to him – into his head, that's for sure. He had let his emotions rule his control, his discipline, his professional shield, and it was eating him up from the inside. He's in danger of a serious slide into a dark and deathly place.

"You want this man, your nemesis. You going to let him win?"

He doesn't answer, but there's a perceptible tightening of his eyelids, a look of hate. That'll do.

He has a shower and a shave and gets into his clothes. With the combination of his time off the sauce and the bed rest, he's refreshed physically and mentally. He decides to focus his new energies in doing a proper job in researching this man, and this time while not in a drunken stupor. He gets out the ALDI bag, and pulls out the file with the CID report. He avoids the summary information and goes straight for the chronological history of Johnston, taken at the time of assault by the police. He skims through the information, and it becomes evident this is more than an everyday history taken in an interview context. This is an in-depth and detailed assessment. The writer was a professional, able to extract personal and intimate information from his interviewee.

"OK, what does it say?"

He would usually ignore me, but he decides to indulge me this time.

"The CID file, it's chapter and verse on Johnston."

"Really?"

He continues in a steady cadence. "He was born in Cape Breton, in Canada. His father James Johnston was a diplomat, a Canadian with a long Scot's lineage. He led the family and the young Johnston around the major cities in Europe. They were constantly on the move. His mother Louisa, a French Canadian academic, taught Breton and Celtic studies, wherever they were obliged to live, which seemed to be never more than a few months in any one place at any one time. This eclectic experience created an understanding of many cultures in the young Johnston; and a conversational retention of at least a few languages. It was reported Johnston said his father constantly reminded him of his namesake ancestor, the said Arthur Johnston, seventeen-century principal of Glasgow University, the prestigious Scottish university.

"Arthur. Artorius, Arthur, Ben Arthur, the Cobbler, the Polish family!"

"I get it."

"Think you're good at this?"

"The *file* says Johnston's mother had a temper which was symbolised by an ornate hickory walking stick she used regularly on him, when she wasn't using it to get around following a riding accident. His father was reported to be a manipulative man, manifesting emotional harm which marked the young Johnston, but had also left him with deep resentment of his father's tolerance of his mother's brutality."

"The guy got a lot out of Johnston. No' like you."

"What do you know?"

"The pain and conflict you need in your man?"

"I know this was a mother's brutality towards her son and her authority over his father. This was a father's corruptive influence over his son, his acquiescence over his mother's brutality. This father's insistence, both in his professional and private life, that manipulation was the way to achieve."

"Weakness. Find it. Exploit it."

"Whether it was in the field of international affairs, or at home, his parents were high achievers. They made big demands on their son. Maybe Johnston was never as good as they were. Or never as good as they would have liked him to be."

"Jackie?"

"You keep out of that," he says, continuing. He's on a roll. "The young Johnston developed a precise grasp of Latin. He used it to amuse his ever-critical parents as he habitually translated everyday Latin phrases, for emphasis and to gain some response. Just about the only way to get a reaction or advantage. *'Non revertar insultus.* I shall not return unavenged' was used regularly by his mother. She was well known for her temper and as the parent who meted out cruel punishment."

"An irreconcilable reality, inability to match his parents' expectations?"

"Christ, you're starting to sound like me."

"I am... you."

"They got a lot of personal information from him. He was, though, interviewed by some sharp detectives in the CID," he says. "Throughout his adolescence, it appeared his frustration regularly erupted. Perhaps his only coping mechanism was a perception of what he thought was right, which resulted in him coming off the loser and ultimately suffering injury. One incident in particular was recorded. Outside a Cape Breton bar, perpetrated by an upset suitor of a French woman he had insulted, and from a blade that cut deep into his face and through part of his tongue. It left him with the permanent grimace for a smile and a speech defect that made him speak with a lisp; but, more, it left him with a burning determination to seek retribution. Before he left Cape Breton, he advised the French woman's brother that his attacker, a 'French hating Englishman' made her pregnant. He heard later the brother had stabbed his assailant twice through the heart in a fight outside the same bar; was this his first proxy hit?"

"Your man. You've decided."

"He *is* my man," he says, deciding he needs a cup of tea.

He's pleased to avoid his drinks cabinet, not that there was anything in it; nothing lasted in there. Then back to the chronological stuff he goes.

"Following Johnston's father's posting to the Canadian Embassy in Paris, the young Johnston was accepted into the Sorbonne in Paris. It seemed his parents predicted departure to one or more exotic destinations severed ties between them."

"Away you go."

"At university in Paris, at a time of political unrest, he was drawn into political activity and onto the streets of the Latin Quarter during the student revolts. He was a leading light in the revolts, talking at numerous meetings throughout the left bank."

"He was being watched."

"He gained recognition in a number of organisations of the far left, where he exploited the lack of change, the need for action. He associated with those who would promote greater freedom for suppressed groups such as the Palestinians and black South Africans. He insinuated himself there with them, but saw them as weak and ineffective. He avoided major confrontation with the university authorities and appeared to retain some discretion within his personal and political interests. More importantly, he achieved academic excellence and progressed through his first degree with ease, and on through a Master of Science and a PhD in Urban Conflict. He was by then – so the reports said – identified as a political agitator. He moved to Scotland, to the place of his ancestors, and then here, to Glasgow, to this hotbed of cultural diversity."

"Paris for here?"

"Johnston's personality, already damaged by his parents' influence, was to be shaped by the event in Glasgow forever."

"The kicking."

"The raid on the asylum seekers; Johnston was there and was arrested for obstructing the raid. During intensive questioning an 'over-enthusiastic officer' with a 'deep distrust and dislike of anything alien', enraged by the sullen man with a 'torn face' and an inability to talk in 'proper English', gave Johnston the kicking 'intending to stop short' just enough to 'loosen his resistance to questioning,' the report says. Appears his boot went deep into Johnston's middle, and he bled from his mouth, his stomach, and from his testicles. He was rushed to Glasgow's Gartnavel General Hospital, where he spent the next few weeks. When he left, he was impotent."

"Limp dick."

"Later, Johnston accepted a position as a lecturer at University of Glasgow, his first proper academic post since leaving the Sorbonne. It was reported that his academic success, his powers of persuasion, and some say 'political influence' made the appointment inevitable."

"Glasgow politics!"

"After discharge from the hospital he was welcomed to his post at the university by the Glasgow city fathers, both for the misunderstanding of his involvement with the asylum seekers, and for the 'regrettable incident by the city police officers'. Johnston demanded a public apology from the then chair of the Strathclyde Police Authority, James Muir, soon to become the Lord Provost, the leader of the council. This was never given, despite a campaign of numerous letters and his turning up at the City Chambers one day, where he was denied access to Muir. He made it very evident he would use all his influence to damage the council's position in respect of immigration policies and its heavy-handed approach. He wrote critical articles on council policy, which appeared to create the circumstances that led to his appointment as the first professor of urban conflict at the university. A radical appointment, but this was not unusual for University of Glasgow."

"To shut him up?"

"Having an ancestor principal may have helped too."

"Cronyism."

"From the report, this man exudes calm, resolved, aggression; but there was a change in this man's behaviour. This was a man with a background of fear and abuse, terrified initially, in a situation of threat, who, after traumatic experience, became resolved, and was determined to exact justice and retribution."

"The predisposing factors of your damaged, but very able man well and truly established."

"You got it, bastard, Christ, takes time!"

"So here in Johnston is the man you seek, the man you fear – the man you crave?"

Rooney heads for the Bar-L feeling better equipped with relevant information on Johnston, but shamed still by his lack of professionalism when he was last with him, which led to him letting his guard down and being assaulted.

Jackie has said 'if he so wishes' he is off the case and he should take a break before deciding his future. It wasn't keeping him off the drink anyway; if anything the opposite. He'd to think about getting out of this line of work. He advises Jackie he has to go back to the Bar-L. He *has* to see Johnston. Inside, he knew he had let himself down and he had to face him again. But this time it would be different, it has to be. He's learned a very important lesson about his own vulnerabilities, his rage, and of Johnston's ability to exploit these. This man can control and corrupt. More significantly, he can use a man's feelings.

Rooney is anxious as he enters the high-security block of the Bar-L to interview the man, again, but he can't believe how exposed he had been at the last interview and chastises himself.

"Prove it. Do your job."

He resists the temptation to argue. Talking to himself in the Bar-L could lead to a 'wee holiday'!

"He'll get to you."

Rooney wonders if, in Johnston, he has met his match.

He enters the interview room once more, over two weeks since his last meeting with him. Sitting down he covers his mouth with his hand. His face has healed, but his wound is evident.

Johnston enters by an adjacent door, the officer beckoning him in. There's no introduction and Johnston speaks first as he enters the room, as if nothing had occurred the last time or within the intervening time.

"Now we have similar features," Johnston says.

"Not that you had anything to do with it."

"Shall we continue to cross swords? Have we learned anything?"

It's too early to get into a hostile place. Rooney needs to get this onto a proper psychoanalytical level.

"Empta dolore, etcetera, I have learned much," Rooney returns. "But I am interested in learning what is in your mind. What you... feel, Mr Johnston?"

"No one has ever asked me this. You are an interesting man Mr Rooney," Johnston says. "No one has ever asked how I feel." A rational and ordered response, or a ploy? Anyway, for Rooney, it's worth pursuing.

"Well, what do you feel?"

"Feel?"

"Feel about... people."

"People, don't concern me."

Interesting, he didn't hear the emphasis Rooney put on 'feel', but focused on 'people'.

"No, I don't believe they do," Rooney says. "Who or what concerns you?"

Johnston's eyes pan upwards in feigned indifference. "Look, I am not interested in this tact. You have nothing on me, and I have nothing to fear from the criminal-justice system."

"No, I don't suppose you do," Rooney says. "I doubt if anything would be proven or be directly attributable to you. Would you like to get out of here?"

"I would, when I wish."

When *I* wish!

"When will you so wish?" Rooney asks, not expecting an answer. "What other wishes do you have?"

"My wishes... you *are* trying hard," Johnston says, then pauses. "My wish – "

"Yes?"

" – is to get to the root. To remove the pain you need to get to its source. The root, I need to get to the root."

"The root of what?"

"The root... of this city's problems," he says, lowering his voice and sitting down. "A dentist needs to pull a tooth to destroy a deceased root. Some necessary pain, the root is destroyed."

A bit out of context. Rooney wonders if he's telling him something important, or what Johnston thinks he needs to know. Or is he just winding him up?

"I think you are giving me what you think I want to hear," Rooney says, "but let's see where you intend going with it; with your teasing analogies, metaphors, whatever. The tooth?"

"The tooth is what is rotten in this city."

Thinking in the abstract, he isn't psychotic.

"And who will pull the tooth, this dentist?"

"Don't insult me, you know who will."

Did he?

"Sorry?" Rooney asks, trying to get some clarity.

"*Qui gladio ferit, gladio perit,* he who lives by the sword dies by the sword."

Gold!

"You need to be more specific?"

"Those who impose their will on the people will perish by the people's will."

"I'm not clear on this?"

"You will, in time..., when they act."

Rooney is getting irritated over these metaphors, expressions; he needs something more concrete.

"You have a history Johnston, the Latin, your namesake ancestor, Arthur Johnston, Arthur... Johnston." He deliberately splits the Arthur and the Johnston. "Arthur, the Cobbler, and the councillor and her family."

No answer, he continues.

"Parentage, the incident, the correspondence with the Lord Provost, your wife's murder; the Murphy family. A fair linkage, I think."

He's quiet, as if to absorb the words. Then, deciding not to take the session any further, Johnston turns to the wall, Rooney hopes, provoked by his words.

"Arthur, slaughter with a clear conscience," Rooney says. "Are you *the* Arthur, Arthur Johnston?"

Johnston turns back towards Rooney.

"Why do you say this? Why do you dithlike me? Why do you want to condemn me?"

"Because I know who you are."

Johnston turns to Rooney, looking directly into his eyes with a dispassionate stare. As he does, Rooney hears Irena's voice, 'Those eyes... dead eyes?' Johnston moves to within inches of his face; with his slight smile, the faint grin, the eyes. "Dead eyes... funny face, funny voice, without being funny... do you know what I mean?" He does now, Irena. Rooney looks into these eyes to the point it becomes so uncomfortable, but only for him. The more he looks, the more he sees his own father's eyes, eyes full of hate. This is just too much. He has to get out of there.

Back in his flat, Rooney collapses onto his bed like a Douglas Fir crashing to the ground. He rests his head on his hands. Johnston's words reverberate and rattle around in his mind in chunks. He can still see Johnston's eyes drilling into his. His father's eyes appear in a repeating cycle in his mind.

"Your man, or your delusion, Rooney?"

He could do with a drink, at least to steady his head, to dull those visions. He tries to reassure himself. Johnston is locked up after all, and he can't do any damage in there. Can't he?

Rooney's hobby is photography and, as with his painting, it grounds him, gives him something solid. He decides to print the photograph of Johnston that he has avoided developing since he took it in the interview room on *that* day. Using the enlarger, he makes an A4 print. In the cupboard he uses for developing his prints he passes the photo paper from tray to tray. In the developing fluid-filled tray the face gradually materialises in front of him. As it emerges, he feels shivers running down his spine and back up. It's if Johnston was expecting the shot, almost like a picture from a passport booth. He can make out a smile; or is it the grin caused by his disfigurement? Whatever it is, it's disconcerting; there's no way he can stick this on his sitting room wall, not even on his wall of killers. He couldn't cope with man's dominance, bearing down on him as he sits down for his dinner.

"Your man, Rooney?"

Supported by some books, he props the picture up on his coffee table next to the canvas of his man's face, the one he painted in oils: the dark Nosferatu. His visual profile: black face, red eyes, white mouth, red scar, gold and yellow hands, splayed fingers, etcetera. He takes a large gulp of breath as he downs another swallow of water, conveniently set on a pile of books on his bedside cabinet. His eyes move laterally to the bookshelf near the window, the one with the bottle of The Famous Grouse tucked behind some textbooks.

"Your man's getting to you; take a drink, take a drink..."

He has that drink and falls asleep on his sofa, with these pictures bearing down on him, watched by two pairs of eyes. Then, abruptly, he's woken up to the sound of the phone.

"Jackie, no doubt," he says, as he reaches for it.

"You've seen him again. You're still in," Jackie says.

"Suppose," he says, trying not to sound too committal.

"Good, Muir will be pleased."

"Sure he will."

"Have you heard the news?"

"What news?"

"An email, straight into Muir's inbox. It said, '*Jacobus Rex*, a strike to the heart.'"

"Gold."

"Gold; god you're weird, you drinking again?"

"The email."

"Arrived as Muir began his latest press conference."

"Oh indeed, more of the same Johnston's the man stuff."

"Well, there have been no incidents since Johnston was detained, and no further family activity. Muir was relaxed in the media centre, evident from the way he sauntered in, almost casually. Even Hurley wasn't going to get to him that day. Then, just as he was about to deliver his press statement saying security was to be relaxed, his press secretary pushes forward to whisper into his ear."

"Your fly's open, Lord Provost."

"As he did...," she says, with a smile in her voice, "Hurley called out, as he has done at every press session since the incidents occurred. 'Mr Muir, it's been over four weeks since the last incident. Could you confirm it's all over?' Muir turned to the hack audience, and with a shaky voice, he says, 'I... I have to curtail this conference.'"

"Less relaxed now," Rooney says.

"Hurley's insistent, 'Lord Provost you haven't addressed my question. Is it over?'"

"Muir came back. 'You are aware of the city's determination in this Mr Hurley, and you will appreciate I have important business to attend to.' And that was it. The news of the threat quickly spread through the media centre."

"No incident."

"No, just a threat, so far; most probably a shithole crank organisation looking for air time."

"Johnston?"

"No mention of."

"A strike to the heart?"

"Fuck knows, but keep an eye on him."

"An eye for an eye, Jackie."

"Makes all the world blind, hon," she says, signing off.

Rooney phones the Bar-L. Openly pleased and animated, Johnston had been pacing his cell for hours. A microphone in his cell picks up him quietly singing a tune from the film *Cabaret*. "Maybe this time, I'll be lucky, maybe this time

..."

Next he phones Jackie. She says all top-level council business has been cancelled, all diplomatic activity curtailed, and all non-essential travel postponed. The population of the city holds its collective breath. Then another email arrives into the Lord Provost's inbox in the now distinctive font from Easy Everything, a massive Internet café in St Vincent Street in Glasgow. It says, 'Jacobus Rex: the time has yet to come.'

Back in his cell, Johnston appears settled, yet he has no access to external information and had no way of knowing the relief of all outside. Rooney isn't sure about the extent of this, nor the means, but he's determined to probe as deep and as far as Johnston will allow. Following the photographing incident, he knows this might not be very far or deep.

Johnston appears impervious to Rooney's questions in subsequent interviews, and it's three days before he allows him access to any more of his thoughts, not that he doesn't appear every day to sit in his now-familiar seat. There are no further hostile or hurtful words from either of them, as if a steady state had been reached; there's palpable tension.

The last time Rooney was there the seat felt uncomfortable under him, but this time it feels secure, although slightly shaky. He manipulates it to soothe his need, rocking in a comforting rhythm. He thinks about his mother rocking him to sleep in her arms. He recalls the warmth of her holding him and the feel of her skin. Johnston had long left the room, but he enjoyed the atmosphere of it, the peace of it. He thinks of Irena on the hill. He is aware of a palpable sense of insecurity at large. If Johnston is indeed behind this, his power and control of the city's psyche appears total; like a global Svengali, exerting his power, causing great distress.

"So, I've to 'advise' Muir on Johnston," Rooney murmurs to himself.

"Sounds like something you'd want to do."

"He's been harassing Jackie for reports."

"You're just so desperate to help."

"I need to get closer to the man's thoughts, his anger, and maybe even his pain. If I can understand his psychology, then I can develop the picture further, fill in the gaps."

"There are no clear associations."

"I'm hoping that'll be confirmed through the Latin phrases, linking to Johnston."

"So you think. Tell that to Muir."

"A meeting with the Lord Provost is an interesting opportunity. It'll further my understanding of psychopaths."

"Freak."

CHAPTER SIXTEEN

Rooney travels through to the City Chambers in a posh corpy car sent for him, to be escorted in and through security. He waits longer than necessary before being escorted into Muir's rooms. He wonders if Muir would have treated his hero, Nelson Gray, the great Glasgow artist, poet, writer, and voice of the people, like that.

"Mr Rooney, Sir," the PA says, ushering Rooney into Muir's room. He sits him in a hardback seat at Muir's desk. Muir's there at the other side; and, as if to indicate to him he has more important matters before him, he ignores his presence there as he continues to read his papers.

After a while, Muir speaks. "Mr Rooney, please," he says, as in the last time they met, inviting him over to a large sofa where each take up position at opposite ends.

"Tea or coffee?" Muir says, gesturing to the coffee table, which contains a silver platter.

"For your head."

"Shushed," Rooney says.

"Excuse me," Muir says.

"Nothing. Coffee black, thanks."

Muir obliges, and a long pause ensues.

"Never speak first, use the silence. Control the silence, control the discussion."

Rooney understands the power of silence, the pauses, the silences, the para-verbals – his stock-in-trade.

"Your face, you were attacked."

"I was," Rooney says. "By a man released prematurely from a psychiatric hospital."

"Seems it was thought he could be managed in the community," Muir says. Rooney nearly goes into his rant about the failure of care in the community, where many mentally ill ex-patients are living on the streets and in large hostels, rather than safe, caring places. "We have information Harte killed himself."

"Nothing shocks me."

"He jumped into the Clyde."

"I know the area well." Rooney rubs his face.

"Apparently, there was a note in his pocket. It said, 'You are a failed clinician,' then in Latin *'pulvis et umbra sumas'*. I am informed this means, 'In the end we are nothing.' Has this anything to do with our man?"

"Our man. Your man?"

Sensing the hiatus, Muir fires off the operative questions. "What is this man like, Sean? What makes him tick? Is he crazy or sane, dangerous or pathetic?" Then he settles back in the sofa.

"He's sizing you up. He'll work through you. The way your man uses his proxies, you will be his proxy. His way to get to know Johnston."

"I don't know," Rooney replies, a futile attempt at a proper answer.

"You *don't* know!" Muir's incredulity is matched by his scorn.

"No, I do not know anything yet. It is early days in my... inquiry."

Muir is on his feet. "You don't know, don't know. I think I may have underestimated you, your skill, your knowledge of this man."

"Doesn't think much of you."

"He is a complex individual," Rooney says. "It takes time to unpick a mind such as his."

"I was told you were the best, maybe I was misled Mr Rooney," Muir says, moving towards the door.

"Mr Rooney."

"You will excuse me," Muir says in dismissal. "I have some matters to attend to. You have been... helpful."

Muir opens the door as his PA arrives to usher Rooney out. On reaching the door, Rooney does his inimitable stuff. "One thing Mr Muir," he says. "If he is indeed our man, I think he wants to harm you."

"You want to abuse him, not to warn him."

"Harm me? Harm me, why would he want to harm me?" Muir says. This possibility hadn't entered his mind.

"I don't know; maybe you have... upset him."

"Upset him, I don't understand. I know nothing of this man."

"The Rooney-foot-in-mouth disease."

"I had... contact with this man, years ago," Muir says. "You would've read the reports."

"Yes, I have. But I think there is more, much more. Something deeper."

Muir asks him to sit down and the silence returns. He's now behind Rooney at the window and looking out onto a populated George Square, like a roman emperor observing his minions.

"This man is a crazy pathological killer."

"He may well be if it is him." Rooney's talking to an empty chair.

"If that's your shorthand for a mentally disordered offender."

Muir returns to his seat. "Indeed, a psychopath."

"Severe personality disorder. It's the definition in the Mental Health Act, of the narcissistic type."

"A psychopath," Muir says, determined to control the language they're using.

"We don't use the word. But, if you must, this is a psychopath with a big interest in making a big name for himself."

"A serial killer?"

"Who knows? Maybe a serial killer with a slight difference."

Muir raises a determined eyebrow. "Is he a clever man, Rooney?"

"If you're into IQ tests, yes, "Rooney replies. "Johnston is also very able. You need to understand this." In saying this, Rooney declares he has no respect for IQ tests, which had been discredited years ago. For him, years of practice had confirmed an IQ test gave no measure of real intelligence: social, emotional, or practical. "He can make things happen," Rooney says.

"Indeed," Muir says. Rooney gets the silence again. Then, "What, when?"

"I don't know."

Of course he didn't know, but he's not sure why Muir asked. How could *he* know where this man would attack, or when this would be? Although, part of his profiling was about prediction, and there was a pattern. The man had targeted political events, people with links with politics, Muir in particular. This was followed up with his signatures, the people and the places he left his messages. He has his modus operandi, which was the use of others and groups. He had an idea of his victimology, which included Muir, but he had no idea of why he does all of this. Rooney has a hunch that the man would up-the-ante, and something big would come next, something closer to the source of his primary objective.

"Oh, back to 'I don't know' again," Muir says. "I don't know where and I don't know when..."

"But I know we'll meet again some sunny day..."

"I need to know what you do know," he continues.

"I can't confirm anything."

Muir moves back to the window. A long silence confirms the meeting is over.

"When you do, or when you can, you will let me know," Muir says dispatching him. "Goodbye."

"Aye, goodbye," Rooney replies, heading out.

How demeaning this man's 'goodbye' sounded. How bloody Kelvinside and patronising, Rooney thinks, calculated to reduce him to one of his minions.

Rooney arrives home in the early hours. He's tempted to open a bottle, again to sort out his head, his thoughts and his feelings. He had been a forensic psychologist, before coming a train crash of a man and professional. Now he has the chance to get back and to pursue this proxy killer, but the challenge is threatening to take him back into his drinking, deeper than ever before. He sits in his favourite chair, the old leather job he got in the Barras, leans back and thinks. He doesn't need to shut his eyes to find that dark space where thoughts float around. Some music helps and his Vivaldi Collection provides the musical backdrop. It's conducive.

He phones Jackie. There's no answer. Johnston's laptop intrigues him. If he was his man, why would he leave all those files around to be found, in particular 'The Muirs'? Did he want them to be found, and if so, why?

"The Muirs," Rooney says aloud, as his mind drifts to Kelvinside to the home of the Muir Family. Mary, the Provost's English wife, is a lover of all things Scottish. Educated at St Andrews, she had lived a long time in Glasgow, in particular near the river Kelvin, her favourite spot.

CHAPTER SEVENTEEN

Rooney decides to take himself off to London. Following Geraldine's recommendation: "You need to split from the drinking culture for a while," he books the flight. He also needs some information while he's there. Before travelling, however, Rooney checks with the Bar-L. Johnston's reported to be animated, pacing the cell, continually looking at his watch. He's observed circling the calendar on the drab cell wall, stabbing inside it with his finger, like a dart puncturing a bull's eye. This is disconcerting to Rooney.

He arrives at the Celtic Hotel, just off Russell Square in London's city centre. At £45 a night, it's perfect, barren, but what did it matter to him. It's warm and smells clean, and it's quiet and detached from people, which is fine. Once there, he can't resist immediately heading out to the reading room of the old British Library, but only after spending most of the day in the reading rooms of the new Library in St Pancras, where he found some interesting information. He loves the old place where he had spent many an afternoon on visits there. He arrives in the midst of a tour of Chinese executives on a London junket. He groans at their hubbub, hushed by the attendant who reminds the tour guide of the sanctity of the place. He muses at the incongruity of the occasion, this seat of learning and study of Adams and Marx, their respective impact on the 'wealth of nations' and resultant industrial revolution, arriving at the Chinese contribution to the mass production culture of the world.

He's pleased to get a pass into the seating areas which provide controlled access, away from the tourists mulling around the entrance, under the wonderful cupola and blue sky above. He loves this and often visualises it: sitting in Row L seat 14, a seat he remembers well as a student in London many years before. The lush gold leather feels good; it's soft and inviting, as is the leather-covered desk.

Rooney's visit to the reading rooms is fruitful. A librarian helps him to go through the leather bound catalogues, searching name and subject indexes. Subjects: Latin, links with Scotland, Jacobus Rex. Names: Johnston, and, just for the hell of it, the Muirs. There, in the old place, he loves to be surrounded by the rows of books, the smell of them.

Then Jackie phones, and as clear as 'what would you like to drink?' she says, "Mary Muir's dead." That's all she needs to say and that's all Rooney needs to hear. He heads back to the Celtic Hotel, where he calls her back. "She fell into the river," she says. "The river, fuck's sake, she fucking drowned."

"I get the message. I've to curtail my sojourn in the big smoke?"

"Aye!" He gets the message.

Through Joycy, Jackie arranges a hurried flight back to Glasgow the following morning, and she's waiting for him when he arrives through domestic arrivals. He has brought some duty free, and didn't forget to collect some Prada Infusion De Fleur D'Oranger as he meandered through. It didn't appear much cheaper at £49.95.

"Did you enjoy your *short* break?" she says, as he gets into her car.

"It was interesting, no more than that," he says, passing her the gift.

She pops it into her glove compartment. "Thanks hon, very kind."

They don't say much as she drives along the M8 into Glasgow. She refuses to say anything about Mary until they get to Pitt Street. They get to her office and she goes into action mode.

"Right," she says, throwing her jacket over the back of her chair. She goes straight into it. "This is what happened." Rooney has been here before. He takes the desk chair at the receiving end of the table. He remembers well the hard desk chair compared to her high back manager's chair. Strategic, he thinks: keep your interviewee on edge, stay comfortable yourself; a way of showing authority and demanding full attention.

"Right," she said. "She was walking by the Kelvin with Hunter, at the weir next to the old Woodside Flint Mill, and she fell in. She fuckin' fell in."

"That is it?" Rooney says, trying to make himself more comfortable by resting his elbows on the desk, his hands clasped in front of this mouth.

"That is it. The river was swollen and in spate by heavy rainfall. She fought to the surface, choked for air, and tried to swim towards the bank. She reached for Hunter, but she was caught fast. Her left leg tied by weed to the bottom of the river, the current dragged her under. Hunter reached out to her and he fell in too."

"Hunter?"

"Her minder." Her chair squeaked as she balanced backwards to allow her to get her feet on the edge of the desk – part of the power dynamic.

"New shoes, Jackie?" Rooney rests his chin on his knuckles.

"Jimmy Choos," she says. A display of fashion rather than of power, Rooney wonders.

"*Fuck me shoes.*"

"Very nice."

"Thanks. We offered protection for her, but Muir was insistent in having his own."

"Clever," Rooney says, thinking that indeed he would. Muir had no respect for the local police.

"Anyway, they held onto each other and struggled just under the surface. Surfacing, he cried for help, gulping air and spitting out water. Conversely, she was gulping in water, spitting out air, and drowning fast. Twenty five minutes later, he was found alive downstream, dragged there by the force of the river. She was removed at the spot where she drowned."

"Hunter?"

"Hunter. Our people have interviewed him, in hospital. After debriefing and some sedation, he was taken home. Mutterings are the council will commend him for his bravery. Some say he could have saved her, but no one doubts that he tried. She slipped on the wet bank."

"Trustworthy?"

"Angus Hunter's been council staff for over thirty years. His grandfather was aide to Ramsey MacDonald. His family has been trusted and loyal servants of the government, local and national, for generations."

"Really?"

"Really. It happened as Mary took her usual walk along the banks of the Kelvin, as she did at three thirty every day when at home."

"The only exceptions being the Hamilton races, Ayr, and the Grand National; her wee flutters."

"Aye," Jackie says, hesitating. "Her walk this afternoon was no exception. Seems she talked incessantly about her horses: Blake, Benjamin, Nigel Campbell – "

"Called after her weakness for high profile trainers, some say."

"Interesting that," she says, irritated at Rooney's defamations. "Then she fell in."

"What a coincidence," he says, thinking about coincidence theory, where the mapping of events and circumstances point to certain conclusions.

"Coincidence?"

"The families, Johnston, the Murphys, Muir, Muir's wife, etcetera."

"Coincidence."

Just then, Jackie's desk phone buzzes. She swings her feet onto the floor and reaches over to take the phone. Covering the mouthpiece, she whispers to Rooney, "It's Muir."

"Lovely, do you want me to leave?" he says. "You know, to give you both some... privacy," he whispers back.

She shakes her head as she takes the call. "Yes, two o'clock; yes James," she says. "I am very sorry for your... loss, so soon after..., yes, bye." She puts the receiver back.

"He wants to see us, today," she says, moving around the desk to sit on the corner, crossing her legs, slowly, provocatively, revealing a fair proportion of leg.

146

"Femme Fatale!"

"How is he?" Rooney says, not sympathising. He just wants to see her response.

"He's alright, strangely OK, given his wife and his daughter have been snuffed out."

"Perhaps, not so strange, this man who exudes control... Daughter?"

"Louise," she says.

"Louise, his daughter, the prostitute?"

"Yes, Louise was his daughter."

"Indeed, well," Rooney gasps. "I didn't know about her, because you chose not to tell me Jackie."

"I wasn't mandated to tell you," she says, slipping off the desk to stand provocatively over him, her lithe frame encased in a blue dress with a zip all the way down the front. He still fancies her; he always did, since the first day they met when the team was set up. He still fancied she did too. Whatever messed up their marriage, the sex was good. He wonders if she fantasises about him; he does of her, and she knows that. Is she up for it? Would she go for it there in the office, where there was a danger of being caught in the act by Joycy?"

"Go on Rooney, get in there."

"Am I not to be privy to such information... darling?"

"It was his business... personal."

"Personal?"

"His business, hon."

"An embarrassment more like; a Lord Provost with a daughter in prostitution."

"She was estranged," she says, returning to her side of the desk, after a successful sex-power foray, well aware of her ex's predilection for a letch. "She hit the skids. It wasn't a complete secret."

"It was news to me," Rooney says, clearly annoyed at being left out of the loop.

"It was privileged information."

"Just as well you are around to support him, eh Jackie?" He gets up and turns away from her, to look out the window which faces into the car park; his own way of making a statement.

"Just doing my job hon," she says, into his back.

"Just getting into your knickers Jackie? A wee boost to your career prospects, eh?"

"Fuck... off," she utters. "Right, enough, I'll see you later: two o'clock, city chambers, and don't be late, she says, clearly confirming her authority, and the fact she wanted him –

"The fuck out of there!"

CHAPTER EIGHTEEN

Rooney meets Jackie at the City Chambers. On arrival, they're escorted into the public rooms. Muir makes them wait for over an hour before he appears.

They get to talking about the Glasgow gangs.

"I am now policing them as part of my overall remit. There were too many references to gangland atrocities in the killings for me not to investigate any links with the gangs."

Gang murders are taking on a new sinister face, she says. She explains how they had moved to all out attacks on migrant gangs, taking out as many soldiers as possible in each attack to bring down numbers, creating fear, targeting business outputs such as sex traffickers, prostitutes, getting them off the streets. Drug dealers not in the gangs' control were knee-capped mercilessly. They had moved to targeting gang leaders' homes, cars, premises, and then to attacking families and associates. The migrant gangs for their part were resorting to kidnapping and letter bombs. They were disadvantaged, however, they did not appreciate the diversity or extent of the city's gangland empire, but they were brave and ruthless fighters. Resourced by millionaire international barons they operated from swish Prague and Parisian apartments, where they managed their European empires, which included specialising in cybercrime; growing their businesses at a rate just about impossible for the Glasgow gangs to control.

Jackie says she is caught between a rock and a hard place. Many of the Glasgow gang bosses know her personally. Her father developed a tough but respected relationship with the gang leaders in the schemes. She sympathises with the Glasgow teams, the indigenous ones that is, where there's a code. Before the migrant gangs, balance and business was maintained in an orderly fashion. There was the occasional tit-for-tat hits, but always between the gangs as a show of strength. Now with the growth of the migrant gangs, there's disorder and an unknown quality of violence, and all-out war.

"Well, comes with the turf," Rooney says, "and the inflated salary, Jackie."

"Thank you for your kind understanding, you bastard."

"Kaminski," Muir says, entering the public room, ignoring Rooney as he waves his fingers at them, meaning 'follow me into my office'.

"I need to know and I need to know now," he says, rounding his desk to get into his seat.

"We are continuing our inquiries," Jackie says.

"My wife drowned... accidentally," he growls.

"Indeed, sir, but we want to rule out any possibly of... foul play," she says.

"Foul play?"

"Well, the Latin statement."

"These nuts coming out of the woodwork you mean. She drowned accidentally, and that is the official position."

"*Jacobus Rex*. A strike to the heart?" Rooney adds. "King James?"

"King James... what's the significant of that?" Muir asks. Rooney leaves it hanging in the air.

"I want you to talk to Johnston again," Muir says to Rooney. "You're the only one he communicates with."

"He hardly communicates," Rooney says. "Well, not directly that is."

"Have you any more information... on him?"

"Well, I've established his namesake is Arthur Johnston, a previous Principal of Glasgow University. It's the home of the Scottish Latin poets, a select group of academics. He's from a long line of scholars, apparently."

"Scholars, indeed, apparently."

"Incidentally," Rooney says, now determined to pursue the theme. "Jacobus Rex was James the old pretender, the rightful heir to the British throne." This's the produce of his London trip, and he's intent in exploring any connection with the Muirs.

"Oh, very bloody interesting," Muir says, shaking his head. "That is it, and that is all," he says. Rooney is dismissed; he'll curtail his Johnston genealogy, at the same time avoiding revealing the information he has on Muir.

"Jackie, a word?" Muir says, as he sends Rooney packing.

Rooney makes his way out and hangs around outside long enough to realise Jackie isn't following. Eventually, after twenty-five minutes or so, she appears. Jackie likes her wine bars and off they go to the Boudoir Wine Bar in the Merchant City. A classy joint, Rooney thinks looking around as they enter. They take a couple bar stools. Jackie peruses the extensive wine list, Rooney looks along the bar for a lager. She selects a Pinot Nero sampler with bread and oils. Rooney settles for a pint of Kronenbourg.

"He talked at me," Jackie says. "'Three things Jackie,' he said. 'One, bring this investigation to a close, understand. Second, the official inquiry will say Mary drowned, got that? This Jacobus stuff, discredit it. And third, I am losing confidence in Rooney. He is voicing delusional trash about ancient Kings and Latin poets. Can he do this job?'"

"Bastard."

"Yes, I'm still here."

The waiter casts a look to Rooney as he places the plate of the bread and oils on the bar.

"It's OK, he's with me," Jackie says to him. Then turns to Rooney, "Well, I told Muir that you knew your job, and you know the minds of these people."

"Delusional... these people!"

"Then he says." Jackie dips a piece of crusty bread into oil and continues. "'Right, but disassociate with him personally. I know about you two, how you were... together,' he says, after a long look at me. 'You got it?'"

"For god's sake Jackie, hea... vy," Rooney says, wondering if this is all he said to her. "Jackie, Jacobus Rex, Latin for King James. It refers to him," he adds. "King James Muir, get it?"

Either Jackie didn't hear him or she didn't wish to hear him. "Rooney, my reputation is on the line here, get it," she says, pointing a manicured forefinger towards him. "Either you or Muir's off it. I don't know and I don't fucking care."

She moves closer to him, shoulder to shoulder, on the bar. Her perfume's sharp, powerful and warm.

"Rooney, I have to tell you," she says. "I am concerned... about us."

"Here it comes!"

"Us?" Rooney didn't think there was an 'us' anymore.

"I mean us now."

"Go on then." Rooney knows there's something to come.

"I have to tell you, I have a problem."

"With 'us'?"

"You, hon, are a serious problem for me, *you* are a... liability."

Sure, he knows he is, at times, but this statement has more depth than just the being an occasional liability, pain-in-the-arse, erstwhile lover or friend.

"Go on, I'm sure there's more." He's expecting it.

"OK, I intend to," she says. "You know I feel about you,"

"You said you still love me."

"I said I *may* still love you, get it right."

"Beware Black Widow spiders!"

"I may still love you too Jackie."

She bites her lip, shakes her head, and gazes askance at the range of wines on offer. For a second Rooney wonders why, at this important moment, she is more interested in updated her knowledge on contemporary wines.

She turns back to face him, clearly using the pause for emphasis. "We may feel many things Rooney; it doesn't make things... right."

"No, you're right, but it's something Jackie."

"You are not listening Rooney."

"Sorry, you know I don't, I can't."

She picks up the wine list and deliberately starts to read out the ones that interest her. "Le Petit Balthazar Merlot, Malbec, Barbera d'Asti Superiore, Picpoul de Pinet..."

"Jackie, you were about to say something... important. Now you are perusing the wines!"

"Hark the connoisseur of every kind of rot gut known to mankind, but doesn't know a Bordeaux from a bottle of Buckfast."

"You said I was a 'liability'! I understand love implies a certain... responsibility, but a liability!"

She doesn't answer.

"I'm waiting."

"*You* are a danger to me."

"*Love, danger, liability?*"

"Oh, a danger and a liability, and you may love me."

"Rooney, you threaten me." The warmth of the 'love' word is cooling fast.

"I never laid a hand on you Jackie, not aggressively." He doesn't know why he would have to say this, but also understand this is not what she means.

"You threaten me in different ways."

"God, you're playing with my balls."

"Chance would be a fine thing for you pal. I am trying to be serious."

"I am all ears darling," he says, knowing she has the floor.

"You, my feelings for you –"

"Are, will, mess up your career?" He risks the hypothesis, knowing he wouldn't be far from the mark.

"Not quite what I wanted to say, but close."

"*Tell her to get to fuck. Like you should have done when she chucked you.*"

"Get to fuck Jackie," he says, not literally meaning 'get *to* fuck', but '*get* to fuck' she did. However, one minute she's there, the next she isn't. The bar man looks none too pleased at Rooney's language. He can't help thinking it wouldn't have mattered what he had said. She was intent in saying what she was going to say, i.e. loving him is a problem for her, her career, her life.

"*You're a problem pal.*"

"What the fuck do you know about... life, love or women, bastard?"

"Fuck or be fucked!"

Rooney's confused, disconcerted and hurt by Jackie's remarks. He walks. He enjoys the energy exuding from the streets of Glasgow. He'll wallow in it, like he wallows in the drink, let it wash over him, salving his jangled emotions. He takes in the atmosphere, enjoys the fear factor. He sits in a café in Queen Street station. It's as intoxicating as a bar with free booze. The hubbub is about where and when next. Buchanan Street scared people, of being in an enclosed public space where a bomb could go off, or a gun used. Airport type security screening has been installed in the under- and over-ground stations, police check points are set up at the main points of access to the center at Sauchiehall Street, the Trongate, Argyle Street. Random car searches are commonplace, causing massive queues and delays during rush hour for an increasingly disgruntled Glasgow public. The cops are everywhere, instilling some sense of comfort, but the big concern is the possibility of gang killings, the public being caught up in sporadic gunfire.

He moves to the Babbity Bowster bar, to have a couple before heading back. He needs to get his head around this 'love and liability' thing. It's afternoon and it's quiet, and he has a table to himself. This gives him time to mull over his thoughts and to tackle a pint of Peroni; no wine menu for him. He's tempted by the Cullen Skink, but that would leave less room for the beer. He finds a table in the corner by the fire. Cosy and warm.

He's conflicted about Jackie's pronouncement and confused about the whole Muir thing. Her reputation and career are on the line, so she says; she says she loves him but he's a danger to her. Jackie and Muir have made it clear he's to extract material which will convict Johnston, not to try to understand him. He must obtain the information that will bring him and what he does to a timely conclusion.

"Jesus, this one's for me." He takes a large swallow, feeling he deserves it.

He'll focus on his task and to move away from the emotional stuff with Jackie, which he doesn't feel like addressing. Thinking about work will help divert his brain into a more comfortable place.

He drags his ALDI bag up on to his table and pulls out his writing pad, some four by three inch cards, a marker pen, etcetera. Using a black marker, he writes a word or two on each of them. As he does routinely, he lays them out on the table as if to play Solitaire: a line of key cards, with a number of cards with particular points stemming outwards. As he considers each in turn, he presses his pen hard into each indenting them, taking notes on his pad as he does.

He starts with CHRONOLOGY, and in sequence, lays out cards with COBBLER, BUCHANAN ST UNDERGROUND, LOUISE, GROSVENOR,

LORD OWEN, SMSU (Springburn Medium Secure Unit), BRUCE, MARY, and NEXT, and then with a card he marks with a '?'. Using these cards, stopping at each, he considers the progression of the killings, applying the statements from the Latin signature cards, trying to ascertain what they are they saying.

"What are the patterns and associations?"

In his KEY PLAYERS line, he has JOHNSTON, with stem cards such as PERSONALITY, DRIVES, FEARS, MOTIVES, STRENGTHS, WEAKNESSES. He stops on each, making notes. He knows something of Johnston's background and circumstances, and something of his politics, and he has a good idea of his personality, but what are his drives, fears, motives, strengths, weaknesses? He has his ancestor Arthur Johnston, the 17th century Latin scholar, but what links him with Muir?

He turns to the MUIR line, with KILLINGS, where he explores the links and relationships; why Muir features so strongly in the killings. He has LINEAGE, where he is considers Patrick Sellar, the hated bailiff of the clearances in Sutherland, in the early nineteenth century, who just happens to be James Muir's great great grandfather.

"How did Muir manage to keep that out of the gutter press?"

And JACOBUS REX, James the King; what's the significance of that with the Lord Provost, he wonders.

For the hell of it, he adds JACKIE, her MOTIVES, and RELATIONSHIPS considering MUIR and ME, wondering why she drew him into this whole scenario, and, indeed, why he did; what were his motives for being involved in all of this.

He lays out the row of hits in sequences as they had happened. He then places the Latin statements under each incident in a way they correspond. He ponders the cards, sure he'll find some direction, some symbolism, in them.

He returns to the bar for another Peroni, keeping his eye on his table and the laid out cards. It would just take the waitress to arrive to clean the table to ruin his whole framework. He gets back and thinks about a case where he had struggled with a hypothesis that a paedophile he worked with was an unfulfilled homosexual who feared men. This man chose adolescent boys who may have been mature sexually, but not emotionally or mentally. He befriended them and exploited their needs for gadgets, new experiences, and money. Rooney used the cards to confirm common characteristics and to identify a pattern and ultimately to test his hypothesis. He did this by demeaning the man's ability to form adult relationships and, when he'd broken through his defences, he suggested a way to desensitise him from exploiting young men. He referred him to a group at the hospital that focused on adult relationships and in 'coming out' appropriately, and the man developed a long-term gay relationship.

"He relapsed."

"But the cards helped."

In this case, he considers the associations, connections, relationships between Johnston, Muir, Jackie, the families, the hits, the Latin, and himself. On one card he overwrites heavily a large '?', filling the card.

The what, why, how helps. The 'what' happened to the victims was clear, the victims were shot, bombed, battered, or drowned. He knew some of the who, but there was more to the 'how', he believes. The apparent how and what, on the surface, were hit men, the mob, or downright killers perpetrating murder on innocent people, but there was something, someone, behind these perpetrators, and there was another 'how', something more sinister, corruptive – how his man persuaded those to kill on his behalf. This is real power and control; not for *him* to get his hands dirty, but not so easy to get others to do it for you. There was more to the 'why' too; why these people, their association with the Lord Provost.

He ponders this, and, while the Peroni did the trick, he guesses he needs some more. Carefully he places the cards in his bag, so he would be able to place them out in their shape. He leaves and wanders into the Counting House, a large bar on George Square, where he imbibes a while longer.

He arrives home a couple of hours later. There's message on the answering machine. "Phone me." He does.

"Jackie, I didn't mean to say –"

"I know."

"I won't fuck up your career?"

"Hunter's dead."

"Shite." The personal stuff would have to wait.

"We talked to his wife, Joan Hunter," Jackie says.

"To offer condolences."

"Not quite."

"What happened?"

There's a pause, as she fiddles with her notes. "Well, she says her husband had answered the door to an official sounding voice. 'We need to talk to you again Mr Hunter,' she heard the person at the door say. Hunter said, 'Christ not again, you have nothing on me. I've given you everything I know,' on opening the door. Then she heard a single shot and his body crash to the floor in the hall. She hesitated before going out there, but when she reached him he was dead, a single entry hole on his temple and a note in his hand. The words, let's see... *culpam maiorum posteri luunt*, the sins of the fathers ...," she says.

"I know it," Rooney says, "... visiting the iniquity of the fathers upon the children unto the third and fourth generation... Basically, the descendants pay for the sins of their ancestors, the sins of the fathers."

"There's more. We traced a Swiss bank account in Hunter's name through Interpol, easily, almost too easily, as if the normal data protection barriers were down. He had received £20,000 into his bank account, transferred from an unknown Swiss account."

"Murder?"

"Don't jump to conclusions Rooney."

"Bit of a bombshell, don't you think?"

"We don't know where the money came from; it still has to be confirmed."

"Go on."

"I intend to," she says. "Joan Hunter described the incident. 'Mary always talked to him as she faced the river,' she said. 'She liked to look at the rough water as it went over the weir, looking out for salmon, then she slipped'. 'Did he push her?' I asked her. 'He jumped in,' she said. 'And held her under?' I asked. 'He was a strong swimmer and she wasn't, and he could get out.'"

"Did he do it?"

"Joan said there was a phone call."

"The one that made him do it."

"Joan said he was having his dram and talking about their meagre savings. He thought of escape, of turning his back on servitude, and the constant touching of the forelock. He thought it was a hoax at first, a crazy phone call, but later that day he checked his bank account and there was the money. He could have questioned it and had it investigated by the bank. He could have sent it back, that is if he knew who it came from, but he wanted the money... badly."

"A gift he couldn't refuse."

"Joan said that later that day he received a letter from a lawyer in Zurich explaining it was the proceeds of a payment from St James' Palace. She said it explained that no one would question a payment for a loyal life's service. The following morning, as advised in the letter, he transferred it to a dedicated Swiss account."

"Wow, quite an investment... He did it for the money."

"That was one reason, but these people don't do these things for one reason. Most big things need two or more reasons."

"Who's the psychologist here?" Rooney asks. "The other reason?"

"Well, she liked and trusted him, and he liked her personally. But Joan said she represented something he despised, something that had held his family in blind deference for many years. We – "

"We!"

"We need to keep our thoughts to ourselves. James has prepared a press statement."

"Oh James has. So, what happens now?"

"Maybe nothing, publicly; as far as the official findings are concerned, she drowned; a terrible accident. I've to pursue the investigation, covertly.

You need to find out if Johnston was involved."

"Well there is some interesting stuff, historical; kind of links Johnston with Muir; deserves some thought."

"Just leave Muir's... links out of this Rooney."

"So much for my research in London, on the Johnstons and the Muirs."

"Too much of a leap, Rooney; you know that. No more hypothesizing, right. Remember, facts."

"Do we have anything else?"

"We have Johnston."

"And what do *we* have?" Rooney tries to get back to where they were, before he told her to 'get to fuck'.

"Just stay in touch hon," she says, no more than that.

CHAPTER NINETEEN

It's late, something after nine, but he can't resist seeing Johnston. He travels by taxi to the Bar-L and demands to see him. Muir had ensured free rein to interview Johnston, although it wasn't unusual for Rooney to see prisoners in the evening. He sits down at the table as Johnston enters the interview room and moves to the other seat. The prison officer finds his usual place in the corner.

"Well Rooney," Johnston says. "I presume you have a reason for seeing me at this hour." He gets a whiff of Rooney's breath. "But you've been drinking, so don't expect me to say anything to you."

Rooney holds back from answering him, or to start a discussion that wouldn't go anywhere and only confirm that Johnston is right about the drink. Instead, he takes out his cards and places them in the order on the table in the format he had constructed earlier. He presumes Johnston's interest and that he would investigate the cards. Johnston looks at them up and down and from side to side. Then, like a Las Vegas croupier, Johnston deliberately hits each card with his forefinger, so Rooney can see where he hit. Johnston taps firmly as he moves from one card to the other. Rooney notices he doesn't follow a straight up or down or side-to-side pattern, but randomly skips between the cards, like a purposeful glass on an Ouija board. He tries to follow the sequence, almost like a screenplay moving between scenes. Then Johnston stops on the card with the question mark. Pressing hard on the card, he slides the card close to the card with 'Mary'. Rooney feels a shiver go down his back as he realises the question mark card is on the line of hits and Johnston is teasing him with the possibility of the next one.

"And what will it be Mr Johnston?"

Rooney doesn't expect him to say anything, but he does.

"Oh, I don't know. Maybe a coordinated letter bomb campaign to all local authority departments in the city, some nasty stuff introduced into the school dinners, maybe some biological warfare material introduced in the city centre, or common old car bombs in dear old Glasgow toon. Ah, the possibilities are endless." He pauses. "Is this what you want to hear?"

"Par for the course," Rooney says. "All to do with the city, the council, Muir? Look, you can see the same relationships in the cards," he says, pointing to the cards.

Johnston flicks a card off the table towards Rooney, landing in his lap. He picks it up, sees the '?' and places it back on the table. It remains the focus of both of their attentions, but Rooney holds a stare into Johnston's eyes. Johnston returns the stare, before he gets up and walks to the door, while all the time maintaining his own gaze on Rooney. Rooney agrees on him being taken back to his cell. He'll get no more from him this night.

Rooney arrives home and phones Jackie.

"Jackie, it's me." He balances the mobile between his shoulder and jaw, and fumbles with the cards.

"It's nearly midnight Rooney."

"Just listen, right. He's planning something – "

"You have proof of this? You now know it's him, do you?"

"I know it's him, but no proof... yet."

"I'm going to sleep. Where and when?"

"I don't know."

"You don't fucking know."

"I don't know the where or when, but it'll be... significant."

There's a sigh from the other end.

"Who then, and by whom?"

"I have no idea."

"Well, with respect, until you do, all of this is mere fuckin' speculation."

It's Rooney's turn to take a sigh.

"Indeed, but it's a SWAG."

"Oh your... 'wild-arse-guesses'. Are you on the drink again?"

"With respect," he says, nearly saying 'fuck off', but he knows he's treading a fine line. "This man is responsible for all this stuff, and being on the booze isn't a bad idea."

"Well, you keep talking to him, and get right back to me when you come up with anything more concrete; you got that?"

His phone goes dead, and he allows it to slip to the floor. "What the... fuck is she up to?" he asks himself, apart from knowing his pride, once stirred, would push him on. This is the only chance of him getting far enough into Johnston's head to find out what's going on, but she isn't going to prompt Red Alert across the city on a hunch of his. He is on his own. Armed with a lethal hypothesis, it's for him alone to act.

Shortly afterwards she phones back. He struggles to locate the phone, which lies on the floor.

"I forgot to tell you," she says. "There was an emergency council meeting. The Lord Provost gathered us short notice, to discuss 'matters of major importance'. He had information concerning *security*. By the end of the meeting, the elected members were given clear instructions on their own individual and collective safety. They were to agree a response to Mary's death and to enact special powers. Watch this space."

"Completely riveted."

"One more thing."

"What's that?"

"I'm in the pay of the crime families, apparently."

"Sounds like a lucrative prospect."

"Hon, I've been suspended, for the meantime, until an investigation's carried out. It's a set up. They're saying I've been taking bribes, from the families."

"Well, have you?"

"Thanks for the confidence in me Rooney. They're trying to set me up. Do you not see that?"

"Well, the investigation'll prove it's all shite, I'm sure."

"Aye, so it will."

"What's the story?"

"They say I've been feeding the families information."

"On what?"

"On drug busts," she says. "When and where. We mounted a sting. A large amount of mephedrone was allowed to land at Glasgow Airport and followed to demand. Drug Enforcement raided a number of addresses in Ayrshire and found nothing. Lots of empty drugs factories, cleared out. It was a tip off, and it wasn't fuckin' me. Rooney, I'm being fitted up and I'm going to prove it."

"Just claptrap," he says. "What about your friends in high places?"

"Thanks."

"Jackie?"

She clicks off.

Next morning, he's back in Barlinnie Prison, an environment now comfortable to him. He's to stay in the waiting room until the officer brings Johnston out. This gives him time to prepare and think. Although he wasn't a psychiatrist, Rooney has been around forensic psychiatry long enough to 'diagnose' Johnston.

"Now a consultant forensic psychiatrist: more delusional activity?"

"Well, bastard," he whispers, not a place to be heard talking to himself. "*I* believe he has a narcissistic personality disorder, which I intend using."

"You believe."

"He meets all the traits." He crosses his arms, and, under his arms and out of sight, he counts them out using all of his fingers. "One, an exaggerated sense of self-importance, and he has that. Two, a preoccupation with fantasies of unlimited power. Three, a belief he is special. Four, he believes he can only be understood by, or should associate with, special or high-status people. This I intend exploiting. Five, he believes he has a sense of entitlement. Six, he selfishly takes advantage of others to achieve his own ends. This is definite. Seven, he lacks empathy, no doubt. Eight, he requires excessive admiration. Nine, he believes others are envious of him. Ten, he shows arrogant, haughty, patronising, or contemptuous behaviours or attitudes."

"He has all of these?"

"Abso-bloody-lutely, he has every fuckin' one."

"He also has an intelligence way above most NPDs you have ever come across Rooney."

"He's a nihilist. He believes his existence has no value, but he gives himself purpose: to kill others, through others."

"You got your proxy killer man!"

Rooney's whispers are beginning to draw the attention of the officer in waiting room duty, who is about to approach him to check if he is talking into a mobile, or is on drugs. Just then, though, another officer arrives and ushers Rooney into an interview room. Johnston's there, sitting at a table. Rooney takes an adjacent seat.

Exploiting the first three NPD traits, Rooney cuts to the chase. "You'll be pleased with yourself for your... achievements."

"Fishing again?" Johnston says, sitting up straight in his chair, to gain a clear perspective on Rooney. Whatever his traits, Rooney feels Johnston enjoys the jousts with him. He interests him.

"I'm just guddling," Rooney says, with a bit of disarming humour in his voice. He wonders if Johnston will understand the significance of the term 'guddling', where a trout is caressed under water and lured to relax before being scooped out to land squirming on the bank. He wonders if Johnston will indulge him. "I feel you are moving forward, towards a... kill," Rooney says, deliberately using the word 'kill'. He gets up and moves around behind Johnston to fire it directly at the back of his head. There's a pause, not unusual in itself, but this is an atmosphere of intrigue and excitement. Rooney likes the feeling of the hiatus while waiting a reaction from Johnston, but this pause is different. Rooney feels instinctively he's touching something. The atmosphere in the room changes steadily and becomes tense. Johnston gets up, but this time he stays in the room. Rooney finds a corner and nestles into it, his shoulders resting on the protruding walls. He has an open perspective there and a safe place, like a gunslinger making sure no one can come at him from the side or behind.

"How would you know where I am physically or metaphysically for that matter," Johnston says. "What makes you think you know anything about me?"

There's something here. Rooney'll pursue it.

"I think you are achieving your aims and getting a great deal of satisfaction out of it. Is this your raison d'être?"

"My reason for existing is much more metaphysical."

"Intelligence way above most NPDs!"

"An intelligent answer."

"I wish you wouldn't patronise me."

"I don't think you can stop."

"Stop what?"

"Stop what you do."

"What I do?"

"What you do best."

"Do, Rooney, I don't do."

"No you don't do directly, but you make things happen."

"And how do I do this?"

"I'm not sure, but I'll find out," Rooney tries to gain some presence.

"Oh, you'll find out. I see."

"Can I ask you something?" Rooney guddles with the theory of NPDs having predisposing developmental factors. "When you retreat into your mind are you transported back to your childhood? Do you think of your father and mother? Did you feel fashioned by your parents' idea of what you should be, should have been, have become?"

"You know nothing about me." There's another pause by Johnston, but this time a different pause, as if he's organising his thoughts, forming a response. "You think I am formed of familial thircumstances?" Rooney notices the drop in Johnston's tone that follows the pause, as in the safe house.

"We are all influenced by... familial experience." Rooney's pleased to be able to sound like a psychologist for a change. He's intent on teasing out any potential vulnerability in this man. He also wants to explore how this links to Johnston's deeds. "I think you are formed of a whole range of... conflicts and the only way you can ameliorate this is to articulate it, to manifest it on others."

"He's not a willing patient. You can't analyse him."

"What do you know of my life? Indeed what do you know of me at all?"

"There's pain behind all of this." There has to be, there always is.

"My pain, Rooney, is my pain."

"Your pain, Johnston, is everyone's pain."

"Naïve. He'll never provide anything of evidence."

"Your pain, Rooney, is your weakness, my pain is my strength." Rooney knows he'll go on, and he does. "You drink to cope with your pain Rooney. What is your pain?"

"Yours multiplies, touches everyone."

"And yours is exorcised with the booze."

Rooney feels threatened, something he's allowed.

"You're rusty; that's clear to both of you."

Johnston senses Rooney's fear, like a dog sensing a time to attack. Rooney feels confident though he'll not attack him, not directly. *He'll* control the context, the silence, just long enough, to make his own stab, at Johnston's psyche.

"It is manifested by anger, yet you don't want to or can't hurt directly." There's no immediate reaction to Rooney's thrust. "Were there times as a child when you desperately wanted to hit back, but couldn't?" he says, going deeper still.

Johnston's tone drops. "Were there timeth as a child when you wanted to harm your father... as he harmed you?"

"This has nothing to do with..." Rooney tries not to get drawn down that road.

"No? Why then are you doing this?"

"It's my job."

"Your job is to get into the minds of other people? Why do you need to do that?"

"Met your match?"

"It's what I do."

"What... you do. Is it easier to look into other people's heads rather than your own?"

"Suppose."

"Suppose." The pause is longer this time. There's more to come.

"One day you will take a life."

"I... I could never do such a thing."

"Always the good boy."

"The day will come Rooney, when you... will... change," Johnston says, a sinister timbre in his tone.

"Change?"

"Yes, change. And then you, will, harm, kill." He almost spells out the words.

"Change, harm, kill?"

"I could never harm anyone, let alone kill someone. That's something I know of myself."

"You know yourself Rooney?"

"I do."

"Do you?"

"You've spent so much time trying to understand others that you've never tried to understand you."

"I know enough about myself to know I can't kill."

"You will, when you realise to do it is easier than not doing it."

"I can... control my... actions."

"You will do it when you realise you have no control. When you realise you'll have to do it, that you can't not do it. Then you'll change. If you don't, you'll not survive... as a person."

"Who is the thychologitht here?"

He needs to move away from this uncomfortable place.

"I think your objectives are... progressing," Rooney says. "Using people out there, vicariously..." His own guddling swoop. "To get James Muir."

Johnston gazes at Rooney quietly. His hand rests over his mouth. Maybe, maybe, he's getting there. He has to chance the question mark on the card is 'Muir'.

"Muir?" Johnston returns, almost frivolously.

"Jacobus Rex, Johnston. King James?"

Rooney moves slowly towards Johnston. "He's everywhere in your... acts. His friend Bruce, his wife, his daughter..." He pauses there, to check for a reaction. There's none. "The convention, councillor Zysk, Lord Owen. You want to destroy things that are his. Now you will destroy him."

Johnston's breathing is controlled, his tenor defined, slightly more anxious. Is Rooney getting through, so much so, to move from the subconscious to the ego, then to the conscious. Time for some ego massage. "I know you can do it," Rooney says. "I know you have the kind of power over the people who can do it, who do it."

Johnston moves around the table to get the best perspective of Rooney. "And who is important to you... mostly?"

"None of your business."

"It's OK. I know you and Ms Kaminski failed. Who do you... respect... most in your life?"

What's this? A diversion, a message, something else? There's danger in this, but he has to go with it, let it roll. "Nelson Gray, a good man," he says.

"Gray... interesting," Johnston says, with a smile in his voice.

Rooney reveres Gray. He exemplifies everything he believes in. He comes from an ordinary background and became a great writer and artist. He describes the human experience and exemplifies the common good better than any living person in Scotland.

"Muir... equally interesting," Rooney says. "What would it take to stop you killing... people?"

"Infamo, to put to shame, disgrace."

"Disgrace... of Muir?"

Johnston remains silent indicating assent.

"Are you admitting to the fact you could disgrace him?" Was this evidence coming Rooney's way, he wonders.

"I can do things – can you?"

"He is the leader of this city." Rooney wonders why Johnston has moved away from the 'Gray' question; not doubting he has parked this in his head.

"Muir and his kind don't... care," Johnston says. "To him you are scum, lowlifes, drunks with a death wish; he is not wrong there."

Is this his way; to manipulate people, brainwash them into believing they need to destroy for their own ends, when really it is his? Rooney wants to see how far this would, or could, go.

"Would you kill him?"

"Why would it be necessary to kill him?" Johnston says, like a skilful torturer who would apply brutality, cruelty to extend the pain.

"Oh, and what good would disgracing him do?"

"Could benefit this city," says Johnston, almost justifying the act.

"Could I be sure it would end there?" Is this his objective, his goal?

"What reason would there be to go on?"

"Why would it end there?"

"Times gone past."

"Indeed, past times like getting your balls well flattened, and even older, the Clearances."

"You've been doing your research." This is almost complementary.

"Indeed, *'culpam maiorum posteri luunt'*, the sins of the fathers, found on Angus Hunter. It's clear what you were saying there."

"And what was that?"

"Descendants will pay for the shortcomings of their ancestors. It's from the King James Bible; descendants paying for past misdemeanours. You are saying who and you are saying why."

"You have quite an imagination."

"I know, I'll never be bored."

"Disgrace, Rooney."

"Would you leave the country?"

"I'd like to leave this dark place." 'This dark place,' where is this, Rooney wonders: his life, Glasgow, the world?

"I'll have you sent down, enough evidence on you now Mr," Rooney says.

Johnston leans across, close enough for Rooney to smell his breakfast. "Do you think that would stop things... happening?"

"It'll keep you off the streets."

"To observe the destruction of this city from the comfort of a cosy garret at the expense of the most majestic majesty."

Could he do such a thing? To pull his strings from wherever he was? Would Rooney dangle on the end of them?

"And how would you do it, this disgrace?"

"I won't."

"Who will?"

"You will."

"You'll be his proxy."

"And how would you make me to do this?"

"You are a sick, alcoholic man; you don't have any alternative."

"You don't offer alternatives, do you?"

"No."

"And why do you think I would do it?"

"Maybe this city and many of its inhabitants will perish."

"Muir is the leader of the council."

"The city father who sets his sons against each other." Rooney decides to keep quiet. He knows where he's going with this. "The sons: the blue-eyed, the waywards, the prodigals; those who hate and destroy each other; the father who manipulates, controls and punishes, and strengthens one over the other."

"The sons?"

"Please. Don't insult either of our intelligences, especially not mine. The migrants and the indigenous groups; the gangs, Rooney, the gangs. I would prefer not to spell it out for you?"

"Metaphors. The 'fathers', 'sons', et al.; you don't understand that?"

"Muir and the gangs?" Rooney says, confirming a new understanding and pushing it one last step.

"He takes their money. He gives them favours," Johnston says. "He favours the migrants, because they are paid by the Euro-barons. The Glasgow gangs are fighting with the resources they have." They were now in a solid place; much more comfortable.

"Including you?" Rooney guesses it's time to get controversial. It's getting too cosy, too intellectual; and it's good to get away from the emotional stuff.

"The gangs and the migrants will destroy this city," Johnston says. "Muir will play his fiddle as it burns."

Rooney wonders whether Johnston intends this Nero analogy.

"His disgrace'll halt this." Is this evidence he's involved in the Muir–Mob, dynamic. Is he is risking something here, Can Rooney only do what he expects him to do.

"How would it be done?"

"Information."

"What 'information'?"

"He has a thecret."

"A 'thecret'."

"That'll destroy him?" He needs to know this man, not that he's agreeing to it.

"Are you big enough to do it?"

"What?"

"Are you big enough?"

It's time to leave, but Rooney has to ask... again. "The secret?"

"The thecret!"

"When you get me out of here."

"He has you. This is how he does it."

Johnston turns and follows the prison officer out, only turning to Rooney with that grin on his face.

"You going to sit there all day?"

"As long as it takes to get you out of my head."

"Et tu Brute!"

CHAPTER TWENTY

"You have some influence after all."

"Indeed, bastard?"

"Johnston's been transferred from Barlinnie to the State – "

"On an Interim Hospital Order, for long-term assessment under the Mental Health Act 2003, with 'paranoid delusions of a seriously dangerous kind, with particular reference to the Lord Provost'."

"So it's reported. Doesn't mean to say it's right."

"In clinical terms an 'anti-social personality disorder', told you."

"The psychiatrists say Johnston isn't treatable and shouldn't have been transferred."

"Well, the First Minister, informed by Jackie, demanded the move. If only to offer an assurance Muir will remain safe."

"The real reason to detain Johnston?"

"To dislocate him from proxies, families, to which he has access in prison."

"There's no evidence to implicate him with the incidents."

"He needs to be held."

"There's no link with others. No group or family involvement there."

"Well, we'll see how he manages to wield his power in there."

"You had him moved from prison to the State Hospital so you can get him out."

"If you know what's in my mind, why are you asking me?"

"I just want you to show you how wrong you can be."

Rooney is well acquainted with the State Hospital. He worked there and knew the security systems at the hospital well, having been on the hospital security committee for years. The hospital had had a major escape some twenty years earlier. Then two psychopaths escaped and killed a local police officer and a passer-by who just happened to be in the wrong place at the wrong time. The hospital had gone through a major security review, resulting in security taking precedence over care. This Rooney protested against, unsuccessfully, as public opinion demanded the new security regime. He knows that with its current elaborate security system, getting out of the State is impossible, but getting in, less so.

Rooney speaks aloud and writes notes when he is planning something. "To get in, the person has to be identified. OK. Then he's linked with a purpose, a social worker to interview Johnston. He'll say he's doing a report for the Sheriff Principal to consider an appeal. He'll present an ID card. He'll verify the reason for the visit and confirm the patient to be interviewed. He'll be issued with a four-digit number to re-enter the reception area after the interview. After going through an airport type security screen to identify weapons he'll be free to leave the reception area and go into the grounds of the hospital. On reaching a pavilion ward, he'll show his ID to staff again, and entry will be allowed into the ward. Access to the patient will be given under supervision by staff, although staff don't always stay in the room, because patients complain if they do. After the interview, steps will be retraced through the reception area and out of the hospital. During this, he'll be watched by cameras which cover every blade of grass and follow every step."

"Daft plan."

"What do you know?"

Indeed, what do *I* know? Just so happens he is right.

A social worker enters the hospital and Johnston exits as the social worker. The supervising member of staff, by a well-timed phone call, is called away for a few minutes. The social worker is advised to press the alarm if he's threatened. The switchover is immediate. Respective masks and clothing are donned in seconds in the corner of the room and out of sight of staff. Johnston, or who it was thought to be Johnston, goes back to his room. The social worker, now a faux social worker, heads out to the hospital car park and into his car. Three hours later, the social worker, a very well paid housebreaker up on charges with a long spell in jail pending, explains all, including the expert ID forgery. He'll go down for another few years, but the money will see him into his old age and buy him that bar in Marbella. Johnston procured both the money and the man. There's no need to find out where his resources come from. Rooney guesses it's from the crime families who utilise him. They have untold amounts of cash they need laundered or spent.

"What happens now?"

"Now, I meet Johnston."

"Ah, though a different relationship, and circumstances."

"Makes life interesting."

His mobile goes off again, Jackie, no doubt. "Where are you Rooney, and what's more, where the fuck is Johnston?"

"Calm down dear, why do you think I know where Johnston is?"

"Listen, you disgusting wee man. I can only assume you are doing this for the right reasons."

"Absolutely, you can be assured of that."

"Where are you hon?"

"I can't tell you," he says, which feels good.

"You can't tell me. I supported you. Don't turn on me. Rooney. Do you hear me?"

"Indeed dear, I hear you, loud and clear," he says, switching off the mobile, before she has the chance to do so herself. "She thinks she owns me. We're no' married no more Jackie," he calls out, not that she can hear him.

Rooney meets Johnston at Ben's house in Partick, their prearranged meeting place.

"A cuppa?" Rooney enquires from the kitchen, switches off the kettle, and pours two large mugs of coffee. He hears Johnston walking around the sitting room.

"Who lives here, a moron?" Johnston says, obviously scanning the bookshelves.

"This happens to be my friend's house," Rooney says coming in with the mugs.

"Doethn't read much doth he; your friend. I assume it is a he?" he says, kicking through a pile of football books on the floor.

"He enjoys a game of football. That doesn't mean to say he is a moron."

"Oh no, what about this?"

"What?"

"The Daily Record."

"Ben is hardly a Herald reader."

"Reader? Ben is hardly a reader." Johnston talks as he wanders around the flat. "Ben, the social worker, the social controller, the counsellor, the man who intrudes into normal people's lives."

There's a pattern here: provoke an argument, demean and denigrate the point or the person, to evoke a defensive response, if only to prompt the proving of the point. And this man has informants of the kind who seem able to uncover facts about absolutely anyone. Rooney doesn't rise to this attack on his friend. He isn't going to be drawn.

"Are you pleased to be out?" Rooney tries to engage him in lighter conversation.

"Yes." Rooney doesn't expect any kind of thanks.

"Fine. The secret?" Let's get down to it.

"You will do it?" This's more of a demand than a question.

"I got you out. Is that not enough?"

"I need more. You need to – "

"You'll use me."

"You'll do what I want?"

"What *you* want."

"You'll have help."

"From whom, you?"

"To some extent, but you know – "

"You don't get... involved. Who?"

"Jackie." Now this he didn't expect.

"Jackie, don't be daft my deranged friend," Rooney says, trying to pour scorn on this.

"Good. She'll help you."

"You... are mad," Rooney says, though thinking, although deranged, this man isn't psychotic. "Why the fuck do you think Jackie would do this? She's a police officer, for god's sake."

"She'll do it."

"What have you got on her?" Rooney asks, knowing there'll be something.

"There's no need for you to know, for now."

He's exhibiting number two in the NPD profile: a preoccupation with fantasies of unlimited power, Rooney decides to exploit number three: a belief he is special. "OK, you the expert. I know nothing about harming a... a Lord Provost," Rooney says. "I don't harm."

"No, I don't suppose you do," Johnston says. "Hardly something you do... every day."

An attempt at humour, Rooney wonders, questioning the NPD's 'don't do humour' point. "Well, how would you suppose it is done?" he says. He wonders if he can resist assisting the destruction of the man he despises.

"Blow him up, poison him, shoot him, or fuck him to death. Take your pick Rooney."

"Go away."

"Talking to yourself Rooney. Is this a ... symptom?"

"What would *you* do?" Rooney knows this'll tempt a NPD, i.e. number one, an exaggerated sense of self-importance.

"What would I do?" This is a way to understand how he does it. "Disgrathe, Rooney, disgrathe." Johnston moves closer to him, inches from his face. This time there's no prison officer around, and he's going to exploit this. "Now, for obvious reasons, we have to leave this place, and we will both do what we will have to do."

"Obvious reasons?"

"Your call will have been localised to this area." Johnston confirms for all who need to know they are at Ben's house. "You are naïve; and you will cope with the enormity of this by doing what you do under these circumstances: get blitzed, due to your obvious limitations. Just make sure you are fit and able by the time I contact you next, because, believe me, you will need your head well and truly on. For now, Muir's killers are on their way here, and I do not intend to be here when they arrive."

Johnston's half-way through the door. Rooney tries to follow. Johnston puts the palm of his hand on Rooney's chest. "No. Now we go our separate ways."

Johnston keeps his hand there longer than necessary to do to stop Rooney. Although this is a light touch, to Rooney, it could have been a knife, inches away from his heart, ready to plunge deep inside him.

Rooney moves back, releasing the hand. "How do I stay in contact with you?"

"You don't. I contact you. I doubt you could maintain contact with your own reality," Johnston says, with an NPD 10, exhibiting arrogance and patronising him at the same time. "You cannot go home."

"I have to go home, where can I go?"

Johnston passes a card. "*CUI FIDAS VIDE*," Rooney reads aloud, with the backdrop of gold in his mind.

"Be careful of who you trust, Mr Rooney."

On the back of the card is an address: ROOM 21, THE KELVIN HOTEL, ARGYLE STREET.

They leave there together, Johnston disappearing along Dumbarton Road towards Partick Cross. Rooney could follow him, to find out where he is going, but he know he's more than able to elude him, or turn to confront him.

Rooney settles for the Lismore Bar. The Lismore or in the Gaelic, *Lhios Mhor*, named after the Hebridean isle. Here, he can observe the spectrum of Glasgow life, where you can find university professors (he wonders if Johnston ever drank there) alongside artists such as Nelson Gray, musicians, ex-ship builders, shoppers, chancers and poets. Here, he can find solace in the stained glass windows alone, providing an insight into the clearances and the highlanders who were forced to move to Canada, America, wherever. The irony of an exiled Johnston family with no control, no options, leading to the repatriated Johnston and the power he now has, is evident.

Rooney pulls up a stool and orders a drink: a soft drink. Still on the wagon, he reminds himself proudly, but for how long. He's shaken by seeing Johnston and he needs one. His mobile buzzes into life with 'Ben' on the screen.

"Are you alright Roon?"

"Fine Ben, thanks for the use of the flat."

"Anytime," Ben says. "Rooney, I know you're into something...

dangerous. Just watch yourself OK."

"Just don't go there tonight."

"Don't you worry," Ben believes him.

"Talk soon. Remember, until it's safe."

"Aye sure, when it's safe."

Rooney texts Jackie to say they had left their 'safe place'.

A text returns: 'Booked you into the Kelvin Hotel, Room 21. Argyle Street. Near to the park. Go there. Wait for further information. J x.'

"It's the address on the card," Rooney says to himself.

"Be careful of who you trust."

His mind drifts to Jackie. Three things go through his head. One, are his feelings for her; he wants her, but does he still love her? Two, does Johnston know how much she means to him, even more than he knows himself? If he does, she's at risk and this can be used to control both of them. And three, what does he have on her that would force her to help him destroy Muir? He has to find a way to stop him; but, as usual, he'll be one-step ahead. He's introduced more conflict for Rooney – and in him – than he can handle. He looks at his drink. "Fuck sobriety, it gives you fuckall," he says aloud, resigning himself to a booze induced conflict zone, promising himself, whatever happens, he'll ultimately get this man, one way or another.

"So you think!"

Rooney staggers along Dumbarton Road and onto Argyle Street. He reaches the Kelvin Hotel. Near the Kelvingrove Park, this is a dive, a budget hotel offering cheap rooms, by the night or by the hour, whatever the need or circumstance. It'll do, he's had worse.

The room had been reserved and booked for a five-day stay. In there, he finds a toilet bag and a change of clothing on the bed. The room is small with a single bed; no ensuite here, and a high-backed chair, the kind found in nursing homes. He pulls himself under the thin duvet of the bed and falls asleep, fully clothed.

He wakes up to the mobile about to buzz off the bedside table. It indicates a text from an unidentified number: *CUI FIDAS VIDE*. He notices the time on the mobile as 4.15 a.m. and that there's an unopened text. It's from Jackie. The text had arrived at 8.45 p.m., the night before. He was too drunk to notice or even read it. It says: 'Johnston's been traced in Dublin meeting with crime families. Hon, he's planning something big. J x.'

When drunk Rooney has no insight into the possibility of arrest or his safety; but sobering up he ponders the possibility that either two big officers arriving at his flat to arrest him for the Johnston escape, or two black coated hit men'll turning up to take him out. He believes Johnston has a reason to keep him safe, which offers some cold comfort.

He makes some coffee from the single sachets on the 'refreshment' tray. "This is going to be a heavy day," he moans, settling down on the corner of the bed in the corner. He knows two things: one, he has to keep his head down, and two, both Jackie and Johnston will be in touch. The rest – "What the fuck," he says, he'll leave to serendipity.

Around six, Jackie calls.

"Did you get my text? I'm back on the case," she says. "Dad stormed into Muir's office and put himself on the line for me. He said he'd fight him all the way to prove I was set up. 'OK, but you owe me one', Muir said to him."

Rooney's in no mood for conversation.

She reiterates the intelligence about Johnston being in Dublin, where he's at the Sherbourne Hotel on St Stephens Green, the meeting, and how Muir has a SAS assault team en-route there to take out Johnston.

"All very interesting."

"I could do you for assisting an escape, miscarriage of justice, harbouring a criminal, contempt of court, and a few more things, you know."

"Indeed, throw away the fecking key; what do I care?"

"Well, you're on a... suspended arrest."

"I'll try to be good. I believe we have to get Muir."

"Seems like something you would want to do," she says.

"Seems if we don't, Johnston will destroy this... city."

"He can't kill a city."

"Listen, he can bring this city down, not that matters to me, but he'll kill a few folk on the way."

"We'll see."

"You've to help me, *he* says."

"I guess I have to," she says. He expects a rebuke, a 'don't be bloody loopy,' or 'are you on something' but no, this is an affirmation. "Are you in the Hotel?"

"You have to! Just like that. What is this Jackie? This is the last thing you would have to do."

"I just have to."

"You have no choice, you mean. How did he do it? You Jackie?"

"He knows something about me. That's all I'm going to say."

"What could it be; a threat to kill you, your father, your dog; no, not that important; your career, that job, losing your pension, maybe; or something else?"

From her "Enough pal" he knows he'll get nothing from her. Then it comes to him.

"Muir slighted you."

From her lack of response, he knows he's right. Time to change direction.

"Jackie, the restricted file... the Johnston incident folder." Rooney has a hunch that there's more to that file, especially due to her determination to protect it.

"Aye?"

"The intervention by Muir; the detail?"

"What detail?"

"The letters. Tell me, you know how important this is."

"Are you in the Kelvin Hotel?"

Something tells him he should not say where he is.

"I'll get back to you," she says, and she's gone. But he knows she will.

An hour later, she calls back.

"Right, OK, one from Johnston to Muir, here it is. 'Dear Mr Muir... blah blah blah' all sort of complaints, etcetera, and at the end, *'non revertar insultus*, yours Johnston.'"

Rooney gets blue-gold-red in undulating waves in his mind.

"The Latin, directed at Muir; as clear as 'what's your poison?'"

"Aye, 'I shall not return unavenged'. I googled it after the last time it was used."

"The last time –"

"Springburn, Bruce –"

"Freckin'-frock. This is the link between Johnston, Bruce, Simpson and Muir."

"A crank using Latin doesn't make a conviction; what good would it do?"

"Johnston's letter?"

"It's a letter of response to Muir's letter. Copied in the file ever since."

"Muir's letter?" Rooney says. There's more to come.

"Let's see; yes, I have a copy," she says, rifling through the file.

"Read it to me."

"OK, hold on, here it is: 'Dear Mr Johnston ...'."

"I don't need the compliment stuff, cut to the chase."

"All right, stay cool... let's see, 'We have investigated your complaint and see no justification for your complaint against the council. The police officer was doing his duty by protecting our city...'."

"Wow, the rotten bastard."

"Heah!"

"Der Führer."

"Don't Rooney, just don't," she says, ending the conversation.

"Oh, so sorry for being a rude bastard," he says, pacing the floor, "as opposed to being a rotten bastard." He checks the door is locked. "As opposed to being a stupid bastard," he says, as he looks out of the net curtains.

"No where's safe no more."

Home is as safe as anywhere and Rooney decides to go there. The Gribben is there, after all. She appears as he goes up the stairs.

"Oh, the wanderer has returned."

"Could I stay away from you, mine host?"

Rooney says to the Gribben that some psychos have made threats to his life. She says they'll have to get past her first. He doubts not her ability to handle most attackers, but impresses on her that to answer the door would result in her being shot in the head. She gets it this time and double bolts the outside door. Inside, he grabs a bottle from his kitchen, drags his old chair into his bathroom, has a couple, and falls asleep.

Around an hour later, his mobile goes off. He doesn't recognize the number. He opens it and a mechanical voice like a 'you have just won a holiday in Bermuda' sounds out. He hears: "The hit was in the Kelvin Hotel, Room 21. Are you listening Rooney?"

As intended, this secures Rooney's interest. He listens.

"The SAS procured the necessary information from his colleague."

"Ben, Jackie?"

"Our assault team, armed with Airsop assault weapons, moved along the corridor towards the target's room. They stopped outside the door and waited for the order to go. A covert camera was threaded through the wall at around twelve inches from the floor. Our screen was in Control, a white van parked in an adjacent street. Our lit screen in the dark of the van revealed a darkened room, minimal furniture, and a high-backed chair with a male figure with an AK45 resting across his lap. The latch lock gave way to the door hammer, two stun grenades followed, and our team were in. They entered the room where a phone call was made minutes before. The back of a winged high back chair was towards them. A figure could be made out in the chair. They fired a number of rounds into the back of the chair, and the figure slumped. The leader of the team moved to the front of the chair, knocking the gun from the figure in the chair to the floor."

"That was to be you."

"The body was upright but the head was slumped to the side, virtually unrecognisable, tied up with a gag in the mouth. Our soldier stepped back in horror as he recognised his own father in front of him. Just then, the room exploded with a force that disintegrated all there. A massive explosive device, attached to the kidnapped man's chest. The trigger, a probe sensitive to the man's heartbeat, timed to activate fifteen seconds after his heart stopped."

"Revenge is sweet!"

"The windows blew out onto Argyle Street, where a car three-point-turned and escaped the scene. In the car there were four members of a heavy Glasgow firm with a score to settle."

The message and the call end there. Rooney tries to find the caller's number, but it's an unassigned Pay-As-You-Go. He phones Jackie, his hands shaking.

Tom O. Keenan

"Someone's... tried... t-to k-kill me."
"Correct, but someone's protecting you."
"What do you know about this?"
"Get some sleep hon. You've some disgracing to do."
"Jackie—"
The phone goes dead.
"You're on borrowed time Rooney."

CHAPTER TWENTY-ONE

Rooney finds a digital message on his answering machine. 'Mark' it says, then a phone number is read out and two dates are digitally described: one, nearly three months previous: 'Wednesday 20/11/2010'; the other, two days hence: 'Thursday 24/02/2011'; and then 'trust no one'. This must have been the most cryptic message he's ever had. He doesn't understand the significance of the first date; the other he understands as an ultimatum. It must be done by then, whatever it is; and 'Trust no one'. Who could he trust?

He calls the 'Mark' number, and indeed a Mark answers. "Mark Casey here, can I help you?"

"Hello Mr Casey, my name's Rooney," he says. "I think we may have something in common."

"And what is that?" Casey says, sounding effeminate.

"I am not sure, but does this date mean anything to you?"

Rooney spells out the date to a stunned silence from the other end.

Then Casey asks, "Are you from a newspaper?"

"No."

"What do you want me to do?"

Rooney realises this man is being controlled.

"Don't know yet, tell me about you."

Over the next forty odd minutes, Casey explains he'd been heavily into the Glasgow gay scene and was a high-class male prostitute, serving some important public figures. Muir, Rooney wonders. He's very reluctant to explain the full detail and significance of the date, but he agrees to meet him later that evening in the Ben Nevis bar.

Rooney is anxious as he asks the cabby to drop him at the door of the bar, but if whoever wants to get him, they'll have no problem finding him. Where could he hide? Jackie had mentioned he'd be looked after; but what the hell, he just doesn't care.

He finds a corner table in the bar, and chews on a beer mat as he waits. Casey's late. After forty minutes or so and, just as he is about to leave, he hears a woman's voice above him. "You should listen to this," she says as she pressed a small hand-held tape recorder into his hand.

He looks at the tape recorder and then up to ask, "And who might you be?" but she's gone. There's a voice from the tape recorder. He places it against his ear to listen and fumbles with it, rewinding it, and pressing play.

He hears Casey's voice: "I carry a terrible secret and you, or whoever you work for, knows this and of a date which will lead to my death." What kind of date, he wonders. "I can no longer carry the responsibility of this. It is just too much. The knowledge you have will destroy Muir, and I cannot cope with that. My life is now worthless, but before you do anything, you need to talk to someone who will explain things to you. For my family's sake, please leave my name out of all of this."

The woman who delivered the recorder is now sitting in front of him, glass of white in hand. She removes a Berghaus jacket and folds it over a nearby stool. No other jacket makes the crinkling sound like a Berghaus. Nice perfume too.

"Hello," she says, through a sip of her drink.

"Hello, who are you?" he says, wondering if he's quids in.

"I'm here to... help you."

"It's OK, I can reach the bar?"

She smiles and introduces herself as 'Jean Dempsie'. "Just Jean," she says. She's a short dumpy type with a northeast English accent, maybe North Yorkshire; looks a bit like the Julie Walters character from *Billy Elliot*.

"I know of Mark Casey," Jean says. "I was called in... to interview him."

"Called in?"

"You don't need to know."

"Oh." Rooney goes off to the toilet, wondering if he should slip out, but intrigue holds him there.

"He was an actor waiting for his big break," she says, on his return. "But he also enjoyed the casino and played way above his means. He had heavy debts and was desperate to make quick, uncomplicated money."

Rooney senses she's leading to Casey's date.

She talks about a hotel in Glasgow, the Ambassador, which is well known for 'discreet pleasures' of the high and mighty. She says the hotel caters for special status guests, their needs and their wants.

"There was a... a party," she says, "in the Ambassador. Not the normal kind, but not so unusual either; it involved some high-class call girls or male prostitutes. Mark wasn't to know who the party was for, only that it required a suite, drink and food, certain equipment, and a man, a gay man, who was prepared to do anything demanded of him... in a sexual way. He agreed to do it."

"What's this got to do with me?"

"This has everything to do with you," she says. "Now listen!"

This woman has a bite.

"Mark was scared, very scared," Jean says. "Before the party, he was told he would not see the man he would yield to, not initially. But clearly his 'client' would be a high-ranking public figure and most likely a politician. He was advised should any information of this encounter be released into the public domain, whether through the media or any other 'kiss and tell' story, he and his family would be publicly dishonoured. They did their homework well on Mark, well aware of his debts and his predilection to gay sex for cash. He, his wife, and their two children would be made unwelcome in their community; his wife is a local schoolteacher, and he is a community councillor. He signed a statement to agree to anything at the party, and to maintain complete secrecy."

"The party?"

"It involved bondage and domination. The high profile guest had his own doctor in the hotel that night, a sign that said violence was likely. Later, there was a considerable loss of blood in the particular room, and I can tell you not from the guest."

"Muir."

"I know bastard."

"Indeed... Rooney," Jean says. "I am informed of your... illness."

"So pleased."

"So am I."

She explains Mark Casey has been offered considerable cash to 'out Muir' in public and how this is to be done, and what is expected of Rooney and Jackie. Then she, the jacket, and the perfume, are gone; all is left is the empty glass.

"How to make friends..."

Back in his flat, Rooney calls Jackie.

"We've to set up Muir. A Jean Dempsie said so."

"I know."

"Do you know her? Does she work for you?"

"I know her and no, she works... elsewhere."

"Are you going to do it?"

"We have to hon."

"It's to be a classic outing of Muir, during a council debate; tomorrow, in the council chamber."

"I know, it can be done."

"Let's do it then."

"Rooney, I think you're enjoying this."

"Beats crosswords Jackie."

Jean's first to ring the morning of the 'outing'. She arranged Mark's access to the visitors' gallery area overlooking the debating chamber. She says BBC and

Sky will be there to broadcast the debate over 'matters of security'.

Rooney's anxious, and voicing out to himself: "The City Chambers – "

"Remember the Chambers, one of those afternoon tours, when you led a normal life?"

"I remember it well. It's laid out in a semicircle of banked carved mahogany seats, all large and imposing, with built-in armrests and embossed gold city crests on the red leather.

"Sound like a tour guide."

"I sound like I sound. There's a big King Arthur type round table, and the seating is supposed to be 'non-adversarial'. It was built in the late nineteenth century, in an ornate Renaissance Italian classical mode at the time when Glasgow was rich in trading and manufacture."

"Second city of the Empire."

"Indeed. The chamber has six rows of seats in an arc before the Lord Provost's chair on the west side of the chamber, set two steps above floor level behind an ornate desk which holds the ceremonial mace. The visitors' gallery accessed from the third floor."

"Where Casey will appear."

"You got it."

Rooney switches on his radio at 13.45. Muir is making preliminary statements in answer to 'serious matters concerning the Glasgow people'. All await the key questions to be put by Henry Smith, leader of the SNP and the opposition. On plan at 14.00 he opens up with "Would the Lord Provost respond to the view taken throughout the city that this council's flawed policies on gang control are behind the rise of violence."

There's uproar. Muir's supporters criticise Smith for 'unfair', 'uncalled for', and 'disgraceful' remarks. SNP and Labour party members are shouting 'tell the truth... you are to blame'. This is fantastic, fabulous politics. He hopes Mark Casey won't come in at this time. He wants to hear what Muir has to say. But it's time for Casey's entrance onto the stage of history, with a ready-made audience of thousands.

"Mr Smith is sensationalising very serious matters, only political point scoring, and trivialising some very serious and sensitive matters for the city," Muir says, his voice resonating through the chamber.

The arrogant bastard doesn't believe this is a problem. Then, from the galleries, Rooney hears Mark's voice.

"I have some very important things to say about the Lord Provost."

There's no reaction.

This time he roars it out. "I said, I have some very important things to say about the Lord Provost."

The hubbub in the room is silenced.

"The Lord Provost is a homosexual predator who abused me," he shouts;

for Rooney, as clear as 'last orders at the bar'.

Rooney guesses security has moved to grab Casey. "Let him speak," he hears people shout.

"This is an outrage," Muir says.

"The outrage is you are a liar," Casey shouts. "And I have to kill you. I have to."

Then Rooney hears "He's got a gun."

"Here we go!"

"He'll destroy me and my family," Casey roars.

"Put the gun down man, you need help," Muir calls back.

"You used me and you hurt me." Casey sounds like the sick man Muir describes. This's a sound Rooney knows well: a scared man forced into something outwith his control.

"You will put the gun down," someone calls, presumably one of a number of security men moving in on Casey.

"Stay back," Casey says. He sounds scared. Then two shots ring out.

The broadcast ceases abruptly. A couple of minutes later Rooney hears a voice-over statement. "This is a BBC announcement. There has been an unsuccessful assassination attempt on the leader of Glasgow City Council. He is unharmed. The gunman's been killed. There will be a full report in the national news at two thirty," it says.

This has not gone to plan. The mobile in Rooney's pocket vibrates. He opens a non-identified text just delivered, the words: *"Defectio mihi robur dat."* Gold! He goes straight onto his computer. 'Failure gives me strength,' he confirms through Google.

"No need to analyse that, clear enough," he says.

"Muir will survive this."

"Do you think so?"

BBC Radio Scotland have many radio broadcasts, some supportive of Muir, some saying he had a shady side to him. Muir admits to being bisexual and that Casey was a mistake. He admits to having an affair with him that he, himself, ended. There's no evidence of Casey's claims, just a suggestion Casey was obsessively disturbed after Muir had rejected him in favour of staying with his wife. Muir is asking for privacy and time to sort things outwith his family, already bereaved after Mary's death.

"People'll see through that."

Contrary to the city turning on Muir, however, there are sympathetic murmurings he acted with dignity after being the subject of a political attempt to disgrace him.

"Some plan Rooney?"

"Some fucking mess you mean."

CHAPTER TWENTY-TWO

Rooney goes off to meet Jackie in Tennents. Being Friday, it's habitual; but he only agrees to meet on the basis she too is now also implicated in 'subversive activities'. He needs the 'assurance' he'll be safe from arrest *and* attack. He's there an hour before her. She arrives, notices his empty glass, and goes off to the bar.

"It failed," Rooney says as she returns. She places a replenished beer in front of him.

"Aye, I know," she says, joining him at the table. "Casey using the gun only confirmed he was mad, and discredited everything he had to say about Muir."

"We needed Casey rational, alive and determined to prove Muir's abuse of him. He's dead and his case has been obliterated."

"There've been meetings in the Chambers and with us," she says. "The case is closed. Casey has no links with organised crime, nor any suggestion he was part of the recent incidents."

Rooney's mobile buzzes, 'Johnston' on the screen.

"Hello."

"You failed," he says. "But you had no hand in Casey's stupid act. He deserved to die. I will now move to… direct action."

"Johnston – "

"No more Rooney. No more discussion and no more contact between us. The next time we meet will be in very different circumstances."

He ends the call, and Rooney supposes, any communication, for then.

"That's that Rooney," Jackie says.

"That's what Jackie?"

"He knows he can use you."

"Any-old-body can use me… Jackie, you know that."

She predicts an attack of self-loathing, and the inevitable binge. "I *am* trying to help you Rooney." She pulls her coat from the back of the chair and pushes through the crowd out of the pub onto Byres Road.

"Johnston can use you, Muir can use you. And Jackie...?"

Rooney wakes up at home with the inevitable hangover. He's also on an equally inevitable downer. As he does on these occasions, he selects Vivaldi's *Four Seasons: Spring* vinyl and places it on his old Garrard turntable, the only thing of his student days he protects. *Four Seasons* helps control the vivid colours and gives him warm ones, and it manages to hold his depression from plummeting further; recently, the black dog has been arriving every day. He loses himself in Vivaldi, as the waterfall of soft colours cascades over his pained mind. He descends the stairs to collect his mail, mostly unsolicited rubbish, from the old bureau Gribben polices. He gets back to his kitchen table and clicks the radio on. The radio headlines Muir's lucky escape and his 'murky past'. Muir *will* survive this.

Muir apologises publicly to his family, the council, and to the Glasgow people. "I am a respectable man with normal needs, but I gave into temptations, and for that, and for letting everyone down, in particular, my deceased wife and my family. I am deeply sorry." The matter passes.

Rooney fans the mail out on his table and feels the envelopes, avoiding the A5 ones; they generally mean bills and reminders. One small 5 by 3 inch envelope looks interesting. This is a card. For him recently, cards have been significant. Tentatively, he opens the envelope and picks out the card. '*Crede ut intelligas*: Believe, so you may understand,' it says.

He drops the card and gets onto his knees to collect the card from the floor. "Jesus, what the fuck do I do?" he gripes loudly, knowing it would never be over for this man. His insatiable desire to abuse, exploit and kill would not let him rest.

He hears the weight of steps in his hall, as he kneels there. He wonders if he closed the door. He crawls around behind the breakfast bar and reaches inside a drawer for as big a knife as he can find. "Where are you now Gribben?" he murmurs.

"Off your knees Rooney. You don't need to grovel to me." Jackie bears down on him from over the bar. The exuding smoke precedes her words.

"And how the fuck did you get in?"

"Your door was open. I walked in. Not very clever for a man people want to kill."

She's right. "You...," she says, then stops. "Is it Vivaldi?"

"It keeps me sane," he says, going through to the sitting room to turn it down. "So?"

"You... we're still on the case," she says, taking that last big draw smokers have as they are about to stub out. She drops her attaché case on the coffee table, pulling out a file. "Jesus Rooney, how do you live like this," she says, scanning the room.

"Well, seems alright to me," he says, repeating the scan.

"Not surprised."

"Muir got away with it."

"Apparently," she says, "in diplomatic and private terms Muir's predilections to... gay sex caught up with him. In public terms, he and the city are to be spared the disgrace."

"A perfect cover up."

"Yes," she says, but she was 'well and truly charged' with apprehending Johnston and bringing him to a certain justice.

"As Muir demands, Jackie."

"As is necessary."

He reaches for her arm but she pulls it away, then escapes outside for another smoke.

"Losing your touch."

"Just par for the course, bastard."

Jackie both enthralls and unsettles him. Had she a hand in setting up the SWAT to kill him in the Kelvin Hotel, or had Johnston taken them out via a family group? It was clear though they had conspired over the Mark Casey scenario. He's becoming concerned about Jackie, yet he can't stop wanting her.

"You need her."

He shakes his head and goes off for a leak. Then he hears the chink of cups, indicating she's back and making coffee.

"That'll not, as you well know, be enough for Johnston," he says, arriving there. "He'll go on, and on."

"We'll just have to predict his next move."

He passes her the card.

"Well, you should know his mind better than most," she says, reading from the card. "'Believe, so you may understand.' Strikes me you have to believe in him."

"Or believe him, when he tells me something."

"Where will he hit next, that is the question," she says. "A pattern, a system."

"I don't think he's finished with Muir."

"Tell that to the city when the next hotel or subway station is hit. We need to know where," she says. "And stop being so... introspective."

"Dear, it's what we psychologists do."

"Aye, we know that Rooney. I met with the Chief. Archie's been promoted to DCI. He's taking over some of my brief."

"Fantastic, no waiting around there for the fat dude, eh? Better watch Jackie, he's a man, he might get there before you."

"Just listen hon," she says with a serious manicured finger sporting a lethally pointed nail, positioned right between his eyes. "I am a woman; a woman in the most machismo organisation in the country; where to get anywhere you need to be many things: one of the boys, better than the boys, bigger than the boys." Her voice reaches a crescendo way above Vivaldi on the word 'bigger'. "The glass ceiling in this organisation is steel-reinforced concrete and for a woman to break through she has to be ruthless, bloody ruthless. Which I intend to fucking-well be."

"Just like dear old dad?" he says, knowing he's close to losing an eye. She doesn't answer, but turns away to top up her cup. Enough said, this is not the place to re-stir the father-daughter scenario. They need to get back to Johnston, and the where and when of his continuing campaign. The radio gives some respite and draws Rooney's attention. One in particular catches his ear.

"The two day summit to determine migration policy will be held on Monday 7th of March at the Grand Central Hotel in Glasgow."

"The newly refurbished five star joint," she says. "We know about it."

"*You* would, knowing your liking for classy hotel weekend breaks."

"It's a national summit on Muir's turf. He, as Provost, is hosting. It'll involve the First Minister."

"Big PR exercise, a good place to recover some semblance of cred, how could Johnston could resist this?"

"A sumptuous theme," she adds. "A multicultural society."

"Indeed, in the context of civil unrest." Rooney adds necessary grit. "Migrants are being attacked and they're giving as good as they get."

"All under control Rooney. What do you think he'll be doing now if he's targeted the Grand Central?"

His experience and guesswork kick in, boosted by self-esteem due to his being consulted. "Well his plans are time accurate. Too soon, and his proxies are in danger of being caught or losing heart. Too late, and they're unprepared. Timing is everything. If he's up for this one, he'll have confirmed the plans months ago and would've set up the communications. The group or groups will have been briefed. The location, means of approach, and retreat."

"*Get to fuck!*"

"Retreat isn't on for these families," she says. "No losing face for them, too many others to move into any vacuum created."

"He'll maintain contact with the family right up to the hit, then fade into the background, to let them get on with is."

"Then we have just over a week to find the group and the man."

"This time if we find the team, we'll find the man."

"You, you mean."

"Me?"

"*Aye, you.*"

"Right, listen," she says. "OK, we may have three things. One: Johnston, and we could never know enough about him. Two: a family, a favoured group, or a family appropriate to the task. And three: the Grand Central Hotel, and how it could be targeted."

"A good framework, I'm impressed."

"I try," she says. "And when you… we get to understand his influence, we'll have a chance to end this once and for all."

"Before then we need to know who'll do it and how they'll do it."

"Do you think he'll be in touch?"

"He's made it clear there'll be no contact."

"Well, we'll need you to make contacts, establish links, and find out how he operates."

"Within the criminal fraternity – me!"

"Don't worry we'll be watching you."

This doesn't quite fill him with confidence.

"Jackie," he says. "In case I need to remind you, I am predominately a decent man. I pride myself on – as well as being a model human being – staying within society's rules."

She sniggers.

"Are you a good man?"

"I'm sure you'll have no problem bringing out your bad side, hon, not that it'll take much," she says, knowing him better than he thinks. Then she says he is a deep, challenging, but unpredictable man; but, nevertheless, she's sure he'll do what he has to do.

Rooney wonders where Johnston or any family group would get the necessary information about the Grand Central and the Summit security to get anywhere near. Then, by way of a message from deep within his subconscious:

"Trust no one."

"Who can I trust, bastard?"

"I don't think you're referring to *me*," she says. "But you have to trust someone Rooney… particularly me. You're going to be exposed to some serious risk in days to come."

"Funny that these words don't fill me with confidence Jackie."

Jackie looks him in that way she does, as if she's reading his face.

"I look after my own."

Then she says she is way ahead on the Summit preparations. She is taking no chances. She has orders to go to the Grand Central, to maintain security, and to be there all the way through. On a parallel basis, she's making inroads with the families with which Johnston has contact. Rooney wonders how much contact she has with them.

She gets up and leaves, and for then he's glad to see her go. He needs to think. Her 'glass ceiling' soliloquy impresses him, though. He always knew she was bright, but his renewed understanding of this is doing things for him in places that are devoid of intellect, and even less conscience.

"*You want her.*"

"I want her."

He's also excited about the challenge ahead, to understand who he uses, and *how* he uses: his modus operandi.

"If I get this right, and get the job done, success will be back."

"*Mess it up and you'll return to be the sad, mad, miserable drunk.*"

He turns Vivaldi back up and, far from the madding crowd, he spends the day getting his head into shape to face the trials that lie ahead – though even the black dog feels good. This worries him. Feeling good for him is associated with him heading in a direction of elation and losing insight, not with plumbing the depths of despair and depression, and reaching for the drink to ameliorate its effects. At the same time, the 'trust no one' feeling becomes more entrenched, more potent.

"*Paranoia?*"

The next day, as if on cue, the Gribben delivers an envelope. Rooney opens it to find a CD rom Johnston. He sticks it into his CD player. A disembodied voice echoes through his sitting room.

"Hello Rooney, you may have established I am at the Hotel Grand Central. After roughing it in seedy hotels rooms across the land, I am now enjoying the complete luxury of this high-class hotel. I was part of the last intake of guests before the hotel closed to normal everyday millionaires. I sit happily in reception, in my recently adopted persona, sipping Glenmorangie, as has been my usual pattern since I arrived here yesterday. I study the faces of people arriving and leaving, taking mental notes of staff changes and shift patterns. I know the type of people who use this establishment, why they do so, and what they get up to when here. I enjoy the large range of national and international newspapers. Some are heralding the advent of the Summit, and some are discussing the state of the city. Indeed. My eyes drift from the grand foyer, which would sport the type of hotel to be found in the Cote d'Azur, or Paris, to the exquisite fireplace. Ah, this is the Grand, Rooney, a fine backdrop, a symbolic and rightful place to destroy the very thing it symbolises – "

"Indeed, a honey pot for a sociopath, you bastard," Rooney says loudly, pausing the CD and prompting an "Are you alright Rooney?" from the Gribben at the bottom of the stairs. "Yes, my sweet," he calls back. "Come hither to me and I'll give you what you need."

"*Disinhibition.*"

He returns to the CD and presses play. Johnston's voice bellows out through the room. "Muir is a part of the establishment, after all," he says.

"Not only does he need to be destroyed, but also what he stands for needs to go too and what made him needs to die. They come and they go, but establishments have a life of their own, perpetuated by those who seek to ensure they survive and prosper. What I will do here will shake the fabric of this city, to destroy its very bedrock. This city lives on its rich cultural history, its relationship with the rest of the developed world, which it had no small part in creating. Muir's place in its success, of course, is his legacy of cultural integration, I don't think."

"Here we go again," Rooney says. "Muir's legacy? Next, it'll be a statue on George Square, next to Sir Walter Scott."

Johnston, via the CD, continues. "Now, I will exercise a form of aggression which brings down the mighty, ruins reputations, destroys the very basis of the establishment. I'm getting bored with physical acts on people. Sure they hurt, but they have a transient effect. The healing begins, and you are back to where you were."

Am I getting through to him, Rooney wonders. "My counselling talents are succeeding," he says to himself.

"Grandiosity."

"Rooney, I am worried about you. Will I call Jackie?" says Mrs Gribben from outside the door.

Rooney presses pause. "Mrs Gribben, I am enjoying the fruits of my intellect and you want to bring in the flying squad. If you remain there for a moment longer I will drag you in here and do serious damage to your yoni." Off she goes.

He presses play. "My new approach will be much more determined and long lasting," Johnston's voice reveals. "I now seek real power rather than authority gained from violent actions. The Grand Central will initiate this new approach and will be a backdrop to the biggest disgrace in the developed world. Here civic leaders will lose reputations, and subsequently their place in history. A more fitting epitaph for the systems I despise I cannot think of."

Rooney replies to the CD player. "Oh yes, Mr Johnston, so you think, but you underestimate the power of the Rooneyman, the caped crusader of the mental ones, the one sent here from above to be your nemesis, the one to de... stroy... you."

"Here we go, here we go, and here we go."

"Soon, I will also destroy you too, bastard."

So you think 'Rooneyman'. The Gribben is listening from the bottom of the stairs. Rooney being sectioned is a strong possibility. The CD finishes and he's left thinking what he should do. He'll pop it in an envelope and send it to Jackie.

He is vortexing up and feeling no pain, what a welcome relief to the months of misery. The suit goes into the cleaners and comes out shining white, the white fedora comes out of the wardrobe, and the shoes polished to a sparkling jet black. A Hawaiian shirt and his long college scarf finish it off. He buys white emulsion from B&Q and sets about painting the flat, confirming for the Gribben he is 'off it'.

Jackie calls him from the foyer of the Hotel Grand Central. She says she's struggling with her role in protecting Muir. She says his policies will lead to an ethnic backlash in the city and, as the daughter of an immigrant herself, she can't contemplate that. This'll prompt an era of instability, where all sorts of factions'll take their chance: families, clans, gangs.

"Have you seen Johnston?" he asks her. "He's there, my dear. A tourist, businessman, or something, sipping whisky, reading newspapers – "

"Give us a break. I've just struggled through stair-rod-rain and the bloody impossible doors here with my... luggage, and with no bloody help... And don't call me 'my dear' in that way; it's so... patronising."

"All on the expense of the Glasgow taxpayer, my dear?"

"Rooney, just shut it. I am on duty 24/7. Such are the concerns and the status of the guests here. I am in a reception area full of rubber-neckers and those political people with a capital and a small P. I am tired, and I am not happy. And you are saying I may be close to the man I have never set eyes on. So how the fuck would I know if he were here?"

"You have not had the pleasure?"

"Apparently not," she says, "do you remember having the discussion about reinforcing his feelings of authority, grandiosity, etcetera? Archie interviewed him, I never clapped eyes on him, not in person that is, just saw his pictures from the files. Then the trial was delayed until his secrets, his associates and his proxies, were confirmed. Evidence Rooney, remember? I delayed the pleasure of eyeballing him until I faced him in court. As fate would have it, or more how you determined it pal, he was never to face trial and, ultimately, I missed that opportunity."

"Jackie, if you knew how close you are to look into the eyes of this man, you would never believe the irony of it. Mr Johnston, I am sure, will have anticipated your arrival and more. He'll have not taken the chance you would recognise him. He'll know the CID has his profile, sent to police forces throughout the land. He'll have adopted a disguise; maybe a newly grown beard, dyed hair. I might even do so myself."

"What are you on Rooney, or off, for that matter; like medication, for example?"

"I am in my zone dear, where I am destined to be."

"You're away wi' the fairies."

"I think you are heading to Hillwood hon, but I'll give you the benefit of the doubt until I see you. Now I intend heading upstairs to a warm and welcoming bath. I have a major security meeting early tomorrow morning, and I look forward to a good dinner and an early night. You keep a grip on reality, right?"

"Yes, dear," he says, going back to redecorating the flat.

He expects her to call back that night, and she does.

"Rooney," she says. "I was soaking in my bath when the telephone rang – "

"You are trying to turn me on young lady. You know I have a particular thing about you in a bath, us in a bath, together. A master bath big enough for two no doubt, soap, water, bubbles, making a big splash." The words are spilling out rapid-fire.

"Would you stop and listen? I had to walk dripping into the bedroom to pick it up. 'Hello,' I asked, I have to say fuckin' bluntly. 'We had an interesting phone call from the reception area of the hotel,' the hotel manager said. It appears thirty minutes earlier, Johnston made a call from the public telephones in the lobby to the City Chambers. The hotel's now been screened for any unusual phone calls, and the CID picked up this was one immediately. Well, half way through being told this, which was literally minutes before I stood there myself, I squeezed soaking wet into my suit and, only finding my slippers, nothing else, I ran through the first floor, down the stairs and into the foyer. I attempted to compose myself as I entered the lobby, going past the public phone booths. As I did, a man pushed past me. I spun around and fell towards the reception desk. Asking the desk manager if he knew who the man was, I searched inside for my ID, and realised I had left it upstairs next to my phone and keys. The desk manager looked at me, agitated because I had a large amount of tit sticking out of a badly buttoned jacket. Then, he looked over the desk at me to see my bare legs and 'inappropriate footwear'."

"I like the image, Jackie."

"Letch!"

"Shut up arse. 'Excuse me madam,' he says, as he pressed his security button. 'Oh forget it,' I muttered, as I was off after the man who had headed up the stairs, only to be stopped at the bottom of the stairs and dragged into the security office, as I tried to proclaim my high-ranking police status."

Johnston would've recognised Jackie immediately she entered the lobby. He'll have studied her and every aspect of her position and circumstance. She's an adversary, and he'll know everything about her. He made his point, and it'd be time to leave.

"Well," she said. "The hotel manager confirmed my identity and, despite having around three hundred guests, he provided details of everyone in the hotel that day. I searched the telephone booth, the one from which I saw the man leave. Anyway, I flicked through the telephone book looking for torn pages."

Johnston would never leave anything, unless he intended to. If he had intended leaving a message, where would he leave it? She's about to find out.

"I found the hotel in the Yellow Pages, but there was nothing there, and in the phone book, under Johnston, there was nothing; but there it was, in a post-it note stuck directly between the Js and the Ks: '*veritus temporis filia*: the truth will out'. Johnston's teasing us."

Who in the City Chambers had been talking to this man in the Grand Central and why? Jackie puts a man on the entrance and tells him to keep his eyes peeled.

"Anyway, *I* am now back in my bath," she says. "And *you* have work to do."

"Wish I were there darling," Rooney says, as a tingling sensation courses through his veins into his crotch, leading to an extended masturbation session; the better now he can get a hard-on, having decided to stop his medication, which had left him as limp as a rope.

"*Having a good time Rooney, feeling no pain?*"

"I'm a man in his zone."

CHAPTER TWENTY-THREE

"You're off it pal."
"Wrong, I'm on it. Hold on for the ride!"

He's away with no clear plan in mind, but with a particular objective, and a few drinks'll fuel his journey. He's been in the Lismore Bar in Glasgow's Partick for around twenty-five minutes, and he's flying. The Lismore is a haunt for the Gaelic speaking community in Glasgow and one of the better traditional music venues. He double-takes as he catches the smell of an evocative perfume, instantly transporting him back to the Ben Nevis and this woman's role in 'outing' Muir, ultimately leading to Mark Casey's death. But this is not the time to break cover and talk to her. He places himself behind a pillar and locks himself into the Irish music. Magically, he's taken back to a place three or four generations when his immigrant ancestors arrived in Glasgow in their thousands. Then the soliloquy begins. He finds a corner of the lounge and launches forth to the folk around the bar. *He's* the entertainment now. *They* think he's drunk, mad, or both.

"And they're not so far wrong."

"My fellow Glaswegians," he spouts forth. "Think about the ragged starved people who arrived here – out there," he points, "during and after the great Irish famine of 1845. They came in small packed boats, a floating bridge between Ireland and Scotland. Boats of head and faces, bringing a mass invasion of Irish that would change the face of Glasgow forever." He amplifies his voice to gain attention. "But be aware, there's a new cultural invasion of Glasgow where many thousands of asylum seekers and incomer families are piling in. They seek a better life, as did the Irish. Some, though, seek to continue old feuds transferred from their homelands."

"Gezz a break, wull ye," comes from a boozer on a barstool. Rooney allows a snigger, but not enough to deter him from his spiel.

"The migrants and asylum seekers are now, as the Irish in the early days, only intent in survival. In the developing urban areas and the regenerated schemes, it is less about survival and more about having a life. Many settlers moved here to escape the London burghs, populated by Bengali and Afro-Caribbean immigrants. New migrant groups from Eastern Europe have arrived. Back in time, the indigenous population largely accommodated the Irish, but there were those who sought to send them back to their homeland and racist attacks were commonplace. It's the same now."

"Pushing it Rooney, this is a multicultural, multi-bampot pub!"

"Very good, professor," comes from a couple of young folk from beyond the bar; students trying to muscle in on a bit of controversy.

He continues regardless. "The asylum seekers have come from lands fraught with instability, where homogeneity does not exist. They bring new power bases. They challenge the traditional gang culture. There are street battles in Glasgow and throughout West Central Scotland. There are bloody battles between the local gangs, the Eastern Europeans, and the Asians. Now it's guns, not traditional weapons such as knives, hammers, or iron bars. Incidents abound and blood flows like in the city. The authorities do nothing to stem the violence. Funded by big money barons of their own, the cabal of gangs demand control. They exploit the fear of the indigenous population. Whether they be Protestants, Catholics, or the Buckie fraternity." This brings a laugh from his booze-buddy at the bar, snorting into his beer. "The new fighters are raising their profile, demanding greater recognition, greater power, and a greater hold in this brave new city of Glasgow."

Then the perfume returns and with it a voice from over his shoulder. "Good speech, Rooney," she says. "Are you finished?"

"Jean Dempsie?" he says to the woman who appears to know things.

Rooney's about to go into Part Two, when she says, "Come with me." He obeys and follows her through to the back lounge of the bar. "I don't like the look," she says, running his lapel through her fingers. "Drink?"

"I don't give a …. Glenfiddich thanks," he says; thinking, so she didn't like his attire, so she's dull. But it's no coincidence she's there. "Muir?"

"Sorry about the chambers fiasco," she says, dropping two lumps of ice into his drink, and handing in over.

"I don't take ice," he says. This confirms his suspicions: a set up. "It hardly worked to plan," he says, leading her to a table.

"Poor Mark, he didn't need to die." She seems warmer than before, as if she's no longer in role. They clinks glasses. "Sorry about the ice, waters down the whisky I believe."

"You did your best. No one was to know what he would do."

"Not a happy outcome though."

"Sorry, he had a gun in the debating chamber. He was going to kill Muir."

"Sorry yourself, Rooney. Mark was given the gun and prompted to say what he said, and there was a marksman with him in his sights all of the time. As soon as he brought the gun out he was a dead man."

This hits Rooney like a pile of empty words, a double cross.

"And why didn't Jackie tell me?"

193

"Why would she?"

"She didn't trust me?"

"Trust ..."

"Well, where is trust when Johnston finds out everything in time? It was Muir's orders, to save his reputation."

"Indeed, good for him. Though, he took it right to the wire."

"Muir knew he wasn't at risk. He was told Mark's gun held blanks."

"Great... now what happens?"

"You've to go underground."

"Underground! He's bad enough on the ground."

"And what do you mean by underground?"

"Wait and see. We need to go. Get rid of the hat."

"This, my dear, is a symbol of my virility," he says, determined to remain in his zone.

"Hats like that are knocked off in Partick."

"And where are we going?"

"You've to come with me," she says, as she plucks the hat from his head. "Here," she says, passing it to a passing barman. "He'll be back for that in a few days. If not, hand it into the Salvation Army."

"I'll be back," Rooney says, Arnie style.

They gulp their drinks and they're away through and out of the pub, her warmth changing to a harsh task-like determination. Rooney has recognised this fervour before. He's out of breath by the time they're halfway up Gardner Street, only one of the steepest streets in Partick. There she turns and stops him at a controlled access of a tenement close.

"It's me, Maggie, let me in," she whispers into the access panel to the left of the door.

"Maggie?" comes from the panel.

"Shushed," she says as they get inside and head up the close stairs where she turns to him and says, "You follow my lead, right; and you agree to everything that comes out of my mouth and say nothing, you got that." Rooney nods. There's clanking of bolts and locks, and discussion through the door, before an aggressive young man allows them in. "In there, right," he says. They head in, passing the kitchen area. Rooney smells food being prepared with lots of ginger and coriander. Someone's making Glasgow's national dish: curry. Some men there stop talking. Rooney smells strong tea.

"Maggie, welcome back ma wee darling," comes from an older man who steps into the hall to greet her.

The man stilts his greeting when he sees Rooney and urges 'Maggie' into a side room,

"It's fine Davy, he's safe; he's a friend, he'll be useful to us," Rooney hears her say.

"How do you know he's safe?" he hears the man ask.

"He's queer and stupid."

"Have you had him checked out?" he hears Davy ask. "Where's he from? Who does he work for?"

There's a hushed discussion for around ten minutes before they re-enter the hall.

'Maggie' introduces Rooney. "Davy, this is Ian MacDonald."

"Good to meet you sir," Rooney says.

"Good to meet you too, Mr MacDonald."

Great, me a chookter, Rooney thinks, shaking his hand. This is a strong, but warm handshake. Rooney wonders how many bones had cracked under these knuckles.

"Mr McGinn is the head of the family," 'Maggie' says to Rooney, then to Davy, "Ian wants to help and has knowledge which will be useful to use in our plans."

"Aye, good son," Davy says, inviting them into the sitting room where he pours black tea into mugs. "You have to understand somethin' MacDonald," he directs at Rooney. "When you enter here there are certain things –" He pauses as he pours the tea, but it's clear Rooney has to listen intently. As he does, another man enters the room and snarls, " – If you come in with us, you place your life in our hands. You become ours. You share our aims and you'll share our fate. And, if you deceive us, you're deid. You got that?" This man kids not and leaves as abruptly as he enters. Rooney is to learn his name is Thomas. Davy passes Rooney a mug.

These are the McGinns, a heavy Glasgow firm, and Rooney spends the next three days getting to know them, their ways and objectives, but not their mission. Davy McGinn, the father of the family, is a Glasgow hard-man. Now in his sixties, an older man with a grey beard, he maintains a reputation second to none in Glasgow. Mick and Thomas McGinn, his sons, are his lieutenants. Rooney grows to like this man. There's no messing with him, he's straight down the line. Though a bit of an anachronism these days, he's protective of his community, and not to be crossed. He's an intelligent man and Rooney enjoys talking to him about books they have read, and wines and spirits they had enjoyed. He seems to accept Rooney's 'weird ways' and his 'high' manner.

Rooney hasn't intended this route into the dark world of the criminal fraternity, but he has to use it just the same. They're a heavy underworld family; feared by many, including the Strathclyde Police, who have a working relationship with it. They seek an increased control of the West of Scotland and are happy to move into politics to achieve this. Indeed, some say they had the leaders of the council in their pockets.

Johnston is picked up at a taxi rank at the Central Station, just outside the

Grand Central. Inside, Jackie, boobs in danger of falling out, was racing through the reception area trying to find him.

A black four-by-four with blackened windows draws up, prompting a few of the Saturday afternoon revellers to fire off some Glaswegian comments, like "Give's a lift to Castlemulk, will ye? The man's got his own bus!" Johnston ignores them and has a quiet thought as he launches himself into the large back seat of the land cruiser. "Why do I live among these people?" he asks himself. Though he understands why: Glasgow is the place to be at this time; it has all the elements of a cauldron of fear. It has aggression, it always had, it has a melting pot atmosphere of cultures, and it has polarised factions. Ideal for his purposes. He knows why he chose Glasgow.

Jackie says the information received from the City Chambers connection drew a complete blank. The only confirmation she has is that someone there had talked to Johnston that day in that phone call. She could have only imagined what was discussed, she says, but she would have bet her last pound it had something to do with the Summit.

Johnston arrives at his destination. The 'family of families' will muster there, or the *'familia familias'* as he prefers, in Latin. They need him, his expertise and contacts, but more than anything, they need his mind. This is a grouping of the most feared crime families in the country, which includes the McGinns. He had met their leaders in his meeting in Dublin. He provides their motto: *'bellum lethale'*, a 'deadly war'. Their first hit was the Murphys who had become too big, an outlaw clan. They were a means of accessing Johnston, and their demise was a down payment for his assistance. Johnston's reputation within the dark depths of the city's criminal fraternity is well confirmed. He'd facilitated some major hits and was seen as the major player in the new urban wars; however, it's known he has his own needs. That afternoon there would be an agreement on the strategy, but there'd also be discord over how they would implement it. Johnston would provide both the 'how' and the 'what' they would need, but would his price be too much? They know, however, that Johnston's motives are not strictly financial.

Johnston has no idea where he is, unusual for him and something he doesn't like, but he has to risk it and put his head into the lion's den. He tries to establish his location by identifying the passing streets. It could be somewhere in the south side of Glasgow, possibly Pollokshields, an area he knows well from the political meetings he had attended in the area soon after he arrived in Glasgow. This is an Asian area, generally peaceful, but a target of British unionist extremists such as the British National Party. The car enters a close – he hears a solid gate close behind it – where it stops. Then he hears another gate slide open smoothly along well-oiled tracks. The car moves into a court, illuminated by natural light. Fine, the door will now open, and he'll be escorted inside. But no, he hears yet another gate slide open and the car stops.

Then he feels the car going down. He's in a vehicle lift. What he doesn't expect is the lift not only goes down, but down and down, seven or eight levels before coming to rest. Then two large, heavily armed and hooded men gesture him out and, grasping each of his arms, hustle him from the darkened space into what looks like a hangar containing an arms dump. He identifies crates of AK47s and ammunition, and some very ominous looking black transit vans with blacked out windows. He's pleased there's enough equipment to arm a small army – the right impression. From the look of the underground scene, this must be a disused factory, a large underground garage, or a vehicle storage base.

He passes between the crates assisted by the two heavyset men, then physically lifted up a set of metal stairs, down a long corridor and dispatched unceremoniously into a small anteroom. This room contains a table and a smattering of office type chairs around the walls which are covered in gangland graffiti. The men sit him in a chair and stand back, arms folded, behind him. They're reminiscent of the Murphy men he had recent experience of, as they form an impenetrable wall between him and any way out.

He revels in the mystery and drama of it all. He adores the environment, the buzz and excitement that make it all worthwhile. Then an adjacent door opens and within seconds the room's full of hard looking men. Some fall into a shape around the walls. Some sit down taking up most of the seats. A short pause, and four heavily armed men, automatic weapons close to their chests, escort in seven more men. Good, these guys are in power.

They sit grouped around the table, almost like an interview panel – which in a sense they are. They're interviewing this man for their greatest trial, and he has to be right for the job. He smells their breath and their body odour, reminiscent of a fish market in Paris he used as a student.

This is the core group, the leadership, he assumes. They're made up the leaders of the respective families and their right hand men. Some wear suits but speak in broad Glasgow.

"We're pleased you're here," Thomas McGinn, the largest of the group says, speaking first. He's brash and dominant. He looks like a pub bouncer, all punch and no brains; but the way he looks around deferentially at the rest of the group indicates he's not important enough to warrant an answer. He waits. After a couple of minutes, the silence is broken by Davy McGinn. He sits back from the table and, with an authority that ensues from way deep inside his chest, says, "It's good to see you again, Mr Johnston." He reaches over and offers an outstretched hand. Johnston shakes it, feeling slightly off-footed by this wise man. He's not familiar with warm greetings in these circumstances.

"You too," Johnston says, "and I'm pleased to be here; to be of thervice to you."

"We will see," Davy says. "We are from different backgrounds, but we share similar interests. As for objectives, we will also see." It is clear *he* is setting the boundaries.

"Are you all Glasgow families?" Johnston asks.

"We are the McGinns," Davy says. "The Binghams, the Ferris Clan, the Tim Team, the Stevensons, what's left of the Taylors, and a few others. The family of families is an entity, a grouping; we now act, collectively – "

"The time has come. We want a war; let's get to it," Thomas barks.

"Yes, great," Johnston says, ignoring him. "My objective is to help you strike at the very heart of power in this city." He'll be direct. They didn't invite him there to mess around, and he isn't there to mess around.

"Could you be a bit more specific, Mr Johnston?" Like a well-experienced interviewer, Davy invites Johnston to reveal his potential.

"You have decided to collaborate across faiths and cultures – Tims and Billys – highly unusual." He has the floor. "You have decided to set aside any local rivalry, to unite, to fight, and to confirm the families' power base, against a threat which is intent in destroying you." There's more movement now, a shuffling of feet and a clearing of throats. "You need to send a message so strong that no one, no group, team or fraternity, including the authorities, will ever face up to you again." Not quite true, but let's stroke their egos.

"Ah, if this were only true Mr Johnston," Davy says. "You are right. We are *the* family, but we know our limitations against greater powers." He appears resigned, but not fully committed.

"You need...," Johnston says, "someone to lead you."

"*We* need a war," Thomas says. "If we don't act together, the pakis, chinks, and poles will take right over, and destroy us." Johnston senses approval from around the room. He needs to exploit this, but he does not want discord, this would not ensure his plans are met. They need to be organised, committed and together, otherwise they'd never be able to see through his greatest challenge.

"Yes, you do," Johnston replies, briefly answering Thomas then referring quickly to Davy. "But there are different ways to fight a battle," he says, before pausing. "And there has never been a greater war to win."

Davy is pleased. He sees the maturity in Johnston's eyes, hears the experience in his words, and doubts not his ability to lead them to a glorious outcome. Some, though, voice their support of Thomas, and *his* war.

Rooney arrives early on the fourth day. The atmosphere in the house is tense. As he enters the sitting room, he sees Thomas at the table, sitting next to the man he knows as Mick, who rises and moves towards him. Just then, strong arms from behind grab him and force him down on a chair. His head is pulled back by the hair, and his hands held out over the table. He feels a searing pain, almost at the same time as he hears a chopper take the end of the forefinger off his right-hand. He screams in agony as his pain is amplified, as what is left of his finger is pressed into a lit cigar. He feels as if he'll pass out. He's never known such pain. It rages up his arm. It feels as if his whole body's on fire.

Thomas, the perpetrator now towers over him. "Now you know me," he says, as he sits down and pulls out another cigar. He lights it, blows smoke in Rooney's face, and leans over the table and continues. "For our mission, you need to feel and acknowledge pain." He leans over farther, almost in his face. Rooney smells his stinking breath. "And an early death is all is on offer, Mr MacDonald."

"Enjoying it now?"

He's released and can do nothing or say nothing in response. He's escorted outside, his hand wrapped in a kitchen towel. He feels something being placed in his jacket pocket and is told to 'walk away'.

He staggers down Gardner Street like the drunken man he wishes he was; not out of place in this part of Glasgow.

"Trust no one," he voices to himself.

There's a pharmacy on Dumbarton Road and he reaches there with his injured hand in his pocket. He manages to pass over some money for the strongest non-prescription painkillers available. He shuffles along Dumbarton Road and finally reaches his destination, the Western Infirmary, A and E. In contrast to his last visit to an accident and emergency department, he's taken immediately. Not because of his wound, but more because he's dripping blood over the floor, prompting a degree of disgust from others there who complain to an old battle-axe of a receptionist behind a glass partition. A nurse grabs him by the wrist, holds his hand up to stop the blood dropping on the floor, and pulls him into a small cubicle, where she pulls a plastic curtain behind him. She's friendly, but says little as she removes the blood sodden kitchen towel. His account is a fight after that day's Celtic and Rangers game outside the notorious Rosevale Tavern. His finger end is stitched and dressed, and he's sent unceremoniously out into the Partick night, where he hits the pubs running. Eight whiskies later, he's in the Three Judges Bar at Partick cross, feeling very sore, shocked, and confused. He reaches into his jacket pocket for a hanky and slowly opens it, having only one working hand, and is disgusted to find the end of his finger. Christ, he wishes he had known it was there when he was being stitched. He also finds a note he asks the barman to read.

"Sure pal, here we go," he says, then reads it out. "Mr MacDonald, we're sorry to have had to make a statement to you in this way. You will soon realise our reason for this. You need to do something for us. Only then will we be in a position to bring you into our family."

The barman turns the notepaper over and drops it in disgust, but not before he voices the words on it. "As a gesture, to ensure your conviction to our cause, you will rape an Asian woman, and you will be arrested and charged. We will monitor your progress."

He slaps the paper with his hand down on the bar and says, "You're a funny cunt. Get the fuck out of here." And that is it; he's out on the street and heading along Dumbarton Road to the Lismore to collect his hat.

His sorry state is lost to him as his injury only sends him further into insightless oblivion. As he heads up the Byres Road, he hears comments about his hand, and the red patch of blood silhouetted on his white jacket pocket. The hat and his demeanour are, by this time, strange to say the least, until he moves into Tennents, which was well used to eccentrics in strange attire, having been a locus for transvestites over the years. Rooney in his hat and blooded white suite enters and no false eyelashes are batted.

Back with the family of families, Johnston is quizzed about the Summit.

"What do you know about the Grand Central?" Davy asks.

"Rich, posh clientele, expensive food. Roy Rodgers and Trigger stayed there once; Trigger pranced up the grand staircase two at a time. What do you wish to know?" Johnston feels comfortable enough now to play them a bit.

"Please Mr Johnston," Davy says.

"There're around five hundred police officers and security guards, and three hundred plus delegates. This is a massive security exercise. The main players, not living there, are to be ferried in daily from safe houses and hotels in Glasgow, Edinburgh, and Stirling. Lots of demonstrations, some pretty aggressive I would say. The Glasgow Minorities Consortium, the Citizenship for Asylum Seekers, etcetera. A total no go area from two weeks before the Summit. What do you want to – "

"Kill the fuckers," Thomas says, speaking out of turn.

"That's easy," Johnston says. "But what kind of impression do you want to make, to leave? What is your aim?"

"To show we are together, for the first time. We are an army and we have had enough of them," Davy says.

"They bastards," Thomas says.

'They bastards!' I will need some persuasion on that one, my friend, Johnston thinks. He had to guide them towards *his* objective. Theirs had no chance of making any long lasting effect, far less any chance of success.

"You want to kill people?" How boring and predictable is that?

Thomas leans forward one more time and says, "It is the love of the battle. The come ahead ya' bastards, that's what we like."

Straight from *No Mean City*.

"What if I help you do something – "

"As big as the razor battles of the sixties?" Thomas's now becoming ridiculous.

Johnston says nothing.

"Mr Johnston, our intention is also… big," Davy says.

"I can help you achieve everything you could ever hope for," Johnston says, "But even more, if you follow my advice."

"Father, don't allow this man to control us," Thomas says. "To dictate to us."

"Easy Thomas. Mr Johnston has the kind of experience we need," Davy says, but there are those there not entirely happy with him acquiescing to Johnston.

He needs to drive these people home. "The Summit is about power," Johnston says.

"Aye, Mr Johnston, we know this," Davy says.

"The real agenda… behind the scenes."

"A hidden agenda?"

"Yes, the hidden agenda, if you will," Johnston says. "The council seeks the support of the Scottish Government to develop massive inward migration into Glasgow, to repopulate it."

There's a hush in the room. "You know of this… plan?"

"I do."

"The council will have nothing to do with it. We control them, money talks."

"Bigger money talks louder," Johnston says.

"The bastards, fight the bastards," Thomas says, exercised.

"Thomas, for fuck's sake," Davy says disciplining his son, before turning to Johnston. "We will accept your help, Mr Johnston."

"And your commitment?" Johnston asks.

"That you have," Davy replies, "but there is something Mr Johnston – "
Johnston knows what's coming. He's heard it said many times before.

" – we fail, and you and yours die."

"Agreed," Johnston says.

"And what would you wish? We can give you considerable cash."

"My objective will be satisfied through yours."

They're confused at this, but it's clear to everyone Johnston has his own agenda, and his own needs to satisfy in this task.

"It's agreed," Davy says.

They shake hands and Johnston pulls out a dossier marked GRAND CENTRAL SUMMIT SECURITY – TOP SECRET. This's just what they need: inside information. It'll now be put into good, or bad, use.

CHAPTER TWENTY-FOUR

In Tennents, Rooney moves progressively through a number of double whiskies as he waits for Jackie. He has to rape an Asian woman, be arrested and charged. In his mental state, this's not an unattractive proposition. He takes up a position at the back of the bar. Inconspicuous, standing out like a naked male manikin in Mothercare.

He hopes Jackie can set this up for him: a friendly undercover policewoman, an arrest, and a fake charge; this could be fun. Prosecuting should be relatively easy, except one thing: the informants. He has no knowledge of how deep this group's influence is within the criminal justice world. He has a hunch, given they seem to act with impunity, that this is significant. It would take just one flaw to bring the fake attack down and with it any chance of him getting into the group, and any chance of finding Johnston, and any chance of finding out what he is up to be next; and get him killed to boot.

"Can you do this?"

"Easy. I'm a real Casanova."

"Rape a woman, an act outwith your bounds of reason, decency, morality?"

In a manic high, promiscuity is his drive – no problem.

Jackie arrives in the bar, spots him immediately, and has a go. "Man, you need to improve on the image." She rounds the bar and orders her own drink at the same time.

"Who cares in here?"

"Rooney, are you off your head?"

"I could very well be dear."

"I hear you've fallen in with a bad crowd," she says, picking up her Chenin Blanc; a large glass for the same cost as a small in most Byres Road bars.

"Indeed, you could say that," he says, holding up his bandaged hand.

"Shame about that, hon," she says, both elbows on the bar, looking out for anyone she knows.

"Not sincere enough," he says. "You said I would be OK."

Like a wine connoisseur, Jackie quaffs, but swallows rather than spits. "Well, you will be a maverick," she says.

"I always liked the programme."

"Way before my time old man," she says. "Listen *cowboy*, this is a heavy team. There are important individuals in this family group. These men are more than able to put together an attack without being affiliated or accountable to any one individual or organisation. They draw on their contacts and they link with a wider organisation. They are veterans of the Glasgow gang wars and lead a smattering of teams and a whole range of new recruits, one of which you have now become." Another swig. "And believe me they will test your mettle, as they do with all of their people."

"They want me to rape a woman, an Asian."

"Fuck, why?"

"To show solidarity with them."

"No, why an Asian woman?"

"To reflect power over migrants, of course."

"I don't know if I like the idea of you being with... a woman."

"I've been with you; you're a woman."

"I'm different," she says. "I can cope with your smelly body, breath like a toilet, and touch like a wrestler."

"Must be love."

"This is what I have to do – remember?"

She frowns, as if to say 'do not flatter yourself'. She turns away from him looking out towards the windows onto Byres Road. "Then you must do it," she says after a couple of minutes. "I know a woman. Her name is Afreen Khan. She's an Asian society woman. She'll take you all the way to the Sheriff Court and back. She'll ensure you are spread across the broad sheets. You'll use Hypnovel, the date rape drug."

Rooney had worked with perpetrators who had used this to exert their power over women. In his state of mind, though, he'll be happy to use it.

"Date rape! Why?"

"Because I doubt you would have the bottle for an aggressive act. And I wouldn't agree it."

"Why her?"

She's my stepmother's best friend's daughter, and as far as *they* are concerned, she's made it; that's why."

"Oh, the green-eyed monster."

"She's everything my stepmother hoped I would have been: successful, seniority woman, children at Kelvinside Academy; made it through marriage to a city banker. 'Why couldn't you have been like her?' All my life I got that. Everything she got, she got by her sex. Everything I got, I got by hard work."

It's clear Jackie hates this woman. She's made it over her.

"You want to fuck her through me Jackie."

They both know what he means: assault by proxy.

"Rooney, I'll introduce you; the rest is up to you," she says. "She likes shrinks, so you should get on fine. Just get a shower."

"The Muir lie?"

"Jean Dempsie told you."

"Indeed she did."

"Well, you needed to know sometime."

"Suppose."

"It had to be that way."

"It had to be your way."

"It was Muir's way."

"I was warned about you."

"Warned?"

"Are you trustworthy... dear?"

He says this to hurt, not that it has to be asked; best to get it out into the open. Inevitably, she doesn't answer, but they continue drinking until throwing out time, neither of them saying much. He asks her 'back for coffee', but she says she doesn't have her forensic overalls with her. They'll go to her flat instead.

They are hardly in the door when they grab each other, pulling the clothes off each other as they trip along the hall, falling into the bedroom. They bounce onto the bed and he's up to the hilt in her in seconds.

Being manic has its highs, Rooney!

"Fuck me Rooney, just fuck me," she says roughly into his left ear, digging her nails into his back.

He disengages and sits up. "Fuck you," he says. "Who are *you* fucking here Jackie? Afreen... your mother, your dad?"

"You always were a pathetic bastard Rooney," she says, turning away to fall asleep at the other end of the bed. In minutes, he hears her snoring; but just before this, he hears her slurring "and don't you fucking enjoy it." It takes him a minute to realise she's referring to his 'task' to come.

To him, it's clear his task is now 'their task'. Rooney wonders if she's getting something out of this: a power rush through him. It turns her on.

Two days later, they attend the bash in the Hotel Du Vin at One Devonshire Gardens. It's for the entrepreneurs of Scotland, a Scottish Business Enterprise venture. Normally, the only way he would have contemplated associating with these people would be to get severely drunk. In his mania though, he's up there with them, a 'high flyer'. Jackie introduces him to Afreen Khan, and then disappears. Afreen says she is well used to eccentric gentlemen at these kind of parties.

The chat up is enjoyable. She's interesting and attractive, tall, slim and sexy, but not his type. He says he's a consultant psychiatrist with a private clientele: rich business people with a whole range of neurosis.

"Do sex therapies?" she asks.

"She's flirting with you Rooney, get in there."

"Could be arranged."

She moves closer to him, almost face to face.

"Good, we must make an... appointment."

She smiles at him and asks him to look after her glass as she goes to the Ladies, making a comment about how she has to be careful, after reading about a spate of date rapes.

"It won't happen to me," she says, as she heads off.

Little does she know, he thinks, slipping the Hypnoval into her glass. This was the point he could have walked, but a mix of bad and mad prevents him from doing so. In his mental state, he has an obsessional belief his task has to be done.

He suggests they go for a walk in the Botanic Gardens adjacent to the hotel. She agrees happily. They find a quiet spot behind the Kibble Palace and sit on the grass. By this time, she says she's feeling weary, and she'd like to sleep, not understanding why.

"You wouldn't take advantage of a lady who's had a wee bit too much to drink, would you?" she slurs, succumbing to the drug, as she slides down onto the grass.

"Don't worry, I'll look after you," he says, enjoying the feeling of being a bastard.

"Now you know."

He could have backed off then. In his manic state, he's up for it but deep down in his psyche he knows lives are dependent on him seeing this through. He looks around and the place is empty, quiet, getting dark; the gates might even be closed.

"Can I do this," he asks himself.

"You can do it. You have to do it. You might even enjoy it."

"I'm a good man."

"A good man can be bad."

"I can be bad? It's OK?"

"It's OK to be bad, when you are doing good."

He'll do it and he'll be clinical in the task. He lifts her long party dress to find fish net stockings reaching up to a small thong. He wonders if she had dressed this way in the hope of a sexual encounter. He moves her thong aside as deftly as he can; then, getting on top of her, moves her legs apart, and eases himself inside her. He finds the encounter impersonal, but not without pleasure, and it achieves his task; and, in his grandiosity, he feels at one with her, with her class. He could have used a condom, but his DNA has to be found inside her. Even in his insightless state, he hopes she's on the pill.

He stays with her until she comes around, then they move to a park bench. She's groggy when he explains what he has done to her. She appears calm, though, which is somewhat disconcerting for him. She should be screaming the houses down.

"You raped me," she says calmly

"I did."

She is crouching down, sorting herself.

"Why?"

"I wanted to fuck you."

"Oh, you don't believe in the conventional way?"

"Not this time."

She looks up at him.

"You might have fucked me, but you haven't fucked my mind."

She is a strong woman.

"It's OK, I didn't intend to fuck your mind."

"Why did you do it?"

"I told you."

"I don't believe you."

From her hard stare, Rooney sees she's going to interrogate him on this.

"If I told you, you wouldn't believe me."

"Power over women"

"Can't get it up normally?"

"Eh?"

"Need to have a woman comatose to fuck her?"

"Drink helps."

"Well – "

"Can't look at her face? Can't get a hard-on if a woman is looking you in the eye?"

"It's just – "

"Having to cope with her thinking you can't do it."

"Him thinking he can't do it."

"What are you: an inadequate, a child in a man's body? Asperger's?"

"Getting there."

He's confirming all of these.

"A poof trying to prove something… to himself?" He's looking at the ground. "You're just a pathetic wee boy."

"A pathetic wee boy, Rooney."

He feels a pathetic wee boy. The wee boy that was used by a priest and dominated by his father.

In this brief glimpse of lucidity, he wonders if this is the point where a man might snap and kill. Faced with a psychological assault so impossible to escape, that the only way is to kill the source of it. Ridicule, pride, self-contempt, fear – get her to stop, shut up. He has raped, one-step more and he could walk away, not to hear her anymore. Rooney knows that point. He's interviewed those men, who took that one step too far.

"You are a pitiful bastard, you know that?"

He knows it.

"Guess," he says. "You going to scream?"

He needs her to scream, to bring in the cops.

"What and give you the pleasure in seeing me lose control?"

He looks at her. He doesn't know what to do.

She stands up and, as he lifts his head, she hits him with a blow that nearly takes his head off. Then she reaches inside her pocket and pulls out a mobile.

"Hello George. Yes, I'm OK, I'm in the botanic Gardens. Yes, I'm OK … Yes, yes, George. George… I've been raped, get the Police over here… Yes, right now. Thanks."

She sits down quietly pulls out a packet of cigarettes. She offers Rooney one and they smoke. There's no more aggression from any of them, as if they have both been through something.

He sits there waiting for the police and, although he knows he has achieved his 'task', he feels the one who's been fucked, not the other way around.

"Some rapist you."

Within twenty minutes, Rooney's in Maryhill Police Station, and within six hours and, after forensics, he's charged, to appear in Glasgow Sheriff Court the day after. Afreen Khan's connections in the media will ensure her reputation is protected. She's been date-raped by an 'unsavoury character from Glasgow's low-life'. Jackie sorts out a good lawyer who, exploiting his illness and mental state at the time, gets him bail. He'll return there later for trial.

"Via Hillwood, Rooney?"

For Rooney, being in Court hurts. This place where he'd attend as an expert witness. He's in front of a Sheriff he has served under, who at a later date will convict him. The reality cuts through his mania and his feet hit the ground. He is to return at a later date for trial. He's allowed bail and leaves there feeling deflated and disgusted with himself. However, somewhere inside his head he knows this is necessary. Lives depend on his going down this road, but the reality of his offence hits home. He heads across the Prince Albert Bridge heading for the Scotia Bar; but half way across he spews the entire contents of his stomach over the wall of the bridge into the Clyde.

"Why did I do it?" he says holding on to the wall. "I was a good man. Now what am I?"

"A bad man."

Then a car draws up. He is about to say 'you're alright pal, I'm no' a poof on the make, thanks anyway,' when he hears that voice.

"Get in, MacDonald," comes from within the car.

This's no cab, this's a black four by four; and this's no cabby, this's a voice he recognises immediately. He does what he is told. Inside Mick says nothing at first, but he knows his task in infiltrating the group has been successful. But what he says next concerns him somewhat.

"You're to be a front-line carrier pigeon," Mick says.

"Really," Rooney says.

"Aye, really."

"He's flying anyway!"

CHAPTER TWENTY-FIVE

Back in the midst of the family of families, Johnston is holding court at a wide table, his hands spread over the veneered surface. He scans the faces around its perimeter. He has no respect for these people, but they will achieve his goals; of this, he's convinced.

"You'll construct the devices. Each with 50 lbs. of urea and 4 gallons of nitric acid, mixed to form urea nitrate," he says.

"We don't know this explosive," Davy says.

"It's hardly known," Johnston says. "You'll add aluminium azide and ferric oxide to increase the force. Then cyanide to produce a poison gas following the explosion."

"Ah hah, I like this," Thomas says, now interested.

"The bombs'll be placed strategically in major social, cultural and council centres throughout the city," Johnston says, not directly to Davy, but to the quiet ones behind. He knows they have collective control.

"Not at the Grand Central?" Thomas says.

Moving forward across the table, Johnston opens an A4 sheet of paper. Davy strains his eyes to see the words on it. Thomas switches on the fluorescent lights, sending most of the group farther into the shadows. Davy scowls at him.

"This is not about the Grand Central. This is much bigger than the transient impact we might achieve there," Johnston says, at his persuasive best. "You will present key demands of the Summit, contained in three simple points." He reveals a set of numbered points on the page. "One, stop the migrations. Two, stop the aid to the migrants. Three, stop the local council and police interference in our businesses." He pauses to increase interest, and then continues. "And you'll insist the demands and threats stand for five years, thereby ensuring long-term compliance.

"You'll set off one bomb. The initial one, to show conviction, that'll confirm their commitment."

"When?" Thomas jumps in.

"One minute son," Johnston replies.

"Thomas!" Davy glowers at him.

Johnston says, "You will say if the agreement is reneged upon at any time within this period, the bombs will be set off consecutively at first, then simultaneously through the city."

"Where?" Thomas asks.

"Right in the most prestigious of places," Johnston says.

"Great."

"You'll tell them an estimate of fatalities will be between two to three hundred people. And that the bombs have been placed in sealed airtight undetectable containers."

"Short of shutting every major drop-in centre, museum, and football ground in the city," Thomas says.

Johnston prevails. "Which, of course, no one there will contemplate, given the cost to their reputations."

"There's no way they could remove the threat of disaster?" Davy asks, now interested.

"Absolutely no way," Johnston says.

"And how will we deliver these demands?"

"That's the easy part."

"Can we trust you?" Thomas asks, now almost on top of Johnston.

Johnston's steely eyes bore into Thomas's. He need say no more. Davy knows trust is absolute, but for Thomas is nothing at the same time. Johnston's conviction in this matter is accepted. They believe he has similar motives, though with his own objectives; but more than anything, they believe he'll deliver.

The car heads through George Square. Rooney hopes it's towards the West End or somewhere he can get his bearings. He wonders if Johnston has had a hand in his task. From this situation, he hopes there will be a link to him. He has to get him, but he's running out of time, strength and bottle.

Jackie meticulously takes apart the room held by Johnston before he escaped the Grand Central. "Clues, baits, messages, or trying to mess us up," she says. What the hell is it this time, she wonders, as she rifles the bedside cabinets. "Usual Gideon's Bible." She opens the Bible, to find a post-it stuck on the inside page, and next to it, a statement. She reads it aloud: "And almost all things are by the law purged with blood. Without shedding of blood is no remission. Hebrews, nine, twenty two."

The family of families agree to accept Johnston's plan. Davy's affirmation confirms this. "It's agreed. We will work with you, Mr Johnston. We know of your... skill and contacts. You will help us in our task. You have something to gain, but this does not concern us. You will have served our purpose. The demonstration of our strength –"

"And a message that we are on the march," Thomas adds.

Jackie calls Rooney. She asks if he's recovered from his 'adventures', then enquires if he's clean. He'll get back to her on that one, he says. She was called to Muir's office, she explains, and he was in no mood to thank her for saving his life.

"'Rooney's pursuing Johnston. He knew this was the only way,' I said to him. 'You were correct in this. He's infiltrated a local family, facilitated by myself, which should lead him to Johnston,' he said. I told him Johnston was conspiring on something very big, centered on the Summit at the Grand Central Hotel. He's leaving clues as usual, this time through the Bible."

"'No Latin?' Muir sneered at me.

"'No, only a strange message about killing. A kind of cryptic message as usual,' I said.

"'Carry on,' he said.

"It is here,' I said, opening my note book. 'It says almost all things are by the law purged with blood; and without shedding of blood is no remission.

"'Law purged with blood... I liked that,' he said. 'That would make a good campaign slogan.'

"I stared on, aghast.

"'I am only joking, but I get the idea,' he said. 'Why this message?'"

She had anticipated this question and had armed herself with information obtained by a researcher in the CID.

"I advised him that 'it appears Mafia bosses, many of whom professed to be good Catholics, often use the Bible to construct coded notes, known as pizzini, to communicate with underlings.'

"'Ah the Mafia,' Muir said, sounding relieved. 'We are dealing with the Mafia?'

"'No, though there is a significant family network,' I said. 'Assuming Mafia family structures and proportions.'

"'Family structures, but with none of the powers.'

"'They may be involved at the Grand Central,' I said.

"'They are involved, Jackie,' he said.

"'Cancel the Summit,' I said.

"'Don't be such an idiot madam. This one's mine and it would be seen to be acquiescing to terror. It would be giving encouragement to every local criminal family or group. No, we need to meet. We have matters to discuss.'

"'I fear Johnston may know something,' I said. 'He may have an informant in the City Chambers.'

"'He *has* an informant in the City Chambers, DCI,' he said.

"I knew then that Muir himself, perhaps through a council informant, was feeding Johnston information.

"'We need him to know about our plans,' he said. 'We intend a conflagration, to snuff out the threat... to our interests, forever. We want them to show their hand, then we will we destroy them.'

"'You are taking a big risk,' I said to him. I was stunned at his response."

"*I'm* not," Rooney says. "This man's capable of anything."

"'Well,' he said. 'Even if they get a few bombs off, public opinion would be on their side. The people of the city will see the groups as against their interests and accept... change.'"

"This man's intends sacrificing scores of people," Rooney says.

"'This is my plan,' Muir said. 'We prompt the family's action and we cope with the inevitable attack on the Summit. That's your part, minimise the damage and protect us. Keep as many people alive as possible. Damage limitation, you got it?'"

"The attacks... throughout the city?"

"Aye. 'Sure, some bombs will go off.' Muir said. 'But my people will rise against the families to protect their city. It'll provide a pretext.'"

"Patriotism is a double-sided sword," Rooney says.

Jackie hesitates. "'The council will accept a deal,' Muir said to me. 'They have done deals in the past and will do so again, but this one is different. They will be given responsibility for rooting out and destroying the families and controlling gangland extremism,' he said.

"'An impossible task, sir,' I said.

"'Yes, we know, a Catch 22,' Muir said. 'The gang attacks will continue. The families will be seen to be responsible. We lose a few people or so.'"

Jackie says she was 'impressed by the man's ingenuity' and 'not unwilling to learn from him'; but she has other orders that concern her. She deliberates on their respective tasks: hers, which are Muir and the Summit, and Rooney's, which are Johnston and the family. She knows she can do it, she says, but wonders about him.

She continues, "'*You* deal with Johnston,' Muir said to me. 'Through Rooney, before he has another chance, but not before *he* does *his* bit in our plan. Then you deal with Rooney before he becomes a... liability.'"

"Little does he know how big a liability you have become!"

"That's the confidence you have in me, bastard."

She ignores him and tells him to 'keep her posted'.

He asks if he can 'come over'. Her 'no hon' is unequivocal.

He's confused. "Why am I doing this?"

"Your mother, to save people's lives, Jackie, you?"

Johnston has spent five whole days with the families. Planning has been difficult, with little cohesion and having done nothing to limit 'Tam the bam', as he calls Thomas, who's intent on 'goin' ahead'. Plans are agreed, however, and arrangements across the city are made. Davy's pleased and, deferring to Johnston at the final meeting, says, "It is the will of the family. We must talk now." Johnston knows this is his cue to leave.

Rooney is to find out that Thomas and Mick aren't quite in concert with the families' objectives. Although they pretend they are, they have their own plans.

"You will deliver our demands instead," Thomas says to Rooney.

"And if you mention anything of this it to anyone you are a dead man," Mick adds.

"I'll invite you both to my funeral."

"Three of us will arrive individually at Grand Central," Mick says. "Thomas, Nisby and me. We have three effective bombs, each with enough explosive to kill everything within twenty yards. After the first bomb, you will deliver our terms. If they refuse our demands, or if we do not receive your reply, we will detonate the other bombs."

"The first explosion will seal off the outer perimeter. Those inside will be pushed together within secure areas," Thomas adds.

Rooney appreciates this will kill a fair number of demonstrators.

"I'll do the first bomb," Thomas says. "I've a security pass and I'll enter through the demonstrators." Johnston's hand, no doubt. "Mick and Nisby will enter as catering staff. Again with security passes."

"Demonstrators will die," Rooney says, knowing he's on thin ice.

"You will deliver the message wi' no concern for any demonstrators," Thomas replies. "You got that arsehole."

Rooney is a drunk and rapist on a high who hasn't a cat in hell's chance of getting anywhere near a politician. The rape, useful to get him this far, and a way to make his bones, to provide credibility, leaves him identifiable. For him, though, on his manic phase, anything is possible.

"I could deliver it with a basket of flowers?"

"You'll talk to the right people at the right time," Mick says. "At their weakest point, we'll have the greatest impact and the best chance of an agreement with them. Then our demands will be met."

"What is the message, the demands?" Rooney asks.

"Just our own particular demand."

"Which is what?"

"Fifty million pounds made available through you MacDonald." Wow, these men are motivated by greed.

"What about the family of families' demands? The three point plan?"

"It was never going to happen," Mick says. "From this, we'll build our own family. We'll be stronger than anything before. We'll hit the other families when they are waiting for a response to what they believe to be you delivering their terms."

"When you are really delivering ours," Thomas confirms.

"What about your father, Davy?" Rooney asks. He needs to know where he is in this.

"He's had his day," says Thomas. "He can't take our family where we can take it. He'll understand."

"Sure, but one small thing," Rooney says. "How do you expect me to get into the Grand Central?"

"You have friends."

This nearly sounds supportive.

"We have security details, from inside. And we await instructions."

"From whom?"

"Never mind. Just you understand that if you leak any information we will find everyone important to you. They'll all die."

Rooney contemplates this, wondering if they'll include the Gribben, but knowing they can and will carry out their threat. He wonders if he's getting any closer to Johnston.

They drop him in George Square, saying they'll be in touch and not to do anything to jeopardise his position in the organisation or to threaten the integrity of the task.

Rooney contemplates this as he meanders his way down towards Argyle Street and to another favoured boozer, the Victoria Bar, an old gin palace in Stockwell Street. In there he knows he'll hear the best traditional music and light craic in Glasgow. He doesn't understand he's up to his neck in the kind of shit that might be too much for him to cope with, but backing out now isn't possible. With the mania, has he the bottle to see it through; though, with the inevitability of the black dog arriving through the fugue to drag him downwards into despair and depression, maybe he can't. But, more than anything, he knows he's on his own and wonders how, or if, he can or even should stay in contact with Jackie.

CHAPTER TWENTY-SIX

Jackie, back at the Grand Central, is feeling relaxed, though it's clear her exploration of the Hotel is more than a leisurely pursuit.

Rooney googles the Hotel, previously called the Central Hotel, to establish it was one of the most famous railway hotels in the world.

"Famous guests include Frank Sinatra and Winston Churchill."

"Indeed, and the world's first long-distance television pictures were transmitted to there in 1927 by John Logie Baird."

"And you transmit your thoughts through an antenna in your heid!"

"Shut your geggie!"

"Shut your sorry-heid!"

"The rooms are called after historical Scottish figures and monarchy. The two authorities, the Scottish Government and local councils will meet there soon to discuss local migration policy."

"Monarchy and migration, an interesting mix."

"The House of Hanover comes to mind."

Rooney heads to bed around 2.30 a.m. but, after a heavy night, he can't sleep. He phones Jackie. Is this a good idea, he wonders? By this time, she'll be tucked up in a luxurious bed in her five-star pad.

"Are you high, drunk or looking for a woman?"

"Will you be good-looking in the morning?"

"Sorry?"

"Nothing, I need to talk to you."

"Go on."

"Look, what happened – "

"Forget it hon. We have to do things in the course of our... duties."

"Wow, I get it now Jackie."

Was it a duty to take him to her bed? Was he a duty?

He has wondered why she had fucked him, but fucked by her he was. And still he wants her; though he has an inclination that, in the stark light of day when he comes down and returns to a state of sense and stability, he may feel differently.

He asks Jackie about the demonstrations and the demonstrators. She says she'd get back with information. She understands the phone might be tapped and realises Rooney has the potential for emotional lability. She isn't taking the chance.

At eight the next morning as if to punish him for his late-night call, she phones him from her mobile. Rooney's still up. He's high and has paced the floor most of the night. She says Dissent, the main organising group, is now meeting regularly to make the final arrangements to disrupt the Summit. She sends him a leaflet, which arrives by courier almost at the same time as her call.

She reads aloud from the leaflet. "Dissent, Network and organise anti-expansion action. Dissent, a local network of resistance against migration. The Glasgow Indigenous Peoples' Action Group is calling for a global day of action on the first day of the summit. Dissent, a call for all likeminded groups to converge to disrupt the conference, and for action to be taken simultaneously across Glasgow. Dissent," she says. "Did you get all of that?"

"These people are going to be slaughtered," Rooney says. His morals and professional ethics are punching through his stupor.

"You don't want them killed."

"Can't you do something, without… upsetting things?"

"I'll see what I can do… Johnston?"

"Getting there."

"You will see it through?"

"It's my destiny."

"Delusion."

"It's your chance to stop him."

It's the day before the Summit and Rooney makes his way into the West End. He heads along the Byres Road in deep contemplation. Passing Peckham's Deli, he reminisces of a simpler life. He loved wandering around in there, checking out the French wines and continental meats, the Italian hams. He ponders a normal life back in Hillwood as a relatively problem-free grumpy psychologist. This's never going to be possible again, but he isn't too upset at this.

A four by four draws up, and a voice he well remembers, calls him over. "Mr MacDonald, we will talk to you." If it weren't for the voice, he'd have disregarded this mistaken identity, forgetting his alias which had been provided by Jean Dempsie for making contact with the group. He knows instantly this's Thomas's. He moves to the car.

"Get in," comes from inside the blacked-out car.

He enters the open rear door and decides to speak first, to protect the alias. Thomas is there sitting at the other side of the back seat. He's dressed in black, camouflaged in the car against the black seats. "I wondered when you would make contact. I was getting anxious. It's tomorrow after all," Rooney says, trying to get into role.

"We have a Press pass for you." Thomas is looking straight ahead. He's talking to the driver who's also facing forward.

"Will this get me into the inner areas of the hotel?" Rooney says, taking the pass. Thinking this is a stupid question, but his instincts tell him to act naively with this man.

"It'll allow you into the hotel. When inside you will stay in the reception area. After the bomb goes off, security inside'll be informed, and you'll be identified and taken to the leaders." Three bombers will have a good chance of the success they crave, even if only one succeeds. There's an uncomfortable pause – there's something else coming. "We know about you Rooney and how you were planted wi' us," Thomas says, confirming Rooney's cover has blown.

"Me?"

"*You.*"

"Don't lie, we know about Jean Dempsie, alias Maggie. Or should I say the soon to be late Jean Dempsie," Thomas says, refusing to look him in the face.

"If so, why am I still alive?" To Rooney, this seems a fair question to ask.

"Because you remain useful to us, no more than that," Thomas says. "Sending you in with our message'll confirm our resolve."

"Do I get to know any more?"

"Not if you want to live."

"Fair enough." He knows not to push this, but what the hell. "What if I decide not to go through with it?"

"We've considered this. We've been offered assurance on your behalf that you will. We are content with that."

"Who has spoken for me?" Now this does flummox him. Johnston? Jean? Jackie?

"You'll know soon enough," Thomas says.

"You sure I'll go through with it?" Rooney says. "A threat to kill me will only strengthen my determination to get the fuck out of it." He knows they'll find him, wherever he goes; Thomas would have considered that possibility.

"But you won't," Thomas says, like an ultimatum.

"Why not?"

"Because of Johnston; we know why you are wi' us."

Rooney has to ask. "Will you help me reach him?"

"Johnston has the same task on the same day and in the same place," Thomas says. "There and then you'll find him."

"I'll need a gun, hidden somewhere in the hotel."

"I'll see to it. He needs to die."

No love lost there. He needs the gun to apprehend Johnston, not to kill him. Thomas doesn't need to know this.

"You'll deliver our message Rooney," Thomas says. "Refuse and I'll see to it that Johnston is informed. Then, either he'll have you killed or he'll slip well out of your reach."

"*Or both!*"

No words were necessary to confirm the deal. Then, just as Rooney is about to leave the car, another man, clearly part of the group, pushes in beside him on to the back seat, sandwiching Rooney between them. Thomas says, "This is Nisby, he has been your shadow since we last met." Rooney wonders, while Nisby had been tracking his moves, whether he had tapped his calls.

Nisby leans over and, pointing into Rooney's face, says, "Mind Rooney, you are ours, until after our jobs are done, then it'll be for others to determine your fate." He seems pleased to say these words, upset at having had to follow Rooney for days.

The car speeds down the Byres Road. In his disturbed emotions, Rooney feels an anger he's never felt before; deep set over the thought of death, the lives taken recently, and the lives that'll inevitably be lost in the coming days; including possibly his own. He'd usually succumb to the downs, but not yet; the Rooneyman's on still on the case.

CHAPTER TWENTY-SEVEN

"Big day today. The Summit. You big enough? You bad enough?"

Rooney wakes at my mental telegraph. It's 7.00am. Not that he slept much in the cramped room, only big enough to accommodate a single metal bed and the kit he's been provided with the previous evening. Around the same time, he receives his instructions through the door: "You'll dress as advised and join us downstairs," a voice says.

The stage is set, no going back. This day he'll face some taboos and, hopefully, confront the man he pursues, and end his reign of terror. Rooney goes down the stairs dressed as a photojournalist, armed with a Konica-Minolta, which pampers his passion and delusion. Not that photojournalists have a uniform, but this is chosen to reflect hack attire: a leather jacket and a NEW SOCIALIST PRESS pass with his ID and photo.

Thomas leaves first, wearing more conventional clothes, and with a well-filled holdall. Rooney has no need to establish what it contains. Mick follows shortly after.

In the family of families' camp, from the middle of the stairs, Davy addresses his troops. "You're sodiers of the family and you'll confirm your reputation in Glesca the day," he cries. "Your day has come."

Johnston looks on without saying anything and all there say no more. There's a quiet satisfaction, but also an anxious anticipation. The time has arrived. They have done their jobs. The bombs are set exactly as Johnston specified. This army is now in his hands, and he is just about to confirm it.

"I'm concerned about Thomas," Johnston says, cutting through the aftermath of Davy's rallying call. All there look his way as he grasps their attention, as is his intention.

Like an old bull on the make, Davy roars, "Thomas, he'll be there, Mr Johnston." He slaps his hand on the staircase, which goes off like a shot in the night.

Without a flinch, while retaining a quiet composure, Johnston says,

"Thomas has gone his own way." All there feel the blast of these simple words.

"What the fuck are you saying about my son?" Davy says. "We have no information to suggest this."

"I do Davy," Johnston says. "Thirty pieces of silver, comes to mind."

There's a pause as Davy considers his response. All there anticipate his reaction. He has killed men for less.

Before he does, Johnston comes in with a pre-emptive stab. "Thomas will jeopardise the operation."

"You don't know this," Davy says, moving rapidly down the stairs to face Johnston.

"I do know this and I will deal with it," Johnston says, standing firm.

Johnston feels the spit from Davy's words, "You'll no' harm my son," he says. "You harm him, and you'll have me to deal with."

The army is deathly quiet. They know this is a battle between Davy and Johnston; between Thomas's individual intentions and the families' objectives, and between Johnston's challenge for control and Davy's leadership. But it's clear the families' mission needs to prevail. Johnston will prevail, and he knows it. He knows the family can only back him if they wish their objectives to be met. Without saying anything more, both stare each other out; but where there is not a semblance of a flinch in Johnston's eyes, there's a discernible flick of Davy's eyelids. Then Davy looks around to see if he has support, as if he would ever question this, confirming his defeat.

Johnston, his authority confirmed, says, "Now, we will realise our dreams." Then he leaves, followed briskly by a large proportion of the assembly, and then slowly by Davy. It's clear to all he has acquiesced to Johnston.

It doesn't need to be said, but all there know Johnston is 'the Father."

Rooney is with his team. They'll travel in individual cars. All private taxis, which would normally be salting away the family's monies, but this time transporting its soldiers, presumably, to ensure no individual bomber could blow the lot and himself up, as that would end the mission there and then. To Rooney, this offers some comfort.

Jackie is in the midst of the demonstrators. She has the file on Dissent. She knows the make-up of the core group there, about twenty or so people. She didn't expect the ranks to have swollen to more than a hundred, a success for Dissent. She holds a press statement saying more than five hundred demonstrators have gathered there, some to demonstrate against the Summit, including No More Expansion, some to support Aid for Asylum Seekers, and a variety of disparate groups and individuals tagging on. She also has her intelligence and has a confirmed task there, one of the most difficult and sensitive, even for her.

Her earpiece buzzes. 'Muir' appears on the LCD display of her BlackBerry. "DCI, it's me," comes from the mobile. As usual, Jackie has to listen. "I presume you are engaged in your... operation. I received your dossier regarding your plans for our... safety and feel confident in this, however –" Wait for it, she thinks. "The contact... there is to be a meeting with him and the civic leaders... at 2.00 p.m. today. We are anxious about this, but we have to see him."

"Do you have an identity of this man?" she asks.

"He's been sent by the family," Muir says. "We have information on them. Davy, whom I believe you know, leads them. It may be him, but the contact will reveal himself to us before the meeting. We expect big demands."

"Leave it with me James."

"Jackie, the representative from this group. He will not leave the hotel. Do you understand?"

"I... do."

Jackie ponders the options. This man may try to kill one of the leaders, or to talk and impose demands; most likely the latter. Security will examine every orifice in his body and every lining in his clothes for any possible threat. He will have a gun on him at all times while he is with the leaders. What will he want to talk about? Would it be Johnston, she asks herself. Not his style though; he does his talking through the aggressive actions of others. But this is big and she knows Johnston will be behind the threat this day.

"Jesus, give me strength," Jackie says aloud, prompting some of the demonstrators to turn to her and, as they do, she says, "It's OK, no problem, power to the people." She has alerted her officers to be vigilant and to advise her 'the second IDs are made'. Automatically she unclips the safety catch of her special edition issue. She feels the weight of it holstered against her side, tucked up under her arm, well inside her jacket.

Minutes later, her earpiece buzzes again. "Our targets have arrived. I've transferred their locations to your BlackBerry."

"Thanks, proceed with caution. You know what to do," she replies.

Her officers are briefed to 'remove the targets, involving minimal civilian casualties'. They'll do what they have to.

Rooney arrives with the others from the group. They move into Gordon Street, which is mobbed by demonstrators. Although the area adjacent to the hotel is cordoned off, their IDs get them through with no trouble. They don't talk. They have individual missions and split up there; they will now fail or succeed on their own. He's elated at this adventure and buzzing with energy, but he's to use all he has to see this through. He has a bit of a profile after all and he's about to try to get into one of the most secure places on the planet. As it happens though, when he gets there, he is searched and moves through security and into the hotel with relative ease. He finds a seat in reception, as advised. Now he has to wait.

Thomas also moves easily within the demonstrators. His moment will arrive soon. He'll put the bag down in the midst of the crowd and walk on. And, before the bag is picked up by security, and removed for the bomb disposal people, he'll punch a SIM number into his mobile phone to trigger the bomb in the bag. By that time, he'll be well away from the scene and safe. His thoughts are on building his own family and with it his father's increased respect for him. Davy will forgive his transgression. Thirty years earlier he would have done similar. Thomas's actions will confirm his reputation.

Jackie is now moving in parallel with Thomas. She has three officers also flanking him. Quiet words arrive through their earpieces: "Await my instructions."

One of the three, John Spowart, a crack SAS counter intelligence officer, is well trained in this contemporary type of combat, where surprise and timing are everything. Briefed on Thomas, the team knows his mobile phone will trigger the bomb in the bag. Preventing him from detonating the device will require determined action, getting him to bring his hands out into the open, and then disabling him before he can trigger the device.

Intelligence has been busy. They have information on Thomas. His Achilles heel is children. He loves children. A small boy approaches him. Thomas notices him as he approaches with an out stretched hand offered to him. "Power to the people mister?" Suddenly, the boy stumbles in front of him. Thomas is caught between two instincts: one, to set off the bomb there and then and be done with it; or two, pick up the boy, who is now crying profusely and appears to be in pain. Thomas decides on the latter, with the former following up very quickly after. Spowart calculates perfectly. Thomas takes his hands from his pockets and picks up the boy, to notice there's something strange about this child's face. This's not the face of a child, more of a very young-looking dwarf-like man. He instantly drops the figure; but as he does, his arms are grabbed by two sets of powerful hands. He thrashes wildly for around five seconds, until the small calibre bullet from Spowart's covert weapon neatly enters his brain, accurately and silently, through his left ear. So quick is the action that no one has any inclination it's anything more than an arrest and the use of a police Taser. Some protest loudly, calling out 'police brutality' as Thomas is dragged away.

Thomas's naivety led to his failure. The bomb, which would have created the massive commotion and the opportunity for the others to detonate theirs, is disarmed immediately. His body and the bag are placed on tables side by side in the 'Special Forces body repository', in a local warehouse, commandeered for the purpose, and policed by armed officers.

Mick and Nisby are apprehended as they hold up their passes respectively to apparently shortsighted security men, who ask, "Bring it a bit closer pal." As their arms are outstretched, they are grasped, hand cuffed, and taken into custody. They are not the most proficient of the bombing fraternity and the SAS and Strathclyde Police have been planning this for days. Mick fights well, until a baton drops him to the ground.

Johnston is inside. He has used this disguise once before while infiltrating an IRA cell. He enjoys dressing as an elderly priest and likes the respect he's given. The catholic guests of the hotel had requested mass and Father Doyle had been dispatched from the local diocese of Anderston. His body is to be found later with a Latin note saying he has been sent to a better place. Father Doyle had no concerns about stopping his car to give a stranger on the road a lift.

Rooney knows that no bomb means Thomas has been taken out. He'll resort to the original plan determined by the larger family group. He'll deliver the Three Point Plan and their terms. Johnston'll be unconcerned about Thomas. He interfered with the plans, and he had to go. Johnston had been given the information that secured this. He'll toy with the irony of his preventing a hit rather than causing one, and of assisting the local forces rather than defying them, but it amounts to the same thing: *he's* been in control.

Rooney loiters in the reception area. He has attended two press conferences and inveigled himself into a bunch of official journalists. This pleases him, but it's meaningless at this stage. He keeps a well-honed ear for anything that resembles Johnston's voice, until he hears Jackie at the reception desk. He sees her and wonders whether he should approach her.

"Do not trust anyone."

He decides not to take any chances at this stage.

Then, someone pushes into him and puts something in Rooney's pocket. He reaches in and pulls out a small card. It's headed '*In Nomine Patris*'. "Feel-my-freckin'-frock," he utters, as his eyes run along the Latin words and a number of bullet points, as gold meteors dazzle his already star filled head. The card is signed 'The Father'.

CHAPTER TWENTY-EIGHT

Jackie has set up the room to brief the leaders on security. Muir chairs the briefing and assures them he will ensure their safety. He advises them if the representative so much as flutters an eyelash, 'his people' will put 'two between his eyes'. Jackie proffers a view that Johnston's behind this, and he'll seek notoriety that will underline his great authority among the leaders. She has information to suggest he's in the hotel and is a serious threat, but she's confident he's there to manipulate, rather than attempt any action that will lead to his immediate death. She's more concerned about his bigger plans. She'd have preferred to have discussed this with Rooney and get his opinion on Johnston's intent, but he's incommunicado, although she knows he's nearby. She's confident Rooney'll do what's necessary, what's expected of him.

"So she thinks."

It is getting close to the time, and having confirmed security arrangements, Jackie takes a coffee break in the Champagne Lounge. She values these few minutes to relax, to think, prepare. Then, an old priest decides to share her table, shattering her peace. He apologises and politely asks if she would mind if he sits there. She nearly says she does, but gestures him to sit. As he does, she pulls out a newspaper to set up a screen between them.

Johnston enjoys this moment of playfulness. He nearly talks to her from behind the paper, but this may push things too far, and he does not wish to jeopardise his plans. Another intruder takes the third seat at the small table. Johnston recognises Rooney's disguise, while he doesn't his.

"Do you mind if I sit here?" Rooney says, sitting down. Jackie's had enough. "For god's sake, where can I get some privacy around here," she says, putting the newspaper down to see Rooney sitting across from her.

"Rooney!"

"Nice to see you."

"Aye, nice to see you too hon."

They exchange greetings as they sit next to the man who locks them in common purpose, and common pursuit.

"Sorry, I am intruding," the old priest says.

"No please father," Jackie says, showing respect for the cloth.

"You always had good manners," Rooney says.

"No dear," the old priest says, getting to his feet. "I must take my leave and attend to my... heavenly duties, but, thank you for your kindneth." Johnston is pushing his luck, but this cameo gives him much pleasure. Then, as the old crotchety clergyman moves away, he says, "Bless you my child?" Before she can respond, he says: "*In nomine patris et filii et ...*"

Rooney hears the Latin. He sees the vestments in his mind. And the inside of his head turns into a firestorm of gold lightning bolts.

"Jackie, *in nomine-fuckin-patris...* the Father."

"Cool it hon, he's a priest, that's what they say."

Rooney turns and the old priest is gone.

Jackie pulls Rooney to her. "Where the fuck you been?"

"Good to see you too," he says, his voice shaking, at the same trying to see where the old priest is going.

"We have information, about a major threat. There'll be a meeting. Have you received the information on him?"

"Not yet."

"Lying?"

"You will inform me when you do, immediately. Got that?"

"Indeed, my dear," he says, lying again, as he heads out of the lounge.

The meeting is set and the time approaches. Two corridors separate the leaders from the entrance to the meeting room suite. Jackie stands at the inner door waiting the family's representative. She's pacing the floor. It's now two p.m. and she's nervous. The leaders will react badly if this is a hoax, but Muir's convinced it'll not be. She talks into her mobile, "Any movement out there?" As she does, she notices Rooney being escorted towards her; his arms held at both sides by two of her agents.

"This is Mr MacDonald, he says he has an appointment with the leaders," one officer says.

"Rooney, you, *the* representative," she says.

"I am *he*, and I am *the*."

"Why didn't you fucking-well tell me," she whispers into his ear, incredulity in her voice.

"I *am* undercover," he says, quietly.

"He is under a delusion."

"How can I be sure?" she asks aloud. "Our intelligence suggested a family contact." She has to confirm he is indeed the family's man.

"It is arranged for two p.m.," Rooney says, confirming his knowledge.

"Aye, suppose it is. Please come this way Mr... MacDonald. You fucking didn't tell me?" she says taking his arm, as one of the agents takes his camera.

Rooney says nothing, though he loves the bizarreness of it. Jackie escorts him into the inner corridor, where he's searched carefully, and from there into the Grandroom, which is aptly named.

"This is the representative... Mr MacDonald," she says to the congregation.

Muir is flabbergasted. "We expected... You... Rooney. Is this some kind of a joke?"

"I am not the man you expected, but I am their voice," Rooney says, thinking 'this bastard will give me the respect I deserve.'

"True respect is gained!"

This's a fascinating situation. The most powerful leaders in the country are there. First Minister Campbell is next to Muir, at the middle of the table. There's a lot of shuffling and murmuring. Respective security agents are talking into collar mikes at their back. And here is Rooney, the 'shrink wi' a drink' from Partick; and he's loving it.

The leaders confer with each other. They agree both on Muir as their spokesperson and Rooney as the families' representative.

Muir starts: "We have made considerable efforts to comply with the... request from the family of families to be here and to meet with you, their *envoy*," he says, choking on the word as he turns to Rooney. "So please cut to the chase and tell us what they want to say to us," he says.

"Right, it is this," Rooney says. "The families know of your plan to subjugate the city, increasing the numbers of incomers, which will threaten their power base." He uses his presentational voice, albeit a bit shaky – last used to address a room full of social work students – a lot easier this time applying it to politicians.

There's a distinct intake of breath and anxious fidgeting around the table.

"Is that it?" Muir says. "Is there more?" He senses a disgruntled disquiet around him.

Rooney resumes. "They know of the pretext within which your plans are based." He pauses to gain effect. "Here are their demands," he says, as he holds up the card. "One, stop all migration policy. Two, stop all economic and political aid to the incomers. Three, stop all interference in local affairs. That's it." Fifty million quid would have been much more acceptable.

There's silence throughout the room.

"They have untraceable bombs throughout the city," he adds.

All remain quiet, but he feels they are becoming steadily more uncomfortable.

"Do you wish me to continue?"

Muir gets on his feet. "Of course," he says.

Got the bastard where I want him, Rooney muses.

"No' me Rooney."

"The families are united in this."

The stunned silence continues.

"I have to inform you that the first explosion is set for two thirty p.m.," Rooney says. "I don't have the location, and the other bombs are set to go off simultaneously one hour later at three-thirty."

Most of the leaders are getting to their feet, shuffling around, whispering.

"Gentlemen, please sit." Muir says. "We have no intelligence to confirm the truth of this," He's trying to calm them, to stay in control.

"They expect a media statement from here at three-fifteen," Rooney says. "Then they'll expect a dialogue with them over the removal of the incomers and the consolidation of their cabal. If this statement is made they will desist with the bombing. Unless you renege, of course."

There's major commotion in the room with many anxious but determined comments ringing in Rooney's ears. "This is impossible – it can't be done. No one'll dominate us – we'll deal with this threat. No gang is above the law."

"We must not exaggerate this," Muir says, panning the room for support.

Rooney feels a sense of relief; but more, he enjoys the feeling of power now that the words are out. He is omnipotent. He has completed the task. He reiterates the three demands on the card, and the effect is complete mayhem. Yes!

"Please we need order here," Muir says. "There's no evidence to support this."

They listen to Muir, but they look to Campbell

"We must remain calm. This may be a hoax," Campbell says, speaking with a quiet authority. He leans over towards Rooney. "Mr MacDonald."

"Rooney, First Minister. MacDonald is a name I used to infiltrate them... the group," he says. This's getting better.

"Flying high, Rooney."

"Rooney," he repeats, putting his hand on Rooney's shoulder. He escorts Rooney over to a marble pillar where the both rest their shoulders to talk face to face.

"Mind the last time you were close to a marble pillar Rooney?"

Muir sits down, realising his diminishing authority.

"Rooney, we have heard of you and your... efforts to locate, or more like understand, the man central to all of this," Campbell says.

"Indeed I have sir."

"You know this man well?"

"I suppose, but not entirely. There are things no person will ever know about him."

"Mr Rooney, I want your... opinion."

"My opinion?" This is music to his grandiose ears.

"The demands, the bombs. How real are these threats?"

Enjoying the drama, Rooney is slow to reply. "Well, I can say this, the man… Can we refer to him as the Father? His name is Arthur Johnston, but he has… adopted the name."

"Indeed," Campbell says. "The… Father."

"The… Father has a reputation for action, but you never know what he'll do next. He always has a number of options."

"Who is in control here, the families or… the Father?"

"He is, of that I am sure."

"Shall, or will, the families act independently of him?"

This is a wise man. "Who knows?"

"I think you do, Mr Rooney, but I'll not press you on it." Campbell rests his back on the pillar as he takes in the ornate ceiling.

"What's the risk?" Muir says, pushing into the discussion.

"Given the magnitude of the devices, it may be hundreds," Rooney says. *"Feeling the power?"*

"Sir, it is two-twenty." Robin Clark, Muir's PA, says, interrupting the discussion, loud enough for all to hear.

"We have ten minutes," Campbell says, taking Rooney by the arm and leading him back to the table.

"If we believe what *he* says." Muir scowls at Rooney.

"Trusting no one?"

Once again, Campbell turns to Rooney. "How do we stop this thing?"

"You can't. Not the first one, it seems," Rooney replies, taking an apple from the crystal fruit bowl that sits in the centre of the table.

"Oh we can't?" Muir says. "What if we offer something?"

"The first one, I think, is to show they mean business," Rooney says, munching the apple, thinking '*he* loves killing as much as you love power'.

"Loving this?"

By then Muir is standing over him, agitated. "You think, you think. Thinking is no bloody good here."

"Basil Fawlty mode?"

"Perhaps sir, I have overstayed my welcome." Rooney decides it's time to get out of there.

"Right you are, go," Muir says. "We have talking to do. Jackie!"

Jackie nods to Muir, as if on cue.

"It's a bluff," Rooney hears Muir say, as he leaves the room.

"Bluff? Well, we'll soon see," Rooney murmurs, as Jackie escorts him out to the lobby area.

"So much for you taking Johnston out," Jackie says, directly into his ear.

"Well you know him, he's a slippery character."

"Where is he?"

"He's here."

"Aye, of course he is hon."

There's a pause. It becomes clear she has received a call on her earpiece, to which she replies, "Yes, I'll meet you. Yes, alone," she says to the caller. Rooney has a feeling this is one request she cannot refuse.

"You stay right there," she orders Rooney, as she pushes through the door into the hall. "Watch him," she says, instructing one of the agents at the door.

The agent towers over him, his anxious breath puffing down on him. Rooney wonders what to do next. "Don't even think of it," the agent says.

"Don't worry, my friend. I know my limitations."

"The Rooneyman has no limitations."

"Good," the agent says.

Chaos reigns. People, police – plain clothes and uniformed – are running in every direction. "Code black, code black," screams out of the agent's earpiece.

This is maximum security, only employed in situations of great risk, mainly to politicians. There is an obvious crisis emanating from within the Grandroom. PAs, officials, press secretaries, security, are everywhere; highly exercised, firing instructions into walkie-talkies, mobile phones, emails on handhelds.

A warning goes out across television, internet, and radio stations. The radio behind the reception desk blares out a statement. "This is a Scottish Government announcement. We have information of great importance for the people of West Central Scotland. It is this. Stay indoors. Do not, repeat, do not use public transport. There'll be a statement from the First Minister at three p.m."

All there hold their collective breath. All concentrate on respective clocks, watches, television screens. Two thirty comes and goes. Rooney is taken back in.

Muir is jubilant. "The threat is over," he says, addressing the leaders. "There was never any threat. Their intention is to disrupt our plans. We must now proceed as we said we would." Many there indicate approval.

Campbell is less convinced, saying, "We must be cautious. I believe there's more to this. We must maintain maximum security. We must be vigilant."

"OK, we should await the other deadline at three-thirty," Muir says, acquiescing. "If there are no incidents perhaps then we can relax."

Muir nods to a police officer and Rooney is unceremoniously escorted out again. He's taken into a room just off the reception area and he's there for what feels like an eternity, but in realty could have only been an hour or so. There's pandemonium in the reception area. He can hear the press clamouring for a press release. A group of paparazzi tries to force its way into the room, hearing that a 'hack has been in the Grandroom and he's in that room'. Rooney sees his chance. "I've been in there. I've spoken to them," Rooney calls out loudly. They push in through the door towards him. The officer moves to stop them, giving Rooney one opportunity. The officer turns back to Rooney and he's gone; he's unconcerned, he'll let him go – more important things are happening that day than losing Rooney.

Rooney sidles off and approaches the reception desk where he asks for a package addressed 'John MacDonald'. The desk clerk produces it after Rooney reveals his ID. "It's been security checked," the man says. Has he been paid off, Rooney wonders. Rooney puts the square container inside his jacket gingerly, and then the man says there's also a sealed envelope there for a 'Mr MacDonald'. Rooney asks for directions to the nearest toilet and, once inside the cubicle, he retrieves the gun. It feels light, but it'll do the job he hopes. Right, armed, let's find Johnston. He sticks the gun in his inside pocket, holding it with his arm against his chest. Remembering the envelope, he opens it to find another card. This time, though, all it contains is a room name: King James Suite, in wide Latin font.

"*Jacobus Rex?*"

"I know bastard."

Rooney doesn't intend staying around the reception area long enough to be escorted back in there. But as he walks along the hall, he wonders how Johnston will be at that time. Will he be revelling in the energy there? This meeting, his payback for delivering the message, might be his only chance to stop the man. He looks aimlessly around. "Where the hell is the King James Suite?" As he stands there, a female voice and a well-recognised perfume appear from behind him.

"You need to go to the King James Suite. I'll take you there," she says, this Jean Dempsie.

"You were supposed to have been killed by Thomas's mob," Rooney says.

"Let's say I kept my head down until the three musketeers were taken." She escorts him up the stairs and along the corridor of the first floor. "Though, in my business, death is always a risk. It comes with the job."

"The job?"

"Yes, the job, Rooney."

"You've been part of this all along, the Muir fiasco. You're with Jackie."

"Not quite. I facilitate things."

"Facilitate things!"

"You're here," she says, pointing to the King James Suite. "Now do what is expected of you."

"She *facilitates* things," he says, as he turns to the door, then turns back to question her further, but she's gone.

Hesitating, he listens at the door. He can hear nothing. Will there be a hit team in there waiting to take him out?

"Trust no one."

He could head back down the stairs, out of the hotel. But no, the Rooneyman needs to deliver his mission. He knocks at the door. There's no answer. He tries the door and finds it open. Warily, he enters the room.

The room is dark. He reaches to the left of the doorway on the wall to find a light switch. It's inoperable.

"I'm over here." A soft voice comes from the far corner of the room. This is Johnston's voice. "We meet again."

Rooney takes the gun out and grips it purposely in his right hand. "So it seems, Father Doyle," he says.

"Ah ha, you heard my whisper. You have keen hearing Rooney. Why are you here?"

"I'm here to... stop this."

"I don't stop Rooney."

It's clear this man has no intention of stopping with Muir, the leaders, the city. Rooney removes the gun from inside his jacket.

"You're going in, and I am going to see you off to your permanent placement in the big hoose."

"I'll have power wherever I go. Jackie's death will please me greatly," Johnston says.

This exercises Rooney. A waterfall of gold cascades through his mind, as his index finger squeezes the trigger. He lets off three shots at Johnston. Almost instantly, he says, "Oh my fuck, what have I done?"

Rooney moves through the gloom towards the corner, to the figure of Johnston. The potential this is not Johnston becomes clear the nearer he gets to the figure. Two immediate realisations come to his mind. One, this is Jackie in the chair before him, her mouth gagged; and two, it is Johnston's voice which emanates from a speaker-camera gadget placed at Jackie's throat. He removes the gag from her mouth.

"Very fuckin' good, Rooney," she says.

He expects the worst, but she's uninjured. He releases her arms, and she takes his hand and runs it over her breasts and stomach. He isn't prepared for this, but he makes out bright green paint.

Jackie takes the gun from him. "A paint ball pistol, what a fucking idiot you are."

"Wyatt Earp."

A voice comes from the speaker again. Jackie grasps it. "Rooney, this time you have paint on your hands, not blood. You can kill, now we both know this. It's good to know you would kill me. This will occur sometime soon. On my terms, however, when I am ready. Now you will leave here.

Police detectives have been informed that a colleague has been shot in the King James Suite. You must leave here now."

Should he stay, he wonders. To explain this was not his fault. Jackie will defend him. Will she? He'll get the fuck out of there. Jackie looks on blankly as he leaves.

CHAPTER TWENTY-NINE

Jean Dempsie is outside as he exits the room. "This way, you've to come with me," she says, escorting him down through a staff exit into the underground car park, where they get into a car.

"Right, what's going on?"

"No questions, please," Jean says. "I need to get you out of here. You did what you had to do."

"I've shot Jackie."

"What!"

"I shot Jackie."

"You shot Johnston, Rooney, Johnston. We... I helped... the gun."

"It was paint ball gun and it was Jackie – not Johnston."

"A paint ball..."

"*You fucked up.*"

"I did what was expected of me."

"*Correct, you fucked up.*"

Rooney begins to sob. This is not an expected response. The shock, the trauma, his mood cycling downwards; the abject shame over being used; being made to look a fool in front of Jackie, Johnston, *and* Jean Dempsie?

Jean shakes her head. "I'll get you out of here."

She drives them through the security gate, and out onto Midland Street, this Jean Dempsie woman, who is always around.

Safely outside in the streets of Glasgow, Jean pulls over into a parking space. "Time to bring you up to speed."

"So you know what happened in there?"

"Yes."

"The families?"

"We have an informant."

"Who?"

"Nisby."

"Nisby?"

"He's an agent."

"He was my shadow."

"He was my plant, and the source of our information on the family. He's back with them."

This is a pragmatic woman, and not the woman he thought her to be.

She describes her links with the family groups; and, as she does, she's becomes all officious again. She's back in agent mode.

Jean says, "The family were anxious about the prearranged deadlines which had passed. They wondered if this meant Johnston had made a deal with the leaders. Johnston had insisted they await his instructions before any action was taken. Davy knows about his son, Thomas."

"I mind him," Rooney says, holding up his bandaged hand.

"Never mind Rooney, you have another nine with tips."

"Thanks."

"Relax, you'll get your disability benefit."

"Anyway, Thomas."

"Dead or detained?"

"A bit of both."

"Eh?"

"Shot in the head, unconscious, detained in the Southern General."

"Fuck."

Nisby said Davy's in terrible distress, but he was comforted with the belief he had been brave – a proper street player."

"Indeed, where he was hoping to fuck off with multimillions in the bank. What happened inside?"

"Muir and the others were in considerable debate," she says. "They passed the worrying deadlines. In particular, the three-thirty one and no major incidents were reported.

"Jesus, that's a relief."

They felt confident that Muir, as convener and host, had protected them. The members agreed with Muir this had been an elaborate hoax and they had beaten Johnston by not responding to his threats. They hadn't been his lackeys."

"And that was that?"

"No, the sense of security was short lived, as was Muir's credibility. A television screen had been set up in the Grandroom. Campbell's PA was first to notice something. 'Look,' she said. 'The bomb locations in the city are revealed.' The councillors watched intently as locations in each of their constituencies were given. Chaos followed as they fired orders to their heads of security, police, etcetera."

"How do you know all this?"

"We were watching from a screen in our control room."

"Covert cameras in the Summit, what would the papers pay for that?"

"We needed to... we'd to monitor things in there. It was expected."

"Jackie would have expected it."

"There were bigger forces at play Rooney, than... Jackie."

"What happened in there?" he asks the woman who knows everything.

"Well, three-thirty arrived and there were no reports of explosions."

"Thank fuck."

"Then Muir said, 'This confirms that the objective of this is to manipulate us, control us; now we must prevail.' His voice was shaking, but he was demanding attention. He added, 'We will inform the families we will not negotiate with... jumped-up street neds.'"

"Wait until that gets back to Davy," Rooney says.

"Then fresh information came in," Jean says. "The bombs had been disarmed, but they had been real enough."

"I know that."

"Their size and technical sophistication astounded hardened explosive experts and they had been placed in some highly sensitive areas, such as the Chambers, the Burrell Collection, the Scotstoun Sports Centre. These bombs were calculated to kill hundreds of people."

"The reality of the threats had hit home."

"If this was a hoax, it was a very elaborate hoax," she says. "They knew then they were dealing with some very serious people."

"Well, you know they are."

"We know that Rooney."

"What about Muir, what was he doing?"

"He was trying to retrieve his position," she says. "He admitted they had managed to breach security systems and place the bombs. But they did not detonate, he said. This was an important point. By not giving into the family demands, they had forced their hand. They had surrendered their arms in a very public and exposed way. He said they, the leaders, had confirmed the family network's vulnerability and the weakness of the criminal underworld. 'We have triumphed, so we will now progress *our* plans,' he said."

"Ever the statesman."

"Well, we know different. The leaders, though, were looking towards Campbell. 'That is not how I see it,' Campbell said. 'The family has shown it can reach deep within our walls, expose our vulnerabilities.' He said that Johnston had shown his power, he had galvanised the groups into something very potent, and they were putty in his hands. He said the leaders took a great risk in not reacting to the family's demands. He suggested that may have been Johnston's intent."

"To show his power, his control?"

"Right. Campbell took a long breath, then said, 'In not doing anything Johnston has shown he can.' Then he said, 'I am no longer confident in the stewardship here today.' To which there was a call to remove the Lord Provost from the chair."

"Muir was out?"

"Like a man about to die, Muir's political career passed before him," she said. "The loss of the chair would lead to his downfall. There can be nothing worse than this loss of face."

"Even in taking no action, Johnston has won. This'll finish Muir."

"Morte, In nomine Patris…"

"But you know Muir," she says. "He asked to be allowed to withdraw from this in a dignified way, which would allow him and his party some respect. They were the hosts after all."

"Tricks will out."

"There was silence for some minutes, while they waited Campbell's thoughts."

"Christ, can't stand the suspense."

"Campbell rose and his words cut right through the jangled nerves there. 'We will concentrate the business of the Summit on positive results,' he said. 'We will leave here with accolade. We will confirm for posterity this was indeed a momentous and monumental meeting. Our agenda for aid to the run-down inner cities must show tangible progress. Our plans for homeland migration will be replaced by an agenda of political and social development, embracing legitimate family business, and – ' They all held a collective breath. ' – we will progress real and actual plans for Glasgow to have its own migration aid, policy and control, with substantial development money from the Scottish Government. Special case status.'"

"Wow!"

"Though some, the less significant council leaders and the like, were not fully behind the plans, but felt obliged to comply for… economic reasons."

"Understandably."

"But all there knew Campbell exerted a statesmanlike lead and Muir appeared the defeated man. All his hopes had dissolved before his eyes. He looked lost, but he spoke again to try, at least, to get a secondary position to Campbell, though his words didn't carry much conviction. 'I need an exit plan,' he said. 'I need to preserve my integrity here…. Glasgow needs to be able to hold its own in this.'"

"The man'll use anything, even his city."

"Apparently. Then Campbell replied, 'I have no problem with Glasgow and yourself,' referring to Muir, 'being seen as the honest broker in this momentous breakthrough'. There were nods of agreement. Muir was pleased – "

"But this wouldn't have changed anything. His influence there and within the city is over. Johnston's defeated him."

"A press conference was arranged and a public statement made. There's a sense of relief all round."

"The family would've been pleased Johnston delivered, but perhaps not all he promised."

"They believe their actions have secured a major result, which has preserved their dignity within the criminal underworld."

"Everyone got what they wanted. All except Jackie, that is."

"Well, we... wanted Johnston... but the next time."

"You, we..."

"Next time, it *needs* to happen, Rooney."

"If you, we, ever find him?"

"Where do you think he is now?"

"Well, who knows where he was when he talked through the speaker receiver on Jackie."

"I imagine Jackie's technical team will be working on the receiver, trying to establish where the transmitter was. But not being technical myself I can only imagine this was from a mobile phone somewhere or a Skype call."

"Skype call?"

"Keep up Luddite."

"Through the internet," she says. "Do you think he's still in the hotel?"

"I doubt it," Rooney says. "He'd have dumped the Father Doyle alias. It would have identified him. Dyeing his hair, eyebrows, beard, donning the appropriate uniform, he would have been in another role. A hotel porter, security man, delivery driver – whoever. One thing, he would have had no problem getting out of there."

"Are you glad to be out Rooney?"

"Out of what?"

"The hotel."

"I'm happy to be *out* proper."

"Sorry, Rooney, you're not 'out'."

CHAPTER THIRTY

Rooney gets out of the car and onto Midland Street, within striking distance of the Waysiders Club, well used to providing a shower and soup and sandwiches for down-and-outs. That'll do him.

"Get cleaned up tramp."

"I'm not talking to you," Rooney says. "I'm tired and hungry."

He has a shower, shave, something to eat and a mug of tea. Then he heads off to Clyde Street Hostel for homeless men. All 'no questions asked', and his anonymity preserved. He gets a change of clothes from the Salvation Army clothes bank. He selects a suit from a long line of them. It's over big for him, but it'll do. He's given a shirt and fresh underwear. He has a think these might have been donated by the widow of an old insurance man, but he's grateful for them.

Rooney spends the next two days physically and mentally trying to recover from the experience, and has just about decided to give himself up to London Road police station, to get out of the 'whole-sordid-fucking-business', perhaps to disappear and start again somewhere else, perhaps as a proper analyst and to change his miserable life.

His recent bravado has given way to shame and despair. His mind drifts back to Irena on the hill. Her words echo in his mind: '*In nomine Patris*... I was scared... really scared.' She was so like his mother: quiet, solid, sincere; was, until this monster decided to end her life. Since he found Irena on the hill, he's acquired a Glasgow smile, raped a woman, joined a crime family, and conspired in the biggest gangland act in Scottish history.

He needs to be in Clyde St, his sanctuary. This is what's described as a 'wet hoose' where you can drink and keep your room. He needs this, to immerse himself in a drink culture, to be a proper drinker for a while until he sorts out his head after the Grand Central. In a shitty wee room, he has a bed, a wardrobe and a sink. And he has two bottles of Famous Grouse, procured from Haddows. He gets pissed.

"As you do."

"As I do."

After the first bottle, the words came back. 'Irena... scared... shot Jackie... paint on your hands, not blood... you can kill... you would kill me... when I am ready.'

"As you do."

He has swirling colours of reds, greens and golds, like dyes in white paint spinning around at speed.

"Hold on for the ride!"

He hears his mother's words, "Don't be scared son."

Then Father Healey's, "You'll do as I say."

"As you do."

"I wasn't a bad boy."

"No?"

"I had to... do it."

"Your father condoned it, so it was fine."

"So, it was fine."

"You have to face him, your father."

"Please don't."

"He's in the nursing home. He dominates the staff. As he dominated your mother."

"He's eighty-three and, although he can barely walk, he's lost none of his power."

"You hate him. He abused your mother. You hate him. She killed herself. You hate him. He made you hate yourself. You hate yourself. You didn't protect her or yourself; or tell him you hated him. Hate, fear and domination is your life."

"Please don't."

He's coming down, and drinks through each night. His 'medication' is working. He listens to one commotion after another in the street and in the hall outside. Police walkie-talkies, staff shouting at residents, residents swearing at each other, occasional bottles and glasses being broken, and vitriol, anger and aggression – always aggression.

The word 'father' is constantly in his mind and gold and reds rage in there and in his heart. He seeks out sleazy and grotty places, pubs he would never have gone to before, not that he was ever that fussy. This room with its cheap kitchen units and cardboard wardrobes hanging off the wall, trims missing, its threadbare carpet, its mattress filthy and stained with urine, shite, semen, sweat – which is OK, because he adds his. Filthy and ripped net curtains fail to keep out the light from the streetlights and or from the daylight when he wants complete dark. The noise of men wanking, farting, shitting and pissing comes from the toilet next to his room, as if it's all in his room. He catches the crabs from the bedclothes and has to go to the chemist for Permethrin cream. All of this is conducive to his self-abuse, his self-destruction by drink. He loathes himself, and drink takes him to places he doesn't want to go, but can't stay away from... his mind.

By this time, he doesn't care what he is drinking. He buys six bottles of Buckfast Tonic Wine. He hears it contains caffeine, and 'it's a tonic wine'. He can do with some of that, and it's cheap, which means he can have more of it. Many of his clients drank the stuff, many of the residents in the home live on the stuff. It's cheap and at 15% ABV it's strong. It's known as 'Wreck the Hoose Juice', 'Commotion Lotion', or more commonly known as 'Buckie'. He takes the bottles home concealed in a Peckham's bag.

"No point in damaging your reputation!"

The first bottle hits the mark quickly, by the second he's ranting as the figure of his father appears before him. "Fight me now you blithering-bastard. I'm big now, strong; I can take you, you bastard. Don't let him get too close to grab me. He is strong, the bastard. He'll grab me like a vice and bring me down, bite me, strangle me. I'll stay at arm's length, punch him square on his face, burst his nose, make him bleed, kick his fucking legs away, jump on him, not on his head; not to kill him, but to hurt the bastard; like he hurt me, like he hurt ma mammy – come ahead you bastard."

When drunk, he thinks about him, his father; leading to sobbing, screaming and destroying furniture. When sober, he thinks about Johnston, his control, his need to combat him; his hatred of him, his respect of him, his fear of him, his need to hurt him; his need to understand him. When drunk, he thinks about Jackie, and whether he loves her and can't tell her. She is good to him, but she isn't good for him – she can't give him what he wants. When sober, he thinks about her too, but in a different way. He wants her, but she's too good for him. This is the kind of duality he recognises in his patients.

One night, down on his strength and self-esteem, he reaches rock bottom. Sitting in his barren room, at a laminate top table, he pours a large glass of Buckie. He sucks it through his teeth; and, with the room light creating a reflection on the bottle, he sees the man he has become: a drunk man looking at his reflection though a bottle.

"What do I see? What am I? A mental illness. An alcohol abuse. A destroyed self," he says to the bottle. "What has doing good ever done for me?"

"Nothing."

"What has being a good man, given me? I always did the right thing; 'do the right thing', my father would say, kowtowing to the Roman Catholic establishment, to protect the priest, to respect the priests. What has doing good for others, having feelings, given me? I tried to do the right thing, go along with Jackie, for Johnston, over the Muir outing fiasco. What did it give me, exploitation, getting used. What a pathetic fool I am."

"Indeed."

"What did my doing the right thing by 'going underground' give me? What did my attempts at stopping Johnston in the Central Hotel give me? More abuse, exploitation, and more getting used. My life has been about being used, about doing the 'right thing'. I have lost my sanity, my self-respect, my inner-self, my outer-self. And what about those who have no feelings, what do they get?"

"Success, power, respect, self-respect."

"Me?"

"Failure, disempowerment, disrespect, self-hatred."

"Correct bastard, correct."

He drinks that bottle, he drinks the next, and then he drinks the last. In each bottle, he sees a reflection of the transformation of him to that of his father. Then he reaches for a 500 mg tub of Paracetamol tablets and eats the lot, just as his mother had done three years before.

He drifts off and soon he is unconscious. He has reached that happy place between life and death. He feels no pain, either in his heart, soul, head or body. He isn't going back to that other place; he's going to a better place, as they say. And, just as he is about to take that last step, he hears a voice: "Sean, son, it's me, it's your mammy." He sees his mother approaching him. She isn't old, like he'd last seen her before she died. She's young, strong, vibrant. "Don't do it son, don't go there. There'll be a time for you, but it's not now. Now is not your time." Although the words seem to be coming from her, it's his voice. "Don't let him do this to you, like he did to me. You can live or die in your mind or you can die or live in your life."

This is an ultimatum from himself, from her, from his inner self, in the shape of the person he loved most in his life, who would have understood his pain; she had gone through it herself. She had killed herself at the hands of an abuser. He is about to kill himself at his own hands; a self-abuser who is, was, being abused – his only way out.

"Rooney, Rooney," he hears, like a faraway cry, getting closer, closer. It's Ben. He's tracked him to the hostel to find him in a heap, closer to death than to life. This time, though, it's his own words he hears. "Don't let him do this to you, like he did to me. You can die or live in your mind or you can live or die in your life," he slurs, as he regains some consciousness.

"Aye sure, Rooney," Ben says, getting him into his bed; then alerting the hostel staff of his condition. "Get an ambulance, quick."

He's whizzed off to the Glasgow Royal Infirmary where his stomach is pumped, vitamin B poured into him, and where he spends the next ten days until it's established the Paracetamol hasn't damaged his liver, nor the booze damaged his brain.

On discharge, he goes home with home help support, a community psychiatric nurse, and a support worker from the local mental health project, all of whom get the heave-ho shortly after. Of course, there's the inevitable message waiting for him on his answering machine. But, this time, this's Davy's voice: "This is for Thomas," he says, and leaves an address, no more. He tries to return the call using 1471, but it's a withheld number.

Next day, he travels to Pitt Street. He has to.

"The Sunday Mail to interview the head polis involved in the Grand Central stuff," he says to the desk officer, who clicks an internal phone link and asks the question, "Do you want to talk to a newspaper reporter called Rooney?" He's in, but not before the officer says "go easy on her, or you are *out*."

"Took your time hon." Jackie voice comes from behind her desk, her head in a pile of papers. Where's Joycy, no coffee?

"I was... ill."

"But now I'm well."

"If you are here to give your apology, you would do well to get on with it," she says, lifting her head to face him. "Better sit down, may take time."

"Not worried I may shoot you?"

"Hon, if I was really worried about you, you would be in jail."

Rooney leans over the desk. "I was bloody well used..."

"You were assisted..."

"You have your informants Jackie."

"The woman who knows everything."

"Sit down. I know you've been in hospital. Don't worry, I don't like to see a man crawl. I guess you're coming down Rooney. You're more... reality based?"

"Reality has struck home, Jackie, that is sure." He drops his full weight onto the seat. "I was used by Johnston, and you were in no danger. He didn't intend you to die. I was used by you in the Mark Casey fiasco."

"Human toilet paper."

"Get a grip, Rooney, we've all been used, we are all used... It's just some of us are used more than others." She brings her legs up and onto the edge of her desk.

"Fuck or be fucked Jackie, is that what it is all about?"

"Sometimes it's necessary Rooney."

"You know what happened?"

"I do. Do you think you would be standing there if I didn't?"

"I thought it was him. You, I mean. You were him and he was you. I couldn't see it was you." Joycy arrives with coffee.

"You were blind."

"And now I see!"

"Alright hon, I got it," she says. "You having coffee?" He nods. "Milk?"

He nods again.

"What do you remember?" He takes a mug from her.

"Well, your paint balls ruined my best suit, and I remember feeling lucky it wasn't real bullets."

"How did you happen to be in the room?"

"I was lured there after stupidly agreeing to a private meeting with Johnston. He had obtained my mobile phone number and talked directly to me. I had hoped I could arrest him and stop the bombing. I looked through the spy hole into the room. The glass had been removed and I was hit by a squirt of CS spray. I almost fell inside as the door jerked open. I tried to scream, but he grabbed me. I couldn't believe how quickly he moved. He tied me up and wrapped tape around my mouth, then injected something into my arm. When I came to I was tied to the chair, and there you were at the other end of the darkened room. I heard Johnston's words come from the speaker tied to my throat. I heard everything he said to you, and I felt the paint splat me."

"And Jean Dempsie?"

"She who knows everything?"

"Not sure."

"Not sure?"

"She's not following you orders?"

"No."

"What about the Summit?"

"Well," she says, pushing herself back in her seat. "Appears it's been held up to be a monumental success, the best ever. Muir is viewed to be a great civic leader. Everyone is happy. Immigration policy is to be reviewed. There's to be massive urban aid for the city."

"Everyone gets something."

"Even the families congratulated the leaders on their wisdom," she says.

"Wow, been... compensated then. Cross my palm – "

"We all have our needs Rooney."

"Take more than that to compensate for Thomas. Davy will go to war."

"No war. Davy is saying Thomas died a street player. He won't wage war on... us."

"No? He was about to kill the good people of Glasgow though."

"We are... content the people of Glasgow are safe, Rooney."

"What with me and Johnston still at large, taking a chance eh?"

"We knew where you were Rooney, but we don't know where Johnston is and that worries us."

"Well, maybe I am learning. What about Muir? We both know what Johnston was after. Muir."

"Well, the council's risen against Muir," she says. "His political decline's imminent. He's been fucked by Campbell. Although there's praise for the Summit, he sealed his political future by admitting to the council he was the dissenting voice there. They took a vote of no confidence and offered him one option: to resign, prompting new leadership. His political and personal life is in tatters."

"He's destroyed, just what Johnston wanted."

"What're you going to do now?"

"I do not know." He pauses slightly after each word.

"You have to find him hon."

"I need to do fuckall, dear. I am done with being told what to do."

"Got his balls back Jackie."

"Just don't call me dear... like that," she says loudly, prompting two burly officers to enter the room. "I'll have you arrested. I will. I won't fuck around this time,"

"Go on then, but you won't. You still need me."

"Aye, you. You and your... *analysing* ways."

"It is the only way I know. Though, as said, I am learning Jackie."

"Words won't fucking kill him Rooney."

"Well, he hasn't killed me," he says, as if that mattered.

"He's playing wi' you. Like a cat wi' a mouse."

"They are all playing wi' you. Like a bunch of cats wi' a mouse."

"Apparently."

"Are you mad, deaf, and stupid?"

"Two out of three ain't bad."

"You're on the way down Rooney. I know you hon."

"I am over the hill and heading for home, my sweet," he says, only confirming she's right.

"So pleased. Get on your feckin' tablets."

"I have other medicine."

"Aye, so you have," she says, turning away. "Anyway, you said Muir was all he wanted, and then he would stop."

"Well, so *he* said."

"You were bloody well wrong."

"How do you know I was bloody well wrong?"

"You are *so* wrong," she says. "You thought Muir was the source of his pain. Your psyche brain took you down the wrong road."

Rooney girds himself. Standing up, while pulling his all-too-big jacket together, he says, "Indeed, and your cop brain thought it was his need for greater gratification which forced him always to go further."

"I still think so," she says. "He's a cycle-fucking-path, getting a big kick out of it. He won't stop until someone puts a bullet in his head."

"We're both wrong."

"Both wrong?"

"Indeed, we are both wrong. It's all a diversion."

"A diversion, a diversion from what? Reality, normality?"

"It's… away from something… unbearable in his head. It's his parents, I think."

"You bloody think. His parents? Rooney, are you delusional again or is it the drink? What is it this time?"

"So far none of either. Not today at least… dear. Yes, his parents."

"This just gets worse, idiot. Whatever, he'll keep going."

"Either way he'll have to be stopped."

"We know that, but we have different ideas about how to do it."

"We both want to put something in his head."

"I don't have time for this." She gets up, pushing her seat backwards with the back of her legs.

Rooney stays put.

"You want to put a bullet into his head. I want to put a thought into it."

"And what good would a thought do?" she says, turning the corner of the desk to stand over him.

"The tongue is mightier than the blade," he says, calling on an old proverb.

"The man needs to die hon."

"And what about justice, a right to a fair trial and all that? Remember there is no such thing as the death penalty in this country."

She looks at her sidekicks as if to say 'do you believe this man?' A dispassionate gaze confirms otherwise. She beckons them to leave. "It's OK you can go." She waits until the door closes behind her. "Listen… Mr," she growls. "This man can't go through the courts. He'd play to the crowds. You said so yourself, remember? He'd become a symbol to all the freaks and die a hero in prison. A bullet Rooney – no thought – into his cranium – not his mind – frontal lob – got it?"

"From me, as your stooge."

"What?"

"Well, the CID assassinating a man Jackie? It wouldn't look good, it wouldn't be the done thing. Best to get a stooge to do it for you. Meaning me. You'll use me, again. You're using me. Is this what you do?"

"I do what I have to. A bullet Rooney," she says with an assertiveness he has grown to know of her.

"I'll do it in my way. Something so destructive it will destroy him and what he is. This is more successfully than a bullet in his head."

"You're revelling in this."

"What?"

"You're enjoying this. You are dragging this out for your own perverse ends, i-fucking-e your proxy killer. Is this is the one, Rooney?"

"I am... doing what I need to do."

"And what is this magic bullet?"

"His mother and his father."

"His parents? Jesus, you really are a perverse fuck-up."

A perverse fuck-up.

"There's something in them, the father, the mother, their relationship, something pathological."

"There's that bloody word again," she says. "Sick you mean."

"There's something in the dynamic of them that's destructive."

"He's the destructive one Rooney. Do it. Right?"

"No."

"You will, I'll see to it."

"You will see to nothing ma'am. I won't do it."

"Then you will be complicit, and you'll go to jail." She pulls her seat under her.

Rooney hears the door opening behind him. "The door is open, Rooney," she says, her eyes dropping back into her papers.

"I'll be going to jail anyway."

"You got it hon. The rape and other things, like assisting an escape, harbouring a criminal, etcetera, etcetera."

"Oh well, who the fuck cares? I'll do it my way," he says, waiting to be taken by arm by the uniform.

Jackie gets to her feet. "You, your way. You are putting your perverse needs before this city," she says, leaning over the table, her knuckles pressing down, arms akimbo, showing a fair amount of cleavage.

"And you're putting your ambitions before your thick cop heid," he says, also getting to his feet. "Anyway, I don't give a feckin'-fuck for 'this city'."

"And what do you give a 'feckin'-fuck' for, if not for the city, or its folk. Why are you doing this?"

"I am doing this for me," he says, backing out towards the door. "And who or what are you doing it for, your father, your mother?"

"I do what is necessary," she says, coolly this time.

"What you think is necessary to get there, Jackie?"

"Hon, just go."

She's right. It's time to go. "I'll see you Jackie." He hopes the Red Sea of police at the door will part.

"Not if I see you first," she says. "But you will fuckin' well stay in touch."

"How do I know you won't try to find me, to apprehend me?"

"I might yet, but I... still need you.

"You still need me, conflicted Jackie?"

"Johnston, remember?"

"Indeed, should I forget, sure you do. And maybe I need you too," he says, seeking something from her.

At this, the cops at the door reach saturation point. "Right you, out," one orders Rooney, pointing at the door.

"Hon?" she says, softer now.

"What?"

"You're just a big pile of shite." She moves towards him.

"A pile of shite."

"We'll see."

"Rooney?" she says, reaching out and grabbing his arm. Is she going to say, 'watch yourself', or 'take care', something like that. She approaches him. He feels her sex approaching him; her perfume, her cleavage, her lips. She postures provocatively before him, square on. Her arms reach out. She holds his neck in the fork of her hands. "Hon – "

"I know you love me, but..."

"Maybe some day you'll realise." She takes her hands away and puts something in his pocket.

"Take this. It's a CID listening device. State of the art, Johnston'll never know it's there. It doesn't emit radio waves and is undetectable. You activate it when you like from your mobile phone and listen in. The battery lasts for ages. If you get a chance, use it. It'll help you to keep track of him."

"Indeed."

"You keep in touch right. Right?"

"Right yar, dear."

"And take your fucking tablets."

"All at the one time."

"In fuckin' handfuls," he says, and leaves.

CHAPTER THIRTY-ONE

Rooney checks the address given by Davy, in Cook Street, on Zoopla online. This is an executive apartment in a refurbished industrial site, possibly a self-catering flat taking on an assumed name on a short term let. This's Johnston's place – his place of safety. He's desperate for a drink, but this has to be done first. He arrives at 7.30 p.m., courtesy of a black cab. The cabbie points him towards the door. He presses the controlled access.

"Yes," comes quickly from inside.

"It's Rooney." The outside door opens with a clunk.

"Third floor, at the top, the door on the right."

He gets there, out of puff after six flights of stairs, and there he is. "Ah, Rooney, you're alone. No SAS?" Johnston says.

"Well, you know me by now. I don't need a posse. A real tough guy," Rooney replies, catching his breath as he cautiously enters the hall. "Another safe house?"

"You were given thith address." This could have been a question, but he says it like a statement.

"I was."

"Not by the authorities of course." Johnston wanders into his sitting room, expecting Rooney to follow, which he does. He sits on the edge of a large red sofa without inviting Rooney to sit. There's a solid wooden coffee table. Rooney recognises the birdcage and the Zebra Finches. Johnston's changing their water. There's an adjacent sofa, also red, The table ensures a reasonable distance between them, There's a mobile on it next to the cage. The other sofa will do. Rooney sits there.

"You look like a tramp, Rooney."

"He doesn't give a fuck how he looks."

"I don't give a fuck how I look."

"It was from Davy?"

"A phone message. It mentioned his son."

"He's still smarting over Tam the Bam's death."

"Why hasn't he killed you then?"

"He'd be signing his own death certificate and others in his family, that's why," Johnston says. "There are bigger guys than him in the families' battalions. He knows that."

"He wanted me to reach you," Rooney says, not really at this stage knowing why.

"He knows of your... task."

"Jackie, why did you say you would kill Jackie?" Rooney's determined to challenge him on this, given this was the prompt for him to shoot him.

"She's a gangster's moll," he says, cruelly, also highlighting the link between Davy and Jackie.

Rooney moves to the edge of the sofa. "You're a liar. I'll kill you if you harm her."

"Oh, you would kill me?" Johnston turns the cage to get a better perspective on the birds.

"I would."

"I wouldn't kill her... directly."

"You made a fool of me."

"You didn't have the balls to shoot to the head or heart."

"No balls, only paint balls."

"I still shot though."

"Paintballs from a madman in a manic phase, Rooney," he says slowly, as if to allow the emphasis of this to sink in. He is chastising and ridiculing Rooney. He is baiting him, again, as he did. He lounges back, his focus on the Finches, his eyes through the bars of the cage on Rooney. Like a lion who has eaten its fill, lazing in the afternoon sun, he's watching him, studying him, waiting to see what he will do and say.

"Would you have cared if I had killed her?" Rooney says, breaking the silence.

"Not really. Although you did think she was me."

"Yes, I did."

"So you would have killed me?"

"Yes, I think I would have, to stop you."

"Would you kill me now?"

Rooney doesn't answer, sitting back.

"Is that why you are here?"

"Maybe."

Johnston gets up and turns his back on Rooney, and walks out of the room, another control tactic. Rooney turns to the cage. The birds start chirping as if to greet him. Johnston returns. "Maybe?" he says, moving into the room, a packet of birdseed in his hand.

"Maybe. Are you planning something else?"

"Well the Summit was pretty big. Don't you think?" He says, pouring seed into the container in the cage, then dropping heavily onto the sofa.

"He wants his ego massaged, like back in the prison cell."

"I am not here to congratulate you," Rooney says. "Though Muir's downfall would've pleased you, that being your ultimate goal?"

"Partly. Though his... physical demise was... is clearly... imminent."

Does he know something Rooney should know? "Imminent?"

"Yes, Muir will kill himself," he says. "Soon."

Rooney is confused, but tries not to show it.

"Don't look so surprised, you knew this was my intention," he says. "He'll die by a massive dose of barbiturates. He's chosen not to pursue the political option of leaving office and has decided to take his life. The text I'll send to him now is my usual hallmark. It will present him with a dilemma with one outcome." He lifts his mobile. There's a beep. Then he drops the mobile on the table. "That's a send Rooney," he says.

Rooney feels trapped, again. Should he get out of there, contact the CID, find out if what he said about Muir is true. Who knows might even save the bastard, if indeed this matters to him. Or should he stay there, to see this through, to see where this will go.

"I am not going to ask you to verify this," Rooney says. "I'll find out soon enough though, but why do you think Muir'll kill himself?"

"Thirty minutes ago, he met the council for the last time to confirm his resignation from the Lord Provost post, the city, and from politics."

"Why do you think that will prompt his suicide?"

"Because a major national newspaper now has the full story Rooney – the text was copied there too – including Mark Casey, his days as a predatory homosexual, a small matter of misappropriating party funds, and some big money being transferred into an overseas bank account. Oh yes, and another matter which confirms his death. What else can he do?"

"Muir will answer these accusations. He has done this before, in the past."

"Not this time."

"And if he can't, he'll retire, rebuild his life. The inveterate survivor he is. He'll write a book or ten. Look at Jeffrey Archer. Sleaze doesn't destroy politicians. It makes them interesting. Why not this time?"

"Because he wants his place in history, and this is the only way he can secure it."

"Am I missing something here?"

"I think you are Rooney. You've spent so much time studying me, you hardly know Muir."

"And you have, no doubt."

"You know I have."

"The other matter?"

"Yes, the other matter," he says, knowing Rooney would enquire.

"You said there was another matter thrown in."

"That all of this is a pretext for him to take his own life. Truth is, he either kills himself or MI5 will."

"This gets crazier by the minute."

"He knows they're on his case."

"And why indeed would they?"

"He has stepped over the line."

"And what line has he stepped over?"

"It takes you time to think Rooney, something to do with brain damage caused by alcohol abuse?"

"Alcohol-related brain damage, affecting the thinking process, insight, memory?"

"The line?"

"The plan, the Summit. A complete control of migrants coming and going, playing one faction against the other, lining his pocket," he says, looking at his watch.

Rooney sees this's Johnston's way of increasing the tension. He's in control of the time they have. Rooney needs to prompt, explore, get the information.

"I believe Campbell is promoting this policy."

"Campbell has been led down a road by Muir. He'll do what I say, to prevent a major confrontation.

"What d'you say? Confrontation?"

"The families. They're waiting for my signal."

"The signal from the hill, burn the houses, Johnston. Patrick Seller's clearances, Muir's ancestor?"

Johnston pauses, absorbing this.

"They will destroy this city, and many of its inhabitants," Johnston says. "There will be a war."

"On your signal?"

"On my thignal."

"On your signal, they will destroy the ordinary folk," Rooney says. "Just like Muir's ancestors killing people, like your ancestors? Campbell?"

Johnston is pausing now, reflecting more before he stabs "He has to do what he has to do."

"What you want him to do you mean, to get Muir. Is Campbell now your proxy, *procuratia*? Is he acting for another, you, to get... Muir."

"Interesting Rooney, there's no other way. MI5 is involved, they have given him... advice he cannot refuse."

"I'll make him an offer..."

"Kill yourself, retain something of your reputation," Rooney says.

"Don't, then we'll do the job for you, right?"

"Ah, now you are thinking Rooney. Sobering up, your brain is extricating itself from the shackles of its dependency."

"He's good. Listen and learn."

"You had all those people killed to get to Muir?"

"Ultimately."

"Ultimately. Did you know the MI5 would ultimately kill Muir or Muir would ultimately kill himself?"

"The spooks have no choice. I threaten the state. So does Muir."

"They'll get to you first," Rooney says, knowing they could.

"They have tried. But they know if they touch a hair of my head some bigwigs will fall."

"Funny too!"

"And how will this happen if you are dead?"

"My people have been informed what to do," Johnston says. "Letters will rain down on the civic, political and judicial echelons. Copies sent across the media who will have a field day. Careers, reputations, lives will be destroyed. MI5 can only pursue the course of least resistance, the least damage. The least restrictive option, as they say in mental health law, as you well know Rooney. Given you have been incarcerated under it."

"Trumping and demeaning you at the same time."

"I needed treatment."

"It didn't work Rooney. MI5 will ensure stability, equilibrium, homoeostasis, and Muir is expendable."

"He knows things."

"You know this?"

"Information equals power, and the right information on the right people is real power. He's a liability. I'm doing the city a favour. The people will act. The tooth?"

"Pink-shit, you acting for the city. What about all the death and destruction?"

"All for a reason," Johnston says, then pauses, giving Rooney time to gather his thoughts. He wonders what will be next. "All for a reason," he repeats, his tone dropping in that way.

"Buchanan Street no more. Grosvenor Hotel no more. Argyle Hotel no more. Muir no more."

"Your raison d'être. You make killers," Rooney says. "I thought it was just about Muir, but it's bigger than him. Maybe it started with him, but now making people kill is your reason for everything, for existing, for not being dead, for not killing... yourself."

Rooney says this without any real basis for this, but he's chancing it, winging it. This man has pain he's exorcising on others, he just knows this.

Why would he not want to harm himself?

"Very profound Rooney. Why would I kill myself?"

"Why wouldn't you. You have good cause to?"

There's an eerie calm, then, "I see," comes from Johnston, as he gets up and moves behind Rooney.

"You nearly made me a killer." Rooney gets up and turns to face him.

"I don't *make* killers. I just bring out what is inside them... I'll make you a killer."

"He'll make you kill, Rooney. You'll like that?"

Now they're face to face standing by the window. Rooney wonders if anyone out there in the car park is observing them. If so, they would see two men from the waist up, about a metre apart. Spassky and Fisher come to mind. A great chess game.

"I was no... killer before you came into my life," Rooney says – his move.

"You could've killed me. You thought Jackie was me," Johnston says – his move.

And so on.

"I wanted to kill you. The shot came out. I pulled the trigger."

"I know. You're a killer Rooney."

"I could have been."

"Would you have shot me or taken my picture?"

If this is chess, this is a Johnston strategy, a ploy. Get Rooney to make a wrong move.

"Pardon?"

"Nothing."

Johnston stares him out, another chess tactic. He looks at his watch, another chess tactic. Rooney has to keep his cool, but Irena and his mother's voice, in syncopated rhythm, reverberates through his mind. "I'm scared son. Don't be scared son. Are you scared son? Are you a scared son?"

"He's playing you, with you, like Jackie says."

"Indeed, this is a new tactic."

"You have your fears, Rooney."

"And you have yours."

"Why do you drink, Sean?"

"You don't like this move, the question, not from this man."

"I drink because I drink."

"You drink because your father subjugated you, your mother, it led to her death. It seems a good enough reason to me."

"Check to Johnston."

His words hit Rooney square on the chest.

"Your play to save the game."

"What do you know of me, bastard."

"Everything, you know that."

"Only what has been reported…"

"Trust no one."

Jackie passes through Rooney's mind.

"You know a lot about killers, Rooney," Johnston says. "Is that why you work with them?"

"It is my job."

"Yes, an authority on killers, a PhD, a chartered forensic psychologist."

"Indeed, that's what I do, or what I did, was, more like," Rooney's trying to get to a professional, safe, place.

"And you're a killer none the less," Johnston says. "We're all killers. It's man's primitive and basic nature. Would you have killed your father, Rooney?"

"I can control my… feelings."

"Check saved."

"Yes, so called civilised man manages to repress his instincts."

"And you release them."

"Yes. And you suppress them."

"Yes."

"You only shoot with your camera?"

"Who is psychoanalysing whom Rooney?"

"There's less damage that way."

"A coward's way."

He's baiting him again. This time he refuses to be drawn. Then the text notification sounds on his mobile.

"You have a voice mail, I believe."

Rooney opens the voice mail, keeping it close to his ear, so Johnston can't hear. "Rooney, Muir is dead. You need to finish this. Jackie," it says.

"Check to Johnston?"

"Muir's dead, and she wants you to kill me."

"Indeed you are correct, on both counts."

"Well, go on then, do it now, you can do it." Johnston opens a drawer on the sideboard next to the window.

"And you make me the killer you think I am. The killer you want me to be, to be like you."

"You'll have this chance, one chance only." Johnston pulls a gun from the drawer. "Kill me, like you would've liked to kill your father."

"You want to do it."

Rooney drifts to thoughts of his father, and how he controlled him. His tyrannical regime. How he dominated his mother. How he controlled their lives. *This* man's now trying to control him. Other words come out.

"There may be another way," Rooney suggests.

"Check saved."

"Another way Rooney?" Johnston places the gun in Rooney's hand, the barrel pointing towards him.

"Muir's gone, so you have no further need to kill, no other campaigns. You have nowhere else to go."

"I have many places I can go. I can continue – you know this. I will continue to make killers. I will set up a killer factory."

"You'd never get a patent." Rooney retreats slightly.

"Funny man."

"Take this," Johnston says, holding the gun towards him. "I know you are a weak man, but try. Do it. It is why you are here."

Rooney's trying hard to control his fear, his panic, his pride.

"He's getting to you, like... 'he' did."

"You have no power, no leverage, over me. I don't need to – "

"I may prove to you that I have, and you do." Johnston grabs his arm. Rooney pulls away.

"And who are you out to prove anything to, your parents?" Rooney has to get some balance back, there and then.

Johnston hammers the windowsill with the barrel of the gun.

"Coward," he says.

"Touching a nerve?"

"Take it." Johnston pushes the gun into Rooney's hand. "Feel its power."

Rooney holds the gun. His hand is shaking and for a long few seconds it feels good. He could end this evil now; but he can't do it. He just can't pull the trigger and end this inveterate killer.

"'I don't know why you don't just shoot...,' Gray said."

Red fills Rooney's head. "What, and control me, like all the others?"

There's a palpable pause before Johnston speaks again. "I'll make it impossible for you not to," he says.

"You want me... to kill you as your final act of control."

"Please do it," Johnston says, pausing again. "Show you are not a weak man."

"The man's just a metaphor for your father. You won't kill him; you want to hurt him, to cause him pain."

Rooney drops the gun. "I won't kill what is already dead."

"You weren't big enough, you aren't big enough."

"You were a wee boy. You're still a wee boy."

"Wasn't Muir big enough... for you?"

"Muir and the Summit were more subtle than usual, no massive loss of life. My surrogates may think I am losing my touch. I may need to create some mayhem."

Rooney needs to detach himself. To create some distance, physically and psychologically. He moves to the opposite side of the room. "Do what you like," he says. "I have no interest in who you kill any more. I am getting out of this."

"I'll continue then," Johnston says, returning to the birdcage. "Who will be next? Jackie, Campbell?"

This disturbs Rooney. This man cannot cope with not being at the centre of everyone's consciousness. Rooney's hypothesis, though, is that Johnston wants out – he wants to die; he needs to free himself from the turmoil he feels inside, which manifests in causing pain to, and in, others. Rooney knows his only way to achieve this, his only way out, is to control *him*; to use and exploit a good man.

Then, as if to emphasise his power over living things, Johnston does a strange thing. He picks up a shoebox that lay under the table, carefully takes off two thick elastic bands, slips a thick glove on his right hand and opens it, just enough at first to slip his hand inside. Rooney has no idea what he is doing, but then realises when Johnston removes his hand with a large white rat gripped in it. "Meet Dixy, Rooney," Johnston says. "Dixy, meet Rooney," he says to the rat. Rooney stares on aghast. "Dixy likes small birds Rooney, Finches especially. Don't you Dixy?" he says to the rat.

"Please don't," Rooney says.

"To kill through others, is that it Rooney?"

At the sight of the rat, the Finches desperately crash at the bars of the cage, but there's no escape. Johnston opens the flap on the side of the cage and holds the rat inside.

"Please don – " At that Johnston releases the rat.

Rooney turns away to the squealing of the rat, the screeching of the birds, and the "there, there, now," of Johnston. "*Procuratia*, acting for another, Rooney; now act for me, pleathe?"

Johnson turns to Rooney, the grin, the dead eyes, the glee at killing by proxy; this time through the rat; at other times through confirmed killers; and, if he had his way, through Rooney himself.

"*Check.*"

Rooney moves towards the door.

"You will stay." Johnston blocks his way. No hand on the chest, a gun this time.

"You'll be responsible for the deaths of many, many people."

He needs to go for his Achilles heel. He had held this in abeyance, but this was the time. If he ever needed it, this was the time. "You cannot face the reality of your hopeless life. It's based on pain," Rooney says. "Pain you cannot heal. Pain you can only cope with by diverting your disturbed thoughts, into exercising pain on others. Pain caused by your parents. You destroy others because you cannot destroy your parents for all the pain they caused you."

"Check saved."

"I *will* kill you," Johnston says.

Johnston is holding the gun on Rooney, but Rooney is defiant. This feels good.

"You won't kill me," Rooney says. "My very existence promotes the perverse discomfort you crave. You need me and you'll continue to try to manipulate, control me. Me, the plaything for your damaged ego. But listen to me…"

Rooney moves closer to Johnston, closer than he had ever been before. He smells his breath. He may have detected a smell of vodka. Vodka is drunk sometimes because it is less apparent on the breath. Rooney had used it himself when he had to go into work the day after a binge. Rooney looks into his face, this damaged face. He tries to imagine what he looked like as a child, a child with pain, but he can imagines nothing behind the face. This face is a façade, a front for a damaged man, but the pain is there, nonetheless. He's sure of it.

"If I track you, I'll do it in my way," Rooney says. "For my own reasons and not for yours, and here, I have no further need for this." Rooney stuffs a book into Johnston's hand. It's the Messiner Latin phrase book. "I've no need for this drivel now," he says, as he pushes passed him through his outside door and into the close. "I well understand your modus operandi, the Latin messages, the Mafia metaphor, the families as your proxies, etcetera."

Johnston is standing at the door. Rooney walks out and walks away. He can feel Johnston's eyes drilling into his back.

"Checkmate… to whom?"

Rooney had to get out before Johnston had the chance to come back at him. The thought passes quickly through Rooney's head to be replaced by a certain degree of confusion. He had the chance there to end it. To end Johnston and yet he couldn't do it. He couldn't do it. Not even to protect Jackie. He didn't have the courage. Was it so far from his personal makeup, his own particular ways? Or was it because he's bound by being a professional, a therapist, a profiler?

"A coward?"

At least, he left the phrasebook, which has been so useful to him. It'll have a different use now. It contains the CID listening device, hidden in the spine of the book. Rooney is chancing Johnston would hold onto to it. He's an NPD, he'll see it as a trophy, a memento of his activities.

"What now Rooney? Get pissed?"

"Correct, bastard."

As if my words were necessary to help him decide what he has already decided. He'll make his way along a familiar track.

He finds a convenient bar, where he has a large Coke. He can't do alcohol. His stomach, liver, brain, won't accept it. He thinks about Muir. Let's see the body? There are news reports Muir had indeed killed himself, the loss of his beloved wife was too much for him. A civic funeral is planned and there's talk of a posthumous peerage in the Queen's Honours list.

Rooney will protect Johnston's hideout, though. His perverse determination to understand Johnston would tie him to him, and protect him. Equally, for the same reason, he'll not have him incarcerated; but the listening device indicates he has moved on just the same.

Over the next couple of days, Rooney stays sober, and the DTs return, the rats, and other nasties for a time. He goes into himself in a way he has not allowed before. Something is touching him. This time deep down. Something is changing inside. *"Die or live in your mind or live or die in your life; from death to life; from fucked to fucker; from child to man; from son to father?"*

During that time, Rooney telephones the device and listens in. One time, he hears the rumble of an engine, which sounds like a diesel. Johnston's on the move. He may have been in a taxi. The sound finally stops along with the car, after nearly an hour's drive from Glasgow. If he has gone south, he could have been in Lanark. If north, maybe Perth, Edinburgh to the east or Ayr to the west. Then he hears him talking. "I'm in Arrochar, meet me here," he says. Arrochar, where the Zysk family were found, back to the scene of the crime, where he started of his campaign of terror, a fitting place to take stock and decide his next move.

CHAPTER THIRTY-TWO

Rooney calls Jackie to be told she's 'on compassionate leave'. Not that compassionate! He tries her mobile, leaving messages, which aren't returned.

Rooney needs to see Davy, to understand some things. Mick is a way to Johnston and has obvious links with him, but he is in jail awaiting trial, and he has no way anymore of getting in there. He goes to the flat in Gardner St. It's empty, the door and boarded up. A neighbour says the Police did a drugs bust, crashed the door in. They didn't find anything or anyone. He goes to the Lismore, but the barman wouldn't serve him, not even a ginger beer. He's in a state. The barman lets him sit in a corner, if he 'behaves himself'. Soon, he smells the perfume and hears the crinkly jacket. Jean Dempsie pushes in beside him.

"And how would I know you would be here?" he asks.

"Well, where else would you go?" She gives him an up and down look. "God, you are a state."

"I need your help."

"You need help Rooney, but I'm not going to get you a gun or take you to a room."

"You took me to the family, Mick, etcetera. I need to see Davy."

"Christ, you're a brave man."

"There are things I need to know."

"Rooney, have you seen yourself."

"I don't use a mirror these days."

"Well, you're revolting."

"You don't live with him!"

"I believe so. Can you help?"

"I won't wash you Rooney."

"I want to contact Davy, can you do it?"

"I'll see what I can do, but there's no way he'll see you in this condition."

For a few seconds the reality of his condition hits home. He puts his head in his hands "And what about Jackie?" he asks, turning to face her, but she's gone.

He sits there for a few minutes, but doesn't see the point of being in a pub without a drink in front of him. He'll find a pub where they'll serve a drunk: him. The Quarter Gill pub across the road will. He'll have a few there and then he'll go home, to touch base.

He gets home in the early hours and vomits most of the night. His stomach aches so much he believes he is going to die. He calls NHS 24 and manages to convince the operator that without medical attention he'll expire. Ten minutes later, an out-of-hours doctor arrives and examines him. He says he has blood coming from his stomach, and he wants to admit him. He isn't sure what's happening in there: an ulcer, oesophageal varices, liver damage, blood vessels ruptures. No way is he going to hospital. The doctor says he could bleed to death. Rooney says he'll take the risk. He recommends Antibuse, which he refuses. He'll stay off the booze and heal. The doctor gives him some Ondansetron to stop the vomiting, and he goes to bed.

Next day, he's in the shower, getting the diarrhoea off. He'll wash away the shit, get it out of his hair, off his skin. Sick of it in his mind too, but he can't wash in there. There's something there, something, in the room, wandering around; his paranoia or the DTs, or a predator maybe. It's a small snake. It came out of the shower and fell onto his head. It's trying to get into his ear, into his brain, following the sound of his mind, into his head. He's telling it to get the fuck out of his head. It's ready to go in; but then, there's a sound: breep, breep, breep, stings the air. The moment's gone, so's the predator.

"I'll be back."

He reaches the phone wet, pulling his housecoat on.

He's hoping it'll be Jackie, but not this time.

"Rooney?"

"Hello?"

"It's Davy."

"Davy."

"Aye, Davy."

"Do you want me to call back, some other time. You know, when your heid's OK."

"No, it's OK, my heid's OK. I'm OK," Rooney says, spitting out water.

"You want to talk to me."

"I do. Thanks for calling me. Jean – "

"Careful Rooney, your phone's bugged."

"Right, can we meet?"

"Aye, you'll come to Thomas's funeral, on Monday."

"Monday!"

"Aye, I know nearly three weeks. Sudden death. The PF's just released his body. Violent death by… unknown parties."

"Known to us Davy."

"Aye, son, known to us."

Rooney can't believe this man is inviting him to the funeral of his son, the man who cut off the end of his finger and had forced him into betraying him. He can't refuse.

"But get your heid on," he says. He wasn't kidding.

"I will, thanks." Rooney puts the phone down and shivers his way to the bedroom.

He's shaking, freezing. There's no heating, yet he's sweating. His heart's pumping, going to burst out of his chest. He's panicking, shaking, sweating. He takes Diazepam and Lorazepam, gets into bed, digs under the covers. The snake is there for a time, the insects too.

"The wee men scratching your legs, trying to get into you, up your arse."

He curls up into a ball and waits. He holds on until they leave.

Of all places, Thomas's funeral is in St Mary's, the place of Rooney's abuse. Father Healey had left a long time past. The Priest's predilections towards altar boys had reached the Bishop and he was moved on. No condemnation, no police inquiry; all hushed up and off you go to get on with it elsewhere. Rooney is anxious about returning there. He hasn't been there since his mother's funeral and he's in no condition to confront any of his demons. Purposely, he arrives late, he wants to slip in. The church is surrounded by gangland security: men in black coats ensuring only invited guests are allowed in, and any journalist or threat remains out. Rooney's allowed in on a nod, after declaring his personal invitation by Davy.

He takes a seat in the back row, well out of the way. Damn, the mass is in Latin.

Gold!

Irena's words: 'I knew it was Latin, I'd heard it often at our mass," arrive in his mind. The Latin words bring on shades of gold. He scans the church. Being at the back provides a reasonable vantage point. This's like a Who's Who of Glasgow gangland, with the heads of the other families, and not surprisingly a smattering of Police officials and local councillors. The McGinns are a powerful family in these parts. He'd known of them for some time and had heard of Davy's exploits in his teens; not like him, who managed to get to university and away, he fought his way up and stayed. There's a cavalcade of black limousines. This's both a show of strength and of respect.

He's in a cold sweat all through the service and relieved when Davy takes to the lectern to deliver the Eulogy. He talks of Thomas and his childhood, his liking of fast cars and even faster ladies – pretty privileged, it appears, made possible by Davy's means, which at the time was mostly derived by salting away drugs money into a massive taxi empire. Then it's time for him to make some statements which most people there knew he would.

Davy talks of the community and his family's determination to improve things for the local folk. He almost gets applause for the money he puts into the church, the local community centre, and the nursing home. He reminds those in office, scanning the police and council representatives, of their responsibilities to the ordinary people of this area. It's clear he's just about above the law, which had come to Rooney some time ago when he realised that no charges would be made against him or his family concerning any activity at the Summit or before, such as the elimination of a good proportion of the Murphy family. The Zysks are still an open case, though. With no direct link to the McGinns, it's unclear whether the Taylors or the McGinns or another family had carried out this heinous crime. Then, after thanking all for being there, and reminding those in the local community that he's there to help them and they only have to ask, he makes his ending statement. He says he is proud of his son and has forgiven him for any 'transgressions' and ends with a sign of the cross and a strongly delivered *"In Nomine Patris, et Filii, et Spiritus Sancti."*

Gold explodes in Rooney's head.

He tries to slip out when a strong hand grips his arm. One of the McGinn men whispers into his ear, "Mr McGinn would like to see you at the funeral lunch." He 'escorts' him to a waiting car, where he travels with some local people to the McGinn's palatial villa off the Great Western Road. There's a lot of cash 'invested' in this house. It's a fortress with high walls and a massive gate. They arrive in a large car park and are taken into the garden, where food is served in a large marquee, and, in traditional custom, where whisky for the gentlemen and sherry for the ladies is dished out. Rooney's starting to enjoy this. He observes a growing line of people waiting to go into the house to pay their respects to Davy and realises how much this reminds him of *The Godfather* movie, where, in the wedding scene, people are presented to Don Vito Corleone to pay their respects and to request 'favours'.

Davy calls for Rooney. He's ushered into his office. Davy sits behind a large desk, his subordinates sit around him.

"I am sorry about Thomas," Rooney says.

"Don't worry. No commiserations are necessary," Davy says.

"Mea culpa?"

"I was undercover."

"We knew that. We were advised." Jackie, Jean Dempsie, Johnston?

"I could have betrayed you," Rooney says getting straight to it. This man needs to hear this from Rooney.

"Yes, you could've, though you wouldn't be sitting here today if you had. I knew you had no choice and Thomas's plan had no chance. You did what you were asked to do. You're a made man with us; no hard feelings." He reaches over the desk and offers his hand. Rooney accepts. He didn't expect this. "You wanted to see me?"

"We have some people in common."

"I don't normally do this."

"Johnston and Jackie?"

"Jackie's your wuman?"

"For better or worse!"

"Sure son, one of these modern wimen, who don't keep their man's name."

"Never did, prefers Polish to Irish."

"I won't insult your intelligence by saying I don't know anything, because lots of us know Jackie."

"You know her."

"She helps us."

"You mean she's in your pocket?"

"That has been said, but no. She tried to persuade us to pursue legitimate business and move away from our other activities, but she pushes too hard. She's ruffled a few feathers. She treads a fine line Rooney."

"She hasn't been harmed though."

"We protect her. We need her. We sent out a message if anyone touched her, they'd be dead." He looks at his lieutenants, to ensure they understand this.

"It makes sense."

"She has problems, Rooney."

"Problems?"

"Muir –"

"Muir?"

He doesn't answer. Rooney lets it go.

"Johnston tried to get us to do it, to get to you."

"I thought as much."

"Johnston said it would happen anyway."

Rooney takes time to digest this. He asks to use the toilet. He'll go there to spew.

"You're no' looking so well Rooney," Davy remarks when he returns.

"No, I don't feel so well."

"I'll get you home."

"No, you're alright. I'll get home OK."

"You did what we expected of you Rooney, at the Summit. We are grateful."

"True respect is gained."

"Johnston?"

"Dangerous man, Rooney."

"Johnston got you credit, power, through the Grand Central deal, but you lost your son."

There was a pause indicating Davy was either thinking of this or waiting for Rooney to continue.

"Thomas got greedy."

"Didn't need to die though."

"He had a bomb."

"They had him in a clinch. No way could he have detonated it. He was executed."

Davy stares at Rooney intently, trying to digest this information.

"You know this?"

"I do," Rooney says, revealing inside information.

"I will… consider this Rooney," Davy says. "I am obliged. I owe you one."

"You were prepared to do Johnston's bidding."

"Johnston uses us – we use him. It's a partnership. His work with us brought him some financial rewards from some very rich people in this city. They're pleased with his role at the Summit."

"The gangs and Muir, what was that all about?"

"We were in a corner," he says. "For years we've fought each other for territory, power; now there's a bigger threat. The new gangs are run by international barons. With free movement through Europe, thanks to the EEC, they moved though Paris into London, then Birmingham, Liverpool, and now they're here – thousands of them, Poles, Romanians, Bulgarians, Slavs, Latvians. These guys are mercenaries, moving in, taking over, setting up their own crime syndicates, drugs, trafficking, everything. Everywhere they've gone they've conquered, and now they are attacking Glasgow. But we're standing together; the indigenous teams of Glasgow are coming together to fight them. At the same time the politicians are supporting it for their own reasons. Divide and rule, get us fighting each other. We're fighting the new teams *and* the politicians. Johnston explained the political agendas behind the scenes. He knows things."

"He knows things. It increases his power?"

"I would say that."

"He's the Father."

Davy leans over, almost in Rooney's face. "So called… though no' forever son." It's clear Davy intends regaining his status in the family of families.

Rooney sees an opportunity to find out how the man controls these men.

"How does he do it?" he asks. "You know, getting the families to do his… deeds?"

"He's a persuasive man. You must know this."

"I know that, but what persuades you?"

"He knows things. That's all I'll say, he knows things about all of us."

"'Information is power,' he said to me."

"But it's what you do with it which either makes you great or diminishes you. Anonymous, Rooney."

"Indeed." Rooney has the feeling he has said this before.

"He also… advised us that Muir was playing one against the other – "

"Eh."

The city father who sets his sons against each other Rooney. Johnston said this, mind?

"The father who manipulates, controls and punishes, strengthens one over the other."

"If you want to see it that way."

"The Taylors, et al."

"The Taylors did their own thing, prompted by Johnston of course; not that they needed much of that, the crazy bastards."

"The McGinns: yourselves; the other teams, then the collective, the family of families?"

"You are in dangerous territory, son."

"I know this."

"Rooney, some advice."

"Yes?"

"Get out. Get out before you're killed. You're dealing wi' some serious people here. Now, away," he says, as again he reaches out and takes Rooney's hand. His feels warm and generous; this hand that'd killed others.

Once home, Rooney wraps himself in a blanket and coories up in his chair, the halogen fire full on. He feels like shit, is exhausted, and he doesn't know what to do next. He descends into quiet contemplation, which only highlights his polarities: aggression or passivity; up or down; flat or fun; fight or flight, or just submit, as he would have counselled those with emotional problems,

"I'll take Davy's advice and get out. That will be that. Leave it as is."

"You can't do this?"

"I can stay in, get Johnston, and get my brain sorted through him."

"Or get back to a normal drunk's life."

"Fuck it," he says. "I know a lot about this man. I'm empowered, I have information and information is power."

"Delusional. And I thought you were coming down?"

Johnston is his greatest mentor. He considers him constantly, thinking about how he does things. He learns. It emboldens him. It gives him strength. Though he wonders what Johnston'll do next.

"He'll need more, great exposure, greater control. This man won't settle, to do so would allow the feelings he has to overtake his thinking, to infiltrate his mind. To avoid this, he'll have to act, get the hit he needs."

Rooney's principal source of Johnston information is the listening device, and currently, his only entertainment. He uses it often. He enjoys the voyeurism of it, earwigging on his adversary.

Arrochar is a quiet place, and with a population of around two hundred and fifty souls, he'll be left alone. It's the perfect place for him to think and plan. Johnston has covered his tracks well. After his flat was discovered and the death of Marlene, his job at the university, and with it, the cover he needed to design and deliver his plans is gone, he has gone to ground without a trace... except for the bug! Over the following few weeks, Johnston has had little communication with anyone, but Rooney can hear seagulls, the occasional crashing of waves, and a lot of wind. This suggests he's in a house overlooking the head of the loch – self-catering maybe.

For Rooney, knowing he is there is useful. He's in a trap. Escape from Arrochar or thereabouts would be difficult. With a couple of roads in and out, the troops could be brought in and have him taken in. But, Rooney wonders, what good would that do. He needs to be destroyed not incarcerated.

Occasionally, he hears the sound of music and locals laughing, and guesses he's in the local bar, the Cobbler Bar; also known as the Arthur's Bothy, which is poignant given it's named after Ben Arthur, or the Cobbler Mountain, where the Zysks were found. Arthur! In there, Johnston doesn't talk much. He'll be seen as a loner; maybe a traveller, a visitor, as called, standing on his own at the end of the bar. Rooney hears someone say, "You like that corner pal." He's the 'quiet man' there. He's developing a pattern of going there each evening and, from his discussions and numerous 'same again' requests of the barman, it appears he's drinking heavily. He even hears him getting some cannabis from some Glasgow guys who had 'immigrated' to these parts.

Rooney wonders if he'll need a hit more than he needs the drugs or alcohol he's using. This's a relationship of pain and excitement, an experience many of Rooney's clients understand well, like a paedophile who both craves and hates his actions and has no control. He can't, won't stop, until he is stopped, but for him in a fitting way. He has disposed of Muir, finally, but what will his next big hit be? Through the families, he could ruin multitudes of people, businesses and organisations. This man does big.

He hears him arguing with incomers, then riling the locals not to accept that the majority of the village folk are 'non locals'. "They'll move in, join your community council, make all the decisions, and then they'll destroy your culture and ruin your means to make a living, like the government of the day who cleared this area of people to make way for sheep. They, in Whitehall and in Holyrood, will clear you lot to make way for incomers." He's winding these people up, animating them. He'll soon get them to act on it.

His talk becomes more bizarre. Rooney can hear him conversing with himself incessantly as his footsteps crush mussel shells on the shore of Loch Long. He wonders why he keeps the Latin book close to him. Rooney is probably the closest person to him in a weird sort of way and who bizarrely understands him more than anyone.

Through his perpetual stupor, from his ravings, a plan is developing in his mind that would bring Rooney back to him and draw him, like never before, into his plans.

Last time he wanted Rooney to destroy Muir, or he would have killed all the council members. Now, he rants that 'he would not have such an easy way out'.

Jackie knows Johnston has dropped off the radar and now she can do one of two things. One, await his next move, believing he needs the gratification, that he'll break cover and act. This time CID intelligence is stronger and she has contacts in all the major crime organisations which inhabit the land. If Johnston employs his usual surrogates, she'll know about it. Or two, she could rely on Rooney getting him.

Getting embroiled with Johnston again scares Rooney. He's in no state to cope with him. He could try to stop him, find him, have him arrested, give evidence in Court and have him sent away for good; do his best to prove he's a dangerous psychopath; have him detained in the state hospital. He doesn't have the strength or the bottle to do this. His mental and physical health is on a downward spiral. But if he doesn't kill Johnston, Johnston'll kill him. Either directly, which is a serious proposition, or by stealth where his mental health would give up. Rooney'll give up.

"The bastard's pushed me too far," Rooney says. "I've drawn a line in the sand. The good man is no longer good."

"Good man made bad?"

Johnston also has health problems. Rooney hears him make an appointment with the local doctor, after discovering blood in his urine one morning. He talks to an elderly woman in the waiting area of the surgery.

"That magazine is well out-of-date you know," she says.

"Ah ha," he says. "Nothing is current here in the land where there is no mañana."

Right there, from the magazine presumably, something prompts him to say, "Nelson Gray, the most prestigious writer, artist and bonhomie in the country, his idol. This man exemplifies everything he believes in," he says. This concerns Rooney greatly.

CHAPTER THIRTY-THREE

Rooney has been low, high, gone through the DTs, has massive health problems, and is shit scared he'll go back downwards over the edge. Without the drink his demons are more apparent. Drink used to help, but it now it's killing him and he doesn't have its crutch. What is his life, this blind drunk? What has he achieved with this man, absolutely nothing? He has to prepare, to use his head. He'll soon place him in an impossible position, and he'll be able to respond, to fight him, to match him, to kill him. Could he kill him?

He needs to get away and – thank the sober gods – he has a reason to. He has to follow his hypothesis regarding Johnston's parents. This's an opportunity for him to take stock, get healthy, eat some proper food, get out of the Glasgow drinking culture for a while, and arm himself for what he's convinced will be his final battle with Johnston. He has to take the chance; not to would lead to disaster, or even worse, failure.

Jackie employs her sources through Interpol and traces Johnston's parents easily for Rooney. Now retired from their primary professions, they're living on the north coast of France, in Honfleur in Normandy. James Johnston, once the diplomat, and his wife Louisa, once the French Canadian academic, now run the Hotel Du Dauphin, a small but classy hotel in this small fishing port, close to the Vieux Bassin. Rooney will book in and get to know them better, to better arm him for his next, he hopes ultimate, meeting with Johnston.

Two days later, he flies to Beauvais and arrives in Honfleur. He enjoys it immediately. It's a beautifully preserved 17th century maritime port, an artist's delight, where Eugène Boudin was born and lived. He'll pass himself as an artist as he wanders around carrying his painting pallette and oils, at the same time mixing with a multitude of cultures and nationalities.

He books into their hotel for two weeks, purely for a vacation. To paint pictures, he said at the time. The Johnstons have created a modern but rustic French hotel, well respected by the locals by ensuring the hotel remains in keeping with the mediaeval town. They blend in well there, she more than he.

Louisa's Québécois French is well accepted, her feisty personality appreciated by the locals, especially when she blows her top with truculent guests. James is the perfect host, always the diplomat. He fits in well into the local political scene and quickly developed a reputation for getting things done within the local community, and there's a rumour he'll stand for local office. Rooney takes Chambre Eugène Boudin, a bit pricey at 98 Euros, but he's charging Jackie, or more accurately the CID – the British public is paying. The room overlooks St Catherine's, a 15th century church built by shipwrights, surrounded by cobbled streets and art galleries.

Within a couple of days, he has the Johnstons sussed. At breakfast one morning, he identifies a situation of abuse. Paul, an effete, effeminate, but very stressed French houseboy of sixteen, who looks much more like twelve, seems to do everything, including acting as a hotel cleaner, receptionist, cook. But nothing seems to be good enough for Louisa. She slaps him in front of a guest when he complains his coffee is cold. Anyone would have walked out there and then. It's clear he needs the job, and it's clear Louisa understands this.

Rooney times his walk one day to coincide with Paul's weekly trip to the market for fresh vegetables. He walks with him into the Bassin and asks if he wishes to accompany him for coffee. He appears to acquiesce easily, as if this's a common occurrence. He's hardly going to refuse; Rooney's a guest after all. He's reluctant to say anything about the Johnstons at first, but, after some words of comfort, he opens up. It appears there had been a rapid turnover of young male staff members, aided by a steady recruitment drive facilitated by James. Paul has an ill mother and, as a result, a poor work record, taking time off to care for her. He was surprised to get this job; no other hotel in the area would take him on. If he resigns or is fired, he'll never work in the area again. He realises he has no way out. It's a situation of control, a set-up that can only lead to abuse. This's made crystal clear later the same night when he hears Johnston senior talking to him in the way which confirms Paul is a toy to debase. He chides him for not looking after his mother, saying he's selfish and he should be punished – and he'll punish him. They work him hard for little money, and Louisa thrashes him regularly with her stick while James fires off Latin statements. One, in particular, 'ab asino lanam' he uses on Paul. "You can't get wool from an ass," he says, running him down and demeaning him at the same time.

The context is clear to Rooney: vulnerability giving way to abuse, manipulation, and exploitation. Blame and retribution will come next, and sure enough the following week Paul is sacked. The dismissal comes after Louisa accuses him of stealing. She attacks him with her walking stick, leaving him bruised and bloodied, and running into the night. He hears Johnston senior uttering to his wife, "Compesce mentem," which he understands, because he had heard it said so often in Hillwood, means 'control your temper' – particularly apt.

Paul goes to the Gendarmerie, but no action is taken against them. After all, the Johnstons are well respected in the area, part of the local establishment, paying taxes and adding to the local economy. It appears to Rooney, there, an employer's aggressive response to theft, albeit by a young person, is justifiable and tolerated. If anything, as an example of the context within which the young Johnston grew up, this was it. Rooney finds everything he has sought there, but he can't leave without one last test. He wants to know how much Johnston's parents can control him. Do they think they can have influence over him?

The Johnstons lost contact with their son some years previously – or him from them, more like. Until Jackie got in touch, they had no idea of what he was doing or whom he was doing it to. They thought he was well established in Scottish academia, which pleased them as it rounded the family circle, returning a Johnston to where the ancestral Johnstons originated. Now they cannot believe he's capable of the things Jackie suggests, and write her off as a zealot for an overenthusiastic UK justice system. Rooney wonders if they would want to reach him, to punish him for bringing the long arm of the law to them, besmirching the Johnston name; but more, because he threatens their respectable and respected place in their new found French society.

Rooney leaves it to his last day there. He doesn't want to be thrown out of the hotel prematurely, and he wants to choose the context well for his confrontation. He also doesn't want to be assaulted, being the coward he is. He invites them to lunch in a small café in the harbour, one recommended by them, to 'thank them for their hospitality'. They'll behave themselves there, not wanting to draw attention to themselves. They order seafood platters and a very refreshing bottle of Sancerre. Then he toasts them and their successful hotel, of which he, somewhat disingenuously, says he has enjoyed enormously. He waits until the cheese and Calvados arrive before he drops the bombshell.

"I have to tell you, as well as being a bit of an artist," Rooney says. "I am also a freelance journalist." He sees them looking at each other, perhaps refusing to consider this a threat. After all what would a journalist want with them?

"Oh yes, and what does that entail?" fishes James.

"I do stories and sell them to a variety of newspapers and mags." Rooney drops his head as he breaks the cheese into his mouth, followed by a plentiful swallow of Calvados; but he knows they'll be looking at each other in pursuit of assurance.

"Any interesting stories?" James says.

"Only your son's predilection for killing people." Rooney waits for the response, as they look aghast at him.

"Our son, our son!" Louisa screams, slapping her hand down on the table, smashing a glass.

James quickly cleans up and tries to pacify her. "Now dear, remember where we are." She's fuming, and Rooney's a hair's breadth away from her scratching his eyes out. "What do you want with us, Mr Rooney?" James says.

Where has he heard that before?

"Your son is attracting quite an interest."

"Our son has been convicted of no... crime." Louisa is standing over him in a menacing way.

"Only because he has cleverly concealed his involvement with some... atrocities."

"You are defaming our family. We will... sue you," she says.

"I think we need to curtail this discussion, love," James says, trying to deter his wife from getting more involved than she needs with this man, who is surely a threat to them.

"Don't you try to tell me anything." She reaches over and digs her nails into the back of Rooney's hand, bringing tears to his eyes. Pain control kick in! But he has her. Now he'll introduce his test.

"What would you do if he was convicted as a major international terrorist... responsible for mass murder?"

If Louisa had a knife in her hand, and had she not been in such a public place, she would have enjoyed using it.

"We can do nothing in this situation," James says to his wife.

"And the death of the Muirs? Even you would've heard of them."

"We know of the Muirs, Mr Rooney. From a long way back," James says.

"Indeed, and I am sure your son will have too."

Their parallel silent scowl indicates he's achieved what he intended there. Now he'll use them, in the way their son had used others. He gets up and leaves, abruptly, dropping a card with his phone number on the table as he goes. He's made an impact. He'll call again on the Johnstons. Through them, as *his* proxies, he'll reach right into Johnston. Next time, he'll be armed and ready.

In his Arrochar hideaway, Johnston practises his new role by playing host to a number of teleconferences between high profile gangland bosses. Via his listening device, Rooney hears him do this. He wonders if he's mastered the technology while at the university, to help him link with others interested in urban conflict around the world. He'd developed a sophisticated and secure means of communication, mindful of the possibility of infiltration and hackers into the system, in particular intelligence agents.

They all want to be in the 'Cosa Nostra Scoti,' as he calls it, an interesting play on the term Scottish Mafia. Johnston seeks to become the '*capo di tutti capi*,' the boss of bosses. He is the father of fathers; he is *the* father. Jackie advises the group had grown from the nucleus of the family of families, to include other big players such as the notorious Fox family, and the Taylors, there as per right.

The McGinns are taking a back seat though. He can't see Davy taking his family into unknown territory, seeking national exposure, or any exposure after losing Thomas, and with the possibility of Mick seeking his own family.

The Cosa Nostra Scoti is joined by lesser families such as the Hogans from Dundee, the Fergusons from Aberdeen, and the Anderson family from Edinburgh. Other potential organisations, not quite active in a destructive sense, were to seek apprenticeship status and support for their cause. Through the bug, he hears how pleased they are with Johnston's stewardship; allowing them to retain their individual power bases and not to be seen to be the organisation leading the others. He's an entirely independent convener and has no allegiance with any individual family. The group's constitution seeks to share information and expertise, to maximise the potency of terror, and to shift the balance of power and politics. With their combined strength, they intend overpowering the new groups, leaving them open to being bought off, and their soldiers to be drawn in as new recruits to their ranks, making them stronger yet. They intend going international, spreading their empires down south then into the continent, and into the very heartlands of the international crime bosses.

Johnston's less interested in the development of their ideas or ideologies, which propagates violence, extortion or murder; he's only interested in action. This pleases the families, because it diverts them away from costly inter-cultural and inter-religious clashes. He'll exploit the tools of communication such as the internet, mobile communications, the media, the covert movement of people and funds, and opportunities for identity theft to help them realise their aims.

Armed with ammunition gathered from Johnston's parents, Rooney calls Jackie. Even more so since she sent him a voicemail, which said no more than: "I need to talk to you." Johnston'll be in touch with him too. Of this, he has no doubt. Hearing her voice mail message, he leaves his. "Jackie, I *need* to talk to you."

She phones him right back. "Rooney, thank god you phoned."

"Is this call being traced or recorded?" he says, fearing GCHQ is monitoring their calls.

"No, please believe me."

"Am I a hunted man?"

"Don't worry, there were mitigating circumstances. You were working in the city's best interests."

"Maybe I don't trust the 'city's best interests'."

"And me?"

"And you, Jackie?"

"You got my message?"

"Yes. I'm been trying to reach you, where have you been?"

"I've been... busy hon. Johnston, have you seen him?"

"Indeed, and his parents."

"You have been busy."

"I was with him when you texted me about Muir's death. He knew you would contact me right then, right at the time. How did he know this?"

"He asked me to."

"He asked you to! What is this Jackie?"

"He emailed me to say what Muir was likely to do."

"Why didn't you try to stop Muir?"

"It wasn't possible hon, Muir was determined. It was the best thing for the city."

"The city, the city. Here we go again, with the city."

"He's made a move on Gray."

"Christ."

"No, Gray."

"Same thing."

She reiterates the information she received through the CID.

"This is to get me," he says.

"I know."

"He's manipulating me."

"Kill him Rooney. Do it, damn it."

"Just like that."

"Either way, he wins. Can you no' see this?"

"He'll have made me do it."

"Just do it anyway."

"We'll see."

"Well, if you don't he'll kill Gray."

"Aye, he probably will."

"If he kills Gray, you'll never live wi' yourself Rooney; and you'll never be forgiven if you had that opportunity and hadn't used it. You've got to do it."

"OK Jackie, I get the message. You want me to kill Johnston, nothing to do with your ambitions."

"Rooney, do you want me?" This stops him in his tracks. He refuses to answer, to kowtow to her; but he wants her and she knows that. "Do it then."

Tom O. Keenan

He cuts off. This 'do it' is affirmative. He has to kill Johnston. But if he kills him, could he live with himself? Another bloody dilemma. He needs to think, so off he goes to the place his head works best, the pub. However, he promises Ben, if he intends another bender, to allow him to be there to 'supervise' him.

CHAPTER THIRTY-FOUR

Rooney meets Ben in Tennents around 9.30 p.m. Rooney orders a large Glayva and ice, and Ben has a pint of Deuchars IPA. He can't drink it at first. Then, as the anaesthetic properties of the alcohol starts to work, he can. The pub's its usual rumbustious self, full of all sorts: students in for the cheap real ale, groups of west end women who like to drink pints, older folk in town for shopping who then got waylaid until the last bus will take them off home to Drumchapel, Maryhill, wherever. He enjoys the buzz of this bar, the hubbub, the anonymity – and some nooks and crannies where it's possible to sort things out.

They find a seat, way off in the corner next to the Ladies toilet; less chance of being pestered by the boozers that surrounded the bar there. The pub has zones where, once ventured into, people remain in a routine way forever more – same people, same place, same time, same drinks – same as Rooney. Ben likes his privacy and this corner gives it. There they can talk.

Rooney reveals his dilemma around killing Johnston.

"Rooney, can you do it?" Ben asks.

"Can he not do it?"

Rooney takes time to answer. He rests his head on the back of the seat taking in the wide ceiling, reputedly held up by just three steel pillars that hold up the rest of the three floors above.

"Can I do it? Gray, the great man's in serious danger." He takes a gulp of his drink. "I have to save him. It's straightforward, easy." Another gulp. "All I have to do is kill Johnston."

"But that's what he wants Rooney."

"Indeed it is. Therefore, it's easy."

"You can you kill a man?"

"Can you kill a man?"

Rooney smirks. "I'd shut my feckin' mind to it. Pull the trigger. Administer the poison. Stab him in the gut. Whatever; fifty ways to kill another."

"But what would that make you, this saviour of Gray?"

"The man who rid the world of a fiend. A hero?"

Ben shakes his head. "No, Rooney, it would make you a killer."

"Rooney the killer."

"Well, that's where I've been heading anyway."

"Sorry."

"I wanted to hurt or kill some people I counselled."

"You?"

"You!"

"Me. Time to give up the ethics, the profession. Do the right thing, wipe the fuckers off the face of the feckin' earth. Then, I might feel better inside. That's what most of the public want anyway."

"That would make you what Johnston wants you to be, what he has created."

"I know."

"Could you be a killer on his terms?"

"To be a murderer to save Gray, and to save others who would have followed Gray?"

"For me Rooney, there's one operative question."

"God, you are such a bloody social worker Ben." Rooney notices the weaker the Glayva becomes as the ice melts. "Go on then."

"Could you let Johnston leave the world with a great triumph over his fellow man? To kill himself through a good man. This killer who kills through others."

"Indeed, Johnston, in me, would have had created a killer out of a normal man. Others, possibly his parents, made him a killer. He would have created me, the killer. I would have been as bad as him. Ergo he's as good as me and I'm as good as him."

"Rooney, I'm becoming increasingly worried about you."

"'The Father', the killer, was created. I, the normal everyday drunk, who can kill, has been created. Man creates killers – they are not born. My thesis confirmed."

"Say no more!"

Rooney orders another double and another. By the end of the third, he's sure he can do it.

Ben is not so sure. "You are a good man, Rooney. What makes you think you can do it? I mean it's alright talking about it, but when it comes to – "

"Ben, this isn't a crime, this is sanctioned by him, for him. DCI Jackie Kaminski says I have to do it. There'll be no arrest, no charge, and no conviction. I would remain a just man. Notwithstanding my trial for rape, which, when it comes, will be justified in terms of being sanctioned by the authorities. I will be acquitted. I will remain a... good man."

"A good man ruined!"

"You'll be killing him nonetheless."

Rooney shrugs his shoulders. "He needs to die."

Ben pulls his chair in close. "And does that meet your moral code Rooney? What you live by, what made you, this... task?"

"I'll be dispatching a fiend from the earth Ben, putting him to death on behalf of mankind."

Ben moves back. "Well, I guess it's warranted and necessary then."

"I'm acting on behalf of society, ergo it's fine."

"I don't believe you Rooney. I don't believe you can ignore your morality, to be indifferent to the death of another human being. I mean you, Sean Rooney."

"Indeed, Sean Rooney."

"Well, Johnston is psychologically immune to any moral scruples."

"But can you be Rooney? Your life has been about helping, supporting, healing."

Rooney fidgets in his seat. There in this place where they debriefed after countless incidents. "In being controlled, being his proxy, I am innocent. I am just doing what I have to do; as any other human being would do, only obeying orders."

"Like SS guards?"

"You will kill what you believe in Rooney."

He's now up and on his way to the toilet. Avoidance or a need for a pee, Ben isn't sure. As he departs, he says, "Indeed, when you kill the self, you kill the person, the person's morals, the conscience. You kill the self, you control the person."

He gets back ringing his hands. His time in the toilet has given Ben time to think of a reply.

"Mind your words, Rooney, when you came out of your overdose. "Don't let him do this to you, like he did to me. You can die or live, in your mind, and you can live or die in your life. You can live or die Rooney." He knows this will hit home.

"Live or die Rooney."

He's up for it. "I live or die in my mind. If I am controlled, I die in my mind and I die in my life. I won't let him dominate me as my father dominated my mother."

"To do this you'll have to be like him, be him, be a nihilist, be a proxy killer."

"Christ when two therapists get together!"

"Indeed, then I'll have no direct part in the act. I'll use others, use the power he uses. I'll fuck rather than be fucked. I'll trump his power and raise my nihilism above his. I'll triumph over him. *I'll* be the great proxy killer I have always wanted... needed."

"Fuck or be fucked."

"You'll be no different from him Rooney. You'll just be the same as him, but with less of the success. Rooney, this man – as you yourself have said – has destroyed numerous lives."

"I'll do more."

"Rooney, my friend, this is delusional talk."

"I'll kill him in his way and I'll kill him in my way. I'll kill what he is and then I'll kill him. And this is why I'll triumph over him."

"You're delusional, Rooney. You're developing an NPD. An exaggerated sense of self-importance, a fantasy of unlimited power, and a belief you are special. We know the traits Rooney."

"He's the man. Flying at the speed of sound. The Rooneyman."

"Ben, delusional, narcissistic or not, I *will* do this. Not to do it will be the end of me. He knows that, and he knows I cannot not do it."

"If you kill him you'll have been controlled, used."

"Yes, and I'll lose my self-respect. My inner self'll die. I'll die. Yet, I have to do it, for my self-respect, for my inner self."

"It's your dilemma, Rooney."

"I have to use, rather than be used. This is my resolution. I understand his power and how he exerts it. His proxies were just doing what they had to do. My proxies will be doing what they have to do."

It's as if Ben is reading his mind. "Aye, the Nazis knew how to do this. The officers and guards who corralled, singled out and gassed the Jews, said they were just following orders."

This is Rooney's subject and he's determined to show it. "The Nazi overlords knew how to do it. They dehumanised their proxies, the ones who carried out the act. It's the ideology of war, of taking of life, of killing human beings and absolving oneself of the responsibility, of the guilt of it. You get people to kill when they have no sense of self. Or, to hold onto any sense of self they have at all, they have to kill. This isn't me. I am obeying orders. I'm not responsible. The proxy killers know that all good and normal people are exploitable. We are all fallible to change, and to transform, if faced with the right or wrong type of pressures. They, we, are all able to do heinous things."

"Have you changed Rooney?"

"Changed!"

"Aye, we all change."

"Remember the Milgram experiment in the early sixties," Ben says. "When Stanley Milgram set up experiments to test how much pain an ordinary person would inflict on another person, simply because he was ordered to by a scientist. Flagrant authority was pitted against the subject's strongest moral imperatives against hurting others, and, with the subject's ears ringing to the screams of the victims, authority won more often than not."

"My point. People will go to any lengths on the command of authority."

"Ordinary people, with no particular hostility on their part, can become agents in a destructive process, Rooney. You know that. When asked to carry out actions outwith their fundamental standards of morality, relatively few people have the strength needed to resist this authority."

"Well, *I* can."

"You can use others Rooney?"

"*Tibi seris tibi metis.* I am the master of my fate. I am the captain of my soul."

"Fuck, you have learned from him."

"*The poacher becomes the game keeper!*"

"I have learned."

Ben appreciates his challenge is over. His friend has lost his morality, and he can do no more to dissuade him from his intentions, but he has one last point to make.

"But how do you use others to kill and at the same time save your good friend Gray?" Ben says. "How can you prevent Johnston from giving the order – if you don't kill him, as he demands? How can you prevent the group holding him from killing him? With the cellular structure of these families, there's no clear basis of command, and Johnston may have relinquished control to those who would do the deed."

"Nihilists don't worry about friends Ben."

"Indeed," Ben says, as he gets up and leaves. Defeated, he has lost a friend.

CHAPTER THIRTY-FIVE

Rooney listens into the device and it's clear Johnston, for his part, mulling over his plans in the 'quiet man's corner', believes he has Rooney where he wants him. Rooney can only comply with his demands or the man he admires most in this world will die. 'It's him or me,' is his incessant credo. Johnston believes Rooney can only submit and put aside his beliefs and values. Johnston also knows he has to confirm his resolve to close the deal. He needs to believe Rooney can and will do it.

Rooney keeps up to speed with Johnston's developing profile, mainly through some very dubious 'family' web sites, Facebook and Twitter. He wonders if the CID might have traced him by his browsing habits and would arrive at his place to arrest him as a terrorist suspect.

The crime community now see Johnston, The Father, as its godfather, the 'capo di tutti capi,' the boss of bosses. Whether he likes it or not, many in its ranks see him as the vehicle that unites them in a common purpose. No one person can lead them though. That person will be truly at risk and will ultimately fail. Johnston appears happy though to act as a catalyst for their criminal objectives.

From the newspapers, the Scottish Government's fear of a united crime cabal is almost realised. They never accepted that crime societies with their respective differences, belief systems, cultures and aspirations, could ever find common ground or resolve inter-family feuds. Johnston had masterfully, through the family of families on the one hand and by exerting his influence on Campbell on the other at the Summit, confirmed this pivotal role he has exploited with Cosa Nostra Scoti. Johnston's influence is total. He has delivered something no individual organisation could have hoped to achieve, and he has done it with the ultimate malevolent mechanism: fear, rather than direct action. This is the true nature of marshalled terror, and he has mastered it.

Jackie invites Rooney to dinner – out.
Five weeks have passed without incident in Glasgow. There's a feeling of

respite and a palpable sense of relief. It's late when they arrive at Mother India, on Dumbarton Road, just across from the Galleries. This is his first curry since his stomach problems; he chooses korma and beer, and it stays down.

"You're looking better hon."

"I'm the better for seeing you dear." He stuffs naan into his mouth.

"Missed your ugly coupon."

"Ugly being the operative term."

They move to the Firebird lounge and take a table by the wood-burning stove. To anyone around this is a warm, friendly situation. The discussion belies otherwise. Though as she says, getting Johnston is her greatest test and Rooney both the greatest asset and risk to this. Her career will be over if she fails. Success, though, will crash her through that glass ceiling. Rooney is her ticket to that 'Detective Chief Superintendent job'. She reaches for his hand and coaxes him to lean across the table, as she does herself.

"I... want you hon," she says, holding his hand.

"Madam Machiavelli showing her colours?"

"I want you too, but I know why you want me."

"You want me. I want Johnston. You want Johnston. You need me. I need my career. It all works out."

He fucks her that night, fucks her hard. It does him the world of good. He's on top of her, the fucker, not the fucked. She allows this, almost promotes it, then leaves him in her bed the next morning, saying she's going to London. No good-byes, no "I'll see you soon," only "You know what you have to do."

Next day, she phones from London. "Well, you know I need this," she says. "I booked myself into Ragdale Hall Health Hydro for a weekend spa break, where I am being well pampered, looked after, and I've spent a very satisfying afternoon in Oxford Street, bringing my wardrobe up to date with some latest designer stuff, shoes, makeup, etcetera. The girl is ready, Rooney?"

"Aye, suppose she is. Another wee junket," Rooney says, trying to develop his sarcasm.

"Sure, another fun packed holiday paid by the taxpayer. But I'm worth it hon... Now Gray."

"Yes, he's at risk."

"I've taken steps to protect him, but it's Johnston here. You have a role in securing Gray's safety. You got that Rooney?"

"Indeed dear. I know everything."

"Colin Crossan's in charge of Gray's security. He's dad's choice," she says. "Crossan is a large, gruff, Glaswegian polis. He doesn't take fools gladly. So watch yourself."

"A Glesca bouncer's not enough to protect him, Jackie."

"I've no doubts about his ability. I've also have attached several experienced officers to Gray. We're very much in control of the situation. Gray is protected by the highest possible security. We're doing our part, now you do yours."

"Highest security! Do they know Johnston?"

"I'll make sure they do."

"Are you enjoying yourself?"

"I am indeed. This hotel is style, classic luxury. You'd like it there. Pal… atial. The room's extremely comfortable."

"Do you wish I were there?"

"I hear the BBC's running a story on the Gray death threat."

"I know, nothing like assuming a low profile."

"What do you mean?"

"Well, you're a senior police officer. There's a serious threat to the City. A Lord Provost of Glasgow and his wife are dead. So's his daughter. Johnston's admitted liability. You're in danger of losing all your credibility here Jackie. Every fibre of your being should be fixed on nailing the man. You're acting like a daft hound, and yet you're in charge of the hunt." 'Click'. "That'll get her going."

Rooney listens in to the device. Johnston's enjoying the new authority given to him by the 'Cosa Nostra Scoti'. The early meetings agree a common mission; a strategy of individual objectives and a common identity; a greater collective family power where before they had an individual presence. One evening he hears Johnston mutter to himself, "When I have absolute authority, and an ability to cause the greatest effect, I'll take my leave." He's confirming his objective, and when this's realised, he'll back out. He understands that, before long, Cosa Nostra Scoti will disintegrate, and he'll bail out before it does. The individual interests will be too strong and they'll cause its implosion, with him in the middle. He enjoys the ego boost it gives him, taking the 'godfather' role as far as it can go, then stepping out before it destroys itself.

Jackie calls the next morning. "I'm on my way home. I got a phone call from Crossan. He said Gray developed a stomach complaint. They say it's food poisoning. He's been transferred to the Western Infirmary, as a precaution."

"Food poisoning! What about the security arrangements?"

"Crossan says everything is under control."

"Safe as houses."

Johnston's behind this, is Rooney's immediate thought. His next is to get to the hospital.

"If Johnston gets to Gray and he dies you'll be responsible," he says.

"You'll be every bit responsible," she says. "You know what to do to protect him. "Anyway, Crossan's been briefed on what Johnston's capable of."

He's not so sure.

"*Trust no one.*"

Rooney switches off. He wonders if he is faced with a dilemma from Jackie: both putting Gray at risk and doing Johnston's bidding to save Gray's life. He decides to go to the hospital, not that he can do anything physically to protect Gray, but he needs to see what has happening for himself.

A cab appears and ten minutes later he's at the ward's reception desk. After producing his ID, he's advised Gray's in a side room in the medical ward, but no one's to be allowed access to him.

"Does Mr Gray have control over who he sees?" he asks the ward sister.

"Mr Gray can see who he so wishes, but all visitors are subject to security," she says.

"I want to talk to him."

He waits for around fifteen minutes before she returns.

"He'll see you."

Great, he can talk to him, with no plan other than to explain the great risk he's exposed to. As he walks along the corridors to the medical ward, his mind notes everything relevant to Gray's safety, top of the list being a complete lack of security.

"Where's the security?" he murmurs to a nurse as she escorts him along the corridor. She doesn't answer. On reaching his room, she transfers him to a single plain-clothes police officer who ushers him inside where he's met by a female doctor.

"He's an old man. He's very tired and weak from the food poisoning. Please be brief," she says.

As he enters his room. Gray's propped up in bed silhouetted against the light from the window. Great, a sniper's delight. Gray turns to him and offers his hand. The grip is weak, this hand that produces great works.

"Rooney, my friend, have you come to explain to me why I am being treated like a VIP?" he says, in his inimitable high-pitched voice. "Please sit down," he urges. The medic pushes a chair into the back of his legs beckoning him to sit. He asks the police officer and the doctor to leave. "Apparently, there is a threat to my life," he says.

"Indeed so. What do you know?"

Gray screeches, "I know nothing," like Manuel from Fawlty Towers. "I thought you were going to tell me. Two nights ago, in my diner, after a divine tea of a haggis, tatties and neeps, something happened which indicated all was not quite as it should be." His 'diner' is a particular restaurant which, through his 'teas', repays a debt to this great artist, after he had created a fabulous mural in its unlikeliest of places: on the walls of the stairs to the toilets.

He talks in a professorial way. "I was there, enjoying a small refreshment, a significant glass of whisky. I was in the outer area of the pub, on Ashton Lane, among the hubbub of passers-by. Young people, students, as always, were milling around the pub entrance and spilling into the lane, a meeting place for the students. As usual, I talked to them. They know who I am. I talked about the university and how it was in my day, and my books, of which some had read. Some were fans," he laughs. "It was all very relaxed. I have no fears, although threats had been made on me before, for example, when I spoke up against the invasion of Iraq. Then there had been some death threats. My lecture tour was a bit risky from some nut-cases, but at home there has never been any reason to worry. Then a young lad I hadn't noticed before, approached me, pushing through the others there. 'Nelson?' the boy said. He repeated, 'Nelson.' I smiled, as I thought of my father who named me Nelson after his great hero, the great Mandela, who was called Tata, which in his native Xhosa means 'the father'."

Nelson is aptly named. He is unquestionably the father of cultural life in Glasgow.

"'Come here, young man,' I said to the boy. 'What's your name?' I asked him. He appeared shy and didn't talk, but he handed me an envelope. He smiled at me as I took it from him, and he ran away, disappearing out of view. I thought this was unusual as I opened the envelope." Nelson explains how he pulled out and studied the contents: a card and a photograph. "On the card there was a statement: *'optimi consiliari morti*: learn from the past'. I liked that, I memorised it – "

"Latin." The gold predictably returns to Rooney's head.

"Yes, Latin," he says. "The photograph was clear enough. It was me. It was a good photograph. I pride myself on looking friendly in pictures. In it, I was peacefully sitting at the window of the restaurant looking down along the lane. I was wearing the clothes I had worn earlier that night. I studied the picture carefully. I was drawn to a small red dot on my forehead. I got out my magnifying glass, which I carry with me these days as my eyesight is not as good as it used to be. '*Mein Gott,*' I gasped, as I recognised the red mark as a laser dot used to pinpoint a target. This card was no friendly calling card."

Rooney explains in detail the cards and messages connected to the murders in Glasgow, and of his views of a man with the ability to carry out any threats. Gray laughs again, saying he would be immortalized as a poor artist killed by a notorious killer. "Fame at last," he says.

Rooney tries to impress upon him the seriousness of this. "Nelson, this man will kill you, as he has others." Gray thanks him for his concern for his safety, saying he is tired. He would see him again soon. Rooney leaves the great man there.

Later that day Jackie arrives at his flat. She's been to the hospital to see

Gray. Rooney makes coffee.

"I've arranged increased security for Gray," she says. "I've been to see him, but he refuses to comply."

"Didn't work the last time."

"'I've had death threats before,' Gray said. 'Yes,' I said, 'but nothing like this, I can assure you.' But far from having misgivings he was intrigued by this and demanded to know everything there was about the man who threatened his life."

"Know your enemies."

"Strangely, he said he had a thing about incomers. He said, 'Asylum seekers have been diluting our culture since the eye-ties came here with their ice cream and fish and chip shops. Then came the Jews, Indians, Pakis, Chinks, Serbs and Croats. Every wee nation we try to knock sense into by bombing brings in a new wave of asylum seekers crowding out our natural native food with their foreign restaurants until now Scottish salmon and lobster, Scottish lamb, Aberdeen Angus beef, haggis, black pudding and our venison are for export only.'"

"What!" Rooney gasps.

"He was quoting from one of his plays, you tumshie," she says.

"Wow, that's a close call given everything all that's going on."

"He said he was fascinated by Johnston's role in the Summit. 'This man has real power,' he said. I told him he was in great danger, and he laughed. 'What should I do, hide? No, I am too old for that. I will, as I do with any threat, ignore it,' he said, laughing furiously."

"Passive action, the power of minimal resistance, Gandhi knew that," Rooney adds.

"'Mr Gray,' I said to him, 'you are at great risk from a man with an ability to carry through any threats he makes.' I was trying to introduce some seriousness. 'Thank you,' he said. 'Without freedom to live our lives what are we?' He spoke with his customary conviction. I said to him, 'You have to take... measures against this threat Mr Gray. This man will kill you.' 'With freedom comes responsibilities,' he said, 'and I have my work to do. My journey is not yet over, Miss Kaminski; however, if it is to be curtailed prematurely, then so be it.'"

"His journey," Rooney repeats. "He's talking about his life and his fight against tyranny. Johnston won't control him," he says, "but he may kill him, just-the-same."

"I left my card with my mobile number," she says. "I advised I would be there to assist him if he needed me. He shook my hand and I left the room. Outside, I talked to the doctor and asked about his illness. He said the symptoms were consistent with Salmonella poisoning, possibly caused by infected chicken, meat or eggs."

"I am not convinced."

"You can't protect him, Rooney, not directly."

"I'll do anything for that man," he says. "Anyway, how's you?"

"I've raised my game."

"Pleased to hear it."

"Well, since the new Terrorism Act, my ability to hold and question suspects has increased. I've had members of the families interviewed. Johnston's covered his tracks well. He's gone to ground Rooney, but where? Where is he Rooney?"

He refuses to answer. This is palpable power, and he is enjoying it. Johnston is his to fight and destroy.

"You *will* tell me darling," comes at him, sounding like a threat, a plea, or a flirtatious pass. He can feel her sexual power, eclipsing anything physical.

"He'll be in touch soon. I know he will," he says. "This is a typical build up."

"Dad's been in touch. The First Minister's been in touch. They want answers."

"Look," he says, "you want me to kill him, not bring him in. You know he can't be tried. You want him dead. They want him dead."

"We all have our wants Rooney," she says, heading out.

"Power corrupts Jackie," he says, as she moves through the door. She pauses for a couple of seconds, turns, smiles and leaves.

That night Rooney hears Johnston, still in Arrochar, say: "A three point plan, a three-point plan, a three-point plan," repeatedly, like a mantra. Rooney plays around with what this three-point plan might be. Again a SWAG hypothesis materialises in his mind from the options available: one, Johnston creates a threat on Gray's life; two, he convinces Rooney of the certainty of Gray's death; and three, he forces him to do whatever he wants him to do, thereby confirming for him his lifelong belief that, as is said, 'absolute authority controls absolutely'.

Rooney goes to bed early after a few, and sleeps through Jackie's call. She leaves a voice mail, which he gets as he makes a nocturnal visit to the loo.

"I've made enquiries about the food poisoning," she says. "Gray's chef at the restaurant is livid. He's cooked for him for years and says there's never been a possibility of food poisoning. He's sure Gray's been poisoned. I share your concerns. I'm off to my bath."

Rooney imagines Jackie in her bath, and he admits to being not a little excited; though, for him, a vivid imagination and a repertoire of fantasy vignettes were never a substitute for the real thing. He tries to concentrate, but this's giving him a hard-on as solid as a whisky bottle and his bed beckons.

Next day, he expects the morning call. "Hon, it's me." Her voice echoes out through the peaceful dark of his room. He opens his mobile, feeling more than a little startled.

"Can you no' ring me at a sensible time?" he says, responding with his natural charm.

"Well hello darling, it's eight o-fucking-clock."

"Jesus, that early," he says, pouring a small one from the bottle on his bedside cabinet.

"Rooney, Gray's been kidnapped."

He drops the glass.

"Fuck-it, when, how?"

"About an hour ago, three men, at the hospital, at gunpoint. He tried to resist, but he was too weak. He was bundled into a waiting car and driven off at speed. You have to act now."

"Fuck off, what can I do?"

"Johnston, Rooney, Johnston."

"So we're sure?"

"I got a text message last night, one I opened before I went to bed. It read '*re infecta*, unfinished business'."

"When the fuck will this be over?"

"You know when."

"They've made a statement."

"That it was shite security?"

"They left a message: 'We demand a press release on James Muir, telling the whole story. There will be no civic funeral, no honours. This will be done to show your willingness to work with us.'"

"It's a fait accompli. The council won't do this. It'll bring them down. He knows this."

"Hold on, there's more. 'Failure to meet this demand will result in the summary execution of Nelson Gray, sometime before midnight on the third day from now.'"

"Three days. *I'll* blow the gaff on Muir."

"Aye, you do and he'll definitely kill Gray."

"What's being done to save him?"

"Everything, as you would imagine."

"As you would imagine Jackie?"

"High-powered discussions, a task force, headed by a security committee."

"Didn't do much the last time, did it?"

"I've to lead it. It's overseen by a Scottish Government security committee. To 'negotiate and effect' a safe return of Gray."

"Oh well, just what's needed, another bloody committee."

"This is it hon. This is where we succeed or fail. I'm on my last chance, and you are on your last legs, and you're drinking again, silly bugger."

"Silly bugger."

"Indeed I am; what does it matter?"

"It matters to me." He stops at this. "Does Gray matter to you? Are you no' supposed to be keeping a clear head?"

"Just clearing it after a skin-full last night."

"So much for *my* advice," she says. "Rooney, now you have to do it, you. There's no alternative."

"And what will I do?"

"You have to kill Johnston!"

"I presume it's a local family?"

"Correct."

"What if they kill Gray, regardless of Johnston?"

"I doubt it. He's doing this for you, and *you* can stop it."

"Thanks, I need to know I'm responsible for Gray's life, or more like his death." He pours another drink, in another glass.

"Well, you are. Has *he* been in touch?"

"Not so far."

"Rooney, Gray, your hero, dies in three days' time. Do you want that on your conscience? There's no time for persuasion."

"Fuck you Jackie, you and your fucking police department." He ends the call with a whack of his thumb.

Sure enough, the next call is Johnston.

"You know about Gray. We should meet," Johnston says.

"Why? What do you want me to do about Gray?"

"You know what I want you to do."

"What if the council agree the terms?"

"It won't."

It's clear Johnston's set up an irreconcilable situation, in which Gray could only die.

"We will meet on the third day," he says, "close to the deadline of Gray's demise, and then you will do what I ask of you. I will inform you by the second day of where, and you will not involve the authorities. To do so will lead to an early death for Gray. You are his only chance. And Rooney..."

"I'm listening."

"Keep off the holy water, hon. Gray and I, and you, depend on you having the wherewithal to do what is necessary."

"You'll get yours pal," Rooney says, throwing the mobile into the settee.

"And you'll get yours."

"And I'll get mine," he murmurs, as he gets a bottle and his computer out.

Rooney drinks and browses at the same time. He establishes the Fox family has taken Gray.

"They don't know the great man."

Rooney believes Gray would've have known this family from his contacts in Glasgow, though not the names of his captors. But he is no ordinary captive. He'll seek to establish a relationship with these men. He'll enquire and learn about those who would kill him. Gray also has some information on Johnston. Rooney doubts they'll know this. Maybe Gray will use this at the right time. Gray knows the way of the criminal mind; he encapsulated it in his plays. These men have taken on much when they took Gray.

Jackie appoints the now DCI Archie Paterson to be her partner in crime fighting. They head an executive project team, responsible for interviewing, sifting information from the public, following up leads, leading teams of investigators. They have access to an armed unit ready to leave for any potential Gray location. The special task force will carry the primary armed response. Jackie will lead negotiations with the group.

Jackie posts a notice on the BBC news web page to deliver the terms: WE WISH TO OPEN DISCUSSIONS TO SECURE THE SAFE RETURN OF NELSON GRAY.

Then she attaches contact details and orders an analysis of the primary kidnap terms. The Chief says nothing is to be offered to the group. The first day passes with no leads.

Jackie says Archie has been busy and, through Gray's cook, has traced the source of the meat delivered the day of his stomach complaint. Jackie's team also has some success in locating underworld sources with knowledge of this family.

By day two, Archie has extracted some crucial information from the meat supplier. Apparently, the haggis, destined for Gray's plate, was switched. The supplier was told his family would be killed, unless he acceded. A Johnston touch, no doubt. The meat supplier identified the man responsible for the switch as Joe Macqueen, a Fox family member. A team was sent to his house to apprehend him. His neighbours hadn't seen him for three weeks. Gray would have known Macqueen.

Then there's a breakthrough. Macqueen telephones Jackie. Jackie, through the security group, obtains authority to see Macqueen with Archie. Macqueen is given an assurance he would not be arrested, and a meeting is arranged.

Archie and Jackie meet Macqueen in the conference room of the Holiday Inn. He's ushered in after presenting himself at reception. Archie refuses to shake his hand, but Jackie does. Macqueen says he had been instrumental in Gray's kidnapping.

"We have them," Archie says to Jackie.

"Not quite yet," Jackie replies, reminding him they need to turn off the source of the group's actions.

Then, in an unprecedented move, Jackie orders Archie to arrest Macqueen, to remove him to the Force headquarters, to be held there incommunicado, and not to share the information received there that day with anyone, for fear of Gray's life. Archie is aghast, but bows to her greater experience in these matters as part of her strategy to secure Gray's release. He'll say nothing which might lead to Gray's death, but he's confused over her tactics. Nothing of Jackie's actions surprises Rooney.

CHAPTER THIRTY-SIX

The bug's still operating, although the battery'll go soon. Steeped in his new role, with his Cosa Nostra Scoti, Johnston cements the cohesion between these groups rather than leads them. *"Rex regnat sed non-gubernat.* The king reigns, but does not govern," Rooney says, now toying with Latin, taunting himself with the gold it brings to his mind. Within their respective leaderships, this group includes some very dangerous men.

This's a no-win role. In terms of group development, Johnston will lead the group through the forming stage and step out before the storming stage. This'll cause great disagreement. He knows they will never perform well as a group. They have no real cohesion other than a need for power. No man can hold them together for long, and to lead them is impossible. Johnston would know their very power lies in their individual independence and autonomy, and an ability to strike without a say-so from any authority. Moreover, pulling them together and stepping out, before the group implodes, will be satisfaction enough for him. This will be his swansong. He knows to challenge their individual missions, thereby seeking a communal objective, will be signing his death warrant, especially by the Fox family and the like. He will cut the strings to these groups, but with one last act of control.

Rooney anticipates the text from Johnston: 'King James Library, Day 3, 6.00 p.m.' In receiving this, he's aware this will be the day which will define the rest of his life, or indeed, determine his life or death. There'll be no going back. To go back would be the end of him, his inner self.

He wonders where the hell the King James Library is. Following up his research, he quickly connects this with Arthur Johnston, Johnston's, ancestor. The Deliciæ Poetarum Scotorum is the prestigious Scot's collection of Latin poetry, which is part of Johnston's life's works, held in Glasgow University. "Got it," he says. "A fitting place for the denouement he plans – "

"And you fear."

Jackie meets with the security committee. There's no breakthrough. Though, 'leads are promising,' she says to them.

Soon Rooney will confront Johnston. All he has to do is to end a psychopath's power, put an end to him, save Gray, and become the man he's destined to be. Inevitably, he needs some Dutch courage, but his stomach's aching and his head's thumping. He has the shakes and his skin's yellow. He doesn't need to go to his doctor with these symptoms. This's as good a reason as anything for a drink, but he decides to see Geraldine, his counsellor, instead; then he'll go for a drink. What she tells him deters him. She says he has about a year to live and suggests he sees his GP, who'll confirm this. She'll be right. She asks if he's thought any more about why he drinks so much. He says no, but he knows what she means. She says he has unresolved grief because of his illness, he has trauma from his childhood, and he has a habit. I could have told him that! The first and last ones are easy; the middle one, less so. Colour gold from the Latin and memories of his father marching him to church invades his head. Sort this, she says, and he'll have no reason to drink. "But I need to drink," he tells himself.

He doesn't need a reason to drink; though, he'll go to the pub anyway. The first couple of drinks give some pain, but after that it's easy. His head feels better, stomach feels better, the shakes stop. The hair of the dog helps. That is until about three drinks later when the ground comes up to meet him. He collapses like an old tower block being demolished in a heap at the bar. The folk there try to get him up, but he's like a sack of tatties. He's bleeding from his mouth and through the skin on his throat, and he's thrashing about in an epileptic fit.

They call an ambulance and he's admitted once again to the Western Infirmary. "Tonic-clonic seizure, chronic alcoholic, potential liver failure, question alcohol-related brain damage, stomach ulcers; needs a medical ward and most probably a nursing home for brain-damaged adults," he hears them say. He's transferred to a medical ward and put on a drip, given lots of vitamin B12, and has a few scans which confirm his sorry physical and mental state. Next morning, a consultant neurologist comes to his bed to say he wants to admit him to an alcohol rehabilitation centre and from there to a specialised care unit, where he'll likely stay for the rest of his life.

"Best place for you."

"No thanks," he says.

The consultant says he'll have him detained. That was it, he knows the score, and it's day three, and he has an appointment to keep. It's the 21st of April and he is in hospital. He agrees to stay informally and to take his advice; then, later that day, he dons his clothes and, saying he needs some air, he disappears out onto Byres Road. He walks into the Tinderbox café, directly across from the La Patisserie Françoise, and orders a strong espresso that stings his stomach, to gather his thoughts. He imagines Johnston over there; the Latin man and the hoodie man: a proxy killer and his fatal weapon.

"A fateful day then, an ever more fateful day now, you up to it?"

CHAPTER THIRTY-SEVEN

Rooney, feeling like shit, heads to Glasgow University, arriving there at 5.35 p.m. He can't be late this time. At reception, he's advised he needs a permit to access the university library. This is, though, magically produced after giving his name. He's given a leaflet and a guide to the library, and advised of strict rules concerning 'visiting scholars'. He's then directed towards the special collections department. The visiting hours for the reading room are 12.00 to 6.00 pm. 6.00 pm, he notes. Johnston's cutting it fine. He says to the attendant he has a meeting there at 6.00 p.m., to which he replies, "Oh aye, there's a special request to use the room after normal hours, not unusual for those who want exclusive and private access to the library." He hands him a special pass and directs him to the stairs and onto the first floor.

He's bumping off the tarmac, but he'll do this. He has to.

As he climbs the stairs, he leaves a message on Jackie's voice mail, reiterating the text he received from Johnston. It couldn't do any harm now. He doubts she'll try to prevent the meeting happening, hoping that he'll bring Johnston to book.

A student directs him to the Reading Room and in he goes through an already open door. Entering a dim, musty room, he runs his my hand over a large wooden table which looks like mahogany, positioned in the middle of the room, and drags his fingers along the surrounding columns of bookcases. There's an evocative smell of old manuscripts. He doesn't have long to wait as a familiar voice precedes the man entering.

"Ah good, you have arrived Doctor Rooney." Doctor! "As I expected, on time, two doctors together," Johnston says.

Then Rooney is hit by Vivaldi's *Four Seasons' Spring*, at a louder than comfortable level, prompting crescendos of colour in his mind. How the hell would Johnston know this? It's obvious, this's to disorientate him. Johnston moves into the open. He's wearing an eighteen-century, black frock coat and a doctorate hat. Rooney hopes this won't become a circus. Rooney rises and closes the door. For then, he does not want interruptions. He sits down close to the door for obvious reasons.

"Doctors, PhDs. Just bits of paper," Rooney replies.

"Indeed. Here is where you and I connect. Me, in this shrine to my ancestor's work, and you, in the place of your doctorate. Could there be a better place to achieve our respective goals?"

"I can think of better places I would like to be." Rooney wishes he could have told him to fuck off there and then, but the life of Nelson and others are on the line, as is his sanity, and much more, his self-respect and his pride. He has to see this through.

"I am sure you could," Johnston says, "like a few pubs around here for a start. Whatever, you are here, albeit you look like death."

"I've felt better."

"A delusional, hallucinating alcoholic. Are you a worthy opponent?"

First foray from Johnston. They both understand what he'll do: demean, disable, destroy.

"Let the battle begin," Johnston says. "I win, and you do what I expect of you, and Gray lives. You win, and you don't do what is expected of you, and Gray dies."

"I'm here to destroy you."

"Good, you'll do what you need to do." Johnston moves in closer to him.

"And I'll secure Nelson's release." Rooney keeps his distance.

"This I may allow, Sean, but only if you subscribe to my wishes."

"As you say, I'll do what I need to do."

"*Empta dolore docet experientia*, remember 'experience bought with pain teaches effectively'," Johnston says. "Use your head, kill me, save Gray, and others who would undoubtedly follow."

"*Non vacari*, Johnston. I will not be your puppet. You will not control me."

"*No?*"

"Very good Rooney, a vicarious act of mine. I will deliver my demise through another, which is you my friend. Yet *you* can prevent the death of your friend through another, me."

"Your attempts to break me down, use and manipulate me, destroy my sense of self, destroy me and my determination to challenge you, confounds your control; it minimises and destroys it. They, in turn, will defeat you."

"An interesting dilemma, don't you think?"

"The only dilemma here is us."

"Good, we are agreed."

"*He's no' listening to you?*"

"NPDs don't listen."

"No, we don't Rooney, Johnston says. "I have here a mobile phone." He's thought of everything. "It has a speed call number: number 1. This call will reach the group holding Gray; they'll release him immediately. So easy, don't you think?"

"Easy. What if I fight you, obtain the mobile and send the call?"

"You can hardly hold yourself up. Have you seen yourself? You look like death."

"Death warmed up."

Just about the way he feels.

"It needs a password. You'll receive it when I know my death is imminent. Then you'll have access to the mobile. My intermediaries expect contact from you. No contact and they will kill Gray. Do you understand?"

"I understand it all. I am to be an experiment, a plaything. You want to know if you can manipulate a good man into doing what he is not hardwired to do. Kill a man. This, you're greatest triumph. Sure, you can force others to kill, through money, power, fear, whatever. You use people by offering gains, by blackmail; you use people prone to kill anyway. But me, I'm not open to blackmail."

"Very well, a good man, indeed, but a weak man, a scared man. A man who can't protect himself. A man who cannot... take revenge."

"You, revenge? You wish to exploit, deprave – "

"Interesting words, Rooney."

"Corrupt, control."

"Lie, cheat... fail, Rooney."

"I'll put an end to you in my way, *and* save Gray."

"Put to an end? Your ability to 'put to an end' may be inhibited... by mental illness, your drinking?"

"Churchill fought a war on both of them."

"Ah, but he was a man. Why do you drink Sean?"

"Why do you kill?"

"Any hang-ups you wish to explore Rooney? Any fathers you wish to talk about?"

Ridicule, break down the defences. Like a snake charmer, relax, then control.

"Johnston, *In nomine Patris*; what about *your* father?"

Johnston moves around the room, talking to the bookcases. "Your father, Sean?"

Rooney doesn't answer.

"You hate him."

Again, he doesn't answer.

"He's a man, a man, not like his son." Rooney refuses to go down this road. "Gray, Sean, Gray," Johnston says, breaking into song. "Fre-e Ne-elson Gra-ay. Fre-e-e Ne-elson Gra-ay. Fre-e-e Ne-elson Gra-ay...." Vivaldi is turned up once more. It's clear he's trying to shatter Rooney's train of thought. "Called after Tata, the father," Johnston says. "*In nomine Patris*, Rooney. Do it for the father."

"You know nothing about Gray. He's a good man, a bigger man than you."

"Ah ha, your hero."

Johnston circumambulates the room, constantly chanting "Free Gray, free Gray, free Gray," exacerbating the tension.

"They will save him."

"You think so? I have an assurance which indicates otherwise."

"Assurance?"

"Indeed Sean, power, influence," Johnston says in a slow voice. "*Procuratia*, someone acting for another."

"Proxy, doing the act of another. Just like the rat, Johnston."

"*Patria potestas*. The power of a father."

"*Patria potestas*. The power of *the* father, Johnston."

"The father who didn't protect his son against the Father's cock," Johnston fires at him. "Father Healey. Remember him Rooney, at St Mary's?"

"*Remember him?*"

Gold gushes in. Rooney can hardly speak. This information is only available within the Catholic Church. He presumed would have been destroyed or archived, and protected by the church. How did Johnston get this information?

"*Information is power, Rooney!*"

"Easy to see why you drink Sean," Johnston says. "A real conflict. One father abuses, the other condones."

Rooney's shaking. He has to bat this back.

"Another father condones, while the mother harms. Are you angry? You want to kill, but you can't kill… with your hands."

There's a lull in the battle, both sides take stock, girding themselves for the next assault.

"Jackie's determined to get there. You know that," Johnston says.

"Nothing wrong with ambition."

"No? The mob feed her information, she feeds them information, and gets well paid for it."

"Beats working in Sainsbury's."

"We all have our price, Rooney. Why do you think she appointed you, to track me down?"

"She said that if anyone could track you down, I could."

"You, a drunken wreck of a man-shrink; you could hardly find yourself. I found you, I tracked you." Rooney doesn't want to hear this, but it comes, nonetheless. "She used you because the mob said you would never find me, nor confirm any link with them. You were a front, a distraction, Rooney; something to tell the Chief and Muir that she put a 'forensic profiler' on the case."

"You're a liar."

"She'll do anything to get into the big job, any big job to beat her father at his own game. This is what this is all about Rooney, didn't you know that? Do you trust her Rooney? Think about it, if you can that is. You want her, don't you?"

"You want her, but do you trust her?"

"I trust no one."

"She is playing with you. To play with a doll: *num credis me pupa ludere.* You are a doll, she is playing with you."

"They're all playing wi' you."

"I'm no doll."

"A doll, a puppet, a pawn, a flunky, a lackey. You're on the end of our strings."

"I'm a puppet of no one."

"An instrument, a tool, a lapdog, a cat's paw, a minion. That's you Rooney?"

"A puppet."

"Fuck off."

"Pupa. A developing insect inside a cocoon. An insect at the stage between a larva and an adult in complete metamorphosis, undergoing internal changes. Is this you Sean? Are you undergoing internal changes?"

"I am changing – "

"Are you changing into a man?"

"From child to man; from son to father. Metamorphosis... from good to bad man.

Rooney's psyche is under bombardment and Johnston's using everything to denigrate and destroy it, to shatter his defences. He has to marshal everything to protect himself in this the most challenging time of his professional and personal life. Johnston's trying to take him out from his professional fortifications to a personal place, where he can break him down and exact his control more effectively.

"Stay focused, keep the heid."

"*Nunc est bibendum.* There's a time to drink."

Johnston takes a bottle of claret from a cabinet and a crystal glass.

"Here," he says, pushing the bottle and glass across the table towards Rooney. "You're only a drunk, Rooney; you can only do what is necessary."

Rooney could do with a full glass of wine, to steady his nerve, but recognises this is about control, and he can't fall for that. He is about to slide it back and tell him to "fuck-off, I won't fall for that one." Just then, though, like the last time, he sees his image reflected on a bottle. Last time, he saw the man he had become: a drunk man looking at his reflection though a bottle.

"What do you see? Last time you saw a mental illness, an alcohol abuse, a destroyed self?"

Rooney stares into the bottle. He sees the dark claret. Then his eyes pan outward to focus on his reflection. This time he likes what he sees. Like Narcissus who fell in love with his own image reflected in a pool of water. Narcissism. Rooney sees a new man, a transformed man, a bad man.

"You like what you see Rooney? You're a made man; you're a cold, hard, bad bastard."

He steadies himself, grasps the bottle with both hands, and swipes it and the glass off the table and onto the floor. Magically the bottle remains intact. The glass shatters into pieces.

"You will not kill Gray," Rooney growls. "You *will* do the right thing."

"Challenging, I like that. How do you propose to make me desist, drunk? *You* have to do the right thing."

"I'll reach right inside you, to your inner… feelings. Your deepest fears. The places you would never dare *enter*."

For Johnston, this is discomfort, but not enough. "I don't have feelings. By now, you must know this of me."

"You're an NPD, but feelings drive you."

"A NPD controls his feelings, you know that Rooney. Do you control your… needs?"

"You cannot control the anger you have inside. The rage you have can only be exercised through others. Your actions are governed by feelings that drive you to kill – ego syntonic – you aren't even aware they're there."

"Psychoanalysis, again. It really is boring. Rooney, the healer. Who's healing you?"

Just then, the mobile buzzes in Rooney's pocket. He reaches for it and presses it to his ear.

"It's from the nursing home."

Christ, does he know every-fucking-thing?

It's Chris, the nursing home manager. All Rooney hears before dropping the phone back into his pocket is "I'm sorry Sean. Your father died fifteen minutes ago."

"Your father is dead Sean. Now you are free."

A multitude of questions, emotions, and colours explode inside his head. His father was near to death with his drinking. Like father like son! Is he pleased? Could he have saved him? What now: a church service, having to say nice things about him at the funeral mass? The vestments: gold, gold, and gold. He's screaming inside, and he can't let it out, not with Johnston so near. How did Johnston do this? Though, it wouldn't have taken much, the old man was on borrowed time; his liver about to give up, just a wee something into his drink. 'He slept away,' they'll say. The 'why' is easy, another way to show his power over Rooney's life, a way of manipulating him to do his bidding; or is he doing something for him, something he wanted to do himself?

"Sean, would you kill me now?" he prompts.

"How do you propose I should... kill you?"

Clinically, Johnston replies. "I will explain... carefully; because you have difficulty understanding, remembering things. I have here, in this box, a hypodermic with a substance, a poison, Digitalis, which will quickly and progressively end a life. If you do it, there's a note with a local solicitor confirming you did not administer the drug. I died by my own means. Interested, Rooney?"

'Interested' he is. He has to stop him. Is he able? All through his life he's lacked confidence. Low self-esteem, the teachers said. He overcame it by developing his mind. His intellectual development trumped his emotional development. Now his emotional frailties are overpowering his intellectual abilities.

"Take the bokth, Sean," Johnston says, sliding the box across the table towards Rooney. "It contains a full phial, a hypodermic needle, and the mobile phone. In there, there's everything you need to save Gray. This box will determine our fate. Like a revolver, with a single chamber charged with a bullet, this box has the element of chance. Chance I live, chance I die. Chance Gray lives, chance Gray dies. Chance you live, chance you die."

Rooney feels the box. "This is a toy box for a desperate man," Rooney says, moving around the table. "A toy box for a boy, toying with life, a pathetic wee boy with a cruel parentage. How do you feel about your parents, Johnston?"

"Parents are parents Rooney, you know that, and you are lucky to be free of them."

"Some care, some love, though some hate."

"Some control, some abuse."

"Some hurt, some damage."

"What do you feel about your father now, Rooney?" Johnston moves closer to him. "He was a drunk and you are a drunk. He battered your mother and you let him. He's better dead Rooney. Now be a man."

This is exactly what he wants right then: Rooney, putty in his hands, to do his bidding. Rooney needs to get this back into his territory, not his.

"I would like to confirm some things with you," Rooney says. "I have some ideas."

"Ideas Rooney. You have ideas?"

"Indeed I have," he says. "First, Muir's ancestor, Patrick Sellar, cleared your family from their land. Correct? Muir's descendant, Lord Provost Muir, and his council ironically promote migration policy? Your injury and your hope for an apology, ignored? You hate Muir? You desperately want to kill him? I'm not quite sure why though, whether it be the history or the slight. Whatever, pathological revenge is in the air."

"All very interesting," Johnston says. "You either have a great hypothesis or a wild alcohol-induced imagination."

"And you have a great desire to kill. Louise's death, yes? Mary's death, yes? Then Muir's, yes?"

"As you say Rooney. And Gray will be next, sometime before midnight, yes? Though, I may kill him now. Should I do it Rooney, yeth?"

He's trying everything, and now he's pressing the keys on the mobile phone.

"No you won't," Rooney says. "You'll take this to the brink. That I do know about you." He's desperately trying not to reveal the fear in the pit of his stomach or the Technicolor shower in his mind.

"I have entered the password," Johnston says. Then, talking into the mobile loud enough to be heard, he says, "It's me. Instruct him, or Gray dies in one hour, and your career goes down the Suwannee. Have you got that?" Then he slides the mobile onto the table towards Rooney.

Rooney reaches out and takes the mobile, which he puts to his ear, catching the last sentence. "Put him on, Mr Johnston."

Rooney knows that voice. "Jackie, is that you?"

"You've got to do it Rooney. It's the only way to save Gray," she says. "You!"

"I'm only doing what needs to be done, hon, please do the same."

"Fuck off... darling."

"He said one hour – "

Johnston reaches to take the phone from him, but only manages to grip his hand. This is a scary but strangely intimate feeling as their two hands grasp. Johnston withdraws his hand like he has had an electric shock, takes the mobile, switches it off and drops it into the box.

"Remember, it will only operate with the password," Johnston says.

Sitting down, Rooney runs his hands over the box for what seems to be a long time, but it can only be seconds. He wonders if this man would be willing to give his life, to prove he can corrupt, him.

Johnston takes off the frock coat. "OK, let's combat," he says, imperiously.

In Glasgow University, in the domain of his ancestor, this is where he wants to triumph.

"Let's combat then, "Rooney says. "*You* sir, are controlled, by your fears: you are as much controlled by your innermost terror, as those you would direct to exert this terror and in turn exorcise your anger."

"Fear, terror, pain. It works Rooney, you should try it?"

"Indeed, it's on the cards."

Johnston looks at him strangely, not quite expecting him to say this.

"If you kill, Sean. Then you will be free, and I will be free."

"Your dénouement?"

"Yes, my... dénouement."

"I can't kill – "

"Come on Sean, anyone can kill," Johnston says, almost a sympathetic tone. "Your father could kill, he killed your mother didn't he? If you had the chance, you would have killed your father. OK, I did you a favour, but it was in your heart to do it. You would have killed. You thought you were firing at me, in the Grand Central; you are no different from me."

"You can kill."

"I do kill."

"But don't kill directly, you can't kill directly. You kill through others. You, you're as much a coward as me, you can't even kill yourself."

Johnston remains quiet, as if to absorb the words.

Rooney continues, his dander is up. "You're in pain. A pain caused by your parents, and the only way out of this pain for you is to die. Although you want the satisfaction, or the legacy of control, to achieve this, you can't kill yourself, and you can't kill the source of the pain, your parents. You're so lost."

"Ah, my parents," Johnston says, in a disinterested way.

"Indeed, your parents, "Rooney says. "Your parents created you. They created the monster inside there." He reaches over to Johnston and pokes him of the chest. "You have an irreconcilable conflict. You are extremely angry and you want to cause them pain, to have them feel the pain of a wee boy. But you have no power, no defence against them, and you can't take them on." Rooney drops his voice. "You are angry and you are scared, and you are in blind deference of them. A double bind dilemma known to families of those with narcissistic personality disorder, and there's no way out. Brutality on the one hand and corruptive influence on the other, both symbolising your pain and control, typifying the kind of people that you all are."

"Rooney, you know nothing about... us."

"I know more than you think."

"Really? Time is ticking on your Nelson Gray."

"It's all about them." Johnston is looking at Rooney intently, not as if he's interested, but more in a curious way. "And through them I can get to you, and you know that." Rooney expresses confidence by sprawling over the table, his voice resonating against it, making it sound stronger.

"Ticking, Sean, ticking."

The contretemps is finely balanced, but Rooney has to tip it in more in his favour. "I think you want it all to stop, but you can't, not in the way that'll give you peace."

"I will have peace. Gray will live, and you will kill me," Johnston screams into his face. "Tick, tick, tick."

Rooney measures his words. "You have power, but you don't have peace."

They are now circling the table like pace cyclists at either side, facing each other.

Johnston breaks first. "I don't need peace, I need death. I need people to die. I need, I need, I need... tick, tick, tick."

There's something very bizarre, albeit personal, going on there between these two men at opposite ends of this table – at opposite ends of the spectrum of humanity – but maybe there's more uniting than separating them. This bothers Rooney, but it's reality. Both men, damaged by the abuse of adults: one seeks an internal world to cope with pain and drinks to salve; the other articulates it in actions that cause pain, to cauterize the wound. One self-destructs, one kills, both hurt.

Johnston pushes the box closer to Rooney. "Minutes Sean, you have no more time to counsel me. I cannot be your client, however much you would like me to be. Maybe, if it had been different, maybe, but time's against us. Ticking, Sean, ticking. What are you going to do, let him die?"

"To kill a bad man to prevent the death of a good man, I can live with that..."

"Good, I am getting to through to you. You will do it then." Johnston pulls up his sleeve. "Go on then, do it, do it now." His voice echoes against the serene sound of the Vivaldi violins, creating a crescendo of colours, his words in blocks of colours in Rooney's mind, which feels as if it will explode.

"I will kill what you are... then I'll see about you," Rooney roars, more to hear his own voice above the violins.

"Ah, now you are trying my patience." Johnston gets up and smacks his hands against his head. "Will you stop the psychobabble, gobbledegook? I am getting sick of it. Do it now you poor excuse for a shrink, the shrink with a drink, or I'll kill him now."

"I'll destroy your ability to control, to manipulate, to kill."

Rooney knows well how the potency of a man can be reduced to nothing, of torturers who could break strong foes, leaving them no longer a threat. He knows how mental illness can torture and break a man, as it had him, destroying confidence, leaving him a shadow of his formal self. He sits back and mentally blocks the Vivaldi. He's pleased he's triggered this anger in his 'man' who's now exposing his emotional underbelly. He feels more settled, in control, no longer anxious. He'll torture this man.

"When you realise you can't control me," Rooney says. "You'll realise you have lost your power, you will be... nothing."

Now Johnston appears the more apprehensive, saying, "You... will kill me, me. You will do it. You have little time."

"I will. I'll kill what's... inside you."

"Ah, the coward tries to analyse his way out. You can't change me, shrink. You can't change fate. *Quo fata vocant.* Whither the fates call. Ticking, ticking, ticking."

"Arthur, it's time." Now Rooney uses the first name game.

"Good, let's get down to it." Johnston crashes down on a seat, his arm outstretched across the table.

The mobile intervenes.

"It's for you Rooney, it's Jackie." Johnston pushes the mobile into Rooney's hand. "Don't worry," he says. "I know what she's going to tell you."

"What have you got to say Jackie?" Rooney asks, into the mobile.

"Rooney, I've killed Archie," Jackie says.

"Fuck!"

"He said he would save Gray."

"What!"

"Through Macqueen, he made contact with the Fox family. He was confident he could save Gray. I led him out of the room, along the corridor, into a side room. I said we needed complete privacy to discuss, and a direct line."

Johnston takes the mobile from him. "Thank you *Ms* Kaminski."

"Two shots rang out from the room, Rooney," Johnston says. "Members of the security committee raced to find Jackie slumped over the desk with a gun in one hand and the phone in the other, blood oozing from her arm. Paterson lay behind the desk, a blood pool around his head."

He hands the mobile back to Rooney.

"Archie?" Rooney asks her.

"It had to be done," Jackie says. "Now it's for you to do your bit."

Johnston interjects. "Well, Rooney, what do you think of your Jackie now?"

"You've got something on her," he says. "Jackie," he calls into the phone.

"Please, Rooney, for us," she says, then she's gone.

"Nothing to do with Archie stealing her thunder," Johnston says. "Right, let's do this?"

This is the point of no return; the time for Rooney to turn an unrelenting tide of death towards Johnston.

"Time to introduce the source of your deathly habit and the vehicle of your sure destruction," Rooney says.

"The source of my habit, my sure destruction?"

"Indeed... your parents."

"Ha, my parents," Johnston says, in a flippant, dispassionate way. Not quite what Rooney expected. He was hoping for something more like anger, trepidation, confusion.

"Through them, I'll destroy you." Rooney makes for the door and opens it. This is his signal.

CHAPTER THIRTY-EIGHT

A momentary hush descends on the room, only to be broken by a distinctive voice.

"Arthur," Louisa Johnston says, as they enter, her stick tapping on the floor. Vivaldi is turned off, she's exercising her dominance.

"Two boys together, what is going on here?" she says, like the matriarch she is.

"This is not a good time mother," Johnston says.

"It's a good time for Rooney."

"Mr Rooney asked us to come," James, his father, says. "He wants us... to help you."

Louisa's 'huh' indicates 'don't talk for me'.

She moves to the other side of the table.

"Shut up, James," she says. "He needs more than help."

James gently closes the door to the room and moves to his wife's side. They pull out two chairs and take a position at the middle of the table, as if they're about to chair a meeting.

"Help me, how can you help me?" Johnston asks of them as he walks around the room, purposefully avoiding the side of the table where they sit.

Louisa clatters her stick uncaringly on the lovingly varnished table. She's determined to demand attention.

"Now listen to me boy, we need to talk," she says. "Look at you... dressed like a bloody... actor."

"Don't interfere... mother – "

"I will interfere. You can't do this. We're here to stop you." She's followed by a full minute of hesitation, as if none of them would say anymore.

"Interfere in what? What has he told you?" Johnston says.

"Only what you do," Rooney says.

Louisa snaps back at him. "Shut up, little man."

Uncomfortable with the heightening tension, James moves forward. "Arthur, we can help you," he says, and reverts to his wife's side, who shakes her head disconsolately.

"Help me? The only thing which can help me is this." Johnston stabs his finger on the box. "And him," pointing at Rooney.

Louisa snaps back. "Get a grip, you pathetic boy," she shrieks. "You bring shame on us."

Johnston flinches at the sight of the stick pointing directly at him. She moves closer to him. "You look awful. What is wrong with you, your skin, and your eyes? You look like death." She sniffs his breath. "Have you been drinking boy? Have you? What have you become?"

Rooney has noticed neither a smell of alcohol nor a deteriorated state. This is not good. His stock-in-trade task is observation, his assessment of cues. He has missed this.

"Son." James edges forward and spans the room with his voice, almost as if he's addressing an audience. "We are here, together, in this... this place of our forefathers, where our great family name was established. This is a great moment for us. This is where our own Arthur Johnston, the great Latin poet, had his greatest triumph, where he was venerated. We should not besmirch him, and we cannot defame our family here in this place."

Deliciae Poetarum Scotorum represented the zenith of Scotland's burgeoning Latin culture during the renaissance and reformation. Glasgow University's work, through Johnston's ancestor, provides a translation of the anthology and explained the Latin culture of early modern Scotland.

He's close enough to his son to touch him. Rooney wonders if he will. He preaches softly, then changes his tone.

"Do this, and I will personally rub you out of this family's history," James says. "The Johnston that never was." He moves back to his wife. Jesus, sadism runs in this family. James Johnston's words are soft, but their sound carries through the room, reverberating against the rows of books. "Arthur, remember, *ad fidelis, ad finem*, to the faithful, to the end, remember?" he says.

Johnston seems lulled by this and then – sounding shaken – he turns to Rooney, tapping on the glass of an old wooden clock. "Ticking, ticking, ticking, Rooney. Gray will die, soon."

"He means to kill Nelson Gray," Rooney says.

James calls on his corruptive powers. "Arthur, you will stop this. Is the death of one man worth the shame of the Johnstons?"

"It'th the way it hath to be," Johnston says, his lisp more prominent now.

"We cannot be responsible for you," James says.

"Responsibility hasn't stopped him killing up to now," Rooney says.

Turning to his son, "Is this true? Have you been responsible for... killing people?" James asks.

"Killing, fath – "

"You, our son, killing!" Louisa's words sting. "Do you hear this James? I always told you he would disgrace us," she says.

"My god, what have you become?" James drops to the seat.

"I am what I am," Johnston says.

"*He* is what *you* created," Rooney says.

Rooney needs to mix it, create drama, crisis. Crisis releases the energy – use the energy. He is comfortable with this model. He can get some control here. He says to Johnston, "You are what they created."

Sounding animated, James turns to Rooney. "Mr Rooney, this is not what we expected. You said we could help. To stop him... shaming... us."

"This is what will help," Rooney replies. "This needs to be brought out, into the open, to see it for what it is. Tell them." He turns to Johnston, who is silent, almost contemplative, as if Rooney has opened a door that he has wanted opened for some time.

"Tell them what?" James asks.

"Tell them why you did it."

"Go to hell," Johnston says, indicating Rooney has gone too far.

Rooney needs to grasp the impetus, seize the upper hand, control the joust. He persists. "You did it because of them."

"Shut up, Rooney, or I will end Gray right now," Johnston says, picking up his mobile.

"Us?" His parents yell in unison.

"Yes, you; *you* both," Rooney says. "He kills to exorcise his feelings, the feelings you produced in him, as a child. You know, he is an extremely damaged, angry man."

"Damaged, angry, Rooney?" Johnston replies. "Ticking, Rooney, ticking, decide. Kill me now or Gray dies. There is no other way. Kill me, the damaged individual. Put him out of his misery."

"You cannot do it Arthur," James says. "You cannot do it. For God's sake." He's pleading for some common sense. "And you cannot do it Mr Rooney," he says, turning to him.

Conversely, Louisa is much more cutting and assertive. "You will not do it, boy. You will not do it. And Rooney, don't you even think about it."

James adds his weight. "Son, you are a sick man."

"I can do, I do do." Johnston is determined to reveal something to them, something they did not know about him; and, in saying this, something seems to be released inside him. "I can do it. I do it. I do things that, I have no doubt when Rooney tells you, will shock your petty little world," he says, spitting out the words, like stabs of a knife into their chests. "I do, I do it, I do do it," his voice rising; becoming high pitched, agitated.

Rooney delivers a prompt. "This is your son, your only son, whom you created."

Louisa is disgusted. "I didn't create... this," she says.

Johnston rounds the table and grabs her arm. She shrugs him off as if he's a fly just landed on it. "Get your sordid little hand off me, boy." She raises her hand like a cat with claw out, ready to tear his eyes out. "What have you become? Look at you, look at your face, the way you talk, the way you're dressed," she says. "You hardly even look like us, or like the man we named you after. You are no... Johnston."

Ouch!

Johnston screams at her. "Me? You are no Johnston, you only married a Johnston. This doesn't make you a Johnston. I am a Johnston."

"I am more of a Johnston than you. You are a fraud," she says.

"Listen, you are a Johnston," James says to his son. "You are a Johnston," he says to his wife. "We are all Johnstons, we are Johnstons, now let's all act like it."

This exercises their son greatly, who is now chanting, "You punish, but don't care," to his mother. "You harm and don't heal," to his father. "Me, I kill, but I don't feel. I kill. I kill, and I can't... live," he screams at both of them.

Shit, this is deep stuff coming out. Security will become interested in what's happening in this room. Rooney needs to control this. He can't be dragged off to Partick Police Station nor sectioned under the Mental Health Act. *He* has to be in control of his destiny.

Louisa helps. "You'll stop this. You will save the man Gray. We demand it. Do you hear me?" She rises to her full height over her son, majestically like a King Cobra over an adversary.

"Why don't you kill them?" Rooney asks Johnston. "Surely, you want to." He has to raise the stakes. Time is against him.

"Kill us?" His parents answer in unison.

If this wasn't so serious, this would be funny.

"And what good would that do?" Johnston asks.

"They are the source of your anger, your pain." Rooney calls on all of his gall. "She the abuser of her son and he the conspirator in the act."

"What about the source of your pain, Rooney?" Johnston asks. "Your father's gone, but Father Healey... he may still be alive. I can find him for you. Do you want him?"

"Do you want him Rooney?"

Does he want him?

"In nominee Patris, Johnston, the father's name, Johnston." Rooney appears intentionally trying to get away from the 'fathers' in *his* life.

James interrupts Rooney's golden storm, brought on by the Latin. "Johnston? You know nothing of us, you know nothing of this,"

"I know why people do things," Rooney says to Johnston senior. "And I know a dysfunctional family when I see one."

"It is *he* who caused the problems," Louisa says, referring to her son.

"Yes, problems to this family," James says, agreeing with his wife, now on his feet walking around, referring to the manuscripts.

"He brings shame on our... family, James," Louisa says.

"Johnston, *clarum et venerabile nomen*. An illustrious and vulnerable name, son. It is here, in his works." James refers to the texts. "What do you think he would he say?"

Johnston replies immediately. "He would say '*nil sine mango vita labore debit mortalibius*.'"

Louisa translates: "Indeed, where there is no pain, there is no gain," she says.

"*Expressis verbis*. In explicit terms?" Rooney replies.

"This man knows Latin?" Louisa sounds both surprised and dumbfounded.

James interrupts. "He would say '*empta dolore docet experientia*.'"

The gold flashes are interfering with Rooney's thoughts, but he's determined to trump them with the Latin.

"*Latine dictum*. Experience bought with pain teaches effectively," Rooney says to James. "What kind of pain did you inflict on your son James? What did he learn? That psychological abuse works? Is this what you taught him? That the only way to survive is to fuck the world." James says nothing in response, but there's a look of horror on his face. For Rooney, it feels refreshing, powerful. The coup de grâce is evident.

"*In nomine Patris*, Johnston," Rooney says.

"In the name of the Johnstons," James adds quietly.

"What are you suggesting, you stupid man." Louisa moves aggressively towards Rooney. He steps back. Johnston reaches out for her. "Get your hands off me... boy," she says. "Who do you think you are? You were always an insignificant little nonentity, always the source of our... concerns."

James throws his weight in behind his wife. "Arthur you should not touch your mother," he says.

Not touch!

"*Compesce mentem*," Johnston says, calmly.

Controlling their temper? Either he wants to back off or they should back off. He wants to be in control. Maybe he's worried about them getting the upper hand, as they had done so many times in the past. Rooney has to stir this some more, though time is passing.

"Don't be used by them," Rooney says to him.

This's a tactic and he's intent in keeping his course.

"Rooney, you have ended our... debate, prematurely," Johnston says. "You had your chance and did not take it. I have the mobile open. You will leave. I will end him right now."

"You have a chance here to change things, to deal with them, deal with your pain, their abuse. To feel normal." Rooney is determined to stay part of things.

"Out of the room, Gray dies now. I will do what is necessary." Johnston is unequivocal.

Rooney wonders if Johnston intends seeking some resolution, some retribution, to the pain they have caused him. Would he confront them?

"Johnston, there is a way out of this," Rooney says. "They are the source of your anger, your pain. Deal with them. Gray is no longer the issue here."

Johnston roars back at him. "Gray is as good as dead, dead, and you are responsible." He bangs the mobile phone on the table, repeatedly, as his words bombard Rooney.

Time for a hand grenade of his own.

"*In nomine Patris*," Rooney stabs. "Your calling card, the message left at your murders. In the name of the father; your father's name. That is why you did it?"

The glass on the wall cabinets almost shatter from Louisa's scream. "In the name of the father." She goes in close, her stick pointing at him like a police baton. Will she strike him, Rooney wonders.

"Get out now," she shouts at Rooney.

"Yes, get out now Mr Rooney," James says in support.

Rooney has them where he wants them. He has the chance to administer the final cut, but he is risking Gray's life. Is he prepared to do this to achieve his ends?

"It's clear they don't love you Arthur. They've never loved you. In fact they despise you, deplore you, hate you. They hate you, Arthur. Your parents hate you. All they care about is the family, the family name."

The words sound absurd, but believable. There's a pause. All appear paralysed, as if in a freeze frame. Then Johnston steps up towards Rooney, as if to deflect him and his words.

"*Mors*," Johnston says. "Death. Time to die, time to kill."

"*A time to kill, a time to die. Your turn Rooney.*"

Rooney recognises the dispassion of this man's voice. He's ready to strike. From a shrink's point of view, he loves observing this man. He is magnificent. He's like the white stag, the monarch of the glen in his dream. But Rooney's rage trumps his observations. It's time to act, not to analyse or understand. Fuck the understanding. Instead he feels a surge of adrenaline. Time to dispatch the sad, mad bastard, that's held him down for so long. Himself.

"*Time to fuck rather than be fucked.*"

"I'll do it," Rooney says, grabbing the hypodermic. "I'll kill you and I'll enjoy it." Johnston looks at him strangely, though holds out his arm towards him and pulling his sleeve farther up his arm. Rooney grabs his arm tightly in his left hand, his right hand around the hypo and his thumb on the plunger. As he does, he hears Gray's voice like in his dream. 'Now, go on now, do it, end him, squeeze it.'

"Squeeze it."

They are now where Rooney wants them to be. They're on a point of balance between life and death; between liberty or control. This fulcrum will determine who lives and who dies; but also the life or death of his self-respect, his self-worth, his pride. There's no going back. "Now," he tells himself. "Now, I will not be used. I will be the user."

"Use it."

But they can't allow him to do what they have to do themselves. He knows and he expects the attack, but when it comes it is ferocious. Louisa, with a forearm swipe, hits him square on the side of the head with her stick. Then, in one overall movement, the backhand return hits her son with a thwack against his head. They both slump across the desk. Rooney's head is engulfed with stars, pain, and sharp lights behind his eyes. Johnston droops over the desk; he sees a scared wee boy as his mother's stick rises above him. Rooney sees his father's hand raised to come thwacking down on his face.

"Feel it."

Louisa snaps. "He's ours, now get out, before we... kill you."

She moves towards Rooney with the stick. He draws on every last once of strength he has. He rises and backs out of the door.

"Kill him," Rooney says. "It's the only way, for you, for him..., for the Johnstons."

"Out, you pathetic little man," she says. "Everything was fine until you came into our lives, now we have to act to protect our... family."

Rooney knows they'll do it.

Gray? Is there any way Rooney can save him? Would Rooney sacrifice him for the sake of his own needs to control, to be the controller, to no longer be the sad, mad, drunk shrink? Is Gray's life, a great man's, worth it? Rooney's care of others nearly killed him. His contempt of others will heal him. But he has to try. He can't have people say he didn't try.

"Try it."

"Indeed I will," Rooney says to Louisa, "but get the password, Gray doesn't need to die. Do you want that on your family's name as well, the death of a great writer, caused by the family of a great writer? What would history say about that? It would consign the name of your great ancestor, the Arthur Johnston, the Johnston name, to be forever tainted by the act of his ancestor, your son."

"Get out," she shouts.

Rooney staggers out, knowing she would use the stick on him as readily as earlier, but he has left them with a dilemma, an irreconcilable set of circumstances. They can only do it, he believes. The door slams shut behind him. He pushes back on it, but feels the weight of a large chair behind it.

Rooney gives them sufficient time, ten minutes or so, time to make a call. Then he heads along the corridor, until he reaches the reception desk. "There's a killer in there," he shouts, "someone's been killed." A security guard appears. Both of them rush along towards the room. The guard fumbles with the door. Then, with a hefty shoulder shove, they're in.

They enter and there's a state of calm – like being in the eye of a hurricane. Johnston has regained some consciousness and is sitting at the table expressionless, his face pale, drained of blood, shocked. He's facing his parents, who are sitting directly across from him across the table, as if they aren't there. There's a scary calm, a weird scenario. They're locked in their own psychopathic bubble. If he could capture this, he could make a fortune. He feels for his mobile which has a camera facility, but desists. His hands are shaking so much so that the picture would be ruined.

"We did what was necessary, what *you* suggested," James says, absolving himself of guilt, as he removes the hypo and phial from the box. "See," he says.

"We did it," Louisa adds, triumphantly.

"There was no option," James says. "We did it for the family name."

"*In nomine Patris*," Rooney says to them. "Johnston, you have failed," he says to him, in a cutting voice from where he stands.

A groggy Johnston replies, "You have killed Gray. I gave you the chance, but you would not do what was expected of you. Like most times in your life when you need some courage. Like when you could have done something about your father, you relied on somebody else to do it for you, as you do."

"*Hear it.*"

"Johnston, your parents have killed what they created," Rooney says. "They create a killer and killers they themselves become."

As Johnston looks at Rooney through rheumy, sad, but dispassionate eyes, he says "*In manus tuas commendo spiritum meum*: into your handth I entrust my spirit," and then slowly swings his head around towards his parents, where his despairing gaze prevails.

"Failure has destroyed you as much as the Digitalis administered by your parents," Rooney says. "You have failed to use or control me. Your power is crushed, controlled, mitigated."

Johnston is now speechless, like the words are there but he can't get them out. His confidence in his power is shattered, his control and abuse disabled.

Rooney knows this is the time, his time. He slides down on the table to a position close to Johnston, his face in line with his.

"Through me," Rooney says. "You thought you had determined your destiny; designed, planned and delivered your departure from this sad place; but I made them your killers. Like you, the great proxy killer, I have exploited, manipulated, controlled, and used. You have been a good teacher Johnston. I was in control of them, and they have killed you. I have destroyed you and what you are, were, and I have destroyed you. *Salva conscientia*, with a clear conscience, *Artorius*, Arthur!"

Johnston raises a determined but weary eye.

"Can I help you sir?" The security guard leans over Johnston. Johnston shoos him away with a very weak hand, looking intently at Rooney through bleary eyes.

Rooney whispers to Johnston. "*Procuratia*, someone acting for another..." He leaves the comment hanging in the tension-filled atmosphere of the room. Johnston looks on blankly.

There's a deep and solemn silence. Like the hush which would await a Roman Emperor's decision in the Coliseum: thumbs-up or thumbs down. A kind of emptiness appears in Johnston's eyes, and from his lips, something akin of a smile, or more of a grin. Irena's words come right back to Rooney: "dead eyes... funny face, funny voice without being funny". Back then, on the hill, Rooney didn't know what she meant. He does now.

Johnston tries to speak, but his voice is low. "Gray is dead and you have killed him – "

"No, he's not," Rooney says with gusto into his face. "*Patria potestas*. The power of a father, Johnston. When outside, I called in a favour; he's been saved. The McGinns verses the Foxes, there was no contest. *In nomine Patris*, Johnston."

Johnston slumps down on the table, succumbing to the drug, clearly no longer able to communicate. Rooney gets up slowly, confidently, triumphantly, believing Johnston would say no more, do no more, in his life.

"Come on pal." The guard tries to bring Johnston around.

Rooney turns and looks to the parents.

"He has killed us also." Louisa seems to be losing consciousness too.

"What's happening?" This he didn't expect.

"We have injected each other too," James says, reaching for his wife.

Rooney lifts the empty phial and compares it with its initial weight. He thought it held more than was necessary to kill Johnston.

James continues. "We could only do the right thing here, in the place where our family triumphed. In killing him, we have ended the family's shame, protected the family name. In killing ourselves, we have taken the only way, the right way, out. To reinstate our pride, the pride – "

"Of the Johnstons," Rooney says.

"As you say."

"*Pulvis et umbra sumas*," Louisa slurs.

"We are but dust and shadow," Rooney replies.

They're losing consciousness. A group of people muster around the door. Paramedics shoulder through to reach them, but they're done. Rooney leaves the room. He has to gather his thoughts. He finds a bench and sits down. He holds Johnston's mobile in his hand and considers the disasters he had triggered from this small device. He wonders what lay within the depths of this particular mobile.

"What does it matter?" Rooney asks himself. "It's all in the past. I've killed him by other hands, as he did. I have triumphed over him, in his way. He is dead. They are all dead. My hands are clean. My life has turned. My life has changed. I have changed."

"Metamorphosis... Narcissus... Rooney, the narcissist... Rooney, the Father."

CHAPTER THIRTY-NINE

"You have changed."
"You are so right, bastard."

Rooney saunters out of there, feeling resolved and empowered.
"Bastard, are you there?"
There's no voice.
"Bastard, are you there," he repeats, just to be sure.
I'm gone and so's the self-doubt. He'll miss me, but not the doubt. Success has filled him with feelings of self-worth. *"In nomine Patris,"* he says, and no colours. He's destroyed 'the father' and with this the remnants of the trauma he has suffered for years.
"I've done it, I'm a made man." He skips along through the halls, eventually finding his way back to the reception where two CID investigation officers are waiting along with local police. He'll give them a statement and leave. Though, this could turn, he knows this. He's responsible for the deaths of 'the Johnstons'. He can see the headline: 'Forensic psychologist kills the Father, the primary suspect in the recent atrocities.' He holds on to Johnston's mobile, which he hasn't dared let slip from his grasp.
On his way out, he hears a klaxon. This is an ambulance making its way out of the University car park, not unusual given it's a crime scene. Forensics may well want to check it over, and, who knows, the neurology department might want to do some scans of their brains to establish what lies in the minds of psychopaths. The university might want to avoid any media backlash, encouraging the police to remove the bodies forthwith. Whatever. It appears a bit premature.
He can't go back to his old life. He thinks of Jackie. What is it that draws him to her? Her intelligence, her scheming, her sex?
'You're a danger to me,' she said to him. "I am now," he says to himself.
He feels like a few drinks, which will undoubtedly lead to a few more. But no, he's on a high, he has a new hit. He can feel it cycling upwards, it's fantastic. Then he hears a very distinctive 'boom', and his train of thought is

abruptly shaken. This is a bomb, it can't be anything else, after all this is Johnston country. The best thing to do is to get off the street. He finds a pub in Ashton Lane. It isn't long – nearly half through a pint – before he's told by the bartender that a 'terrible thing has happened': an ambulance has been blown up as it left Glasgow University.

"Shite," he says loudly.

"You're no' kiddin' pal; there's nothing left of the bloody thing. I hope there was nobody needing treatment in the back," he laughs.

This is Glasgow, where black humour and warm sentiments fuse; where everything, including multiple murder, corruption and mayhem, has a way of being treated as normal.

He sits there pondering what's happened, trying to fathom the reality of that day. Johnston's dead, his parents are dead, their bodies blown apart. It's all tied up, they're all dead. He's been instrumental in Johnston's death. He fashioned it, though he hadn't killed him directly. As Johnston had done so many times, *he* had used others to kill.

Johnston had hurt him, as his father had hurt his mother. Johnston tried to use him, as his father had used his mother. Nothing makes sense, nothing except Johnston is gone, his father is gone; and yet everything makes sense. He has asserted himself, he has become the controller, doing to rather than being done to. He is empowered. It feels good to be in charge, empowered, on top. He has, though, just about killed himself with the drink. He bears a scar, his 'Glasgow smile' mouth, not unlike Johnston's, and the loss of the end of his finger. He could easily enter a 'good reason for' binge, but he needs his head to work.

"Let's see what's at the other end of this?" Rooney says, footering with the mobile. He tries to find the password. 'Johnston', then 'Arthur', then 'Gray'. "It's not bloody 'Gray'." Then he tries 'Rooney'. Nothing.

Then, as he is about to try 'Father', it buzzes.

"Hello?"

"Rooney?"

"It sure is, Jackie dear, who did you expect, Johnston?"

"How did you get the mobile Rooney?"

"How do you think I got the mobile?"

"I don't know. I only know Johnston would've never given you access to it, unless you killed him. Did you kill him? Did you do it Rooney?"

"Why are you doing this, Jackie? Your ticket to the big job? Who else have you fucked or killed for that matter to get there?"

"I had to Rooney."

"Indeed Jackie. Why?"

"You know why. Johnston. You know how he works. Information equals knowledge, equals power."

"Tell me."

"You wouldn't want to know."

"I do want to know."

"Well, maybe you'll never know. It's best we stop this... relationship, before someone gets hurt."

"Who Jackie?"

"I think she means physically man."

"Come over here, tonight."

"And you have an SAS squad there to take me out. 'Trust no one,' Jackie."

"Bye Rooney." Click.

Rooney arrives at the West Cemetery in Hamilton around 1.00 pm. He knows the place well, having been here with Jackie many times. He walks past the stone of a soldier who died in the Second World War, one who died in Northern Ireland, one in the Falklands, and one more recently in Afghanistan. When will it ever end. Then he sees her. He approaches her from behind. The afternoon sun makes her hair glisten. It's unmistakably her.

"Jackie," he says, over her shoulder. She's fixing red and white roses in a brass pot, cutting them to size, splaying them outwards.

She doesn't look up. "How did you know I would be here?"

"It's Sunday, Jackie. St Simons until 12.30, then here to where your mother was buried. You're here every week at the same time, putting flowers on your mother's grave."

"Course you would know that." She looks up at him.

"Some things I don't forget."

"You've no right – " She places the brass pot back on the base of the stone.

"I had to talk to you, I – "

"You couldn't trust me?"

"I needed to know some things."

"Well, we better sit down."

She wipes the black marble stone, ending with a final wipe of a small white plaque of her mother's face on the stone. She pauses to look at the plaque of a young woman, smiling, her eyes full of life. She looks so like her mother. She gets up and leads him to a bench on the other side of the graveyard. Rooney sits down at one end and Jackie at the other. He reads the brass inscription plaque in the middle of the bench. In Loving Memory of Irena Zysk, 18.5.1928 – 05.1.2009. Loving Mother and Grandmother. Erected by her Loving Family.

"Irena Zysk."

"Yes, her family erected this bench."

"Kind of seems appropriate given all this stuff started with her."

"Good place to end it hon."

Rooney looks around to see if the SAS is moving up through the headstones.

"Good place to make sense of it." He stands up to face her. "Why did you do it Jackie? Johnston, Archie... and everything else?"

"You look different Rooney, clean, clean shaven." She looks him up and down. He's been to Slaters; a new suit, white shirt, tie, black woollen overcoat, leather gloves, black shoes; haircut. "You going to a funeral? Right place for it. He straightens and looks away across the cemetery grounds. "Beats the filthy white suit, though, the Crombie, the bunnet; less tramp-like, more befitting a – "

"A made man Jackie."

"You seem more... self-assured."

"I feel... better." He dips his hands into his coat pockets and faces away from her. "Why did you – "

"I told you. I had to."

"Your ambitions, your father, Johnston had something on you?"

She folds her arms and rests them on her knees. "I cheated. The Birreli case. He knew this."

"And beating your father at his own game is just a bloody smokescreen; this is about revenge, not about ambition. You want revenge for his... intrusion into your relationship with your mother. The 'beautiful relationship' he shattered."

Again, as in the Horseshoe Bar, he sees the child in these soft green eyes; as she had seen in his. However, while she was torn from her relationship with the person she loved most in the world, he was held in that relationship sharing the abuse of a man, a father. A father, it turns out, abused them both.

"All very... cryptic Rooney."

"You don't even know Jackie."

"Hon, we have a lot in common, you and I."

"I suppose we are bonded."

"Oh, Freudian shit again?"

"Attachment theory. Maybe why we got together in the first place."

"Sorry."

"We share the same neurosis."

"Give us a break Rooney."

"Jackie, we were both fucked as children, and fucked up as adults."

He lets this sink in. There's no response. He looks at her face. She's gone somewhere. She's staring out over the headstones, to where her mother's grave is. There's something different, disengaged... in her eyes.

"Do you love me?"

"Hon," she says, calmly.

"What?"

"The case has to... close."

"Jackie, how can it?"

"Yes hon, as you say "*In nomine...*" And with that she disappears through the rows of graves.

Rooney leaves there, and gets a train from Hamilton West to Partick. He spends the rest of the day in the Ubiquitous Chip, the Chip. He's above Tennents and Jintys now. He plans the rest of his life. A life fulfilled. He drinks good wine. No more whisky, beer, or any other rot gut. Only the best from now on.

It's nearly midnight as he heads out of Ashton Lane onto Byres Road to find a cab. He can walk home, but he can't walk. A taxi tonight pal.

He stands with his hand up to hail a cab. He'll stand there until a cab turns up: a black, a private; any car, he just wants to get home. This time it's a private. He drags himself onto the back seat and makes himself comfortable. He'll explain to the driver he's had a hard night. He's in for a good tip. Just get him home to his bed.

"You're to be a dead man," the driver says.

"We've all got to go sometime." He gets the perfume again! "Jean Dempsie... the woman who knows things."

"Good to see you Rooney."

"I hear you're MI5."

"You are to be assassinated tonight."

"Jesus, who, how?"

"You are to be blown up... in a taxi."

"Where is she?"

"Right now, she's on her way home and heading up Sauchiehall Street. She's walking a bit to clear her head. She's had a good day at the office. As far as she believes, everyone in her way has gone, including you."

"She'll be sorry about me."

"Yes, I think she will, but she'll cope with it. She'll pick up a taxi at the rank on the street. Little does she know it's the one intended for you."

"Bastard."

No answer this time.

"You'll make the call."

Jackie makes herself comfortable on the back seat of the 'taxi'. She opens the mobile to hear a voice she knows well. She feels the mobile becoming strangely warm. Almost at the same time, she gets an explosion of white, yellow and orange; a multi-coloured meteor shower in her head. She has a strange sense of weightlessness, and gets a complete vision of everything around her. Like those dispossessed souls who look down on their bodies from above an operating theatre, before regaining life, she sees the damaged taxi, herself on the ground, just to the side of it. She looks down on Sauchiehall Street, on those anxious folk fighting to get away, or anywhere to get out of Glasgow. It's no longer safe, and she's the most recent casualty.

It's all caught freeze-frame, frozen in time, immortalized. Fear overtakes the drunken banter at the taxi rank. They're no longer singing away to the auld busker with the guitar or tapping their feet to wee Johnny with his fiddle. The driver's looking down on her. The mobile is in bits on the ground, the same mobile that contained a device, triggered by a call. To her side, she sees Rooney.

With tears in his voice, she hears him say, "In the name of the Father..."

Ad finem